Gospel

of the

Forgotten

J. Armand

ISBN: 0996119175, 978-0-9961191-7-7

Cover illustration by Greg Opalinski

Table of Contents

"Darkness cannot drive out darkness;

only light can do that.

Hate cannot drive out hate;

only love can do that."

— Martin Luther King, Jr.

Preface

Deep within us all, there is a fire: raw, primal, and unyielding. It cannot be tamed, and it should not be. This fire is our passion—our driving force—which, when channeled, can unlock a wellspring of creativity or a superhuman compulsion to thrive. But this flame has more to offer than the inspiring embrace of its warmth. When left unchecked, our passions can disfigure us. Feeding these flames with aggression and vitriol can cause a backlash that no longer empowers but consumes all it touches.

Prologue

Peace is a fleeting luxury. Whether through victory or annihilation, it is as inevitable as the conflict that claims it. No matter how far down you stick your head in the sand, eventually, you will be met by something crawling up from below to threaten it. As powerless as we may feel at times to make a difference, there is always a bigger picture. Some believe that life works in mysterious ways, but this only holds true for those who don't take a moment to reflect.

The answers for what the future has in store for us have already been told a thousand times over in our past. We all have the strength to stop history from repeating itself, because in the end, we will each be the harbingers of our own demise—not some supernatural entity casting judgment upon us. Every day that we don't look back is another step forward into darkness.

I had learned firsthand that what had been built could be destroyed and that what had crumbled could be reborn into something even more beautiful with the right vision. I could demolish a building with a thought, but that wasn't what I wanted my contribution to this world to be. I decided to hone my superhuman gift and architectural craft by helping to renovate the apartment building I was staying in with others of my kind. There wasn't much room to be creative while fixing a teardown in Upper Manhattan on a shoestring budget and with basic materials, but the work was fulfilling. My ultimate dream was to design and build a house of my own someday ... maybe one with columns or something fancy like all the elaborate estates I had visited on my travels.

I set up a meditation area in the basement to practice refining my powers with the help of the ambient darkness. Calling it a meditation area might be over-glorifying it; it was a cement room with an old yoga mat, some rocks, and a candle. The low lighting forced me to focus on only what I needed to by feeling along the materials without distractions. Carving basic shapes with telekinesis had soon become as simple as imagining the finished product in my mind and projecting it into reality.

I had saved a neat pile of about fifty rectangular stones, two inches by three inches each, which I stacked into the rough shape of a house. Next to the miniature house was a bunch of rocks in various geometric figures resulting from my attempts to break off pieces on all sides until they were perfectly smooth. Each attempt brought me one step closer ... until tonight, when I finally succeeded in turning a slab of rock into the size and shape of a baseball.

The shadows at the edge of my candlelight fluttered, and I could sense someone standing over me. It was a man—one whom I had not seen in quite some time.

"Welcome back," I said, staring up at the familiar figure emerging from the darkness. "I was starting to worry something bad had happened—"

"Do be cautious how far you wander down the spiral of darkness. For he who speaks with honeyed tongue holds naught but hidden malice, and you have not what it takes to resist the promise of tomorrow."

The filthy undead hobo was no worse for wear than he had been during any of our previous encounters, but something was still off about him, and that was saying something for someone who babbled incoherent nonsense most of the time and regularly had kitty litter and God knows what else matted into his mangy gray beard.

"Octavio, are you feeling okay?" Octavio had the kind of lazy eyes that no matter how directly he was looking at you, they were never focused on the same place. But this was not one of those times. Both eyes stared straight into mine, locked pupil to pupil without blinking. His words were disturbing— even for him.

"There you are!" a girl's voice called from the stairs, chasing Octavio away into the shadows again before he could be seen. "You really need to get out of this basement. It's Thursday night, and we're holding Bible study, if you'd like to join us."

The girl was Emily. Starting at the tender age of sixteen, Emily had been held captive for years by the man she loved after falling victim to the undead curse. His name was William, and his fanatical religious views led him on a crusade against all undead, including her, in an attempt to cover up his own indiscretions. Since I'd rescued her, she had joined the patchwork quilt of an undead coven—the Outsiders—and had taken it upon herself to manage their new hideout with startling efficiency.

"I do need to get out more," I admitted. "I was thinking of heading up to Boston this weekend to put flowers on my parents' grave. It's been a while since I've had the chance to visit." Coming from a family of doctors, my rearing was much more scientific than Emily's devout, and often idyllic, view of the world. However, when I fell face-first into the supernatural, my skepticism for the divine had waned. It was hard to say something didn't exist or couldn't exist when you were fighting dragons, demons, and the undead on a daily basis.

Anything was possible if you opened your eyes wide enough, I suppose, but it was people's often violent interpretations of religion that I had a problem with. When I sat in on one of Emily's Bible studies, the discussion was actually quite inspiring. Those who attended were firm believers in using their faith to help others and spread hope. This was the complete opposite of William, who felt that faith was a weapon to crush those who were different.

Call me a dreamer, but I'd like to think that people were given free will for a purpose.

Chapter One

"Who would do something like this?" Emily exclaimed outside my apartment door as I waded through the crowded hallway to see what was going on. "You always keep your place locked."

"What's going on?" I asked her as I pushed past the people who were gathered in the doorway.

"Oh, Dorian! It's like romantic vandalism," she said with stars in her eyes. Emily was way too enthusiastic and optimistic about pretty much everything. There were dozens, possibly hundreds, of white roses covering every surface of my room. "That's so poetic! Maybe it's someone's way of thanking you for all your hard work. I'll ask around—"

"It's okay. They obviously wanted to remain anonymous. Was my door left open like this?" I already knew who had left the flowers, and they didn't use doors.

"Mia wandered in," Emily confessed.

"Mia? You mean Emilia's going by Mia now?" I asked. "Like 'missing in action'? Very appropriate since I know that something's broken if she's gone missing."

"She's gotten a lot better," Emily said in her defense. Emilia, or Mia, was another undead refugee whom Octavio had taken in, and she had been turned only a few years ago as a child. In the weeks since I'd been there, I'd used my powers to help remodel four apartments on the third floor to provide more individual rooms for people. Mia had set fire to three of them. I'd assembled over a dozen beds that had been purchased at an overstock furniture store. Mia had dismantled about half of them by removing some screws to try to sell them back to me. When I'd painted the rooms, she had finger-painted over them in bright pink.

"You should think about decorating your room," Emily continued. "It's so ... I don't know ... lonely?"

"I'm not really the domestic type." I had lived off the land for two years in the Ōmine Mountains, learning to do without and honing my senses to get a better grasp of my powers. A traditional bed and shelter from the elements were more than enough.

I went to close my door behind me when something stopped it halfway.

"What've we got 'ere? Let ol' Grampy get a look at them whitey-whites." Octavio's moment of clarity from the other day had ceased, returning him to the absentminded codger I was used to. "Grampy," as he was endearingly nicknamed, had a kind heart in a cruel world and had been absent from the hideout on and off since I'd gotten there. He took in the wayward undead who held no coven of their own and who were appropriately named the Outsiders. There was usually sage advice between his muddled words, but it was always hard to differentiate the snippets of clairvoyance from insanity.

He was the one to call on my help when the Outsiders were being slaughtered at the hands of invaders from the Far East. My on-again-off-again friend and mentor, Noah, had taken me for training in Japan, only to defile a sacred temple in a desperate bid to steal a legendary sword that was capable of felling an Ancient. The situation had quickly spun out of control when the guardian spirits of the temple had followed us back to New York to exact their vengeance. Their leader had taken the form of an enormous serpentine dragon when we'd brought the fight back to their land, but once defeated, she'd explained that their purpose was to protect the world, and that they'd mistakenly viewed all the undead, like Noah, as a threat to the purity of death and the afterlife.

"Where've you been?"

"Here ... or maybe over there ... Sometimes both, you know. I found me a nice fishin' pit upstream." He licked his chops to remove whatever foul-smelling substance was encrusted around his lips today. "Too quiet 'round here. Nothin' stirrin'."

"I think you mean fishing hole." Octavio was a lively soul—as lively as a cold dead body could be—but right now, he seemed dull and lethargic. He shuffled away from me down the hall in a daze, ignoring the many weathered vagabonds in his path.

"No, no, this was a pit alrighty. Deep and dark with lots o' the little critters squirming about."

"What are you talking about?" I shouted after him as he waddled around the corner. "Never mind."

"Gianni? Are you there?" I asked in a loud whisper once my door was closed. There was no response, and I hadn't really expected one. It had been weeks since I had last seen him, but Gianluca still managed to make his presence known while guarding Yomi as part of our truce with the guardian spirits. He seemed to enjoy presenting me with gifts of pure white. Maybe it was some Roman courtship ritual I was unaware of, or it could have been the association with my pasty complexion, which he claimed Romans viewed as greatly attractive in comparison to his more common tan olive skin.

A former Roman soldier turned undead warlord of the shadows, Gianluca was fated to become an evil like no other. It took an incredible amount of willpower to pull away from the dark masters who had sent him to terrorize mankind. While he had not been in control, his horrible acts had placed a stain on his soul and a sadness in his heart that couldn't be silenced.

Gianluca had plunged himself into the endless abyss of the Nether Realm, where he'd slept for centuries so he could do no more harm. The world had changed so much in the time he'd slept, but Gianluca was a fast learner. When he found me, I had no idea that we were from different worlds. He was chivalrous and always in high spirits, but best of all was the undeniable spark between us that continued to grow from more than just a mutual physical attraction.

He showed interest in me from the start, but I had put up so many walls to protect myself from being hurt that even someone as charismatic as he was had trouble breaking through. It wasn't easy for me to trust others. The idea that love is a weakness was forced down my throat since I'd first interacted with other supernaturals, but he made the risk worth it.

I laid the flowers out to dry so they could be saved before I headed out to catch my train to Boston. Beside the white roses sat a stack of books on Ancient Rome and learning Latin. Gianluca told me that Latin was easy and that it was English that was confusing. That was a lie. He learned English in a couple of years by listening through the shadows; I couldn't learn a sentence of Latin in a week with a guidebook. I was hoping he didn't see the books, because I knew he would be amused listening to me butcher the language.

Down on the first floor, Emily's Sunday group was in session. This was the nicest area in the building. It had needed the least amount of remodeling, and Emily had done a great job collecting refurbished couches and vintage lounge chairs accented with an abundance of pillows to give it a welcoming feel.

I snuck by the mixed congregation, wondering how clueless the humans were to the undead amongst them.

"Mia, don't you dare," I scolded as I walked past the front desk. The little imp was going through our money box, replacing the bills with play money.

"Aw, but I want to buy a unicorn!" she squeaked.

"You have more toys than Santa's workshop."

"Santa's not even real," she said with indignation.

"Neither are unicorns, I think."

I left the comfortable warmth of the shelter for the frozen tundra that Manhattan had been transformed into by an unusually relentless winter. In my white hoodie, jacket, gloves, and hat, all of which had been given to me by Gianluca, I was a ghost against the freshly powdered terrain. The subway was only two blocks north, but under these conditions, it felt more like a ten-mile hike.

The streets were quiet. We lived far enough north that late-night traffic was minimal since there was nothing up here for tourists. Leftover Christmas lights blinked in some apartment windows, casting eerie reflections against the snow and projecting warped silhouettes of discarded Santa Claus decorations on the buildings, which kept my peripheral vision at constant attention. I had fought monsters that would make the best horror movies look like comedies, but all it took was the right lighting to send chills down my spine. I convinced myself that it was only in response to the bitter midnight air until the lighting was no longer an issue. The lights died, and everything faded into an overcast gloom around me as the sound of someone approaching came from ahead.

"There you are." It was my favorite deep Italian voice drawing me in from down the sidewalk. I went forward into the darkness and was immediately held in Gianluca's tight embrace. "I think you hide from me in all the white."

He tugged my knitted hat down over my eyes and kissed me on the lips.

"What are you doing here?" I asked and pulled my hat back so I could look up at him as the darkness from which he had arrived cleared. "Are you done guarding Yomi?"

"No. I take a rest to come see you." He rested his chin on top of my head. There was a good six-inch height difference between us that made me feel tiny. He leaned his body weight on me as a joke to make me try to support him, and then he picked me up like I weighed nothing.

"Gianni, you're freezing," I said, talking into his chest. His skin and clothes were like ice, and his eyes looked weary.

"Yes, the shadows do not keep me warm. I do not like such cold places." He was talking about his clothes, which he'd made from tangible darkness.

"Let's go inside somewhere. I can go back out in the morning."

Gianni transported us through the shadows, and in a flash of blackness, we were back in my room. I took him by the hand to sit on my bed and threw a blanket around us, completely forgetting about the train I should be on.

"I am ... very tired." He lay down with his head on my lap and looked up at me with his vibrant green eyes. "I fight always and never sleep. The devils come to steal the souls in Yomi because they know the empress is weak. I do not know how many days it is because there is no sun and no time."

"Send me there. I can take your place while you rest." I ran my fingers through his jet-black hair.

"The shadows guard for me while I come see you." He reached up and touched my face. "It is too big for you. The land never ends, and I must look through all the shadows to be sure the souls are safe."

"I can help at least."

"No." He yawned. "I come to see your face with my eyes, not with my dreams. I want you to be safe here, and Yomi ... it does not need another little devil."

I poked him in the ribs in retaliation.

"You like the flowers?" He turned his head to the collection I had displayed on the desk.

"Yes, thank you! But you don't have to keep bringing me things. Spending time together is enough."

"For you, I will do both, *ab imo pectore*, from the bottom of my chest—ah—the heart." He smiled and kissed my hand. "When I am a child, my father brings these flowers to my mother. He tells me red is for the passion, but the passion can burn too hot and leave you scars. This is not the love you want. To be happy, there must be more … you must have respect. White is pure, and you must cherish it always to stay this way. This is real love."

Gianni's eyes were starting to close. It was snowing outside my window again, so I used my powers to turn up the radiator without disturbing him.

"That's good advice," I said. "Your dad was a wise man for two thousand years ago."

"Love does not change."

"What were your parents like? Did your dad teach you how to use a sword when you were a little Gianni?" It was almost impossible to picture this man as a little kid running around with a wooden sword. I wished there was some way to see back then as proof that he hadn't just been spat out of the darkness as some muscular Roman warrior.

"No." He smiled. "When I am born, they are old and tired. I think they do not want me."

"Don't say that. That can't be true. My parents adopted me when they were older because they really wanted a child. If they went out of their way to have you later in life, they definitely wanted you."

"It is not hard to have a child if you always try. They love each other very much, this I know. I had a brother before me. He is a very strong soldier ... the best. But he die in battle before I am born. I do not think my parents know they can have another child so many years later."

"That doesn't mean they didn't want you." I lowered my voice as his eyes closed.

"I try to bring honor to my family and to make them proud. I practice the fighting with the other boys in Roma, but my parents punish me. They want to send me away so I cannot join the army. To them, I am never as strong as my brother, but I join and am almost a centurion in my last year."

"I think they were trying to protect you. They didn't want to lose another son to war. Just like how you don't want me to fight because you lost someone you cared about before."

There was nothing but silence from Gianni for some time as he started falling asleep.

"When I am a soldier, is the first time I feel someone want me. All of Roma want me to protect them ... the caesar want me to conquer for him, my brothers in the army want me to fight with them ..." Gianni fell silent again, and his breathing slowed as he finally drifted off. He looked so peaceful. I still found it hard to believe that this was the man whom so many had feared in the past. I knew what he was capable of; yet, to me, he was a different person.

I summoned the history book on Ancient Rome to my hand from under the bed, but the room was growing darker by the second until I couldn't see my hand in front of my face. *This must be some sort of subconscious effect of Gianni's powers when he falls asleep. The only thing to do now is take a nap myself.* It had been a while since I had slept, and the darkness was very comforting to me now.

Chapter Two

Gianni and his shadows were gone when I woke up tucked in snuggly under the covers. The Outsiders, who were sharing the rooms on either side of me, were blasting metalcore music along with their video games. Most of the Outsiders had been turned when they'd been teenagers, homeless, or a combination of the two. The other covens must have had no use for such humans among their ranks. It seemed that the Outsiders rarely knew who turned them. In most cases, it was either by accident or curiosity and, even more rarely, to spare a life from the clutches of death.

They were all generally good-natured and lacked the manipulative machinations of the other more unified covens, but it made survival that much more difficult in this existence. They were undead rebels without a cause and couldn't be happier with the simplest of traditionally mortal pleasures. Those pleasures were giving me a headache right now, though.

I grabbed the book on Ancient Rome and took the fire escape outside my window up to the roof. It was serene up here with the distant sound of steady traffic keeping rhythm like a heartbeat. I had begun to enjoy city life and didn't feel as restless here anymore since I'd found my place in it.

"The Romans had no word in Latin to distinguish between modern-day concepts of sexuality," I read to myself. "It was relatively commonplace for males to enter into both sexual and romantic couplings with each other up through the infancy of the empire. Even the young Emperor Nero famously married two men during his reign."

Interesting. Gianluca had told me about this in his own words when I'd questioned his confidence in public displays of affection toward me.

"The Romans were not alone in their acceptance of same-gender relations. The Ancient Greeks were known to have a well-respected army comprising one hundred and fifty pairs of male lovers known as The Sacred Band of Thebes. They were thought to have fought with greater vigor than even the legendary Spartans to protect their lovers at their sides."

Wow. I had grown up in the wrong century. But maybe I was here now to make a difference where it was needed most.

The Outsiders' racket was starting to penetrate my little oasis on the roof as more of them woke up. I closed my book and decided to find a place in Central Park that had enough light for me to continue reading.

"Ah! H-ii ..." I was startled by a figure staring at me from the shadows when I got up. It wasn't easy to sneak up on me. I had been trained by the best and had developed a sort of sixth sense—or psionic sonar—that let me feel out the immediate area with my powers. "Something wrong, Grampy?"

Octavio didn't answer. He stepped further into the shadows and left through the door on the roof. I went to check on him but stopped at the sound of several pairs of footsteps coming up the fire escapes around the building. They were faint as a result of the effort to go unnoticed. I could hear the jingling of metal. Maybe keys? Nobody ever came up here and certainly not in groups. If it was anyone who belonged here, they would come up the stairs or maybe a single fire escape.

I hid in the dark, growing more suspicious as I tried to use my powers to feel out how many were coming. Two. No, three. Now ... four ... one on each side of the building. Suddenly, I was surrounded.

"Found one." There was a gruff, muffled voice following a bright light to my eyes. Four figures in futuristic SWAT gear surrounded me. Were these humans? I couldn't see their faces behind the sleek black helmets, and their guns looked nothing like what a normal soldier would have. What would SWAT be doing here?

I had seconds to decide whether to use my powers to escape or to pretend I was just a normal human. The soldiers all had the lights on their guns pointed at me now, and I could see a fifth up on the roof next door, watching me through the scope of a sniper rifle. If they managed to shoot me, they'd see that I was supernatural when I healed from the bullet wound. And then there were the Outsiders ... I couldn't let them get hurt. But was I prepared to kill humans, assuming that was what they were?

I'd have to get them to chase me. I could scare them off then go back to warn the Outsiders to clear out in case they came back.

"Your orders, lieutenant?" The soldier in the lead took a cautious step toward me while looking down the sights of his high-tech rifle. I threw him to the ground with a telekinetic push and bolted to the edge of the roof to fly off.

"Stand down!" A sixth soldier shouted as he walked out on to the roof from the same door through which Octavio had retreated. They were already inside the building. I had to go back.

I pulled the soldiers' guns from their hands and aimed them at their heads.

"Dorian, wait!" The sixth one shouted and removed his helmet.

"No way—" I froze. "It can't be ..." I had had many hallucinations of moments like these while suffering from PTSD, but that was behind me ... or so I thought. "Is this real?"

"Of course I'm real, man. Drop the guns. We're not here to hurt you."

It had been over three years since I had last seen him. We'd ended our friendship over a petty argument when I'd felt like he hadn't understood me. I'd regretted it every day since.

"Lyle, what are you doing here?"

"I'm here for you, dude! We've been looking everywhere for you." It was him all right: Blond, blue-eyed, and three years older than I remembered. He looked a bit more mature. Maybe it was the facial hair that he'd lacked before. "Can you put our guns down?"

I complied, still in a daze, and flew over to him for a better look. I was surprised when he hugged me like our fallout had never happened. Back then, I'd felt like I'd had no place in the world, especially around humans. He'd been like a brother to me and had tried to encourage me to lead a normal lifestyle after we'd survived a supernatural war in Manhattan together. I hadn't been ready then and had chosen to run away instead.

"What are you wearing?" I asked, upon inspecting his all-black combat gear. It appeared to be made of a dense plastic and heavy-duty bulletproof Kevlar mesh. The design looked like it had come right out of a science fiction movie.

"Like it?"

"Uh, I guess." The super-soldier armor must have been ridiculously expensive. There was even a screen inside the helmet he was holding.

"Well screw you. It's cool. Why are you dressed like a snowflake?" he asked, taking note of my all-white ensemble.

"Because I'm unique."

"That's one word for it." He smiled and hit me on the shoulder. "C'mon, let's get out of here. Pack some underwear 'cause it's gonna be a trip."

"Where are we going?" The other soldiers, who were still wearing their helmets and were standing around like I was under arrest, were making me uneasy. "I kind of live here now."

"Incoming. It's an undead," announced a female soldier. The pitter-patter of little feet was led by Mia's squeal as she charged across the roof and jumped at Lyle.

"Don't shoot!" I shouted and grabbed their guns away again as they took aim. Mia latched on to Lyle, trying to hug him around his gear, but her arms were too short to make it.

"Stand down, everyone," Lyle ordered and picked Mia up. "Hey there, little lady. Long time no see."

"Can I see your badge?" she asked as her feet dangled in the air.

Mia had been a big fan of Lyle since first meeting him back when she was human during the Carpathians' invasion of Manhattan.

"Sorry, but I'm not a police officer anymore," he apologized and set her down.

"What *are* you now exactly?" I asked and returned the guns a second time. "I never thought you'd quit the force. I thought something happened."

"Yeah, one of my best friends went missing." He didn't sound like he was joking. Whether I was around or not, I wound up influencing his life. Part of why I stayed away was because I was scared of bringing trouble to his door. Saying the supernatural world was cutthroat would be a severe understatement.

"Sorry." I felt embarrassed now and wondered how much the other soldiers knew.

"We should be moving out, lieutenant." The sniper from the other building had made his way over during our conversation and had addressed Lyle. I thought the mortal world was simple and predictable, but I had more questions about all this than anything in my supernatural life.

"Right," Lyle agreed. "It was good seeing you, Emilia! We'll be back. I just have to borrow Dorian for a while, if that's okay with you."

"It's Mia now! Can I come?" She hopped back and forth excitedly.

"Next time! Our plane doesn't have enough seats for all of us," he explained. "Now go inside so you don't turn into a Mia-cicle."

"Plane?" I questioned.

"You'll see." I could tell Lyle was trying to contain his enthusiasm and play it cool.

"Tell Emily I'm going on a trip, Mia."

"'Kay!" She obliged and scampered back inside.

"Don't you want to pack anything to take with you? I wasn't kidding about the underwear," Lyle asked.

"Nah, they always wind up flying off or setting on fire in battle."

"Um, that sounds like a problem."

"Not for me. I've gotten used to it."

Lyle and his space cadet squad escorted me to an unmarked gray van they had waiting in an alley a block away. If I didn't trust Lyle, this would surely have raised a few red flags.

"So, you're military now?" I asked him as we got in the back of the van with three of the other troops. The remaining two took the front seats and didn't waste any time getting us out of the city. "I thought you said NYPD for life ... police help people; soldiers kill them."

"We're not the military. Not exactly."

The soldiers, or whatever they were, removed their helmets to relax. The three in the back with us were women, and two guys were up front. Lyle introduced me to them, but I had zoned out and was paying more attention to their suits. The fact that he wouldn't explain what was going on was now beginning to get on my nerves. It also didn't help that the others kept looking at me through the corners of their eyes like I was going to bite them. They obviously knew I was a freak, and their false smiles weren't concealing that.

"Lyle, tell me what's going on," I demanded.

"We're called PROJECT: UNITY," he declared with the same pride that he'd had for the NYPD. "We're an independent organization that specializes in human–supernatural justice."

"Aren't you against vigilantism?" I remembered the argument that had divided us. I used to use my powers to stop crimes and let him take the credit as a police officer, but when people started getting suspicious, he wanted me to stop. At the time, it was my only outlet to be who I was, and I took his reaction as more of an attack on my person than as the result of the repercussions of what I was doing.

"I am. But we aren't taking the law into our own hands; we handle what the law doesn't: supernaturals."

"Am I under arrest or something?"

"No, man, we've been trying to track you down to make sure you're safe."

"Why?"

"Because we're friends, Dorian, and that's what friends do."

But I hadn't done that. I'd let Lyle go so I wouldn't bring him anymore trouble, and still he'd wound up getting himself involved in this world again.

"When you disappeared, I figured you just needed time," he continued. "I got worried when you didn't come back, so I went looking for you. That's how I got involved with these guys. We knew Noah was after you, but you never stayed in one place long enough for us to catch up. We came out here locked and loaded because I was afraid you had been kidnapped again."

"It wasn't like that. I went with him willingly," I explained. "He's taught me a lot."

"The guy's dangerous and completely unstable. Not to mention a total prick. I'm just glad you got away."

"Don't talk about him like that. He's my friend, and you don't really know him like I do." I couldn't believe I was standing up for Noah, but it had to be said.

"I don't want to know him anymore than I already do. I'm glad we didn't have to deal with him."

"Deal with him? What were you gonna do? Arrest him for kidnapping?"

"That was one possibility, but I doubted he'd come quietly."

I broke out into laughter, picturing that go down. It wasn't easy. Lyle and the others weren't laughing, though, and he even looked a bit offended.

"Oh God ... you weren't joking." My laughter stopped abruptly. "Do you have any idea what he would do to you? Not that you could ever catch him—"

"We've handled worse, all right?" Lyle snapped in his own defense. "We take care of werewolves on a regular basis. When they get too close to the cities and go berserk from all the lights and noise, *we* catch and release them back into the wild so nobody gets hurt."

"I've still never seen a werewolf ... I fought a dragon, though."

"Wait, really? Or are you being sarcastic?" he asked, moving past his aggravation.

"Seriously. But it's a long story, and you owe me yours first."

We pulled up along the shore of the East River near a water treatment plant, where Lyle had a plane waiting. It was just in time too, because as we arrived, two tires blew out, scaring us half to death. The soldiers were suspicious of foul play and put on their helmets to scan the area through their computerized visor screens. These guys took their job way too seriously for a piece-of-crap van. What did they expect when driving off road in an industrial area?

The plane, on the other hand, was no laughing matter. It looked like a cross between a fighter jet and a small cargo plane modified to hold more, or larger, passengers.

"Wow," I exclaimed as I checked out the inside and took a seat.

"Like it?" the driver from the van asked and sat in the cockpit with one of the women.

"Yeah, I've never seen one of these close up." I was scared to brush against anything. There were buttons, lights, and touchscreens everywhere. It looked more like an alien spaceship than a plane from Earth.

"I wouldn't think so. This baby is only one of four, and they're all owned and manufactured by PROJECT: UNITY," the driver-turned-pilot said.

"Lieutenant?" One of the female soldiers whispered to Lyle and indicated something on a touchscreen tablet.

"Yeah, I know. It's fine. Just ignore it until we get to base," he answered.

"What's wrong?" I asked.

"Nothing. Just e-mails."

"So, who thought it was a good idea to put you in charge of women? Doesn't PROJECT: UNITY do background checks?" I teased. The female soldiers cracked a smile between them like they knew exactly what I was talking about. If there was anything Lyle loved more than the NYPD, it was beautiful women. He was a total gentleman—the type who would hold doors open and pull chairs out for them, but his priorities were hilarious to me. Even in the thick of a city-wide crisis, he found the time to flirt. Then again, maybe I was being a bit hypocritical, considering my newfound Roman interest.

"You should get strapped in," Lyle advised. "Or I might throw you from the plane."

"We better be going someplace warm."

"How's the southeast end of Greenland sound?" the pilot asked as we took off. The engines were much quieter than any commercial plane I had been on.

"Terrible."

"It's not much of a vacation spot, but it makes a great place to hide a base." The pilot smiled back at me. He had a faint accent—Australian maybe—but it was too subtle to tell for sure. "Low population, lots of space, rough terrain to deter visitors, and right in between Europe and the Americas for quick travel to both."

"And covered in ice ..." I sighed. "Who organized you guys?"

"It started as a coalition in response to the surge of global terrorism after the turn of the century," one of the female soldiers explained. She was in her late thirties, maybe early forties, and had short, spikey blond hair; I wondered how it maintained its shape under the helmet.

"Terrorism is a human creation. A cowardly human creation," I said. "Any of the supernaturals I've had the pleasure of dealing with that despise humanity would rather squash mankind in one blow than waste time setting off car bombs and crashing planes."

"With respect, you're wrong," another of the girls spoke out in an easily distinguishable Spanish accent. She didn't look like she could take Emily in a fight, let alone chase werewolves. But I guess the state-of-the-art assault rifle evened the score. "There's more going on behind the scenes that we've been working to piece together. Governments and private investors from around the world have been funding us for over a decade to put the puzzle together, but we have no official affiliation with any of them."

"Why am I getting the feeling that this wasn't a social call to catch up and show me your new place?" I turned to Lyle, who was looking pensively at something on his tablet.

"Because it's not. We need your help."

Chapter Three

We landed at our icy destination after a short flight. The trip had been filled with empty small talk in a transparent attempt by Lyle to avoid further questions about PROJECT: UNITY before we arrived. It wasn't like him to be so secretive.

There was nothing around for miles, except the sporadic gatherings of tiny, snow-covered houses we passed. Along the coast of the frigid waters stood a rather unassuming bunker atop a manmade tunnel covered in rime. The tunnel was closed off by hangar doors that opened just enough to let the jet in.

Inside was far less spectacular than I had been anticipating after seeing the technology of PROJECT: UNITY thus far. It was just an ordinary airplane hangar with three other jets, a helicopter, and a few ATVs, which were all impressive but didn't merit the cloak and dagger act. Lyle led us to a touchscreen console mounted beside an interior metal door that put my disappointment to rest. A computer-generated female face popped up on the screen to greet us as we approached.

"Welcome, Lieutenant Turner," the program recited in a synthesized voice. I couldn't decide if it was fascinating or creepy. Its eyes seemed to track his, but it may have been my hopeful imagination filling in the blanks where I wanted there to be something more. "Clearance granted. Please proceed to debriefing with Commander Rudgar here."

The face was replaced with a three-dimensional layout of the base, highlighting a path to his rendezvous point. I was starting to wonder if I had fallen asleep at some point on the way there and if this was all a dream. No one was talking, and I didn't know if it was because this was business as usual or if they were on edge about something.

"You guys go first so I can get Dorian into the system," Lyle told the others. Once they had been let through without any specific orders of their own, he instructed the computer to scan the area for "unknowns."

"Two unregistered presences detected," the face announced. It was somewhat off-putting to see the program mimic lifelike expressions when you knew there was no actual emotion or reasoning behind it. "Error. One unregistered presence detected."

I looked at Lyle, who just sighed and rolled his eyes.

"Um, is your cyber girlfriend feeling okay? Because if she goes haywire and kills us all, I just want to say I called it first."

"Very funny," he said without a smile. Lyle tapped away at the on-screen keyboard. I watched him click "Assign to file," where there was a whole profile on me with basic information such as height, weight, and "assumed birthdate," which I found amusing. Nothing like being stalked by a secret military organization, but I trusted Lyle.

"Stand here so she can scan you." Lyle pulled me over in front of the screen.

"You're really calling it 'she'?"

In a few seconds, the computer had a picture of me on file, along with a polygon image of my frame and "updated statistics," correcting my height from five eleven to five ten.

"Hey, change that back. I'm five eleven," I lied. Online I could be anything I wanted, and I wanted to be taller.

"You're five six with four inches of hair." Lyle laughed at his own joke. "This is PARAGON, by the way." He pointed to the screen.

"Oh, she has a name. Have you brought her home to meet the family yet, or do you just use her to look up porn?"

"It stands for Paranormal GUI Operating Network."

"What the heck is a 'gooey'?" I asked.

"Graphical User Interface. She's the most advanced artificial intelligence program out there, and she oversees all the technology we have. There are PARAGON terminals all around the base. You can use them to look stuff up, including where people are in case you need to find me for some reason."

"That wasn't a 'no' about the porn then?" I teased.

"I'm going to punch you."

"You can't. I'm an endangered species."

"Not endangered enough. Come on, I wanna show you around." We finally got inside the door, after I received my official welcome from PARAGON. The face on the screen rotated to watch us leave the hangar. It was unsettling, but what I saw next helped me forget. In fact, it completely blew my mind. I felt like I was on a space station a thousand years in the future. Lyle took such amusement in my bewilderment that he shook me by the shoulders to snap me out of it and dragged me down the hall.

For a military base, I was expecting something industrial with plenty of gray metal fixtures, florescent overhead lighting, and sharp corners around tight walkways. This was nothing like that.

"Pretty cool, huh?" Lyle asked, noticing me staring at the illuminated walls. I had no idea what to investigate first, so I started with what was right in front of me; call it the inner architect in me. "It's made of backlit plastic paneling that mimics the sun's good rays since a lot of us spend so much time down here. It triggers the same energizing feeling as if you were outside at the beach all day. At night, it turns blue and gives off waves to help relax us, and the LED track lighting between the panels illuminates."

"That is ... awesome. Does it burn the undead like the sun?" I asked.

"Nah. They're only affected by the real thing."

"Cool. Well maybe I'll get a tan during my stay."

"You couldn't get a tan if you walked on the sun."

The arched hallway was wide enough to fit four people side by side. Ahead of us was a central hub branching off into other hallways and a glass elevator encircled by a clear staircase that led down to the other levels. Mechanical drones no bigger than basketballs buzzed quietly through the air, carrying packages from one part of the base to the next.

From my bird's-eye view looking over the guardrail, the residents weren't as militant as my first impression of the soldiers. Many of them were dressed in matching dark blue sweatpants and hoodies with the "PROJECT: UNITY" logo, a few were wearing lab coats, and even fewer were in actual riot gear. They chatted and waved to each other while others joked and laughed. People paused to interact with the PARAGON terminals and others watched the flat screens at the end of the corridors that displayed schedules, directions, and messages in various languages. This was like being on a futuristic college campus.

"What's down the other halls on this floor?" I asked Lyle. I wanted to make sure I didn't miss anything before moving on. I was never a fan of ultramodern architecture, but this was an exception. I noticed a lot of the framework of the base was done in columns, domes, and arches, not unlike the Greco–Roman style. Gianni would have been fascinated by this as well.

"Storage ... maintenance ... nothing really exciting. Most of it's a mess right now. This base is new. The original is off the coast of New Zealand on a small island, and there are two other satellite bases in Hawaii and Madagascar. They're still in operation, but most people like Shaun transferred over here to get things up and running and just never went back since it's nowhere near as cool."

"Who?" I felt like I should know the name, but if I pretended to remember, I knew it would come back to bite me.

"Our pilot?"

"Oh, right." I watched someone sitting on an ergonomically designed bench, cleaning their gun. "Let's go down!"

"Directly below us is the common area: mess hall, lounge, a gym, general meeting area for unimportant stuff." I waited impatiently for the elevator while he explained. With all this technology, you'd think they could have invented something faster. "Under that is the armory. I can take you through part of it, but nothing much to see there except guns, ammo, and armor."

"Okay, see you there."

"Where are you going?"

I let my enthusiasm take over and jumped the guardrail to fly down to the next floor.

"Hi." I greeted the passersby who stopped to see the floating guy with the freaky eyes. None of them screamed or seemed too surprised. This was a good sign. Their tolerance was admirable. Nobody was gawking, but there was as much curiosity in their expression as you'd expect. A couple of them said hello back, but not before Lyle shouted down to us.

"He's with me! It's okay!"

"We know!" a middle-aged man in sweats shouted back. "Dorian, right?"

"Yeah, how'd you know?" I didn't think everyone knew about me yet.

"I read your file. Welcome aboard," he replied as others gathered around. This guy knew me from my approximate height and weight? A picture hadn't even been added until a few minutes ago. News traveled fast.

"Sorry, everyone," Lyle apologized to the crowd around me as he sprinted from the elevator. "He's just a little excited."

"Yeah, I've never seen a real human before," I quipped as Lyle dragged me to a less populated hallway.

"Cool it with the powers while you're here," he warned. "They don't know you're not a threat, so you might spook some people. I wanted to show you around before we go to meet the commander, so don't make a scene."

"Yes, sir." I landed back on my feet, looking chastened.

"I'm just trying to look out for you. You're like a little brother to me, and I don't want you running off again because of a bad experience."

It was nice hearing Lyle say that. I had considered him a brother for sometime too.

"I thought PROJECT: UNITY was used to supernaturals. They seemed fine with me."

"We are, but I don't want anyone getting the wrong idea. I want you to like your new home."

"New home?" I questioned. "I have a home back in New York."

"Oh," Lyle sounded disappointed. "I thought you were just squatting there."

"Nope. I was helping fix it up. I mean, this place is great too, but I'm not a soldier."

"You don't have to be. Not everyone is. I didn't want to say it yet, but you're kinda like a VIP here." Lyle walked me back out to the hub, and I noticed the lighting start to dim. The daylight glow before wasn't obnoxious on the eyes. It was actually quite pleasant and made you feel like you were in some tropical area, expecting to see the sun if you looked up the elevator shaft. The common area we strolled by had potted trees and plants in between benches that gave it an outdoor feel. Even the circulated air smelled nice and fresh, unlike the clinical scent of disinfectant I would have expected from someplace so technological, like a hospital or laboratory.

"I've talked about you a lot to the team," Lyle continued. "We spent a lot of time and resources tracking you down, and they've seen some of the stuff you've done, like back in New York a few years ago. I was hoping you'd stick around. This was everything you wanted, right? People to accept you and a way to use your powers to help others."

I was content with the Outsiders in New York, but I didn't really have any emotional attachment to them. I wanted them safe and wished them the best, but we hardly interacted. We didn't have much in common, except for not being human. With Lyle, it was different. We were like brothers, as he said, and we could talk and joke around and be ourselves. I couldn't keep pushing away a real friend and blaming myself for him being involved in this world when he had made his choice to stay.

"I don't like fighting if I don't have to. I learned new ways to use my powers, and I've been practicing building things."

"That's great, man. But you have a gift—one that can save billions of lives and already has in the past. You're a superhero."

I laughed at the thought of that. For years, I was a filthy homeless kid, with no friends or family, who couldn't get out of his own way. Hardly a hero, but I did have some pretty interesting adventures. I had never told him in so many words, but I always considered Lyle a hero for selflessly helping to pull me out of a dark time when we met.

"I'm serious," Lyle pleaded. "You can do so much good, and we've all got your back. I won't make you do anything you don't want to, but just think about it."

"I will." This was suddenly getting a lot heavier than I was prepared to deal with at the moment. I had a hard time paying attention as Lyle continued the tour, and it didn't take him long to notice. We had skipped over most of the armory and were in the barracks the next floor down when he stopped.

"Here. This is my room. Let's go inside so we can talk."

The automatic door slid open the moment his hand touched the electronic panel beside it. Inside was a room with a computer desk attached to the wall and two twin-sized beds with flat-screen monitors mounted at the foot of each. There wasn't much else unique about it, except the smooth, curved aesthetic of molded plastic, along with the strip of LED lights in the walls and ceiling. It was still cozy in some way; maybe it was the familiarity of seeing Lyle's mess like when we had lived together in New York.

"I figured you could room with me since the barracks are all built for doubles."

"No one else could put up with you?" I joked and cleared away stacks of magazines, laundry, and empty soda cans so I could sit down.

"Something like that. Nobody likes to be roomies with their commanding officer, and I'm still kinda new." He sounded a little sore about the subject. When I'd met him, he had been a rookie in the NYPD. He'd moved up fast, but every step forward had been like starting all over again.

"How'd you become a lieutenant?"

"I was snooping around the city for supernaturals that might give me a lead on where you had gone when the commander approached me. He said they had been watching me since the battle with the Carpathians in New York. They knew about my involvement with you going vigilante and offered to help find you.

"PROJECT: UNITY tries to recruit people who come in contact with supernaturals before they get killed or have their memories erased. They look for certain skill sets, like military background, law enforcement, science, and medicine, and they place you based on experience. After a year of training out in the field, he made me lieutenant since I knew what I was doing."

"What's the commander like?" I asked as Lyle changed out of his gear.

"He's intense. He isn't going to take no for an answer, so that's why I wanted to ease you into everything and talk first. The job is equal parts compassion as it is combat. Just like being a cop."

"I'm not your job, Lyle."

"That's not what I meant. I'm saying we're not about going to war and fighting. It's about taking care of the people involved. I think you'd like it. We're trying to bridge the gap between mankind and supernatural ... prevent a war *before* it happens."

"Have you been taking steroids?" With all his armor on, I wasn't able to see that he had gained at least twenty pounds of lean muscle. Lyle had been pretty athletic to begin with, but when we'd last seen each other, he hadn't looked like a guy who spent his life in the gym.

"Why? You think I look bigger?" He beamed at himself in the mirror. "Gotta stay shredded in this line of work."

"Nah, I take it back. It's just fat."

"Screw you." He laughed and threw his rolled-up shirt at me. "I'll have a better body than your buddy Noah, and it won't take me a hundred years to get it either."

"I don't think that's a physical possibility …"

A chime sounded from the door. Lyle went to answer it but tripped on something and banged his head on a desk.

"Are you all right? You've gotta clean your room. When was the last time you saw the floor in here?"

"I'm fine," he grumbled and opened the door for another man about our age.

"The commander wants to see you immediately, Lieutenant. And you're bleeding, sir."

Chapter Four

"That's the Medical Ward and the R&D Lab across from it." Lyle pointed out as we took the glass elevator to go meet his commander. "We can go there later. I wanna introduce you to somebody."

By the smile growing on his face, I could tell that the somebody must be of the female gender. "Another robot girlfriend?"

"Nope. A real one."

"You have a girlfriend?!" I exclaimed.

"Why do you sound so surprised? And we're not official or anything. I haven't really had time to ask her out, but we've been getting to know each other."

We exited on to the last floor—the Command Center. This floor wasn't as inviting as the rest. Several of the PARAGON terminals we passed were off-line, and the air was cooler down here. The lighting was darker, and most of the plastic paneling on the walls and ceiling was missing, exposing the infrastructure of pipes and wires. Now I really felt like I was inside a military base. The Command Center was also not as opened up as the previous floor plans, making it almost claustrophobic to walk the corridors.

"He's either going to be really enthusiastic to meet you or not say a word," Lyle continued to prepare me. "I know he's not gonna be happy I didn't bring you to him first."

"Jeez, you're making me nervous."

We were almost at the door labeled "Alpha Command" when Lyle stumbled over the metal grating, garnering the attention of two troops guarding the door.

"What's going on with you?" I asked. "Are you dizzy from hitting your head?"

"Lieutenant?" one of the guards inquired to offer help.

"I'm fine."

We entered the commander's office, which was little more than a vault with a metal desk cluttered by paperwork, a few chairs, and a computer. The man behind the desk stood to greet me with a handshake right away. He was in his early forties, in great shape, and quite handsome for his age, with short salt-and-pepper hair that matched his goatee. He had a hardened expression and definitely seemed to fit the military stereotype.

"Commander, this is—"

"Dorian, yes, I know." He cut Lyle off. The armed guards came in and locked the door behind them. That was ominous. "Please, sit. I was just recalibrating my sidearm, waiting for you to make your way down here. I thought the elevator might be broken, so I sent maintenance to check so it won't stop at every floor on the way down next time."

The commander was of German descent, based on his accent, but he spoke perfect English. He made me want to laugh about the elevator remark, but I refrained.

"Sorry, I thought—" Lyle attempted to explain himself.

"It's an honor to finally meet you," the commander redirected to me.

"Oh, thanks, Commander ... sir." I didn't think he was being sarcastic, but it sounded like an exaggeration.

"Call me Lars." A stack of papers suddenly fell off his desk. He glanced up at the two guards standing behind me and then sat back down to fiddle with his gun while we talked.

"That wasn't me," I jumped to defend myself.

"I know," Lars said and motioned to his eyes without looking up. "You have the eyes that change."

There was this tension in the room that I couldn't explain; it was making me uneasy. My anxiety peaked when the commander's finger slipped and fired his gun at the vacant chair next to me. I leaped out of my seat as the guards behind me drew their weapons. And then I saw it. The bullet was floating in midair.

Lyle and the commander kept their cool, but I was in shock.

"Noah?!"

"Hey." He grinned at me and embedded the bullet into the wall with a flick of his finger.

"What are you doing here?" I looked at the others, who didn't seem the least bit surprised.

"Being bored out of my mind." He had his feet kicked up on the commander's desk where the papers had fallen. "I got tired of slapping this guy with my dick after about a hundred times." He nodded to Lyle.

"Noah!" I shouted at him.

"I'm kidding! I did trip him a couple times though."

"And slashed our tires," Lyle added.

Noah flexed his arms behind his head. "By the way, your body ever looking as good as *this?* Never gonna happen."

"That was you with the van?" I glared at him. He shrugged, trying to look innocent. "What are you doing here?"

"What are *you* doing here?" he retorted.

"I was invited."

"I'm Noah Burckhardt. That's all the invitation I need."

"The only thing you need is to leave," Lyle demanded.

"Not so fast, Lieutenant," Lars interrupted. "We welcome all superhumans who are willing to be civil."

"I'm the most civil guy you're ever gonna meet," Noah bragged. "Now whose neck do I have to tear into to get a drink around here?"

"Noah, stop causing problems," I chided.

"Are you telling me what to do?" He stood up over me to intimidate me, so I floated up to stare at him face to face.

"Yes."

"Pfft. Whatever."

"Lieutenant, why don't you go up to Medical to get our guest a drink from the blood bank?" the commander suggested. Lyle was fuming, but he followed orders. I felt bad for him.

"Make sure to warm it up, rookie. It's chilly down here," Noah mocked.

"Maybe if you put a shirt on ..." Lyle mumbled under his breath.

"And cover up all this? Don't you wanna see what you aspire to be?"

"Noah!" I shouted again.

"All right, all right. I'm just kidding!" He smiled devilishly.

"That was impressive catching that bullet." Lars dismissed the two guards after Lyle left. "Our firearms use magnetic force to fire rounds. It's up to fifteen times faster than a standard assault rifle and fifty percent quieter. They were specially designed to hit targets with supernatural speed."

"Didn't feel any faster to me." Noah smirked and looked over at me. He seemed in an uncharacteristically good mood.

"How come I'm the only one who didn't seem to know you were here?" I asked.

"Because you don't pay attention."

"Our scanners picked him up," Lars explained. "They're built into the helmets, portable devices, and all over the base ... monitored by PARAGON. The sensors scan the full electromagnetic spectrum, including body heat or lack of it, and DNA remnants. Mr. Burckhardt may become invisible, or turn to mist, but he still leaves an energy trail that can be locked on to even if for a split second. We know all about him, but it was still impressive to see him in action with my own eyes."

"I'm famous." Through the corner of my eye, I saw Noah's smug smile still plastered across his face. I didn't want to give him the benefit of acknowledging that.

"Actually, it's Dorian who's rather famous," the commander corrected. "It's something I wanted to discuss."

He brought up pictures on a tablet. It was me at the Colosseum when the guardian spirit of fire from Yomi—Kamiko—attacked. There were dozens of shots and videos taken with cell phones of me flying and levitating falling rubble away from innocent bystanders.

A knot formed in my stomach. I had known that it was going to get out, but I'd had to save those people. There were no repercussions at the time, so I had hoped that nothing would come of it.

"Your secret is out," Lars said. Noah was quiet and just raised an eyebrow at the pictures. There were more of me in Manhattan flying and even some taken through my window as I fixed up the Outsiders' hideout with my powers.

"It isn't only supernaturals who have been keeping things under wraps. PROJECT: UNITY has plenty of reason to keep things quiet too. If everything was out in the open, there would be riots without guidelines on how to contain situations peacefully. Governments would panic and turn to hostility, no doubt. This would make our job impossible.

"PROJECT: UNITY was funded in part by backdoor government agencies when it started. Since then, we've slowly disassociated with them to avoid being investigated and having to answer to a governing body that lacks the understanding of the depth of our work. It has been wealthy and grateful supernaturals who have contributed to helping us expand further. They, too, want no official ties to us, but the comfort of knowing trustworthy human allies are working to keep their secret is there."

"Oh please," Noah scoffed. "Dorian's not the first one to do something like this. I bet if he didn't save those humans, you'd be calling him evil."

"I didn't say what he did was wrong or that he was the only one. Anyone with good intentions has merit. We brought him here to offer him sanctuary from those who might not feel the same way. I'm more aware than you know about how violent your lives are. Your own kind wouldn't hesitate to kill you over secrecy."

"Neither would humans. Only they do it out of stupidity." Noah rolled his eyes and leaned back in his chair.

"I'd hope after spending some time here, you'd think differently about some of us. We certainly don't feel the same way about all of you."

"So what's going to happen?" I asked, nervous about the consequences of being exposed. I was confident at the time, but I didn't think there would be a blood hunt in my name. The undead always seemed to just cover things up like it was routine and go about their business. It was the humans I was more worried about coming after me for being noticed up to now.

"Nothing," Noah said. "No one's going to fuck with you over a few pictures. The only ones who'd care are those who aren't powerful enough to deal with being outed, and it's not like they're any threat to you. The only ones strong enough to bother you aren't going to care and will do what they always have for centuries."

"How can you be so sure?" Lars asked.

"Because I'm one of the strong ones and probably the only one not hiding away in some castle."

"I'd like to believe that, but are you willing to risk your friendship on it?"

"Yeah. There's no risk. Dorian's fought a lot worse than some undead who are going to bitch like their existence is so important it was disrupted by this."

I looked over at Noah. Had he just admitted that we were friends? Had he just *complimented* me?

"The offer still stands," Lars redirected the conversation to me. "I know you have an interest in helping people and exercising your powers. We could use someone like you on our side, and it wouldn't be the first time we've had a supernatural member on the team. Working together, we can make sure things stay discreet and organized. I extend the same offer to you, Mr. Burckhardt."

"I'm not really a teamwork kinda guy," Noah said. "And I don't like helping people."

"I'll think about it ... I guess," I said, trying not to be rude and sound too reluctant.

"Once we find the rest of your siblings, you'll feel more at home. Now that we've found you, it should be easier."

"My siblings? What are you ...? No. You mean the others from the Strigoi? You can't." The sorcerous undead coven known as the Strigoi had created me and several others as living weapons to serve them. It took a significant amount of violence to dissuade them from pursuing us any further and I was at ease thinking that the issue had been laid to rest. The last thing I wanted was for any more innocent lives to be disrupted.

"We've already been searching for them. I was under the impression this was something you'd want. They could be in danger with the Strigoi hunting them."

"They're not," said Noah. "Trust me. The Strigoi got more than they bargained for with this one. They don't want anything to do with the others. If the kids survived this long on their own, they're fine."

"Yeah, please don't go after them," I echoed.

"We already have people on the field, and we're close to—"

Noah stood up and leaned over the desk with his knuckles down on it. "Then get them far away," he demanded and squinted into the commander's eyes.

"We've already spent a great deal of time and money—"

"I'll cut off one of your fingers for every day you keep the search up." Noah unsheathed one of his wakizashi from his hip and slammed it on the desk between them. "Starting with your trigger finger."

I wanted to stop him, but I also wanted PROJECT: UNITY to leave the others alone even more, and I didn't know how much convincing it would take.

"You can't bargain through threats." Lars didn't back down. He was pretty brave for someone who'd just met Noah and who had experienced what it was like to have him get in his face.

"I don't bluff."

"He really doesn't," I reinforced.

"Fine," Lars agreed. "If you feel this strongly about the situation, then we'll call it off. We were only trying to help to our fullest capacity."

I thanked him as the door opened for Lyle, who was looking miserable and holding a blood pack.

"What? No straw?" Noah snatched it out of his hand. He bit off the top and spit it at Lyle before downing the contents and throwing the empty bag at him. Lyle looked like he was about to explode. The commander excused himself and took Lyle with him, leaving Noah and me in his office.

"Can you leave Lyle alone?" I asked.

"Yeah." Noah sheathed his wakizashi. "But I don't want to."

"He hasn't done anything to you. Why are you even here?"

"I'm just fooling around. The guy is so self-important. What's with you and not letting me have fun? I'm bored."

"Did you take care of your problem that you needed the Muramasa for?" I asked, noticing he didn't have the cursed sword with him.

"Don't worry about it."

"Don't give me that crap again after what I went through to get it for you." It was Gianluca and me who had put an end to the fight with the guardian spirits that had been awakened by Noah's attempt to steal the sword. Once it was over, we'd bargained for it, knowing that he'd needed it to defeat his master—Aurelia—and secure his freedom after over a century of enslavement.

"It's not done yet. She left after the spirits trashed her chateau, and she hasn't returned. The sword is someplace safe. Trust me." He wasn't an easy person to trust, and it didn't help that he wouldn't look me in the eyes when he said it. "I'm gonna see what there is to do around here for fun. Maybe drop Lieutenant Loser down the elevator shaft."

"Leave him alone!" I shouted after him as he disappeared.

"Try and stop me!" he shouted back. "It'll be just like old times!"

Chapter Five

"Do you guys know where Lyle, er, Lieutenant Turner, went?" I asked the guards outside the commander's office.

"No, but if you were registered with PARAGON, you can use the terminals to locate him. I'll show you," the guard offered. She wasn't at the screen long before alarms started going off all over the base. The terminal screen flashed red, and PARAGON's virtual face popped up.

"Security breach in ... Medical Ward, Operating Room 1

"Security breach in ... Medical Ward, Laboratory 3

"Security breach in ... Barracks, East Wing

"Security breach in ... Research Laboratory 4

"Security breach in ... Armory, Small Arms

"Security breach in ... Armory, Artillery

"Security breach in ... Elevator Maintenance Shaft

"Security breach in ... Barrack, West Wing

"Security breach in ... Unknown.

"Security breach in ... Main Server Room

"Rebooting ..."

The alarms and terminal went dead.

"What the hell is going on? How many of them are there?" The other guard joined us as footsteps stampeded back and forth on the floors above. "That doesn't make any sense. The server room is behind us!"

"I think I broke your friend's girlfriend." Noah appeared with a half-empty blood bag dangling from his mouth and tapping away on one of PROJECT: UNITY's tablet devices. "She couldn't handle all this."

The guards pulled their guns on him.

"Don't bother," I told them, knowing the more they confronted him, the more he'd be tempted to start trouble. "Noah, what did you do?"

"Nothing. I was just taking a look around. Here, hold this." He handed me the blood bag after sucking it dry so he could concentrate on the tablet. "How do you watch TV on this thing?"

"Our security could use some work." The commander came out of the elevator with Lyle.

"It got annoying, so I broke it with my fist," Noah said nonchalantly. "Is anyone gonna tell me how to get TV on this piece of crap?"

"He needs to go! He's already a problem," Lyle argued.

"I'm really sorry." I didn't know why, but I felt like I had to apologize for him. "He's needy and kind of an idiot."

Noah slapped me upside the head with the tablet.

"Exact opposite, actually," Lars disagreed. "If he had been a real enemy, we would've been caught with our pants down. This was a great drill to expose our weaknesses."

"Sir, you can't be serious," Lyle protested.

"If you're interested in watching television, the lieutenant can show you to a room, or there are those in the common area." Lars ignored Lyle's rebuke. "That particular tablet you're holding is a prototype for the onboard missile defense system of our helicopter."

"Nah, I know where his room is. I'll let myself in." Noah shoved the tablet into my hands. "Here … you like blowing shit up."

"I'll register you so you don't set off security, but if it says restricted, please respect that." Lars's warning was falling on deaf ears. Noah was busy flexing with his arms up to show off his biceps as PARAGON finished scanning his image.

"Why don't you take Dorian up to Medical to get checked out, Lieutenant?" Lars said after Noah had disappeared again.

"Why do I need to be checked out? I'm the last person to ever need a doctor."

"It's procedure ... just a physical and some blood work to keep on file," he explained.

"No thanks. I'll pass."

"It only takes a few minutes. Lieutenant Turner can stay with you."

"I'm not five years old. I don't need my hand held. I just don't like being examined."

"You'll be in good hands with Dr. Sullivan," Lars insisted and walked away like it was a done deal.

Lyle waited until the commander was out of earshot to speak. "Don't worry. You don't have to do it. They like to make sure everyone is healthy and you aren't bringing anything contagious in."

"They want to see what makes me tick." I wasn't gullible enough to fall for Lyle's excuse, but I knew he was saying it to make me feel better.

"Rebecca—I mean Dr. Sullivan—isn't like that. C'mon. I still want you to meet her."

We barely got our foot in the door when the security alarm sounded momentarily.

"Security breach in ... Research Laboratory 1."

"I don't care what you say about him, Dorian, but I can't stand that guy. I can't stand bullies ... never could."

"He's not a bully, he's just—"

Noah was sitting perched on the guardrail near the elevator when we stepped out.

"There was nothing on TV," he said.

"So, you went into the research lab?" I questioned.

"I was looking for something to sharpen my swords with."

Lyle headed toward the medical area without me, clearly frustrated by Noah's antics.

"What's his problem?" Noah asked. "I haven't even thrown him down the elevator shaft yet."

"Just stop. I don't know why you're here or what you want, but get it over with and go."

"I don't want anything. I was bored, so I figured I'd see what trouble you were getting yourself into. If it wasn't for me, these toy soldiers would still be hunting down your test-tube family."

He may be right, but Noah never did anything without some purpose, no matter how random it seemed at the time. I knew it wouldn't come out until later when it hit the fan. He was still in a better mood than I'd ever seen him, so there was that to be thankful for.

"I know. Thanks. Can you at least try not to get these guys worked up? It's only going to make it harder on both of us while we're here."

"Stress brings true colors to light." Noah vanished without being followed by the sound of alarms—for now.

The medical area started out decent enough. It lacked the stinging scent of bleach used to mask the despair beneath. Everything from the plastic walls to the ceilings and floors was nauseatingly white. The furniture, terminal screens, desks, and even the pens were white. I liked white; I just didn't like clinical settings and what they represented: questions, false hope, and memories. People very rarely went to doctors and hospitals for a friendly visit. They entered with the hope of salvation; but if death wants you, it will find a way.

"Dorian! Over here," Lyle called from a doorway with a sign overhead that read "Implants."

My parents were doctors. I didn't want to follow in their footsteps, because I couldn't take the sight of blood. This was ironic, considering all the gore I had been through in my adulthood so far. After their tragic death, my showdown with the Carpathians took me to my breaking point in a hospital.

But I was a different person now. I wouldn't panic and accidentally maim everyone by losing control of my powers.

"What's in there?" I asked, already feeling queasy.

"I'll show you. Come in. I want to introduce you to Dr. Sullivan."

"Nah, I'm fine here."

"That's okay; I'll come out there. I was just finishing up." A woman in her early thirties who was wearing a lab coat stepped out behind him. She fastened her pen to the clipboard she was holding and extended her hand in greeting. "It's nice to finally meet you, Dorian. I was beginning to think

Lieutenant Turner had forgotten about me in all the excitement."

"Oh, I wouldn't be too worried about that," I said and shook her hand.

"I understand you're not keen on getting a checkup. I won't pressure you, but I'm sure you value the importance of our work in the medical field. The anomaly that granted your immortality is something mankind has been in search of forever. It's the ultimate goal of any medical professional."

"It doesn't have anything to do with biology or medical technology, though. It was magic."

"Are they really so different? Technology is humans' answer to magic. Different tools, yes, but the outcomes are often the same or similar. A thousand years ago, if we showed the general population a routine heart transplant or bionic limbs, they would have called it witchcraft."

The doctor had posed a good question. When I came here, I was fascinated the same way I was when first witnessing supernatural occurrences. The techniques may be different, but the results are similar, like healing or harnessing the elements.

"Can I show you something in the lab?" she asked. I nodded in agreement with an encouraging look from Lyle, who barely took his eyes off the doctor.

Inside the implants room were two operating tables with multiple robotic arms looming over each and computer screens everywhere. It looked more like a factory assembly line for cars. Dr. Sullivan directed me to a table full of surgical equipment and handed me what appeared to be a small grain of rice.

"This is a neural implant that all members of PROJECT: UNITY have at the base of their skulls. It transmits vitals for PARAGON to monitor using the body's own electric current for power. It's made from a pliable semi-organic polymer and is embedded with a digital code. We engineered it by altering the genetic material of simple bacteria to act like a computer program with layers of basic, self-replicating commands. The combat suits and weaponry will also only respond to those with these implants, and PARAGON can detect an impostor when scanning for it.

"Most importantly, it's our only line of defense against telepathic powers. We've found that the undead read and control minds through synchronizing brainwaves. The implant constantly scrambles the frequency of those brainwaves before they leave the body, making it virtually impossible for any common undead to lock on."

"Wow. All that in a grain of rice?" I put it back down before possibly breaking it.

"Magical, isn't it?"

"Rebecca's a genius. She's the one who invented it," Lyle boasted, trying to score points.

"Oh, stop, Lieutenant. You're too flattering. I think the other four doctors and fifteen research scientists on staff would wholeheartedly agree it was a team effort," she corrected. "And it's Dr. Sullivan. You know how Commander Rudgar is about protocol if he were to hear us."

I laughed at Lyle being shut down. Poor guy. She was probably completely unaware that he almost considered them an item.

"Oh, yeah. I know. I meant that this was like your specialty." Lyle stumbled over his words, trying to make a smooth recovery.

"Actually, it was more of Dr. Hessler's pet project," she corrected again. "I'm a neurosurgeon, not a biomedical engineer like him; although, lately, I find myself doing a little bit of everything around here to help out where I can. I was just the operating physician on staff for the first few implants. But I appreciate the kind words."

A simple thank-you was enough to elevate Lyle's mood again, but it was getting painful watching him flounder. I had to bail him out.

"Anyway, it was nice to meet you. But I'm getting hungry and have no idea how to get food around here ..."

"I was just closing up here for the night too. Maybe we can talk more tomorrow if you get the chance?" Dr. Sullivan asked. "I have so many questions after hearing all about your exploits."

"Couldn't have done it without Lyle," I said, trying to throw him a bone.

"Why don't you join us for dinner?" Lyle's voice was full of hope.

"Thank you, Lieutenant. I ate in the lab just before this, but if Dorian feels more comfortable, we don't have to meet in Medical."

"I'm staying in Lyle's room. We can talk there." My suggestion perked Lyle up. "If he cleans it."

"Then maybe the common area," Dr. Sullivan suggested instead.

I left with Lyle to head up to the mess hall. The base had changed over to nighttime colors while we had been inside the Medical Ward. The lighted paneling was now a deep blue that was darker by the floor and then gradually brighter as it curved up and around to the top of the ceiling. The LED strip that ran the length of the halls twinkled subdued white like a trail of stars, and the PARAGON terminals and mounted flatscreens also changed to reflect the night sky.

"This is really cool," I said as we got into the elevator. The central light above the cylindrical hub glowed with a pale sheen like the moon and even had craters projected onto the surface. "I feel very relaxed."

"Yeah it's all alpha, delta ... whatever ... brain-wave stuff like the walls. I don't know. Science. The moon up there tracks the actual phases in real time. Werewolves love it."

"You've brought them on base?"

"Once or twice for medical assistance when they've gotten silver stuck in them from a fight with a hunter. They can't heal from the stuff, so it's pretty much lethal," Lyle explained as we got off the elevator. "We've found they like raw hotdogs. Can never get enough. It's gross, but it's like candy to them."

The mess hall's name was inappropriately militaristic. I was expecting a step-down from a high school cafeteria, but this was like a picnic under the stars. Maybe things were different during the daytime ambiance, but it was still immaculately clean and smelled like delicious barbecue was coming from the open kitchen.

"Nice. Thompson's on tonight. He's an artist behind the grill." Lyle's third love in life, after women and justice, was one we shared without question: food. Halfway through dinner, some of the troops who had come with him to get me joined us.

"What's it like to fly?" asked the woman with the spikey hair, who now introduced herself as Ericka.

"Oh, it's great. You should get your ass out of the passenger seat and into the cockpit sometime." The Australian pilot hopped into the seat next to me and put his hand out for me to shake. "Shaun."

"Dorian." I returned his handshake. He was about Lyle's age and build, with sandy brown hair and freckles across his nose that smiled along with him.

"The real question is: How fast can you fly?" Shaun asked me.

"I don't know. I've never had a way of measuring it. Noah's the one to talk to if speed is your thing."

"Going fast isn't always better. Sometimes it's more fun to go slow and see who finishes last." Shaun and the others snickered amongst each other.

"I don't get it. Oh, a sex joke. Clever."

We chatted for another hour until Lyle suggested we bring the conversation over to the lounge to get drinks. They had an informal bar setup that some of the members took turns working at, like in the kitchen.

"I don't really drink," I said after being asked by Shaun for the fifth time if I wanted anything. "I can't get drunk. My body heals it off too quickly, so there's really no point."

I never drank before gaining the accelerated healing either, but I left that part out.

"Well I can't fly, so I guess we're even," Ericka said and pounded down another shot with Lyle.

"I can do both, so I got ya both beat," Shaun joked. "Hey, Dorian. Lyle tells me you can build stuff with your powers too. Maybe you can help me out on the jet sometime."

"Word travels fast. I don't think Lyle and I have been apart for more than five minutes since I got here. A jet might be a little out of my league, though. I've been practicing on sculpting with stone and wood."

"It's just following a diagram. After that, it's just screwing and lifting."

"Is that another sex joke?"

"No, but it can be." Shaun was a funny guy. Too bad his jokes weren't. I liked hanging out with all of them. They made me feel more important than I was with all their questions.

After a few more hours, it was just him and me talking. He had started to sober up while Lyle was passed out on a bench. Ericka and some of the others who had joined us had returned to their rooms over an hour ago.

"Do you like it here? Is everyone treating you good?" Shaun asked.

"Yeah, it's been fun so far. It's been a long day. I'm not used to meeting so many people who don't want to kill me."

"Everyone wants a piece of you, huh? You couldn't be in a better place, as long as you don't mind the celebrity treatment. It must be tough being a superhero."

"You're crazy." I laughed, unsure if this was another bad joke.

"Maybe. I am a big fan, though. Probably your biggest fan, ya know? It might be your accent."

"My accent? I don't have an accent." I was genuinely surprised to hear that. "*You* have the accent, Aussie."

"You must have read my file, because I *know* I don't sound Australian. In fact, people get me confused for a New Yorker all the time. They think Lyle and I grew up together ... never believe it when I tell them they're wrong!"

Lyle had just peeled himself off the bench and wandered over, still plastered.

"Hey, let's ... go ... up," he slurred.

"You mean down? To the barracks?" I asked. It was sunrise, according to the clock, and the lighting had changed back to daylight mode.

"What?" He stared blankly at me, fighting to stay on his feet.

"I'll help you bring him down to his room," Shaun offered. "You two are staying together, right?"

"I can handle him. I'll just fly us there."

I said goodbye to Shaun and brought Lyle to his door. Along the way, he had drunkenly confessed several times how happy he was that we were friends again.

"What the fuck, man? What is he doing here?" Lyle swore. Noah had pushed both beds together and was sprawled out asleep facedown on them.

"Aw, he looks so peaceful." It was odd to see Noah sleeping. He always disappeared somewhere during the day. I assumed he turned to mist in a hiding spot so he wouldn't be bothered.

"Fuck him! This is my room!" Lyle shouted. It was a miracle he hadn't woken Noah.

"I'll deal with him. Just stand back; he's going to throw his sword at us."

I used my telekinesis to nudge him to one bed, and my prediction came true. He sprung up and threw a wakizashi at my head, but I stopped it mid-flight.

"Oh, it's you," he grumbled and went facedown again. "This is my room. Go find your own."

"It's Lyle's room. Move over so he can have his bed back."

"Forget it," Lyle said from the hall. "I'm not sleeping in the same room as him. I'll go use one of the beds in Medical."

Every time I nudged Noah to get him to move over, I was met with a growl, until I finally just shoved him onto one of the beds and separated the other for myself. There was some more grumbling and light swearing into the pillow, but he didn't try to stab me, so I was fine with that. What a weirdo. He was still after something, and it was bugging me now more than ever not knowing what it was.

Chapter Six

I woke up disoriented under a collection of tablet devices. The door had been barricaded with the furniture in the room, and Noah was reclined on the other bed, sucking down another blood pack while watching TV with the volume all the way down.

"What's going on?" I asked.

"Not much." He tossed the empty blood pack on to a pile of them on the floor.

"I mean, why am I covered in these things, and why is the door like that?"

"Oh, yeah. The toy soldiers probably want them back. I wanted to see what the rest of them do, but they shut them off from out there."

"Why'd you block the door instead of just giving them back?"

"So they wouldn't wake you." His eyes were glued to the TV, and I couldn't tell if he was joking. I dug myself out from the heap of electronics and unblocked the door.

"You drool a lot in your sleep, by the way. It's pretty gross," Noah said right as I opened the door to let in several of the soldiers. They looked at me and then at him, not sure if they should approach. The rooms must have been soundproof, because the base was buzzing with activity that I had been unable to hear from inside.

"Why do you guys have jail cells and torture chambers that weren't part of the tour? Seems kinda hypocritical if you're all about peace and justice," Noah asked one of the men who had built up the courage to come in for the tablets.

"I don't know anything about it. I can't talk about it." The soldier froze and then collected the tablets as fast as he could so he could get out. Meanwhile, in the hall, I heard one of the others calling the commander and Lyle to come up right away.

"Don't know, or can't talk about it? Those are two different things," I said. "Where'd you see this, Noah?"

"There's a hidden basement. Looks pretty heavy-duty too. Not what you'd be using on humans."

Commander Rudgar and Lyle came just in time to spare the soldier from being further interrogated. I asked them the same question, feeling a bit betrayed that they had failed to mention any of that. It was all sunshine and happiness up top, but what else were they hiding?

"They're holding cells, and that is medical equipment—not torture devices," the commander explained.

"Pliers?" Noah questioned. "That sounds more like something you'd use to pull out fangs."

"They're used to extract silver bullets lodged in werewolves. We can't bring them to the medical lab or they would destroy it. It isn't equipped to handle something their size."

"Why hide it, though?" I asked, looking straight at Lyle.

"I didn't want you to get the idea that we'd put you down there," Lyle answered. "The cells are for dangerous criminals or, like the commander said, werewolves until they heal and can be released."

"Why would I think it was for me?"

"I don't know, Dorian. I thought it might make you uncomfortable and take it personally that we have to detain supernaturals sometimes. That's all."

"He just didn't want you to see where they planned on throwing you once they got scared their guns couldn't stop you," Noah argued. "Ya know, in case you acted out or questioned their authority."

"It isn't like that, and you know it." Lyle pointed angrily at Noah. "You've already caused more than enough shit around here to be thrown down there, and we haven't."

"You can't even catch me; how do you expect to lock me up?" Noah laughed.

"How did you manage to access the area without setting off security?" Lars asked him.

"Don't worry about it."

"What do you do with the criminals?" I asked. "It's not like you could enforce a life sentence or anything meaningful."

"We do what needs to be done," the commander recited a very scripted answer.

"That means they kill them after they get what they want," said Noah.

"This is nonsense," Lars retorted. "And you've never killed anyone? Either of you? We are on the same side. The only difference is that we hold the enemy until we are certain without a doubt that they are guilty and without possibility of rehabilitation before we sentence them."

"You want us to wait around until you invent a way to sentence us for everyone we killed without a fair trial?" Noah asked. "Or was bringing Dorian here your way of 'rehabilitating' him before he becomes a bigger threat?"

"He would be a valued member of the team ... the same as anyone else who volunteers, including yourself, if you choose. This conversation is over. You are welcomed here, but not if you insist on question—"

"Questioning what? Your authority? Just what I said." Noah grabbed the commander by the arm and twisted it against the joint to pin him to the desk. He drew his blade and pressed it down along the commander's fingers as he whispered into his ear. "I still counted the same sixty-three people on base since yesterday. Did you forget our deal?"

He dragged the blade across the skin until it started bleeding. Lyle pulled his gun and shouted to release Commander Rudgar, who was fighting to break free.

"They're coming from Germany! They'll be back by tomorrow!" The commander yelled.

"Wrong answer. It doesn't take two days to get here from Germany. You're only saying that because you know the Strigoi are there, but they would've gotten to them first years ago." Noah pressed down on the wakizashi until blood started squirting out from the base of the commander's pointer finger.

"Noah, stop!" I shouted over the commander's screams.

"You only have four planes and one helicopter, all of which are here right now," he continued. "How were they supposed to get back? And don't say civilian transportation carrying those weapons and armor, or it'll be two fingers today."

Lyle opened fire, but Noah just leaned out of the way of the bullets and whipped his sword back to cut the barrel from the gun.

"You told them to bring the others to the base in New Zealand instead, didn't you?" Noah returned the blade to the commander's hand and dragged it down harder, cutting into the meat and letting blood gush out everywhere. The commander let out an agonized wail that was interrupted by PARAGON.

"Do you require medical attention, Commander?" PARAGON turned on the screen in the wall, but Noah broke it with the hilt of his sword.

"Yes! Yes, okay?! I just thought that Dorian would change his mind after staying with us for a while. We've spent years and tons of resources to give up looking for them now. It was for their own good!"

"How many do you have?" I asked.

"Only one. Another male from the US."

"Release him," I demanded.

"Fine, fine! It was only for his own good to begin with," he choked out in between exclamations of pain.

"You wanted more powerful soldiers and things to study in your labs," Noah asserted.

"It wasn't like that," Lars pleaded. "You can meet him yourself ... take him wherever."

"No. I don't want to get involved," I said. "Just return him home."

"That's if he even has a home," the commander commented, but he quickly retracted his statement when Noah started to apply the final amount of pressure needed before severing his finger. "All right! He'll be returned immediately!"

"Let him go, Noah." I pulled on Noah's arm, hoping to stop him from going through with permanently maiming the commander. He hesitated, but then complied and kicked Lars out of the room by his backside.

"I didn't know." Lyle stared at me, his face turned almost as pale as mine.

"He's not lying," Noah confirmed and licked his blade clean. "One, he's too stupid. And two, I saw the commander sending the order to change transport to New Zealand on one of his tablets this morning."

"It doesn't excuse what you did," Lyle said to him.

"Yeah, well arrest me then." Noah vanished from the room in a gust of wind.

"We really are the good guys," Lyle tried to convince me. "I know the commander just wanted to do what was best."

"It's not up to him to decide that."

Lyle cleaned his room in silence for hours after one of the computer techs came to replace the screen while I sat in bed watching TV. I knew Lyle was embarrassed and distracted by doubt. I wasn't sure who or what to believe either. Jumping to conclusions wasn't going to benefit anyone.

"What do you think of Rebecca?" Lyle asked.

"She seems nice. She's like a human Strigoi in some ways."

"She's nothing like them. She's compassionate and wants to help people." Lyle sounded offended.

"I just meant she's smart and curious about all that stuff. Like how she was talking about magic and technology being the same."

"That's true." He finished returning the room to a livable condition and lay on his bed. "What's the deal with you and Noah?"

"I'm not sure what you mean."

"Why's he not an abusive dick with you anymore like he is with everyone else? Last we left off with him in New York, he would have killed us if we looked at him wrong. He only backed off when Vivi said so. I thought he was after you to finish the job and kill you like Aurelia wanted, but it's like he's looking out for you and listens to you now."

"He knows I respect him, I guess. We've been through a lot together." It did surprise me how adamantly Noah had been in my corner earlier that day, but maybe it shouldn't have. I knew about his reluctance to trust anyone and his hatred for those who manipulated others.

What would he gain from coming here in the first place? Was he biding his time until his master returned to meet her end? The chateau he stayed at in France had been destroyed by the spirits of the Far East. His shred of solace in the Japanese mountains had also been tainted by our turmoil with them. The only person he had been close to was another slave of Aurelia's named Vivian that had fallen in battle three years ago right in front of him. Could it be that he was finally tired of being lonely?

I'd never say it to anyone, because it would be impossible to explain, but I did more than respect him. I understood him. It was weird to think so, considering who he was and how he acted.

"It'd be easier to respect him if he wasn't a psychopath," Lyle said.

"That's exactly why he gives you a hard time. You two stand for totally opposite things. He doesn't like authority and being controlled. You're all about order and rules; he wants to be free and left alone. Authoritative types always look at people who don't follow their rules as bad, but he just has a different way of going about things.

"He has his own strict code of honor he follows. It took me a while to see that. I care about him as a person, and I think he knows that. I don't see him as a problem that needs to be solved or made to obey. He helped train me, I think, because he saw I wanted to be free like he does."

"Rules are there to help people," Lyle countered. "That's what the justice system is for. That's what PROJECT: UNITY is for. Running around making threats and acting out only adds more fuel to the fire."

"Sometimes, you have to fight fire with fire. PROJECT: UNITY might have good intentions, but they'll never be able to peacefully contain some of the things out there and make them abide by your laws. Noah has a good heart. I think I'm the only one who sees that now and doesn't judge him in the moment. He's told me in the past about there being a bigger picture, but it didn't click until recently."

The PARAGON terminal in the room came to life with an announcement. "Lieutenant Lyle Turner, Dorian Benoit, please report to Operations Room 3 for mission briefing."

"Since when did I agree to go on a mission?"

"Man ... I didn't get a chance to fill you in." Lyle collected his gear in a hurry.

I followed Lyle down to the command floor, where Commander Rudgar waited in an assembly room with his hand bandaged. Over a dozen other troops, including Ericka and Shaun from Lyle's squad, came in after us.

"Glad you're joining us." The commander nodded to me. "I assume Lieutenant Turner has already filled you in on the details."

"Not exactly, sir." Lyle addressed him.

"What were you doing then for four hours, Lieutenant?"

"I was sleeping. Just spit it out," I interrupted before Lyle could be embarrassed anymore.

"We've been monitoring a company known as Gestalt Industries. We have evidence of their involvement in the occult and that they commit crimes against supernaturals."

"*Coming together to care for you.* That Gestalt?" I asked, reciting their slogan, which I had seen plenty of times on TV and plastered all over New York City and Boston in the past. "Don't they sell makeup?"

Their generic-looking company logo was three interlaced hexagons, one of each primary color, arranged in a triangle. It made me think of a rainbow honeycomb. "Are they testing lipstick on werewolves or something?"

I got a laugh out of some of the troops, but I wasn't completely joking. Commander Rudgar carried on with his briefing after a moment.

"They're a pharmaceutical conglomerate that sells everything from makeup to painkillers to household supplies under their subsidiaries. They have around sixty thousand employees worldwide and reported a revenue of fifty billion US dollars last year. We're dealing with an entity that is both widespread and has access to nearly limitless resources hiding behind a reputable public face.

"Recently, Gestalt Industries has been reporting spectacular headway on the genetic manipulation front—more specifically, stem cell research. They've reported more than ten cutting-edge developments in under a year. That is more than double the results of their competition, which declared similar, or better, sales figures for the same year. That alone was enough to draw suspicion from several medical ethics boards.

"This kind of research with results of this degree takes significant funding—more funding than a private company could supply on its own while still making a substantial profit. The research they are conducting is heavily regulated by twelve out of the twenty countries they have labs in, so government grants are out of the question. It isn't uncommon for wealthy investors to make sizable donations, but Gestalt has refused to reveal the names of any such parties, citing a confidentiality clause.

"Gestalt is notorious for being secretive with their infrastructure. It wasn't until a month ago that they released the names of their board of directors, many of whom have had little business experience for such a profitable company."

"I don't see what the big deal is. There are tons of shady, corrupt businesses out there," I said. "Where's the proof they're involved in the supernatural?"

"Lieutenant Turner has been diligent in his own research. Information gleaned from multiple sources has shown Gestalt to be obtaining the bodies of werewolves for experimentation. Our own catch-and-release tactical response teams have been headed off by operatives believed to be working for Gestalt to collect specimens.

"Before joining us, our very own Dr. Rebecca Sullivan was approached by representatives of Gestalt Industries while on a medical review panel. They pitched a revolutionary new steroidal injection said to regenerate damaged muscle tissue and nerve synapses; hinting at its potential to get wounded soldiers back up and fighting in no time. No one on the review panel had prior experience with supernatural beings, so the sample they presented didn't raise any red flags; it simply appeared to be a genetic mutation at the hands of the drug.

"Dr. Sullivan was later approached to join Gestalt, but she declined, citing displeasure with their failure to supply the detailed process used to synthesize their wonder drug. When studying werewolf blood samples in PROJECT: UNITY's database later, she immediately recognized the correlation with Gestalt's drug. The rest of the review panel is now under the employment of Gestalt and has declined to comment on any of their findings."

"Are we going to blow up their headquarters then or something?" I asked.

"This is a noncombat assignment. Destroying one building would do nothing to a company that has dozens more around the world, except draw unwanted attention to ourselves and put our enemy on high alert. Any attempt to infiltrate them in the past has been a complete failure. We've sent some of our best and most loyal members to gain employment as double agents, but we've had unsettling results."

"Wouldn't that be drawing unwanted attention to themselves if they're killing employees?"

"They aren't killing them. That's what is unsettling. After becoming employed, they all cut off contact with us and decide to change allegiance to Gestalt with no explanation other than being happy there.

"Any attempt to hack their servers, even with the assistance of PARAGON, has proven futile. They use a secure, heavily encrypted intranet that can only be accessed from within their own buildings. We can't even get the names of their cleaning staff.

"Your mission tonight is to infiltrate one of their smaller facilities in Lewiston, Maine and obtain whatever information possible on their investors."

"How come we aren't going for anything on their experiments?" Shaun asked from his seat next to me.

"Because we don't think it'll be that easy." Lyle stood up. "If they're that tight-assed about people giving them money, they aren't going to have information on their hidden research lying around where anyone in the company can see it.

"Our goal is to start small and isolate their investors from them. If they are outside the company, it's unlikely that they know what's going on behind the scenes and are just being drawn in by the front they're being shown. We need to starve Gestalt out by cutting their funding as much as possible and causing them to downsize, get sloppy, and make mistakes. Then we'll have a way in by setting up an investment deal of our own when they're hungry, get inside when they're weak, and take them out."

"So why bring me?" I questioned. "I typically just smash stuff until it stops moving."

"We want you to see that's not all we're about," Commander Rudgar answered. "If you see how we operate, maybe you'll be more interested in staying with us full time. The only weapons we'll be bringing are light nonlethal rounds, including tranqs in case they have live werewolves detained that need to be released. These are scientists and bureaucrats—not soldiers—and any supernaturals you find inside are most likely victims. We're not looking to rack up a body count for no reason."

"Nah, we're not doing it." Noah appeared in front of me. The commander was a brave man. He didn't even flinch at the sight of Noah after having almost lost a finger to him.

"We?" I floated over to face him.

"Yeah. You're not actually gonna do this, are you?" he asked with an eyebrow raised in question.

"I was considering it."

The rest of the soldiers in the room shifted in their seats, waiting for something violent to go down, as it usually did with Noah.

"You're welcomed to join too," Commander Rudgar extended his invitation. "Your speed and stealth could accomplish the objective before the plane even lands."

"You're right about that." Noah grinned. "We're not going, though."

"I'm going," I said and turned to the commander and Lyle. "Maybe not for future missions, but I'll give it a shot. I want to see what this Gestalt is about."

"You're being dumb," Noah argued. "These monkeys are just pissed off someone is giving them competition."

"Come with us," I said. I felt the whole room watching us go back and forth. I think Noah enjoyed the attention.

"What did I just say? We're not going."

"Fine. Go back to watching TV." I shrugged. "When do we leave, Lyle?"

"You don't tell me what to do, kid." Noah fumed and poked me in the chest hard enough to hurt. "I'm gonna watch TV, but it's because *I* want to."

"We're moving out now," Lyle announced to the room. "I'll only be taking nine of you, so listen for your name."

While Lyle did the roll call, Noah zipped me outside the room to continue persuading me against getting involved.

"Let's get outta here," he said. "It's boring. We should check out Malaysia or something."

I really wanted to confront him on my suspicions that he was finally accepting the fact that friendship wasn't always a weakness, but I knew if I did, he'd deny it. "Come help with this first. Don't tell me you're willing to give up a chance to show off your skills."

"I don't give a fuck what these humans think about me." He squinted and crossed his arms, seeing through my plan to use his own ego against him. "I could just knock you out and take you with me. Figured I'd give you the option first this time."

"If this turns out to be a waste, I'll go," I agreed. "But don't tell me it doesn't bother you that supernaturals are possibly being experimented on and held against their will."

"Not really. They're just dogs."

"Sure. Whatever, Noah."

"Yeah, whatever, *kid.* I'm moving on then. Have fun playing soldier boy."

Chapter Seven

"Can we stop for coffee on the way?" I asked as we entered the hangar. "I can't save the world without it."

"Dorian, come sit shotty." Shaun waved me down from the cockpit of the dual-propeller helicopter. "If we crash, the best copilot is one who can fly on his own."

"Why do you always have to talk about crashing before every flight?" Ericka grimaced and boarded after me.

"It's good luck in the Outback. I used to be in the Royal Australian Air Force," Shaun smiled and handed me a helmet, "four years before these blokes kidnapped me and forced me to fly for them."

"I was there when you were begging to join us after seeing the aircrafts we had," Lyle said.

"I was being polite. I didn't wanna make you guys feel bad." Shaun put his own helmet on and looked at what I was wearing. "Hey, Lieutenant, we need to get Dorian here a suit."

"I want to, if he'll stay with us," Lyle said. "But I don't think he's big on the implants to make it work."

"I can still hear you under the helmet," I said as they talked as if I wasn't there.

We made it to Maine in over an hour. The building we were supposed to be infiltrating was a nondescript three-story office in the heart of the industrial sector of the city. Even though it was the dead of night, a military helicopter flying over was sure to garner some unwanted attention. Shaun landed us far enough away to take one of the ATVs off the helicopter right up to the building.

I flew us to the roof to save them the trouble of grappling, which got me a fair amount of praise. For such a secretive company with billions of dollars at their disposal, Gestalt couldn't even buy a padlock for their roof entrance.

"I'm gonna set up the transmitter so PARAGON can intercept any security calls or silent alarms." Lyle took out an adhesive microchip from his suit and stuck it to the wall outside the door. "Remember: nonlethal combat only."

I rolled my eyes, thinking how seriously they were all taking this while I was standing here in sweats and a jacket, both of which I'd borrowed from Lyle. We got inside without any issues, and I tagged along as the team swept the building for any security or cleaning staff who might get in their way. But everyone had already cleared out for the night.

For an innovative company with such extensive resources, the layout on each level lacked originality and didn't seem to encourage creativity. This wasn't the main headquarters, so maybe they hadn't wanted to waste profit on a more inspired developer. The floors were all perfect squares with a men's bathroom in one corner, a women's in the opposite corner, a supply room in the next, and finally an employee break area with two couches back to back that looked like they had never been used, a small refrigerator, a watercooler, and a coffee machine. Offices sectioned off by glass along the perimeter had a bright red accent wall made of plastic with a raised cubic pattern and their logo displayed in the middle.

How anyone could figure out what floor they were on without going back to the elevator in the middle to check was in on some trick I had yet to figure out.

Contemporary stainless steel desks in widely spaced rows of three lined the white tiles of the main area without any partition for privacy. The way the workspaces were arranged to face the back of the person in front of you didn't quite evoke the sense of teambuilding you'd expect from such an open floor plan.

"All clear," Lyle reported to the team over his helmet's microphone. "Regroup at my position."

He had explained to me earlier that the heads-up display in their suits had been uploaded with the full blueprint of the building. PARAGON was able to track each team member's location and show it to the others along with their vitals.

I sat next to Lyle and played with office supplies while he tried bypassing a computer firewall. I didn't have gloves to avoid leaving fingerprints like the rest of them, but good luck to the local police ever tracking me down considering it had taken PROJECT: UNITY years.

"Isn't this all a little illegal?" I asked half-jokingly because of Lyle's previous career.

"Look around for any files that could have passwords in them," Lyle ordered the team.

"Move over, Lieutenant. It needs a woman's touch," Ericka told him.

"Too bad we didn't bring one," Shaun joked. "We can't go back now and get one, though, so you'll have to give it a shot."

In a few minutes, Ericka got into the system.

"I can only get basic access, but I have a phone list, employee roster, and possibly ... bankroll records. This may lead us to their investors with some cross-referencing."

Espionage was kind of exciting. There was a certain rush to it, even though nothing was happening ... except me spinning in an office chair in the dark. I peeked into one of the desk drawers and found a stress ball in the shape of an anatomical human heart. It made me laugh, and I thought about giving it to Noah.

"You should've seen me in my Air Force days," Shaun told me mid-spin in a chair of his own. "I have a picture back on base. I was so skinny then, you'd never believe how much I got in shape in two years."

"Can you keep watch with the rest of the squad, pilot?" Lyle suggested firmly.

"Sorry, Lieutenant."

"What's that sound?" one of the soldiers asked from their lookout. There was an irritating high-pitched noise coming from above us. No one was upstairs, though, and their security alarm had been disabled.

"I'll check it out," Lyle said and left the office.

"I think I've got a list of bank accounts that have only made major deposits to Gestalt in the past five years," Ericka told the rest of the team over her mic. I looked over, not expecting any of it to mean much to me, but I was wrong.

"Blackbourne," I said out loud after seeing the name on the list.

"You know them?" she asked with distrust in her voice. "It figures they would be in bed together."

"That is a very appropriate choice of words," I told her. The noise was getting louder and more obnoxious. I could barely hear the soldiers' footsteps patrolling the floor.

"Lyle?" I stuck my head out the door.

"What's happening?" Someone shouted right before darkness washed out everything in sight.

I woke up ... or at least I *thought* I woke up. I couldn't remember being knocked out. I couldn't remember much of anything. I couldn't see or feel anything either, but I could hear movement ... voices ... a strange squishing sound.

My mind was hazy. Was I dreaming? I thought the mission with Lyle had been real. It had seemed so at the time, but now I wasn't so sure.

My thoughts were so clouded ... If I was awake, my powers weren't working.

Am I in the Nether Realm? I wanted to call out to Gianni, but my body wasn't responding. It wasn't a bad feeling. I felt peaceful, like I could just close my eyes and go back to sleep at any time ... if they were even open.

What was that squishing sound? It was so wet, but there was a weight to it, like slapping soggy laundry down on the table or cooked noodles into a bowl.

Whose voices were those in the distance? I think they were speaking English. I understood the words but not the context. Were they reciting numbers?

Something about this wasn't right. The peacefulness ... it ... it hurt my stomach. The numbers ... it was the numbers. I didn't know what they meant, but I wanted them to stop. Something about them was making me ill.

The feeling in my stomach was getting worse. I could taste something, but my mouth hadn't opened. It was metallic. Whatever was going on, I wanted it to end.

I must be having a nightmare. It's been a while since I've had one. It'll be over soon. It isn't real.

The disconcerting sensation began to subside. It ebbed and flowed in a pattern like a raging tide transitioning to calm waters and then back again. I had no way of telling how long I had been like this. Seconds? Maybe minutes?

"Consistent thirty-six seconds on bone tissue."

Finally, a voice I could understand. I tried to call out to it, but there was still no response from my body.

"Take these down to cold storage."

Another voice. *Who are these people? Where am I?*

"Fourteen identical hearts. This thing is saving us millions and years in cloning time."

"Wait. Don't damage it before it has a chance to finish regrowing."

"We're at just under sixty liters of blood. I'll send for another canister."

What am I listening to? I was screaming inside my own head, hoping to communicate in some way.

"Take another set of its eyes, but use the bone saw and brace the skull so you can get the full optic nerve before it seals."

Instantly, I could see again. It started as a piercing white light, but the room came into view. I was lying down with people standing over me.

Doctors in scrubs and face masks with rubber gloves covered in blood. I still couldn't move my body or even blink. My eyes were being held open until they watered and obscured my vision again.

"I think it's waking up."

The figure of one of the doctors leaned over my face with something in his hand. I felt a pressure in my left eye. There was a moist, snapping sound, and then I could no longer see out of it.

"It's not getting out of the restraints. We're almost done with it for now. When the pump is out of anesthesia, we'll take this thing down to cryogenics."

In a few seconds, I could see again, just in time for the doctor to bear down on my other eye with a hooked surgical instrument. I tried to use my powers, but they wouldn't work. My mind was still too scrambled to concentrate. I could look down enough to see another doctor pick something up from the table and drop it into a cooler.

It was a liver. My liver. They were dissecting me.

Several others in the room were taking notes on clipboards and transporting coolers on a cart out of the room. A mixture of panic and rage claimed me, but I couldn't do a damn thing about it.

"Do we have enough for the skin grafts? A three-and-a-half second recovery window is making it difficult to remove without tearing."

I started to black out. The numbness was every bit as intolerable as if I had felt all the pain.

The pressure in my eye socket became more acute as the doctor rotated some medical tool around inside. Then the anesthesia wore off, and along with it, my hope that this was all a bad dream.

"Did you want to chance taking a biopsy of this thing's brain while we have it out? The cranium keeps sealing closed around my instruments. I have to crack it free every time."

There came a crunching sound as the doctor rotated the instrument in my skull to demonstrate. My body shook as it came out of its drugged state, but not soon enough. Consciousness slipped away from me once more.

A pounding in my head grew louder and louder. I could taste something in my mouth again, but it wasn't the same as before. It was a peculiar taste and kind of familiar ... sweet ... or maybe salty. I couldn't be sure with all my senses skewed.

The noise was deafening, but I didn't know if it was inside or outside my head.

"COME ON!" The voice was so thunderous, I couldn't tell whose it was. "Wake up!"

Is that Lyle ...?

"You're supposed to be able to heal—" The shouting quieted as I stirred.

I didn't know if my eyes had been opened the whole time, but my vision flickered back into view now. Noah was slamming his fist down next to my head on the operating table while trying to threaten the life back into me. I strained to move and let him know I was alive until, finally, I managed to get myself to blink.

"Stop playing dead on me, you brat." Noah tore the metal restraints from my arms and legs. My body was stiff, but I was quickly regaining enough control to sit up and see that I had been left in only my underwear. Considering what I had just been through, it was surprising the doctors had allowed me any shred of dignity.

I wiped blood from my mouth. It was Noah's blood. I remembered the distinct taste, which was sweeter than regular blood, from when he'd used it to heal me in the past. The amount of drugs that had been constantly pumped through my system while my body had been traumatized must have pushed my regeneration past its limit.

"We're getting out of here. Can you walk?" He picked me up under my arms like a ragdoll. "Or fly?"

Scraps of the doctors' bodies littered the floor. They had been sliced into so many pieces that I couldn't tell what was what when looking at the remains. What appeared to be a severed head was very deformed, and it had broken glasses and a clipboard firmly implanted in it by some tremendous force—Noah's fist perhaps.

Speaking wasn't coming easy. I tried to croak out some words as I glanced around, but Noah grabbed me by the neck to keep me from turning my head.

"You don't wanna do that," he said and carried me out of the room. I think this was the first time he didn't drag me behind him or throw me over his shoulder like dead weight.

"What happened?" I asked. "What are you doing here?"

"You didn't think I'd let my number-one student die to a few humans, did you?"

"I'm your only student."

"Yeah, well, don't get too excited. I made an investment in you that I'd like to not turn out to be a waste of my time."

"I can walk now. Thanks." The feeling of vertigo from the anesthesia wearing off had passed. Noah set me down on my feet, but I still felt weak in the knees. It wasn't from the drugs but from disgust as I looked back into the room. Numbered glass jars containing hearts and various other internal organs, along with canisters of blood, lined a countertop and rolling cart. Several pairs of my own gray eyes stared back at me from a clear receptacle. I wanted to vomit, cry, pass out, and smash something all at once.

"What did I just say about looking in there?!" Noah picked me up again to remove me from the area. "We gotta find a way out. After I killed those guys, the place went into lockdown. Even the vents are sealed tight, so I can't leave using mist."

"I ... I can't believe this. How could they do something like that? They called me 'it' and treated me like I was—"

"Don't lose it. I'm gonna get us out of—Get back here!"

I returned to the room where I had been operated on and stared at the organs as they stared back at me.

"Where are the others?" I asked without turning away.

"I don't know. Probably dead."

"Can you find them?" My eyes weren't blinking ... on purpose this time. I wanted to be sure I took it all in, but I couldn't say I knew why.

"Look, we're getting out of here," Noah demanded. "I'm not sticking around to help those dipshits who walked into this."

"Then go. But I'm not leaving until I'm sure everything here is dead ... one way or another."

I returned to where my vital organs were on display. It pained me in a way I couldn't describe, but I knew what I had to do, and so I smashed the jars until there was nothing left of me inside them. I had been violated beyond any definition of the word previously known to me. Violated by *humans*.

The rising darkness fated to erase humanity was here all right, but it wasn't a supernatural being or any biblical event. It was inside the twisted minds of all these mortals. This doomed species was its own undoing, whether through self-extinction or a corrupt evolution into the monsters they held in their subconscious. Either way I *would* put an end to it, starting here.

I grabbed a clean lab coat hanging in the corner of the room and put it on as I floated over the bloodstained tiled floor.

"Just like the one my father used to wear." I looked at my reflection in a broken mirror.

"There are plenty of humans still here. I can see their auras." Noah hesitated a moment to look me up and down as I floated in my lab coat.

"Why's it so quiet then?" The hallway before us was like in any other hospital: monotonous, impersonal, and dead. There were no gurneys, IV racks, or chairs, however. It was desolate, picked clean of all signs of life, with symmetrical rows of rooms extending as far as the eyes could see.

"The doors are all four-inch-thick solid steel with magnetic locks like soldier boy's base. I can't punch through them, so we're gonna have to wait it out until someone leaves, then cut body parts off them until they release the lockdown."

I put my hand out and motioned backward, tearing the entire doorframe from the wall and chucking it behind me.

"My patience ran out on the operating table." I glided inside to find a body in the middle of an operation and the doctors working on it. From what was still intact, I could tell the victim was a woman with spikey blond hair. There was no way she could live through what they had done to her. She was missing limbs, and they had hollowed out her abdomen. If I had to guess, they were trying to implant parts of supernaturals into regular humans, judging by the plethora of unfamiliar organs waiting tableside.

Noah picked up one of the doctors by the throat. They were nervous, but they were not begging for their lives or fleeing in terror like I'd expect any other human would.

"How do you stop the—?"

A vindictive rage was building steadily inside me as I began to process what had happened to me. I blasted the group of doctors into a fine paste of blood and bone before Noah could finish his question.

"Come on! I was *trying* to conduct an interrogation."

I continued down the hall, pulling doors off two at a time from each side, but the rooms were all empty. "Just so you know: We are four floors underground. If you keep breaking shit, this place is gonna collapse and trap us here for good," Noah warned.

At the very end of the hall, a doctor strolled out from one of the rooms. I tore the floor up under him and crushed him into the ceiling.

"Better?" I asked.

Noah shrugged and disappeared down the hallway to go check out the room that the doctor had exited. He returned after a second while I checked the next set of rooms. Inside was a pile of dead bodies. I recognized them as the soldiers I'd gone there with. They looked like they were being shrink-wrapped for storage. Some were missing body parts, and others had been left cut open from surgery, but they all had the same incision in the backs of their necks from where their implants must have been removed.

"Empty," Noah reported. I ripped off the next set of doors. Inside was Lyle. He was gagged and bleeding, screaming facedown on a table, with doctors standing over him.

"Don't kill these yet," Noah said, but it was too late for them. I crushed them together, deaf to the sounds their bodies made as I compressed them into the size of a beach ball.

"This is exactly why I don't work well with others," Noah complained. "You don't fucking listen." He left to go check the other room while I freed Lyle.

"Are you okay? Can you move?" I asked and snatched gauze and bandages from a tray to wrap his head. He had no other injuries except for where they had cut out his implant.

"I'm alive. That's what matters right now. Where are the others?"

"I don't think any of them made it ..."

Lyle looked the same way I felt: somewhere between anger and sadness. "How'd they get us?" he asked. "I can't remember anything."

Glass started shattering from the room Noah had gone to inspect.

"We're still trying to figure that out. Stay here."

Lyle took one quick glance at my work on the doctors and looked like he was about to be sick. "I'm coming with you. I need to find my gear."

"It was empty." Noah returned before I could go to help.

"What was all the broken glass?" I asked.

"Don't worry about it." That was never what you wanted to hear from Noah, but there was no time to call him out on it. The shrill noise was back from the upstairs office, and if we didn't stop it, we'd be back in the same position again—or worse.

"It's coming from the ceiling," Noah pointed out. "If we had one of those doctors, we could make them turn it off ..."

"Then we just take the ceiling down." I ripped down the floor above us, going room by room down the hall. The calamity from falling rubble and Gestalt employees drowned out the high-pitched noise for a time.

"Are you freakin' crazy?!" Lyle screamed over the mayhem.

"If you have to ask him that, you already know the answer!" Noah shouted back. I looked in the room where the sound of broken glass had come from. Inside were shattered jars that had held more samples that had been taken from me.

All the noise, including the high-pitched tone, started to quiet down.

"Is anyone else still alive?" I asked Noah.

"Yeah, there's another room left with two people." He pointed the way.

"It's Shaun!" Lyle yelled, checking between the debris covering a hole in the wall. Noah and I removed the wreckage. The table Shaun was strapped to had tipped over, leaving him struggling on the floor. He was also bleeding from having his implant removed, along with several other superficial cuts. Beside him was a doctor who was hurrying to inject a black liquid into Shaun's eye through a syringe. I blew the doctor to pieces and freed Shaun.

"Oh shit! Thank God! Oh my God, thank you!" Shaun jumped up after he had been unstrapped and dusted himself off, kicking pieces of the doctor away. "That psycho almost got me ... Lieutenant, where are the others?"

"They didn't make it." Lyle cleared the lump in his throat.

"We've gotta get out of here. This is a nightmare," Shaun rambled on. I bent down and picked up the syringe. The liquid inside was one I had become well acquainted with.

"I would've left a while ago," Noah mumbled.

"Did you know about this?" I asked Lyle and held up the syringe.

"Is that ...?"

The black substance moved on its own. It reacted to my touch through the thick glass. It called to me with impulses sent straight to my mind. It wanted me. It needed to be destroyed.

"You're damn right it is. It's the Carpathians' parasite from the Rift. But what the hell is Gestalt doing with it?"

"None of this was what I thought it would be, man," said Lyle. "I thought they were just playing with werewolf blood to make steroids—not anything this extreme."

"That guy you turned to mush was bonkers. He was talking to himself about making my eyes like yours," Shaun said to me.

The power cut out in the middle of our frenzied conversation.

"Oh good." I heard Noah's voice in the dark. "Now I'm really glad I stuck around ... as if I hadn't already been enjoying this enough."

"Stop whining. I can feel my way around. We're four floors underground, and we have easy access to the one above us." I put my powers to less destructive use and navigated us up through the collapsed ceiling. The next floor had emergency lighting, so the situation was only getting better from there.

"There's more of them alive around here," Noah announced.

"Not for long."

"Dorian, you can't kill them. If we're in control and they're unarmed, we have to take them in for questioning. Murder isn't going to get us anywhere." Lyle's sense of justice was gravely misplaced this time.

Noah just burst out laughing and vanished to go on ahead, but I wasn't having it.

"I hope you're not being serious."

"Yeah, Lieutenant. He saved our lives," Shaun defended me. "Anyone who would do this sick shit to someone doesn't deserve to waste our time questioning them."

"That doesn't mean him doing it back to them makes it better. Dorian, don't lose yourself again. These are humans ... humans who committed a crime and deserve to be punished. But it's not up to you to decide if they live or die."

"Do you know what they did to me, Lyle? They cut me open again and again to harvest my organs. They tore my eyes out and dissected me. Do you have any idea what I just went through for your mission? You'd both be going through it yourself if I didn't get there as fast as I did."

"I ... no ... I'm sorry, man. I didn't know. But you're in control now. It isn't self-defense anymore if they aren't hurting you."

Lyle stopped talking. I heard a thud and looked back to see that Noah had knocked him out.

"I was over it."

"Good," I said. "So was I. But you're carrying him."

"There's an elevator up ahead. Power's out on it, but you can fly these two up to the ground floor, and I'll meet you there. I already took care of the other employees of the month who were busy turning some guy inside out."

We escaped to the ATV parked around the block, but not before I expressed my final act of retribution and ripped down a poster in the lobby of a smiling team of doctors with the caption "Coming together to care for you."

Shaun loaded Lyle into the backseat, and I got out a first aid kit to bandage his head. Shaun claimed he was okay to drive, but he called for backup to fly us to the base.

"Please. Get rid of this thing." I handed Noah the syringe with the parasite. He was the only one I trusted right now to actually destroy it, and I wanted it out of my hands as soon as possible.

As we pulled away and I started to cool down, it struck me: None of the Gestalt employees seemed too concerned with their own well-being. The rooms may have been insulated by heavy walls, but the floors were coming down, and yet they'd still kept toiling away. Surely they'd heard something? They must have known there was danger if that strange high-pitched noise was activated again. Were they that secure in their own lines of defense, or   was   it   something   else?

Chapter Eight

"You okay?" Noah dropped in on me as I waited outside the Medical Ward for Lyle and Shaun to finish getting patched up.

"I'm good." I sat on the floor with my eyes closed and my head down.

"That was a pretty nice show back there. I didn't think you had it in you." A rare compliment from Noah, but a lot of his actions were even more puzzling than usual these days.

"You're the one who taught me to feign weakness and ignorance to get people to underestimate me so they'd be caught off guard."

"I did, didn't I? Damn, I'm awesome."

"Are *you* okay?" I asked.

"Yeah, why wouldn't I be?" Noah had been more rattled at Gestalt than I'd been used to seeing him. It wasn't something that would have been apparent to anybody but those who knew his style well enough. There had been no wisecracks or nauseating machismo. The level of unrestrained savagery that had been used against the doctors had been more out of character for him than it had been for me. Noah was all about precise and efficient movements, not beating people's faces into mashed potatoes.

"Did they ... do anything to you?"

"No. I was in mist form when that noise screwed everyone. You were all gone when I woke up."

"I'm glad you decided to hitch a ride."

"Yeah, well, now we're even for the Muramasa. I just wanted to get that out of the way so you can't keep holding it over my head like I owe you or something."

"I never held it over your head, and you know that."

There was an uncomfortable pause before he continued. "You did the right thing, you know. They deserved to die."

"They were unarmed human civilians. Lyle was right."

"So what? Because they're human they're better than us? Like it would make it better to kill them if they were undead ... or *whatever* you are."

I glared up at him.

"Kidding." He smirked. "You know damn well if those were the Carpathians, you wouldn't be having doubts. I thought you were over the self-pity thing and thinking we're monsters and less than the humans."

"I am over it. I don't like killing in general, and I don't value one of our kind over the other anymore."

"They crossed a line. It wasn't like they robbed a bank. They got themselves involved in our world, and they got what was coming to them. They were human civilians, but on our side of things, they were soldiers in a war."

"You're right."

"Of course I am. I'm always right."

"It's one of the many things I can't stand about you."

Commander Rudgar approached from the elevator, escorted by two guards. "Gentlemen." He nodded to me and Noah. "Thank you for bringing back what was left of my men."

"How about a reward?" Noah asked. I turned to him. *Now it comes out why he's really here.*

"I'm sure something can be arranged. What did you have in mind?"

"I don't know. Can I sign your cast?" Noah sneered at the commander's injured hand from which he had almost cut the finger.

"That's a bandage, not a cast," I corrected. "A cast is for broken bones."

"Fine, I'll break his arm," Noah exclaimed. "Jeez, you put on a lab coat and rearrange a few doctors' faces and suddenly you're a medical expert."

"If you're worried about your counterpart we brought to New Zealand, he's been returned home safely with information on how to contact us if he feels threatened." The commander excused himself and entered the room where Lyle was being worked on, leaving his guards at the door.

"I'm bored again," Noah complained.

"Go watch TV," I suggested.

"Don't tell me what to do."

I rolled my eyes and sat there, trying to hear what was going on with Lyle. It didn't take long for voices to be raised.

"Can you hear what they're saying?" I asked Noah, but he was already gone. After a few minutes of yelling, I started to feel bad for Lyle and decided to go to his defense.

"I'm sorry, we can't let you in," a guard said. I moved them out of the way like the toy soldiers Noah was always mocking them about.

"Lyle didn't do anything wrong. I was the one who killed the Gestalt employees," I interrupted the commander. "I did it on my own."

Lyle looked downtrodden while he was being reprimanded from his bed with his head bandaged. To make it even worse, Rebecca was in the room, trying to make herself invisible while she cleaned him up. He should have been on cloud nine that they were having *any* physical interaction, but it was only making things worse.

"This has nothing to do with that," Lars explained. "Lieutenant Turner has been staking out this facility and the company involved for quite some time. He was completely unprepared and, in his haste to play hero, got many good men and women killed. Not only that, but the mission was a complete failure: No information was retrieved, and worst of all, Gestalt now has our technology, which they can reverse-engineer. They will be on high alert now, on top of knowing all our secrets, while we know none of theirs.

"If you hadn't been there, we would have lost the whole team and possibly our vehicles. We don't rely on ace-in-the-hole plays to get us out of situations. Lieutenant Turner was far too overconfident and underprepared, thinking he could rely on you to pick up the slack. That is not what we are about here at PROJECT: UNITY. We are here to help supernaturals, not hide behind them on the frontlines."

"I acted on my own. Don't blame him for bringing me into it, because even if he'd said not to go, I still would have. I wouldn't be alive if it wasn't for him years ago. He wasn't playing hero; he *is* one. Even heroes need help sometimes."

"That doesn't excuse the multiple deaths and total mission failure under his command."

"Dorian, it's okay, man," Lyle finally spoke up.

"No. It's not. Where's the compassion part of the job you told me about? You don't deserve this. I know you didn't do it on purpose."

"If I had any reason to believe it was more than just a mistake, he would be lying in the morgue, not a hospital bed," Lars said.

"Then treat it as that. A mistake. A horrible mistake. But belittling him won't get us anywhere."

Dr. Sullivan glanced up at me with a very restrained smile. Now she was just pretending to look busy to stick around.

"And it wasn't a total failure. I saw the list of possible investors Ericka brought up on the computer before everything went south. I recognized one of the names: Blackbourne."

"You know who the Blackbournes are?" Both Lyle and the commander asked at the same time. How could I explain that I was an honorary member of a debauched group of hunters that ran amok in England killing supernaturals?

"Maybe." Not my most flawless rebuttal.

"They're an organized crime family, Dorian. How do you 'maybe' know them?" Lyle asked.

"I get around. They're not that bad, though. I know a couple of them. Maybe I can speak to them and find out what they know."

"Not that bad?" Lars raised his voice again. "They are the complete antithesis of everything we stand for ... more so than maybe even Gestalt. They murder and torture for sport. You can't even argue there is some meager benefit to their actions, like Gestalt's steroid."

"That's it. That's how they're involved." I suddenly remembered a conversation I'd had when on their estate. "Owen Blackbourne, the boxer turned MMA fighter … he uses steroids made from werewolf blood. They're customers, not investors."

"They're probably both," said Lars.

"If Gestalt is already past the development stage and selling it on the black market, we have a much bigger problem," Rebecca, who was in distress, broke her silence. "That drug can't get out to the public, Commander."

"I agree, doctor. We can't make a move yet without more information so the same mistakes aren't made. Dorian, I need you to go to the Blackbournes. Find out what you can without letting them know we're after Gestalt. Then—"

"I don't take orders from you." *Oh God. I'm starting to sound like Noah. But if Commander Rudgar thinks he can boss me around after demeaning my friend, he's mistaken.* "I'm going on my own terms."

"I'll have a pilot ready to take you tomorrow." Commander Rudgar and Dr. Sullivan left Lyle and me to talk alone.

"Thanks for that." Lyle let out a sigh of relief. "I thought you'd still be pissed for what I said back there."

"It's just who you are."

"I don't feel like much of anything right now. That wasn't you back there at Gestalt, though. You're not a murderer. That's why I said what I did."

"It's war, Lyle, and if the enemy wants to look down the barrel of my gun, I've got no problem pulling the trigger. I'm not making an excuse for letting my anger take over, but I stand by my decision. Locking them up for a while isn't going to solve the problem. Let Gestalt be on alert and know now they have something to fear."

"I guess you're right. I'm having a hard time not thinking like a cop anymore." Lyle got up from the bed and got dressed. "Let's go up to the lounge. I need a drink. Tomorrow, the Commander wants me to speak at a service for the ones we lost. I get to go break the news to their families after that too. Most of them don't know what they're really doing here, so not only do I have to say their loved ones died, but I get to lie to their faces about how it happened."

We made it a few feet from the lounge when I was tackled to the floor.

"Hey. Come outside and train with me. There's nothing good on TV." Noah was sitting on top of me, grinning like a stupid jackal. I should have learned by now to just always be on guard whenever he was within a hundred miles.

"Get off me! I'm not going out there. It's freezing."

"So what? It's not like you're gonna die from it." The two of us were out in the glacial wasteland before I could hold up my end of the argument anymore.

"I thought we were done with the training thing," I said, shivering and rubbing my sleeves to warm up.

"Oh, what? So you think you're better than me now?"

"No. You just haven't really bothered to teach me anything in a while."

"Sure I have. You just don't pay attention. That's why I brought you out here to fist fight."

"Nope. No way." I headed back inside, but Noah cut in front and clotheslined me into a snow mound.

"What're you afraid of? I'm not using speed or weapons." He removed his wakizashi from his waist and threw them a reasonable distance away. Knowing his agility, it was more of a display of sportsmanship than realistic disarmament. "I want you to use your powers to match my strength, but only to channel it into your movements."

"What's the point of this?"

"Restraint. You're strong after I taught you how to draw out your power, but now it's time to refine it into more practical uses. You need to learn how to defend yourself without exploding everything in a panic. It's also just fun to punch people sometimes."

"I've always dreamed of punching you in the face."

"If you touch my face, I'll rip your arms off to make a snowman. But it's not like you're gonna land a hit." Noah laughed. "Just try not to hurt yourself against *these*, in case you actually do connect." He pointed to his eight-pack abs. The cocky smirk that went along with it was perfect motivation for me.

Noah had trained me in the basics of a variety of martial arts during our time in Japan. He had attained the highest level of mastery in at least

117

a dozen styles that I could remember. I wouldn't say I was a terrible student, but our lessons consisted of him breaking nearly every bone in my body, telling me I sucked, and then speeding off to let me reflect on that while I regenerated. He set the bar high. After two years, I did advance to the point just beyond flailing in fear as he approached me, but after we left, I fell back into using my scorched-earth tactics.

Tonight, we sparred until I was dripping with sweat and could no longer feel the arctic temperatures around me. Noah was kind enough to walk me through a few moves, like the armlock he had used on Rudgar, before we started the real exercise. He brought the pain with each punch, kick, or grapple hold, but he never followed through to the point of breaking anything. His biceps were the size of my head. All it would have taken was a twitch for him to cause lethal damage, but he demonstrated calculated restraint to prove a point and make sure I stayed in the game long enough to learn something.

I expected to perform a lot worse, but I was also still learning not to underestimate myself. I think I may have almost caught Noah off guard one time, but even without him using his speed or mist form, he easily bested me as if I wasn't trying at all. By the end, I was starting to get the hang of focusing my telekinesis into accurate strikes from my fists rather than firing it like a rocket launcher. It wasn't easy to practice on someone as agile as Noah, but it made anything else I'd go up against seem easy by comparison.

Being engaged in fair combat with him was almost surreal. Three years ago, I never would have imagined going toe to toe with him in a contest of strength and skill. Calling it a contest was possibly getting a little ahead of myself. Still, the progress I made, and him recognizing it enough to actually spar and not just humiliate me, was an empowering feeling in itself.

"All right, I'm done with you." Noah punctuated his lesson with a snowball to the back of my head. "Go shower before you make me dry-heave. And remember: Being in control of a situation is always better than wasting your effort trying to overcompensate."

He was out of sight as the first rays of dawn reached the base. Amazing. I'd actually endured a physical encounter with him and wasn't covered in my own blood.

People nodded and smiled at me as I floated down the warm glow of PROJECT: UNITY's halls on my way to Lyle's room. It was nice to feel welcomed and even better to be appreciated after that mission at Gestalt.

"Lyle? Lyle, are you okay?" Immediately upon entering the room, I found Lyle slumped over in a pile of laundry beside his bed. My first thought was that he wasn't supposed to fall asleep without being checked on because of a possible concussion, but the abrasive smell of alcohol filling the room said otherwise.

When I lifted him into bed as gently as I could, he barely woke up, except to slur some words about not being a real hero and disappointing his father. His dad had been a cop in the NYPD who had died in a car chase, trying to save innocent lives. The incident had such a profound impact on Lyle in his childhood that it shaped every step he ever took after that in an attempt to live up to his father's heroics.

There was no one more valiant than Lyle, in my eyes. We were total strangers, but he had saved my life more than once and had believed in me when no one, including myself, had. I was the one with the superpowers, but I looked up to him like a big brother, especially after my parents died and I felt lost in the world. Now, I was worried that the pressure he put on himself was too much. The upstanding rules he lived by in the human world didn't transition well to a life where "kill or be killed" was standard procedure.

Chapter Nine

It was late afternoon when I crawled out of bed. Sleep hadn't come easy. I must have woken up in a cold sweat three or four times after suffering from nightmares of being on that operating table again. They always started the same way—with the sound of my tendons snapping like wet rubber bands as they were plucked from the bone—and then ended with the room spinning as my intestines were sucked out with a slurping noise through a drainage pipe on the table.

"What's up?" I asked with traces of sleep still in my voice. Lyle was at his desk across from me, holding his head in his hands.

"Oh, hey, man. I didn't know you were awake. I'm trying to write this remembrance speech for tonight."

I decided to return to bed and stay under the covers a bit longer after washing my face off in the bathroom. "What've you got so far?" I asked.

"Nothing. All I can think of is how sorry I am and that I wish I could take it all back."

"This isn't about you. It's about them."

"Yeah, I know. I'd rather be going with you to the Blackbournes. They're all on our most-wanted list. Bringing them in for their crimes would make me feel somewhat vindicated."

"Lyle, we're not arresting them. I can talk to them without starting another war. We don't need more enemies."

"Dude, they butcher innocent people like you for sport. They need to answer for what they've done."

"You have to think outside the box. You're one of the most open-minded people I know, but you have these blinders on that prevent you from adapting to a new set of rules."

"I think I adapt pretty well," Lyle disagreed. "I follow my heart. What's right is right, and what's wrong will always be wrong. Hurting good, innocent people is never going to be okay in my eyes."

"I'm not saying it's okay, but there are other ways of dealing with things. I think they'll help if I ask. They just do things for the thrill, not because they're evil. If you redirect that energy, it can be for good."

"Murder isn't a thrill!" he shouted. "Are you hearing yourself right now?"

"They hunted werewolves because they saw them as wild animals. I know it's not a good excuse, but they aren't devoid of emotion. I can reason with some of them."

"I don't get why you're standing up for them when you had a meltdown at Gestalt. You're kinda being a hypocrite, man. Just because they didn't hunt you, you're cool with them? Don't you want to stand up for your own kind? I thought you were better than that."

"One of them did try to hunt me."

"And?" he asked.

"It didn't end well for him," I said, to which Lyle threw up his hands. "I didn't kill him though! He took his own life. Long story. I'll tell you about it when I get back from England."

Gliding casually over the Blackbournes' perimeter wall, I started to doubt how warm a reception I should expect. The Blackbournes were ... well ... simple folk with extravagant tastes and misguided principles. If you pleased them, you were on their good side—easy as that. If you posed a challenge to them, you were in danger. They were thrill seekers: They put the blood in or took it out of blood sports, and they loved a challenge. The Blackbournes weren't just adrenaline junkies. They could smell adrenaline a mile away, hunt you down, and suck it from your veins quicker than any of the undead I knew.

"Good to see you again, Micah." I floated over the emerald green lawn to meet the platinum blond twenty-something-year-old supermodel turned investment banker turned barbaric slayer of the supernatural. Both his kill count and résumé were similarly extensive.

"I'm afraid you're a tad underdressed for the party and far too overdressed to be part of the entertainment." As charming as that polished upper-class English accent was, I knew it was coming from a coiled viper ready to strike at a moment's notice.

"What brings you back to our humble home so soon, mate?" A healthy dose of sarcasm from Micah. His humble home was a sprawling estate just outside the city of Bath, England, with multiple country villas, each of which was owned by a different member of this Blackbourne chapter.

"I won't lie. I need some help in the form of information."

"Honesty? That's refreshing." He took a long drag on his cigarette before putting it out on his front steps. "Never too late to try something new, eh?"

"It's serious. You and Owen could be in trouble. Are the steroids he uses from a company called Gestalt Industries?"

"I don't know anything about that. I'm his manager, not his chemist. That wanker puts a lot of poisons into his body."

"Well, is he here? Can I talk with him?"

"Out on business, I'm afraid." Micah led the way inside to his office, where two scantily clad young women who were wearing more makeup than clothing awaited his return with hungry bedroom eyes from their horizontal positions on a black leather sofa. I hadn't been in here the last time the Blackbournes had offered me their hospitality. Everything was pristine and organized: There wasn't a paper out of place on his desk, the pens were color coordinated, and the books on the shelf were all alphabetized. Bottles of alcohol and glasses were arranged by ascending height at a minibar, along with the contents of the bottles aligned along a matching horizon. All the wood grain of the furniture, floor, and molding was going in the same direction. We were at serial killer-level OCD here.

"You mean on a hunt?" I asked.

"No, I mean *business* business." Micah dismissed the half-naked women with a wave of his hand and sat at his desk. He carefully adjusted the position of a sparkling clean ashtray and then kicked his feet up and gazed out the window. There was a complete shift in the atmosphere.

"Aren't you worried about him? You two are usually attached at the hip. Those steroids he uses are from werewolves ... I know you know that. But the company supplying him is out of their minds. I just had an encounter with them dissecting me on an operating table. They had the parasite there that nearly wiped out Manhattan too. If you're funding them—"

"Owen's a big lad. The poor sod isn't as dim as he looks."

"Are you funding them? If he wants to put his own life at risk, that's one thing, but helping Gestalt expand puts millions in danger."

"Not that I can recall." Arguing with him would get me nowhere, and threatening him would be even worse. I wasn't scared of the Blackbournes, but having them as allies would pay off more.

"Fine." I sighed. "But if you happen to find your conscience and 'remember' anything, you can contact me through here."

I handed him a card that Commander Rudgar had given me before I left; it had PROJECT: UNITY's secure, untraceable phone line.

"What the bloody hell is this? Are you with MI6 now?" He laughed as I showed myself out.

Shaun was waiting for me back at the jet, which had been parked not too inconspicuously nearby. I had told the commander to give me another pilot to let Shaun rest after everything he had been through the night before, but Shaun had insisted. He'd spent the whole flight thanking me for saving him until I'd wanted to jump out and fly myself the rest of the way.

"How'd it go?" he asked as I approached. "You were gone awhile. Was starting to get nervous."

"Not great."

"You shoulda let me come with ya, mate. I know you can handle yourself and all, but I got your back. Not that you need it. I mean, if you did, though, I'd be on it." This was going to be a long flight back. I wished Gianni was here. I had been trying not to let myself think of him so I wouldn't get distracted. All Noah preached to me for the longest time was how love and friendships were meaningless liabilities. I didn't want to prove him right. I also didn't want Gianni to know what had happened at Gestalt. He'd be a huge help, but he'd also disapprove that I was getting involved in something so dangerous instead of practicing my creative side.

"Dorian?"

"Huh?"

"I asked if you wanted to hang out sometime ... off base," Shaun repeated. "I know it's probably going to drive you crazy staying down there all day, and I'm the guy with the wings. We usually take turns visiting family or hanging out together somewhere a bit warmer."

"Oh, yeah sure. Maybe after this Gestalt thing is under control."

It was late by the time we got back to base. PARAGON located Lyle for me so I could talk to him for moral support before going to the commander. After witnessing him chew out Lyle over the last mission, I wasn't looking forward to hearing what Rudgar would have to say about my failure to force the Blackbournes' hand.

"Are you drinking alone in here?" The second I entered his room, I was assailed by such a heavy smell of alcohol in the air again that it could have burned off my eyebrows. Lyle was laying in bed with a beer in his hand and a number of empty cans on the floor around him.

"Where else ... am I gonna do it? No one wants me around. They won't even fucking look ... at me." He was completely hammered. Lyle never really got drunk like this when we used to be roommates and went out with his friends. He was always a happy drunk if he ever did drink. Now, he was just angry.

"I guess the speech didn't go well?" I probably shouldn't have asked, but I didn't know how else to break into conversation with him like this.

"No kidding."

"Well, I didn't have much luck with the Blackbournes either."

"Everyone will still love *you* for it, though. They'd all be a lot happier if I'd died at Gestalt with the rest."

"Lyle, don't say that. It isn't true, and that's just the alcohol talking. Can you stop drinking for tonight?" I spotted another six-pack of beer on a chair; I was hoping he wasn't planning on cracking it open. Even considering the circumstances, this was pretty drastic for him and made me think that it had been brewing for a while.

"No! It's the only thing helping me prepare to go tell Ericka's wife and kid that she's dead in the morning. I gotta come up with an excuse why we don't have a body to bury either."

"Okay, well I'm taking the rest of your beer." I grabbed the six-pack and left a stream of obscenities behind me as Lyle tried following but stumbled and fell over the cans.

I glided down to the command floor, where I knew Commander Rudgar would be waiting for me. On the way, I noticed technicians setting up the luminescent paneling like the other floors had. One of them was adjusting the light show with his laptop. Without the plastic covering, the lights made an annoying buzzing noise.

"If you tune those wrong, can it hurt instead of making you feel relaxed or energized?" I asked the crew.

"Theoretically, it's possible. Why?"

"Can it make you pass out?"

"Didn't Beck's team spontaneously throw up when they calibrated it wrong one time?" one worker asked the other.

"Yes." He chuckled. "We know not to go near that frequency. It *could* make you lose consciousness if dialed up with enough power at exactly the right frequency, I guess."

"Would it sound like a really obnoxious high-pitched whistle?" I asked.

"That, I don't know. We'd have to test it."

"It's okay, thanks. Here, this is for you." I handed over the beer and headed into Commander Rudgar's office.

"Why do you and Gestalt have the same brain wave-altering technology?"

"We have a feeling the members that defected shared our secrets." He extended his hand to offer me a seat. "Our research team is working on customizing the current implants to run interference for the future."

"Wouldn't that have been nice to take care of before people were killed?"

"Lieutenant Turner was in charge of reconnaissance. He assured us the building's structure hadn't been altered in any way that would be deemed suspicious. We had no knowledge at the time what Gestalt had learned from our agents. Maybe now you understand how deep my frustration runs. A little more prep work and we wouldn't be holding remembrance services."

I filled Lars in on the disappointing meeting I had with Micah. He wasn't too surprised, given the Blackbournes' reputation, and I couldn't blame him.

"I've decided the best course of action is that we go into lockdown ourselves. I'm worried Gestalt may lead a strike against us in retaliation. In the meantime, we'll be testing every single product manufactured by Gestalt Industries and their numerous subsidiaries for any trace of them releasing their experiments on the public now that we know they're past the R&D phase. You can still come and go freely, but you'll have to arrange for other transportation."

What did Gestalt want? What did humans ever want? Did they think they were going to enhance the human condition with their experiments? Did they think they could break the mortal coil? I had news for them: It wasn't much better on the other side.

"Before I accept any more of your hospitality, I wanted to say something." As soon as the words left my mouth, I started to wonder if it was a good idea to continue, but I had nothing to lose by manning up and speaking my mind. "Ease up on Lyle, okay? I get that you've got to be the tough guy around here, but it's a lot to put all the blame on one person for what happened back at Gestalt."

"It's simple. Turner is one of those people who work best under pressure. I don't think there's anything he can't do with the right motivation."

"What you're doing is killing him," I said.

"Sometimes you've got to walk through the fire before you become numb to the pain."

"Okay, let me make something clear, Commander. That human means the world to me, and if anything should happen to him because of *you*, there's nowhere you can hide that I won't find you, and I've got all the time in the world to do it."

"I believe that." He nodded, unshaken. "Your loyalty to each other is commendable, but maybe I should explain where I'm coming from."

"Yeah, what got someone like you caught up in this lifestyle?" I asked, trying to drag the conversation out as long as possible in hopes that Lyle would sober up by the time I got back to the room. "You seem too sensible to be the type who goes chasing fairies, so to speak."

"It was that same German sensibility that got me involved in the first place. Since the Second World War, Germany has maintained a quiet interest in the occult. There is some startling evidence that Hitler would perform sacrificial rituals to communicate with a demonic host for power and guidance on how to better achieve his nefarious goals. The Nazis gained a few supernatural allies but turned on them quickly due to overconfidence. Hitler kept extensive personal notes on them, which were recovered by the allies after the war. Even after Germany was demilitarized, the government has kept an interest in these superhumans through today."

Rudgar's story made me think of the Strigoi's arcanum, which was repurposed from an old military bunker in Germany.

"I was moving up the ranks of the First Panzer Division when I was approached to join a covert task force dedicated to monitoring the activities of those remaining supernaturals," he continued. "We were meant to uphold a strict policy of noninterference to avoid antagonizing them, and for the most part, I couldn't see any reason why we would break that. None of our targets were what you would consider a threat, aside from minor thefts.

"They seemed at peace living amongst humans, but I could always tell they didn't feel like they fit in by how they would try their best to stay alone in a crowd. I never spoke with them, but just watching from a distance after so long, I felt as if we knew each other. One happened to save a teammate of mine from a near-fatal car crash and then disappeared before we could speak.

"It wasn't long after that I was given an order I didn't agree with. Something spooked our superiors, and we were given instructions to exterminate all targets. I couldn't bring myself to gun them down in cold blood after we'd spent years confirming their innocence. It was after I made contact to warn them that PROJECT: UNITY enlisted me and helped fake my death to prevent my former task force from pursuing me."

"What do you think made them turn on the supernaturals after all that time?" I asked. "It sounds just like what the Nazis did."

"I haven't given it much thought. There's no point in speculation when every second counts. War is about precision, not daydreaming, and only actions get results. Since enlisting with PROJECT: UNITY, I have sworn that my actions will always be in the best interest of my people, and until the day when I am no longer able to uphold that, I will continue to fight for peace at all costs."

Chapter Ten

Three weeks crept by since the start of the lockdown. Every night was more restless than the last, with persistent nightmares of faceless Gestalt doctors plaguing any attempt I made at getting even a modest amount of sleep. After reaching critical levels of boredom two weeks ago, Noah had left the base without any word of where he was headed. An abundance of products, from Gestalt-brand eyedrops to antihistamines, that PROJECT: UNITY's research team tested came up negative for traces of anything out of the ordinary. Gestalt never made a move, but we had enough problems of our own within these walls.

The soda cans and discarded bags of chips littering Lyle's room were gradually replaced by beer and liquor bottles. Each passing day followed the same routine. His hours of operation were always during the night, when everybody but the research team spent their time mulling around, anxiously waiting for something to happen, and going through training exercises. The first few days, I went to the gym with Lyle and Shaun to help spot them with my powers during weight training and to watch as Shaun taught Lyle Krav Maga.

Only the two of them were allowed to leave the base so that Lyle could deliver the bad news to the deceased agents' families. Those were the days when he drank the heaviest, despite my persistent attempts to cheer him up. While everyone on base grew more comfortable having me around, some even lauding me as their hero over inflated details of my supposedly heroic exploits, my hero and best friend wasted away in his room, and nothing I did was getting through to him.

I watched each night as Lyle's eyes glazed over from downing drink after drink until his thoughts couldn't haunt him anymore. He always managed to wake up and work through his hangover with no one the wiser. His enthusiasm for just about everything except alcohol deteriorated until he was only going through the paces necessary to pass the time until he could put his lips to the glass. I considered staging some kind of intervention, but I feared that the shame would demoralize him even more.

"Hey, Dr. Sullivan." I strolled into the medical area and took a deep breath. Lyle had been avoiding Rebecca in any way he could. Maybe she was the key to getting him to listen.

"Hello, Dorian." She broke away from her colleagues to come greet me. "I'm surprised to see you here. What can I do for you?"

"I realized we never had that talk. I've been getting antsy around here, looking for stuff to do, so if you still have questions for me, now would be a good time if you're free."

It didn't take much to get Dr. Sullivan to take the bait. In no time, we were set up in a break room and chatting privately. She asked all sorts of basic questions that the rest of the team had already repeated hundreds of times by now, such as "When did you start having powers?" and "How did you learn to control them?" But there were some more interesting ones that I hadn't even asked myself.

"How many objects can you manipulate at one time?"

"I have no idea. I haven't tried. I usually only focus on one or two."

"Okay, well how much weight can you lift?"

"Uh, I'm not really sure. I've never measured, but I've never had a problem moving what I needed to when the situation came up."

"Based on the reports of what happened at Gestalt, you're considerably more powerful than anything we had on record. Do you think your power is tied to emotional triggers, or is it static?"

"I don't know that either. I'm more focused when I'm calm, but that's like with anything else. I haven't tried to create things when I was upset though."

"What do you mean create things?"

I explained my ability to carve objects and demonstrated on a rock paperweight by turning it into a pyramid by cleaving off the sides.

"Wow! That's so fascinating. As someone who specializes in studies of the brain, I've always had an interest in supernaturals with telekinetic abilities. It's my belief that, like most other superhuman powers, telekinesis has more to do with mental aptitude than spiritual attunement.

"Commander Rudgar told me that Nazi scientists thought of the brain as a window to another realm where our dreams and thoughts travel from. The human brain naturally filters out much of what it can't comprehend with the five senses in an attempt to process a clear picture of our surroundings. When we sleep, that natural filter relaxes, allowing more information into our minds than we would have the resources to understand during times of consciousness.

"Telekinetics and other psychics may have a clearer filter or 'window' that lets in more from this other world that is then translated into powers such as yours. It's one of the best leads we have in the transhumanism movement."

"The what?" I asked.

"Transhumanism is the concept of evolving mankind through technology. If we could narrow the gap between the natural and the supernatural, it would open a lot of doors toward equality. Unlocking the secrets of the mind and vastly increased lifespans are only the beginning." I wasn't sure I shared the same interest in this transhumanism thing as Rebecca did. It made me think of the Outsiders coexisting with humans in their new place. Why should we all have to be the same to be treated equally? Couldn't we keep our differences and still get along like they did?

"Adolf Hitler had a fascination bordering on obsession with twins of all kinds, especially conjoined twins. Scientifically speaking, when performing an experiment, you always want a control subject to test against the variable of your hypothesis. In the case of human experimentation, ethics aside, you'd want to get two subjects as closely related as possible, which is what made twins so valuable. The madman even tried to create conjoined twins by sewing two together. For centuries, many also believed twins to have latent psychic abilities, such as some degree of telepathy with each other, and even the key to immortality."

Then came the questions about my own immortality, which I figured she was most curious about. I could tell she was itching to run tests. You didn't need twins when I could be my own control subject due to my healing. That was my chance to proceed with my plan.

"I'm sure Lyle's told you most of this stuff himself."

"The lieutenant filled us in on a lot, but it's always better to get a direct account."

"He knows me probably as well as I do. I wouldn't be here without him."

"He's a good man." She nodded politely without relaxing her professional manner for even a second.

"You aren't upset with him over the Gestalt mission too, are you?"

"I wasn't there to judge how he handled things, and honestly, I don't know what he could have done to prepare any better without going in to survey the area in the first place. I'm not one of the agents, but I don't think it's fair to judge someone on a mistake when there are so many variables involved. The lieutenant is very by the book with how he goes about his business. I can't say I'd fault him for breaking procedure when the book hasn't been written yet. I'm just a doctor here, though, so my opinion on the matter counts for very little."

"What do you think about him personally then?" Time to raise the heat and get some real answers.

"I'm not sure what you mean. He seems to be fair, honest, and very dedicated."

"Do you think he's attractive?" My question really threw the doctor for a loop. Her face looked as if she had just heard a clap of thunder for the first time.

"I can't really comment on that," she said, composing herself once again. "He's still technically my superior."

"Oh, come on. I'm not even one of you guys. Protocol doesn't mean anything to me."

"I'll say it this way," she hesitated. "You'd have a hard time finding a woman on staff who doesn't find him attractive in at least some way."

"You should have dinner with him sometime. You know he thinks a lot of people are upset with him over the Gestalt mission. It might make him feel better hearing it from someone on the team directly that they support him."

"Is that why you came down here? I don't know if it's exactly appropriate ..." There was cautious interest in her voice, and she suddenly became an ordinary person with a wider range of emotions than her previous clinical curiosity.

"I'll let you run tests on me," I blurted out and then wanted to retract the offer immediately. "Nothing too invasive though. I mean ... like ... I'll donate blood or something. Leave my brain where it belongs."

She laughed and put down the clipboard she had been taking notes on during our conversation. "This must mean a lot to you," she said with a teasing smile. "You're a good friend to volunteer that for him."

"He's done a lot for me. We're like brothers."

"How about this? I'll draw a small blood sample, and when I end my shift in an hour, I can come by his room so we can get dinner. But please don't let the commander know. He doesn't think highly of fraternizing on base, or I would have had dinner with Lyle months ago if asked."

"Deal."

Rebecca was ready with a needle like it was attached to her.

"You know, I didn't expect you to ever come down, but after Mr. Burckhardt did, I thought you might follow."

"After Noah did what?" I asked.

"He was snooping around the lab a couple of weeks ago when PARAGON picked him up. We were told to ignore him so he isn't provoked, but after a while, he popped into view and asked about the implants. I told him they wouldn't work for the undead since you need a pulse because it uses the body's own electrical current. Then he asked about the blood reserves and offered to donate."

The implants I understood his curiosity in, but giving blood? That was not the Noah I knew.

"Did he say why?"

"No. He only said to save it for an absolute emergency and not to bring anyone back from the dead or he'd have to kill them. I was nervous at first, knowing his reputation for being erratic, but he was very ... what's a good word for it? Civil. It was very distracting just to look at him, but luckily he has really good veins for taking blood."

"Yeah, he's like a road map."

I headed for Lyle's room when Dr. Sullivan was finished. The night shift for both of them would be ending soon. Some of my excitement at getting him a date was clouded over by my curiosity about what Rebecca had told me about Noah.

"Get your finest sweatpants on, because I got you a date with Rebecca!" Lyle was already in his room when I got there. His eyes were glazed over, and he was staring at the TV with a bottle in his hand.

"What're you talking about?" he slurred.

"Are you freakin' kidding me? How are you already drunk? Your shift *just* ended!"

"No it didn't. I told them to break early because there was nothin' to do. Been here two hours by *myself.*"

"We have to sober you up fast. Put the damn bottle down!"

"Leave me alone already. Go fly away somewhere."

"I just got you a date with the woman you like. I literally bled to do it too." I started cleaning up the room with my powers to make it go faster. *Twenty beer cans at once; Rebecca should add that to her notes.* "Can you please just go take a shower? She'll be here any minute. I'll try and stall her until you sober up—"

Lyle got up from the bed and kicked the cans I was gathering all over the room again.

"Get out of my room!" he yelled. "Ever since you came here, you think you're hot shit."

"Lyle, I know this is the alcohol talking, but I swear if you don't stop drinking—"

"What? You'll kill me?" He stepped up so close to me that I could smell the liquor on his breath. "Go ahead! Do it!"

"If you're not gonna straighten out, then I'll tell Rebecca it's off for tonight."

"Ya know, I should've let you pull that trigger on yourself after I blew your parents' brains out!" He threw his beer, narrowly missing me and hitting the wall instead. I spun around and punched him in his face in retaliation so hard that he hit the ground unconscious. I knew he wasn't the real cause of my parents' death. It was a mercy killing that I couldn't bring myself to do when they had been infected with the Carpathians' parasite, but something in me just snapped hearing him speak that way.

"Uh, oh …" He wasn't moving. I went over to make sure he was breathing when an alarm went off on the PARAGON terminal and someone was at the door. I shouldn't have done that. Now I was going to get arrested.

I opened the door to see Rebecca standing there looking radiant in casual wear and out of the medical area's harsh lighting. It was the first time I had seen her in jeans and something other than a lab coat.

"Hi. I know I'm a little early, but I heard the team broke early, so I figured I'd come over."

"Uh." I stared blankly, trying to think of a quick excuse while PARAGON was blaring in the room.

"You're getting an urgent call." She pointed out. "Do you want me to come back later?"

"Lyle's, uh, he's not …"

"Are you drinking in there?" She turned up her nose as the stench escaped the room.

"No! I mean, yes. It was me. He's not feeling well. He wanted me to ask if tomorrow is good."

"Sure …" She was on to me, but I didn't know what else to say. "You should really get that call, though."

I closed the door and ran to the terminal to answer it, all while keeping an eye on Lyle for any movement.

"Dorian," the commander addressed me instantly. "We've just received a message on our secure line from Micah Blackbourne. He wants to meet with you right away. He says you know where to find him."

"I'm on my way. Oh, and ... uh ... Commander? Send someone to check on Lyle in a few minutes. Anyone but Dr. Sullivan."

Chapter Eleven

"Micah." I made it to the Blackbourne estate in record time, thanks to Shaun dropping me off right overhead.

"It's Owen." Micah was waiting for me outside with scotch and a cigarette in hand—a typical Blackbourne breakfast. "He must really be losing the plot after all."

"What happened?" By all the cigarette butts at his feet, he must have been out there chain-smoking for quite some time before I'd arrived.

"He went to that Gestalt with Carter for an investors' meeting. They were going to show them around their facility in the Netherlands."

"When?"

"A week before you stopped by. I haven't heard from either of them since. I don't give two shits about Carter, but if anything happens to that bloody moron ... We're not even related, but we're like brothers, you know?"

"Yeah, I know ... Why didn't you say anything before?" I didn't want to break the news that if Owen had been gone for that long, there was no chance he was still alive. Micah would shut down and not say anything then.

"We signed a strict confidentiality agreement. I would have told you if you didn't come around asking about just that. I figured you'd stick your nose in something and blow it for all of us." Micah started on another cigarette and took a flask out from his jacket to refill his glass. "Owen is never out of touch for more than a day ... two, at most, if he's passed out pissed somewhere."

"Owen is a celebrity, and you have political ties. Why didn't you just go to the police? Gestalt isn't going to want that kind of press."

"Neither do we. The coppers can't find their own arse; do you think they'll dig deep enough to uncover what was going on? The Blackbourne society exists around their ignorance. What's the worst that could happen to Gestalt? They get pinned with some citation for questionable ethics at most? No doubt they do their worst in countries where regulations are more relaxed.

"They'll throw one of their own under the bus to get the cops off their back about the kidnapping and run a PR campaign to cover up the bad press ... build a damn bloody water park for cripples or something. They know as well as we do how to bury our problems, but we have more to lose. We can't put the cork back in the bottle on some of the business we do. The family will be ruined, and they know that. There will be a price on my head that even Her Majesty couldn't pay off."

"Come with me, then, and bring whatever you have on Gestalt. No more secrets."

PROJECT: UNITY had the red carpet rolled out for us as soon as we got back. It took almost as long to talk our escorts into letting Micah keep his firearm and briefcase as it did to get there. They acted as if they were more worried about him causing problems than they had been about Noah. I figured this was just their way of showing their discontent at having to play nice with a criminal.

"You know, I always wanted to be a secret agent for the queen," Micah mused as we made our way down to the command area. "I used to put on my Sunday suit when I was a lad and play pretend. I could tie a tie by age seven."

"Are you telling me this because you're having second thoughts on your life of crime?" I asked.

"I'm wondering why I didn't start sooner."

Our chaperones brought us to a boardroom that was still under construction. The long table sitting in the center had computer screens built into it for each seat and an even larger screen on the wall behind the head of the table.

"Charming," Micah said, looking around. "I'm getting the feeling these boys are all fluff and no substance. If we needed a place to chat, we could have stayed by me."

The automatic door slid open behind us, and Commander Rudgar entered.

"If these arrangements don't suit you, there's a cell down below I'd be more than happy to make available," said Lars.

"Oh, you must be someone important around here. You're the first one with the balls to address me directly." Micah took a seat opposite the head of the table where the commander sat. "Let's get on with it then. You obviously need me more than I need you if you were willing to send Dorian here as a friendly face. Trying to establish rapport ... I know the game."

Lyle's absence from the meeting concerned me. Was he in trouble with the commander for breaking early to get wasted? Was I in trouble for decking him?

Micah and Commander Rudgar bantered back and forth pointlessly for a few minutes until finally we started to get somewhere.

"We started as suppliers, then consumers. Investing was the next logical step. We were selling the beasts' blood on the black market. We used to wash the stuff down the drain, but buyers were offering millions. Then, we got bigger offers: requests for bone marrow, muscles, all that.

"I don't know much about the science of it. It's a growth hormone extracted from the pituitary gland. They're half human, so I suppose it wasn't too troubling to create a drug compatible for people. The trick was, when the beasts die, they turn back to human form, so we had to harvest them alive."

"You make me sick." Commander Rudgar couldn't bring himself to look at Micah's face as he talked about his transgressions. "You're nothing but thugs and butchers in expensive suits."

"Oh please, spare me." Micah rolled his eyes. "Business is business, and that's all it is. They're bloody mutts. Next, you'll be telling me to go vegan."

"Micah, do you know exactly where they planned to meet with Owen and Carter?" I asked.

"Rotterdam. I have the address from their emails, but it doesn't mean they're still there after a month."

"They have two of your own?" asked the commander. "If it's been that long, they're already dead. It didn't take Gestalt more than a few minutes to start experimenting on my agents."

"Owen isn't some brainless foot soldier," Micah snapped at him. "He can take care of himself."

"Then why are you here?" Rudgar asked.

"No one messes with the Blackbournes, and if you're making a move against our enemy, then you have my interest."

"What reassurance can we have of your cooperation?" The commander tapped away at the screen before him.

"The enemy of my enemy is one of the oldest tactics there is. Surely, you learned that in whatever ten-second training you needed to run this little operation."

"That hasn't always gone so well for me in the past," I chimed in, remembering the shaky alliance I'd had with Aurelia's sister—Rozalin—when venturing into Yomi.

"It only applies when one side has something of value to offer to the other," Rudgar said. "As I see it, you've yet to show what you are bringing to the table besides a reckless taste for revenge."

"Oh, bargaining now, are we?" Micah scoffed. "What is it you want? Money? Just tell me where to wire it."

"Donations are always welcomed, but why don't we start with your word to stop butchering innocent creatures?"

"You can't be serious," Micah laughed. "That's your idea of a counteroffer?"

"If we're about to make a strike against your buyer, then you no longer have financial reasons to keep up the hunts. Find another hobby, because after this, we have the same information on you that Gestalt has that you're so worried about getting out."

"You're blackmailing me. You're supposed to be the 'good guys,' but I don't see much of a difference from Gestalt except that they pay well."

"It's just business," Commander Rudgar said coldly. "Of course, with your knowledge and experience with the supernatural kind, we could always use your assistance hunting down certain marks."

"Oh, so your dark side runs deeper than blackmail? Now you really have my interest."

"There's nothing sordid about it. We never turn down help, and if you need a direction to channel your bloodlust, then I'd be more than happy to put it to good use instead of making it a sporting event. It's simple: You get to hunt, we get the bad guys, and both of us stay on good terms."

"Good, bad, whatever. It's all the same to me."

"We can discuss it more later," Rudgar said while clicking on the screen before him. "I've already located Gestalt Industries' facility in Rotterdam and informed the team that we will be making a move today. Our scientists have come up with a way to block their security device that caused us problems last time. It's an adjustment to the implants our agents use, but we developed an external set that work like earplugs for Dorian and will double as a short-range communicator. We'll have a second set prepared for you. I'll have someone show you to a room you can wait in until we're ready to depart."

We filed out of the boardroom, where Lyle was waiting to the side of the hallway. The commander marched right past him, along with the guards escorting Micah.

"Can we speak in private?" Lyle stepped in to ask me. He didn't reek of alcohol, so that was a plus. I followed him back into the boardroom, trying to decide if I was still angry with him or just disappointed.

"I know I have a lot of apologizing to do," he started, looking deflated. "Saying sorry isn't going to cut it, but I don't know where else to start. I said some pretty messed-up stuff, and I want you to know that none of it was true."

"I'm surprised you remember any of it; you were pretty wasted. I've never seen you get like that. How long has this been going on with the excessive drinking?"

"It only started after that mission. I can't even remember what happened tonight, but the rooms have emergency surveillance that's stored on PARAGON. The commander pulled up the video to see why I was passed out on the floor after you left."

"Did Rebecca ...?"

"Yeah." He sighed.

"I told him not to send her."

"I know. She was the closest medical staff member to the scene, though, so she was the first to respond when the call went out for assistance."

"Sorry."

"Don't be, man. You were only trying to help me."

Lyle sat at the table with his hands folded in front of his face. "It just feels like ... no matter what I do, I'll never be half the man my father was.

"That night in your apartment, everything changed. I felt like I was actually making a difference. My dad told me that when I found what I should be doing in life, I'd know it in my heart. I loved the NYPD, but I would start every shift wondering how many teenagers hopping the turnstiles I'd have to catch or how many robberies I'd have to stop before my heart would tell me, 'Yes, this is it. You're doing it.' When is it going to start to matter?"

"Lyle, you're so hard on yourself and set these crazy expectations. Look at what you've done, not what you haven't yet. You have all these plans and dreams, and I'm still living day by day, trying to keep up with what's thrown at me. I wish I had your focus. I've looked up to you since we met."

"I guess part of me envies you," he said. "Everything you do makes you the hero I want to be."

"That's stupid. Everything I've done has been with the help of others like you. Being a hero isn't about keeping score; it's about the intentions behind your actions. You're a lot of people's hero, including mine."

"You mean that, man?" Lyle looked up with hope returning to his face.

"Of course I do. I tell everyone that, including Rebecca. But promise me you won't drink like that anymore. There's a lot more hero stuff to do, and I need your help to do it."

"I promise." He extended his hand to shake on it and gave me a hug. "I'm never gonna stop being sorry for what I said, though. You're family, and I wouldn't even talk to my worst enemy that way."

"And I'm sorry I punched you in the face."

"I had it coming." Lyle smiled. "I'm just glad you didn't use your powers, or I might not be here to apologize."

"Actually, I did," I admitted. "I just held back."

"Oh crap," Lyle exclaimed, realizing how close he had come to testing his own mortality. "Every time I see you in action, I always think I'm glad you're on my side."

"We make a pretty good team," I patted him on the back, "now that you've gotten over trying to handcuff parasitic mutants and read them their rights like that first night in New York."

"Oh man." He laughed. "I did do that, didn't I? How was I supposed to know?"

"I can't believe we've gotten to the point where we can look back on *that* and laugh. Anything really is possible, I guess."

"I screwed things up with Rebecca pretty bad, huh?" Lyle asked as we headed back to his room.

"I'm sure we can convince her to give you another shot. She thinks you're attractive for some reason and that you were going through a lot."

"Hey, what do you mean 'for some reason'? Why do you have to say it like that?"

"I don't know. I thought for a doctor she'd have better taste." I laughed and flew up the central atrium to beat Lyle to the barracks.

Back in his room, we chatted for a few hours about my time at the Blackbournes before the call came over PARAGON to assemble for a mission briefing.

"What do you think about Shaun?" Lyle asked in the elevator on the way down. "He been bothering you a lot?"

"No, why? He seems cool. He's kind of silly from what I expected when I first got a good look at him." For a six-foot Krav Maga expert with a sleeve tattooed on his left arm, he was rather dorky. Other than myself, Shaun was the only person on base who didn't treat Lyle like an outcast for his botched mission. His jokes needed some work, though.

"He's been trying to get me to ask you for an autograph or to hang out or something."

"What? Why?"

"He's a big fan. I've heard a bunch of the agents are, but he's the only one who really talks to me about it." Lyle was being serious, and it was making me uneasy. The thought of that type of attention didn't sit well with someone who'd spent most of his life keeping to himself.

"No way. Why would anyone be a fan of me?" I asked. "Before I came here, I was living in a homeless shelter, and before that, I was on the street or out in the wild, eating whatever I could find laying around."

"That's gross and sad, but you know that's not why they like you. You could really use it to your advantage ... maybe get yourself a date. If there's anyone you have your eye on, I could always find out if they're into you like that."

"I'm already seeing someone." That came out so suddenly, I felt like I may have jinxed it.

"Who? How come you never told me? Is it Myers? I always suspected he might go that way."

"Whoa! Calm down. It's nobody on base. His name is Gianluca, and he's supernatural ... like me, though ... not undead. Well, not exactly like me ... he's alive but immortal." I was getting myself flustered talking about him. I had been trying to hold back any of these thoughts so I wouldn't miss him. It was also strange to be talking about this when I had kept it quiet for so long. "He's from the Roman Empire, or before it ... around that time."

"Are you blushing?" Lyle started to crack up and shook me by the shoulder.

"No!" I denied it, but I knew I was.

"It's hard to hide when you're normally white as a ghost," he teased. "And you're smiling like you won the lotto."

"It's called alabaster," I said, trying to sound as intellectual as possible.

"It's called you need a tan. So how long have you two been dating?"

"I don't know if I'd call it dating. We've only seen each other a few times. He's busy, and he's really old, so I don't know if dating is even something on his mind. I mean, he definitely shows interest, but I don't know how serious a two-thousand-year-old's romantic intentions are. He says I remind him of someone he was in love with during his human years, so I don't know if when he comes to see me it's just a novelty like going to the museum to reminisce."

"This is a whole new side of you. You never talk about this kinda stuff. I'm happy for you, man, but if you've only seen each other a few times and he hasn't been around for a month, he might not be that serious." Lyle may be right. Gianluca had already done so much for me in the short time he'd been in my life. I shouldn't be too upset if he'd decided to move on. But what if Gianni was hurt and all alone with no one to help him? He couldn't count on being so invincible all the time. I had seen hubris get the best of many powerful people. He might be dead, and I'd never know.

"We will be sieging Gestalt's facility in two teams of four, with a third holding their position at transport to secure our evac," Commander Rudgar was announcing as we walked into the assembly room. "All blueprints of the known areas of the building and surrounding sewer system have been uploaded to your suits via PARAGON. That's right, folks. We're going crap diving."

"Why do I always wind up in the sewer?" I sighed.

"We already know what we're looking for will be in the sublevels, so we'll be starting from the bottom up," the commander carried on as we took a seat. "We're not giving them the chance to prepare by going through ground level. The first team will be in charge of disabling their security systems in case they have anything extra-special cooked up. We're using live rounds. If it moves and doesn't respond to commands, shoot it until it does or it's dead. Prisoners are optional; answers are appreciated. After the generators are down, the second team will come in to clear out any security forces converging on the first. This is the real deal. This facility is ten times the size of the last, and if they're taking high-profile prisoners there, you can bet it will be well guarded."

Micah drifted in, donning his black demon leather armor and looking like the executioner from Hell.

"Your cheap imported scotch couldn't give a ten-year-old a buzz," he said. "I hunt better when I'm buzzed."

"I will be leading the Alpha squad for the initial assault," Commander Rudgar continued without pausing to humor Micah. "Benoit, you're with me, along with Sanders and Davidoff. Fredricks, Roberts, and Jackson, you take Blackbourne as the Omega squad to come up behind."

Commander Rudgar rattled off more names, assigning orders until everyone was mentioned, except Lyle.

"Um, sir? What about me?" Lyle asked as everyone cleared out to go to the hangar.

"I think it's best you stayed back on this one, Lieutenant."

"Commander, you can't be serious," Lyle argued. "This is one of the biggest missions PROJECT: UNITY has run. I've been ... we've been working on this for years. You can't expect me to just sit this out."

"You can quit then, if you aren't willing to follow orders. But in case you are, maybe someday you'll survive long enough to be giving them again."

"With all due respect, sir, I don't quit."

"I'm not going without Lyle." I floated over to speak in his defense.

"That's unfortunate. We could have used your help, but we are prepared to proceed without it if that's the case. My squad is the elite of PROJECT: UNITY, and right now Turner is too much of a liability."

"How do you expect me to prove myself and earn back the respect of the team if I'm sitting in my room?" asked Lyle.

"There's a time and place for everything, Turner. Now is neither of those for you."

"Oh screw it," I said. "We'll just go by ourselves then, Lyle."

"Then you'll be deemed a threat for defying orders and will be handled accordingly," Commander Rudgar warned.

"Are you willing to bet your elite toy soldiers are *elite* enough to take me down *and* complete your mission?" I stared the commander down, waiting for a response.

"Fine," he said after some inner deliberation. "Turner can take point with you on Alpha. And bring Blackbourne with you too. I'm not in the mood to deal with him on top of this."

Chapter Twelve

"What does Gestalt have to gain from all this?" one of the agents asked through the earpiece as we waded single file through the sewers of Rotterdam. We had been traveling for what seemed like miles through the network of cramped, 'aromatic' tunnels. The ceilings were too low here to fly above the waterline, forcing me to walk through the slop with everyone else. At least this time I'd been given boots so I wouldn't be soaked through with sewage.

"Crime pays well," Micah answered.

There were no maintenance lights for most of the way, so the only bearings I had were by feeling around in the dark with my powers and following the tiny amount of light given off by the suits. Lyle and the rest had the advantage of night vision and a range of other sight-enabling options built into their helmets.

"Killing your customers by using them as lab rats seems like a bad business model," I said while trying to shake off something that had gotten wrapped around my boot. "I've been wondering the same thing. They have enough money, and they aren't using their experiments to poison the public in some plan for world domination, so what's the point? They aren't even using their own technology to enhance themselves. The employees at the last facility were all regular, unaltered humans."

"You're looking too much into it," said Lyle. "They're bioterrorists looking to sell to the highest bidder. There are plenty of countries out there that would starve their citizens to pay for the latest weapons."

"Is the money really worth it?" I asked.

"It's always worth it until you cross the wrong people," said Micah.

"Did you ever take the steroid?" I asked Micah.

"I tried, but it almost killed me. I've never had a problem with any other drug before."

"Stand back and shut up," Lars commanded as he used a high-powered cutting laser on the tunnel wall to make us an entrance. "On your mark, Turner."

We had to disable security right away and search for anything that could lead us to Owen. PROJECT: UNITY's objectives were a bit more complicated: finding information that could help crumble the entire conglomerate. But all I had to worry about was dealing with any resistance we may encounter. *Maybe someday I'll actually be useful for more than smashing things.*

"Stay close, and keep it tight," Lyle ordered and took the first cautious step through the hole.

"Get bloody on with it," said Micah. We exited the sewers right into the middle of a major corridor twice the size of the previous facility. You could have paraded a herd of elephants down these sterile metallic halls. There wasn't a soul in sight, which had to mean that everyone was hard at work in their rooms.

"How do you open these doors?" Micah asked, inspecting the same symmetrical rows that we'd found in the previous building.

"You can't. They're sealed by airtight magnetic locks," Lyle explained to him. "The scanner above them will only activate for Gestalt personnel. Dorian could tear them open, but we'd risk trapping and killing Owen and any other survivors if the ceilings give way."

"How does anyone find their way around here?" asked Sanders, who had been lucky enough to join us as our fourth. "There are no signs anywhere. None of the doors or halls are labeled. No pictures or acronyms. Nothin'. We're in a stainless steel labyrinth."

He was right. It wasn't something that I would have picked out during the chaos of our last mission, but there wasn't any indications of where we were like you'd find in most buildings.

"We go door by door until we find one that stands out or opens. Don't open fire unless attacked or a victim is in imminent danger," Lyle directed. We took a few steps, and the debilitating security alarm triggered. I held my ears nervously, hoping that the electronic plugs PROJECT: UNITY had given Micah and me would run interference like they were meant to. If not, we'd be out cold in less than a minute.

"Hold your position." Lyle put out his hand. We waited a full minute, my heartbeat quickening with every passing second. "We good?" He nodded toward me.

"Yeah—" I answered just as a door to our left slid open. Out walked three Gestalt employees; they were not fazed in the least by our presence as they chatted with each other over test results in their hands.

"Don't move!" Lyle shouted and raised his weapon at the men. We had them surrounded, but they passed between us without a care in the world. All but Micah's eyes were covered by his hood and face mask, which were more than enough to deliver a quizzical expression. He grabbed one of the scientists by the back of the collar and threw him against the wall with his gun at the man's throat.

"Owen Blackbourne. Where is he?" Micah demanded. The man brushed Micah off like he wasn't even there and tried to walk away. His coworkers didn't stop to wait for him either. Lyle and Sanders had to run back around in front of them to block their way.

"I don't like to be ignored," Micah said calmly, raising his gun to the back of the man's head and pulling the trigger.

"What are you doing?!" Lyle shouted at Micah. The other two employees still weren't concerned by what was going on, even with pieces of their deceased coworker decorating the backs of their lab coats.

"What the bloody hell is wrong with them?" Micah grabbed another and smacked him across the face with his gun. "Where is Owen Blackbourne?"

Still nothing.

"Let him go. We'll follow them," Lyle suggested. Micah stepped back and swept the man's legs out from under him. The scientist hit the floor, got up, and continued on to catch up to his friend, where they started chatting again.

I shuffled through the papers the man had dropped and read from them out loud.

"Patient: RJX-748592.23600

"Status: In-Patient, Day 4

"OR Procedure: Ocular implant

"Pre-Op Review: Patient suffered all the textbook symptoms following the last procedure: nausea, loss of appetite, confusion, hysterics, nightmares, night sweats, and tremors. Patient seems to be recovering well, and mental state has held up, which is better than the other 80% of those who received the same procedure.

"OR Details: The surgical scissors used to extract the patient's eye and clip the optic nerve became lodged halfway in. We had to wait for facilities to bring us a replacement.

"All things considered, patient coped well without the use of anesthesia or sedatives.

"OR Time: 6 hours (including delays)

"Post-Op Notes: Testing the implants during a patient's hysterics coming out of surgery is never easy. However, we were able to confirm the desired secondary vision results along with a much-improved score on his eye exam.

"Additional notes: The left implant failed 4 hours out of surgery. It shriveled and became atrophied in the socket. We immediately replaced it with another from cold storage successfully."

"This is a bloody nuthouse," Micah said.

"The workers in the last facility acted this way too. If they're being mind-controlled, what's doing it?" I asked. "There was no one left in the last building to be in control."

"Anyone I've seen be hypnotized like that acts like a robot. These guys were talking to each other, and they looked us in the eyes. They just didn't care," Lyle said. We were trailing the scientists all around when Micah finally had enough. He pulled one man away and slammed him into a door.

"I'll only say this once!" Micah shouted into the room of doctors gathered around an operating table, mulling over reports. "Tell me where you're keeping Owen Blackbourne."

No one answered. Micah open fired on all the employees, including the one he had hold of.

"Blackbourne!" Lyle yelled. "Killing them doesn't get us anywhere!"

"Neither does leaving them alive." Micah polished his gun on his sleeve and dragged a body to the next door to use under the scanner while I stayed behind to look at the reports.

Patient: OBX-513800.23600

Status: In-Patient, Day 10

Psychological Profile Update: Since last procedure, any interaction with medical personnel has been begging for release. A strong will to live will keep the patient applicable for further operations. By now, most surviving patients have attempted, or succeeded in committing, suicide.

Patient has been moved to a padded room and restrained as a precaution. At this point, we cannot financially afford the risk of damaging the implants due to the patient acting out. Night staff has been specifically instructed not to sedate for any reason. We want the patient's senses to be sharp for testing. As for the past few days, the patient has quieted down.

Patient: CBX-163229.23600

Status: In-Patient, Day 10

OR Procedure: Heart transplant Type-L

OR Time: 4 hours

OR Details: Failed due to patient's body rejecting transplant on the table. Patients of this age are not recommended due to how quickly they go into shock without sedatives. Procedure was still

useful as practice for more applicable subjects. Body
sent for implant removal and termination.

I dropped the papers back on the table,
feeling queasy. There was more than enough
evidence here to shut Gestalt down, but if they'd
made it this far and were this widespread, they
would regroup elsewhere.

I caught up to Micah as he left the room next
door. The room was unoccupied, and Micah marched
on. But what was inside had me more concerned.

"Oil? In a medical research building?"
Sanders asked, upon entering after me. Large vats
of black liquid lined the walls, with tubes reaching
up through the ceiling. The blood in my veins stirred
as if it was trying to sing to me.

"That's not oil," I said, recognizing the liquid.
"We have to destroy it."

"Blackbourne, stay together!" Lyle shouted at
Micah, who carried on murdering his way down the
corridor. "Take cover. I'm gonna blast this stuff back
to where it came from."

Lyle pulled an incendiary grenade off his belt
and tossed it into the room, setting everything
ablaze with a bang.

"What's the Carpathians' parasite doing here
too?" I asked and looked back in at the burning
remains. "A vial of it left over from the situation in
New York maybe, but not in this quantity. It's from
another dimension. Humans can't go there. Not on
their own."

A crackle of static came over our earpieces,
followed by a broken transmission from Rudgar.

"Lieutenant … update."

"Commander, I can barely hear you," Lyle responded. "We found a storage area where Gestalt was keeping the same parasite from the Manhattan incident—"

"Stop playing with fire, Lieutenant," Rudgar cut in over the static. "Where's … Blackbourne?"

"We don't know yet, sir, and Micah ran off," Lyle answered.

"Well split up and find him before he compromises the mission, Lieutenant! This isn't a game."

"I don't think splitting up is a good idea, sir. What about disabling security?"

"That's an order, Lieutenant! Don't mess this up." The commander's transmission ended in a loud hiss of static.

"There's no way we're splitting up," I said to Lyle and Sanders. "That's got to be the first rule in times like these."

"I don't like it either, but those were the commander's orders." Lyle sighed.

"I'm following you whether you like it or not," I told Lyle. "Sanders, you can either be a good soldier and wander around here alone or be alive and follow us too."

"Uh, if it's all the same to you, Lieutenant, I'd like to get out of this alive," said Sanders. "I've got a family back home."

Lyle shrugged at his loss of control over the situation, and we continued down the corridor, using Micah's tactic to open the doors by bringing a body with us.

"How'd Rudgar know you used fire when you said you found the parasite?" I asked. "It's not like he could've heard the grenade from there."

"It's just a figure of speech," said Sanders.

"This was senseless killing," Lyle remarked at the trail of dead employees left behind by Micah. "These people are probably victims too if they're being controlled. Blackbourne is going to jail after this, one way or another."

"I'm not convinced that these employees are victims. They seem totally aware of what they're doing, just not what's going on around them for some reason." I entered the next room. More storage, but this one was different. Body parts, not all of them human, were suspended in jars filled with medical gel. There were not only internal organs of varying inhuman sizes and hues but also appendages: arms and legs with fur and claws, giant canine skulls with four eye sockets, and leathery wings. Some jars also contained entire otherworldly organisms, such as large multi-headed worms and eyeless cephalopod creatures with exoskeletons and human teeth. It was a gruesome sight made no less macabre by how well lit the room was.

"Look at the freak-show buffet," Sanders said, tapping the glass that held an oversized green heart with six ventricles. It still throbbed despite being disembodied. "We're not going to have enough grenades." Next to him was a clipboard with more reports.

Patient: TTX-924710.23600

Status: In-Patient, Day 23

OR Procedure: Allogeneic HSCT-L

OR Time: 18 hours

OR Details: The host patient's red marrow of the scapula, clavicle, tibia, femur, sternum, pelvis, cranium, ribs, ulna, and humerus was extracted without complication by the six-hour mark.

A "healthy" adult male lycanthrope (Specimen BE-209z) that was delivered to us was used for the marrow donation. The rapid level of cellular regeneration in lycanthropes was pinpointed by R&D personnel to stem from their red blood cells. These cells are created by the creatures' red bone marrow while in their primal form. This marrow should successfully grant the host the same regenerative gift using the steroidal cocktail as a catalyst to buffer the transplant.

Fifteen hours in, the patient lapsed into a coma from shock. No signs of infection or septic fluids. The injections prior to the procedure are working well to keep the patient's body from rejecting the transplant.

Post-Op Review: The patient has yet to regain consciousness. We were able to take notes on the impressive tissue recovery by inflicting extensive physical trauma. Surface tissue damage seems to heal over without scarring. The patient's surgical incisions were gone within minutes. Soft tissue organs were healed within three hours.

Muscles and ligaments implanted from the previous operation healed over exceptionally well. Patient's circulatory system shows increased blood flow. Considering this a success. Will proceed with respiratory and cardiac transplants.

"This place is going to make me puke." I threw down the papers, thinking Lyle or Sanders were standing next to me, but the face staring back belonged to neither of them. A head of indiscernible gender floated at eye level in a glass tube filled with liquid. The lips had been stripped from the face, revealing surgical scars above the incisors, which looked too big to fit the skull. Its eyelids were also absent; in their place, extensive scar tissue surrounded the sockets. Eyes of gray and black, matching my own alternative form, were held in with long pins. The torment this person must have gone through in their final moments would have made death a blessing.

I left the room at the sound of gunshots around the corner. We caught up to Micah, who was exiting an operating room with a body in pieces on the table.

"Bring the walls down," Micah told me. "I've waited long enough. Let's see what you can do."

I looked to Lyle. "Every second we spend going one door at a time is one less second Owen and any other victims who are still alive may have. This place is huge."

"All right," he agreed. "Tear it down, but don't go crazy."

I didn't get far in my demolition. "What's that smell?"

In the middle of one room, there was a large tub filled with water that smelled awful. Above it hung medical tools and saws you'd use to cut wood.

"Hydrochloric acid," said Micah. "It's a strong drink. Great for making mistakes disappear ... and bad dates."

We moved on, snaking through the halls to find any variance, but it was always the same: storage rooms of body parts and operating rooms to collect them. I was becoming numb to the horrors the human mind had to offer.

"I can't believe there's no security office by now," Lyle said. "There aren't any security cameras around either. How do they know what's going on around them?"

"It's been almost an hour," Commander Rudgar's voice came in loud and clear over our earpiece. "Omega squad will proceed behind you. If there's no additional resistance by now, I don't know what they're waiting for. We'll sweep any areas you haven't been to and move on to the next floor up until we reach the ground level."

"Roger that, Commander," Lyle responded. "Don't bother wasting ammo on any of the personnel. None of them have been aggressive so far, and that's an understatement."

"This facility ..." Sanders mumbled. "No signs, no cameras, hallways that go on forever, everything symmetrical and identical, staff who wander around working all hours of the night and disregarding their own safety ... This isn't a laboratory. It's like a hive."

Chapter Thirteen

"Last room down this path," Lyle said as we hit the first dead end in an hour. I pulled the door open and was a little shocked to finally find something different.

"Now I'm glad I didn't rip the wall down." I peeked up the elevator shaft. "Isn't this supposed to be the last floor? There's another below us."

"The commander made a mistake," said Lyle.

"I can hear you, Turner," Commander Rudgar spoke over the earpiece. "Save the criticism for debriefing and get down there to check it out."

Micah rolled his eyes under his hood just as another employee came walking up like we didn't exist and called the elevator using the scanner above.

"Well this is going to be awkward." Micah pushed his way in front of the worker. We all stood in the elevator as it went down like it was a casual day of shopping in a department store. I snatched a file the man was holding. He turned and looked for the papers, but when he couldn't get them back, he simply gave up and turned back around.

Patient Registration: OBX-513800.23600

Age: 28

Blood Type: A

Height: 185.5 cm

Weight: 86.2 kg

Eyes: Hazel

Race: Caucasian

Arms: 18"

Chest: 50"

Waist: 30"

Body Fat: 5%

Mentally sound. High potential candidate. Responds well to steroidal enhancement-LSI

"Micah, check this out." I handed him the paper. "I think it's Owen. These sound like his stats from in the ring. He might still be here."

"I already know the wanker is here somewhere. I told you he'd be fine." Micah wouldn't even glance at the paper. Based on the other reports, if this was Owen, they had done a lot more than test a drug. There was a good chance he wouldn't even be remotely human anymore.

"I don't think this is just about money and terrorism," I spoke openly in front of the scientist, as weird as it was. "This is more like the work of the Carpathians. There's no way humans got their hands on that parasite by themselves. Some of those body parts and the reports didn't sound like anything from this world either."

"They hate humans, though," Lyle said. "I can't see them working together, even if they're enslaving them. If this has anything to do with the undead, it's the Strigoi that are running things. You heard Rebecca: Science is just another form of magic."

The elevator doors opened to yet another surprise. Our temporary traveling companion we'd ridden down with didn't seem to notice, but the lights were flickering and were completely out in some places. The steel walls had deep slash marks carved into them, and many of the automatic doors were either broken open or jammed and were trying to close again and again. Stranger still, there was no blood anywhere and no signs of a struggle; such as unattended corpses or wounded personnel.

"What happened here?" Sanders asked, ducking under exposed electrical wires sparking from the ceiling. Personnel in hazmat suits were now added to the wandering drones. But why were these employees so important that they merited any form of protection over the generic lab attire of the medical butchers?

"These are holding cells." Lyle was brave enough to poke his head through past one of the malfunctioning doors. "It doesn't look like anything was inside, though, unless they cleaned up real fast."

"Hey, over here." Sanders waved to us from a room across the hall. "Lieutenant, I think you were right …"

Aisles of glass containment tubes lined the room Sanders had found. Within each one was a body, and not just any body: These were of winged gargoyle-esque humanoids suspended in the same medical gel as the individual body parts we had encountered in the previous rooms.

"Carpathians," I said, touching the glass of one tube. The undead had a large metal screw through its heart that was bolted in place out its back. Multiple IVs attached along its body were transferring fluids of different colors and consistencies in and out. "Even they're being experimented on."

"Then it is the Strigoi," said Lyle. "The Carpathians aren't going to do this to their own kind, and definitely not with the help of humans. Dorian, wait outside."

"Why?"

"You haven't had the best experiences with the Carpathians. I just wanna make sure you keep it together."

"Keep it together? I'm fine, Lyle. They're nothing to me, especially staked." I got that Lyle was looking out for me and the good of the mission, but I had the feeling there was a part of him that was still uneasy around me because of my tendency to lose control.

"That's kinda the point. I wanna talk to them to know what's going on here—"

"Are you out of your flipping mind?" I yelled at Lyle and pulled him away. "They're evil. They want to *destroy* humanity! They don't understand anything but that. They don't even speak English!"

"But it was their leader at the time of the attack in New York that was telling them to hate mankind. Even he was being influenced by a greater evil. They just wanted to be accepted. If we free them, maybe they'll see we're not all their enemies. We can't judge them all based on the actions of their leader or a part of the whole. Innocent until proven guilty. Besides, PARAGON can translate."

"Go ahead," I agreed with extreme reluctance. "But if they even look at me, they're getting their heads blown off."

Lyle shattered the glass containing one of the hideous bat-winged hellspawn and unscrewed the stake in its heart. I kept a close eye on it as it came to life, but a noise in the hall grabbed my attention for a split second. The sound of clicking on the metal floor turned out to be dozens of white mice and lab rats making a run for it.

The Carpathian Lyle released followed suit, knocking us out of the way and yanking the IV tubes out of its gray leathery hide. It hissed something as it flew out of the room and down the hall in the same direction as the rodents.

"What did it say?" Micah asked.

"Run. It was in some Romanian dialect," Lyle translated. "We've gotta get the rest out. Give me a hand, Sanders."

"This is another waste of time." Micah stormed off. I went to go after him, but Lyle stopped me. The Carpathians were more of a danger than the scientists anyway. Every Carpathian that was freed wound up flying the coop without providing us any insight in return.

"Great. That was really worth it," I said.

"They didn't attack us, did they?" Lyle countered. We almost started arguing when Sanders stopped us. Behind the now empty containment tubes was a sectioned-off area of the lab that we'd almost missed. Beyond a partition were more tubes with a different, smaller type of creature inside.

"Are these ... fetuses?" Sanders asked. "The faces are sort of like those Carpathians."

"The undead can't breed," I said.

"They're clones. All of them are labeled 'Lazarus prototype' and numbered one through twelve." Lyle read from a computer that had been left on. They weren't just clones, though. There were two of the fetal creatures crammed into each unit: Some were stitched and pinned together by the side of the skull, and others looked as if they had been born that way based on the lack of scar tissue joining them. They were horribly deformed, even for Carpathians; their gnarled limbs were different lengths, and their chest cavities were underdeveloped, causing their hearts to bulge out from beneath their skin.

"Looks like Gestalt is trying to make Siamese twins out of Carpathians," said Sanders. "This one's only got two heads without a second body."

"This one over here just looks like a mess of congealed afterbirth," I said, fighting back the queasy feeling rising in my throat. Our investigation was cut short when the power went out, leaving us with only the flashlights on Lyle's and Sanders' rifles and the occasional red emergency strobe light.

"The Carpathians are flying out of here like bats out of Hell," Commander Rudgar reported over the earpiece. "Lieutenant, secure the area. I'm moving to your position now. The rest of the Omega squad will be collecting what they can for evidence and leaving. We're about done here once we sweep the floor you're on to check for Blackbourne.

"Gestalt is finished once this gets out. When we're sure there's nothing else dangerous down here, I'll tip off my contacts in the authorities.

"It won't be possible to catch every last person involved; we just don't have that kind of manpower. We'll have to keep an eye out if and when Gestalt tries to reorganize with those who got away. Keep your team in check until I get there, Lieutenant."

"Roger that, Commander," Lyle acknowledged.

As if the atmosphere wasn't unsettling enough, the new crimson glow across the steel sheen of the laboratory drove my peripheral vision wild, chasing dancing shadows. These were not the playful nor seductive shadows I had grown fond of from Gianni. I was starting to wish he was here.

"Dorian?" Lyle stopped in front of me and turned around.

"Huh?"

"I was talking to you, man. Can you start opening these doors again to find Blackbourne and any other survivors? The power's out, but the magnetic locks are still holding."

"What are the authorities going to think when they see this stuff?" I asked and pulled apart another door.

"They won't know what to think. It'll get lost in the paperwork before it can hit the media," Lyle answered. "Gestalt will do everything they can to clear out their other locations before they get raided, but they're finished without financial resources or a reputation. They won't have so much as a scalpel left, and we'll be able to smoke out whoever's behind the staff's weird silence."

Now that Lyle mentioned the staff, I realized that I hadn't seen anybody down here for a while. Hastened footsteps came from ahead as Micah ran around the corner and right past us.

"Run! Just bloody run!"

"Blackbourne, wait!" Lyle shouted and ran after him. "What's going on?"

A clicking sound scuttling toward us made me think of the rodents I had seen earlier, but this was coming from the ceiling, and it was much, much louder. Chasing after him was something I had never seen and could have done without ever knowing existed.

"Get back!" I threw Lyle and Sanders away from the monstrosity closing in on us and immediately regretted feeling almost bored a moment ago.

"Is that … Owen?" I asked Micah. I figured Gestalt had had a field day experimenting on him, but I never expected this. The horror coming into view under the emergency lights was concocted from a depth of depraved human imagination I didn't think possible.

"Not anymore!" said Lyle.

What was once an attractive man was now a bony, seven-foot-tall construct of taut flesh crawling across the ceiling at an alarming pace. He had no hair or face, and any features of gender were gone. An androgynous humanoid shape with skin pulled over a stretched-out skeleton was all that was left of Owen Blackbourne. His arm bones were elongated to reach his feet so that he could move on all fours with ease as he twitched and skittered like an insect. Each finger was segmented in a way that no human's was, with multiple knuckles per digit ending in a pointed claw. It reminded me of the mutation caused by the Carpathians' Rift parasite and no doubt had some related origin.

As the amalgam drew closer, I saw lumps slithering under his tight skin. Whatever they were wasn't restricted to major veins and arteries, as the parasite had been when I had been infected. There was something moving freely about the matrix of his body.

The creature dropped down to face me, except that he no longer had a face of his own—just gray flesh covering a roughly oval-shaped skull. How he could see without eyes was a puzzle to me, but he was clearly "looking" right at me by the way his head tilted and jerked in my direction.

"Owen, if any part of you is still in there, I don't want to hurt you." I didn't get very far in negotiating when he slashed me across the midsection, cutting deep into my torso. The blood on his claws vanished into his being as if absorbed by a sponge. I reeled in pain, but the wound was gone in seconds.

"PARAGON is saying he's undead *and* alive. It doesn't make sense how you can be both," Lyle announced from cover in a doorway. As much as I didn't want to hurt Owen, I knew there was little to nothing left of him now inside this sad, hollow marionette. I tried throwing him back, but my powers had almost no effect. The creature's body absorbed the kinetic energy of my psionic blast, causing it to ripple like a bullet passing through gelatin. It wasn't easy to tell if it was me or just the unnatural twitching and spasms that caused him to move at all.

My next attempt at destroying him, this time by crushing, was similarly thwarted. The harder I squeezed, the more the abomination avoided damage by letting his body ooze through the pressure as clay in a vice. Somehow, this thing Owen had been turned into could turn its bones and razor-sharp claws into an organic putty.

"We, uh, might have a problem here," I called out to the others. "Feel free to help out any time, guys."

Lyle and Sanders opened fire, but their rounds went right through him. The horror bled, but his blood was soaked back up into him before a drop was spilled on the floor. He advanced without concern, but I was becoming increasingly worried after seeing my usual tricks fail.

"Frag out!" Lyle yelled, hurling a grenade straight into the creature's chest. It stuck there a second as I flew out of the way, and then it exploded in a shower of entrails and ashes that coated the metal walls.

"Lyle one, Dorian zero," he said with a laugh. "But seriously, that thing was—"

We were interrupted by a moan from behind a door that had been damaged in the explosion. The Gestalt personnel had all mysteriously vanished with the appearance of the creature. Could this be another one of their eldritch atrocities?

I tore down the remainder of the doorway and checked inside. The pained sounds were coming from a figure that was curled up in the dark recesses of the room.

"I know that sound. It's the sound of a hangover," Micah said, pushing ahead of us into the room. "Owen, is that you?"

"M-Micah?" a man's voice responded in a shaky tone. It was Owen all right. He was in a patient gown and was trembling in a fetal position on the cold floor.

"What are you doing in here?" Micah ran over and helped him up. "Get up, you wanker."

"I was taking a nap. What do you think I'm doing here?" Owen was having trouble standing. "Who's with you?"

"It's me, Owen. Dorian." I was right in front of him, but his eyes were going off to the side a bit where no one was. It was dark in the room, but not that dark.

"They bloody blinded me on top of everything else."

"What?" Micah exclaimed.

"I'm not in good shape," Owen continued. "They did things to me ... Carter's dead, Micah. He was too old to handle the procedures, so they gave him an acid bath. I heard the loons talking about it when they were transporting me."

Micah was quiet; it was as if the situation was just now becoming real.

"How long have you been blind?" I asked. "Because if you're here, and Carter's dead, who or what the hell was that we just fought in the hall?"

"I don't have a clue. Days? Weeks? No way to tell time in here, and the drugs are all a bad trip. I never saw anyone else but the doctors."

"I'm taking you home." Micah snapped out of his daze. "I'll call for the private jet even if it has to land in the bloody parking lot."

"That's not a good idea," said Lyle. "Come back to the base and let our doctors look at him. They might be able to help."

"Who's that?" Owen asked.

"A friend," I told him. "They came to help stop Gestalt."

"Good. You found him," Commander Rudgar said as he joined us.

"Yes, and it's a good thing we didn't split up to do it either," I said. "It took all of us to stop one of Gestalt's lab projects we ran into."

"That's the reason we go in teams." Rudgar brushed off my comment as if he hadn't been responsible for almost getting some of us killed.

"Then why'd you tell us to split up?" I asked. Rudgar turned and looked at me as if I was playing games with him.

"I'd never give that order," he stated with a harsh stare directed at me. "Protocol is to move up Team B, the Omega squad, to rendezvous at Alpha's location before making any moves that would separate a team. We were waiting an hour for you to stop fooling around until I finally gave the command to move up. That was our first communication with you all mission."

I turned to Lyle and Sanders to check that I wasn't hearing things, but their expressions revealed that they were equally baffled.

"Sir, you ordered me to split us up," Lyle said. "We all heard it."

"He didn't, Lieutenant. Our team was waiting to hear from you that you had disabled security," one of Rudgar's Omega squad added.

"Then who was that on the other side trying to split us up?" I asked.

"If you don't mind, we'll be leaving now, and we'll pass on the free checkup. We don't need anymore people playing doctor," Micah declined. "We have our own."

"I doubt you have anyone with the knowledge or technology to wrap their head around what he's been through," said Commander Rudgar. "We're prepared for evac immediately, and our doctors are on standby. Come back to the base, and if we can't do anything for you, then you're free to get help elsewhere. You have nothing to lose."

"Is there an open bar?" Owen asked.

"They don't have anything good," Micah answered.

"I'll take bloody turpentine right now if I can get my lips on it." Owen hobbled out with Micah. The rest of us followed behind, but I stopped to pick up some papers that had been scattered in all the commotion. They were burnt, but I could make out "Patient: OBX-513800.23600 scheduled for implant extraction and termination."

"This is dated tomorrow." I held it up so the others could see. "They were about to kill Owen."

Owen paused and leaned against Micah. "I almost wished they'd just done that at the start."

Chapter Fourteen

"Mm, that feels good. Go a little lower."

"Mr. Blackbourne, need I remind you *again* that this is a medical checkup and that I'm a doctor, not a prostitute?"

"What's the difference?" Owen had been giving Dr. Sullivan a hard time since the moment we'd gotten to her exam room. Micah had been noticeably absent from the conversation, despite sitting in the room for all of it. He hadn't even taken off his mask and hood.

"The difference is that I can put you into a medically induced coma if you keep giving me trouble."

"Show some respect, man," Lyle chimed in. "We could have Dr. Zynes check you out instead."

"What's she look like?" Owen asked.

"He's sixty-five with a lazy eye and a limp."

"Sounds more like Micah's type. Where is the lousy drunkard, anyway? I don't smell scotch."

"I'm here," Micah answered. Owen seemed to be taking everything in stride once we escaped the facility, but Micah was clearly shaken after the unnerving details of his friend's ordeal came out.

"You're head of the household now," Owen told him. "Amy's useless, and I'm not going to be much good with paperwork like this. You've been gunning for this since you were a kid."

"Belt up," Micah said, looking down at his phone.

"We may be able to restore your sight," said Rebecca. "You show no signs of scarring anywhere. It's most likely a disconnect somewhere in the optic nerve. I'll go over the reports obtained from Gestalt's intranet along with our own scans and prepare the OR with the rest of the staff."

Lyle was gritting his teeth, watching Dr. Sullivan touch Owen's near-naked body as she looked for signs of trauma.

"Bring me back a drink, would you, hun? No ice," Owen ordered. "Surgery makes me nervous. You understand."

"Of course," Rebecca said and left his bedside.

"Blackbourne! What did I just say?" Lyle shouted at Owen. "Watch your tongue."

"Love to, but ..." Owen pointed to his eyes and smiled. "I don't need to see it to use it, though, if you know what I mean."

"That's okay, Lieutenant." Rebecca walked back over with a glass of water in her hand and splashed it in Owen's face.

"What is this? It must be American." Owen spit and wiped his face off.

"It's called water," Micah chuckled.

"Oh thank God. I thought my sense of taste was gone too." Owen made it hard to feel bad for him, even when he was lying in a hospital bed with a breathing tube and an IV. PROJECT: UNITY had just finished breathing a sigh of relief to be rid of Noah, and now they had to put up with the British playboys.

I followed Lyle and the doctor out just as Owen started asking Micah to describe her to him in graphic detail.

"Sorry you had to go through that," Lyle apologized to Rebecca. "I'll ask Dr. Zynes to take over so you don't have to deal with them anymore."

"I'll be fine. Patients often exhibit odd behavior in an attempt to cope after suffering from extreme trauma."

Boy, I knew that firsthand. I wished that I had enjoyed myself like Owen was doing after I'd suffered a breakdown. The only thing was that Owen always acted like this.

"Lieutenant," Commander Rudgar approached.

"Security breach in ... Medical Ward, Exam Room 4," PARAGON announced and set off the alarm. It then promptly stopped on its own.

"That's this room," Rebecca pointed back to where Owen and Micah were chatting. "They were both scanned in though."

"Noah?" I called out, thinking it was him, but he didn't appear.

"It must be a glitch from when the other Blackbourne was entered in the database. I'll have the boys downstairs look into it," said the commander. "I came here to congratulate you on a job well done, Lieutenant. The mission was a success."

"Thank you, Commander, but I couldn't have done it without Dorian and the rest of the team."

"I didn't really do anything," I admitted. "I opened some doors, but you were the one who found Owen and stopped that creature."

"That's the good thing about becoming a leader, Lieutenant," said Rudgar. "You take all the blame when you're responsible for failure, but you get the credit when you succeed."

"I don't really think that's fair. I mean everyone worked just as hard."

"Learn to take a compliment, Lieutenant. That's an order. And speaking of orders, the techs ran a diagnostic on PARAGON and think that the communication issue we experienced was Gestalt overriding our frequency with a stronger one of their own like two radio stations crossing. There's no way they could've hacked us. They probably used a high-powered transmitter to cut in like the one they use for that security signal."

"There was a lot of static, but it sounded just like you," I said.

"I'm sure a lot of Germans sound similar to you." I wasn't sure whether that was the commander's attempt at a self-deprecating joke, but fortunately, Rebecca changed the topic before I had to decide how to react.

"Do you think Gestalt will really stop after this, Commander?" Dr. Sullivan asked.

"We've cracked their foundation enough so that they'll cave in under their own weight. Gestalt Industries is finished the second the media starts eating away at it like a cancer. A fitting end, if you ask me, but it doesn't mean the threat behind them is gone. Without resources or personnel to do the dirty work, we'll get a clearer view of who was really running the show.

"Turner thinks it's wise to not rule out the Strigoi, and I'd have to agree. The Carpathians did not seem to be there under their own will, although they could have been grunts that were sacrificed as guinea pigs. If he's correct, it sounds like the Strigoi were trying to replicate and mass produce supernatural bioweapons, like Dorian, with some additional enhancements."

"Just give me a plane and a pilot, and I'll track down my old Strigoi pal Vance," I told Rudgar. "Last time I saw him, he had a whole new book club working on something in a secret lab, but he wouldn't say what it was. He also said I'd never be able to find him again, but I plan on disproving that and beating the answers out of him."

"Perfect. Give it a few days, and we'll help track down this Vance. We want to lie low long enough for the authorities to clear out Gestalt's labs and make them sweat. I'm sending one agent per lab to infiltrate the authorities and provide covert backup just in case."

This would be a good time to have Noah around. He was always able to hunt Vance down like a bloodhound. My own tracking skills left a lot to be desired. Vance wasn't someone who could be lured out with bait. But I did have two hunters next door with a vendetta.

"I'll be in touch." Commander Rudgar bowed out.

"Lieutenant, I was hoping you might be willing to debrief me on what you found at Gestalt," Dr. Sullivan asked. "It could help in diagnosing Owen Blackbourne."

"Sure, I was about to go type it up in PARAGON, but I could do it here."

"Actually, I was thinking maybe a little later. I'm going to finish up around here, so maybe over dinner?" She smiled.

There was a hilariously awkward pause as I could tell fireworks were going off in Lyle's head. I started to float away out of the conversation so I could snicker to myself without interrupting.

"Yes, ma'am. That sounds good to me."

Lyle jogged over to catch up with me by the elevator after they exchanged some pleasantries, and Dr. Sullivan went back in to check on Owen.

"Did you hear that, man?" He shook me in excitement. "Two years I've been wanting to go out with her, and it happens the same day we bring down Gestalt!"

"You deserve it. To the victor goes the spoils, right?" Maybe I was a fool to still be holding out for Gianluca, but patience was a virtue, right? I had other things on my mind I wanted taken care of.

"What's going on, man? You've been quiet since Gestalt. We should be celebrating."

"I'm pissed off thinking about the Strigoi being behind Gestalt. I'm just hoping Vance isn't involved, but it's a slim chance," I said as we rode the elevator to the barracks. "I never trusted him, but I was comfortable considering him neutral. This would be going against everything he's sworn he wouldn't do anymore … and worse."

"We'll take care of it. Together. One step at a time. First, you gotta enjoy what we did accomplish."

I didn't want to ruin his mood, but I felt that what we had accomplished had barely made an impact. Noah's lesson about there being a bigger picture came to mind. Gestalt was just a convenient way to outsource the Strigoi's research. Gestalt may have been big in the human world, but on the other side of the curtain, they were expendable pawns that would be replaced in seconds relative to an immortal's lifespan. I wished I could enjoy the shortsighted victory. Having a broader sense of awareness sucked right now.

"It's too bad there isn't anywhere around here I can take her," Lyle said as we got to his room. "She never leaves the base, and there's nothing but ice for miles."

"One step at a time, Lieutenant. Try starting with a shower."

"You think she'd be up for that?"

"What? No! I meant by yourself!"

"I'm kidding, man! I'm just trying to get you to laugh. You're way too serious right now—"

"Security breach in—" PARAGON's synthesized female voice projected from the terminal in Lyle's room then cut off before it could finish.

"I guess Noah really is back." Lyle sighed.

"I'm surprised he hasn't dropped in on me yet."

I helped Lyle finish cleaning his room while he got ready for dinner with some ridiculous pre-date regimen that ended with push-ups for some reason ... like he needed to get anymore pumped up than he already was.

PARAGON came to life after Lyle left to shower: "Dorian Benoit, please report to the commander's office."

I thought I'd have a few minutes to breathe before searching for Vance. I'm immortal, not a machine.

I glided down the restful cerulean halls, greeted by the usual nods and smiles. It was nice here, but Lyle was right: I did need to get out. For so long, I'd wanted to find my purpose, but now that I had one, it was making me nervous. The responsibility was stifling. I had stopped disastrous events from happening in the past, but it was as a result of my own fight for survival. I hadn't had much choice; it had been kill or be killed.

Now, I was tasked with a more proactive approach: hunting down a problem that didn't directly affect me—not yet at least—and solving it because no one else could. PROJECT: UNITY could have handled Gestalt on their own, albeit with some casualties, but the job would have been done. The Strigoi, however, PROJECT: UNITY had no hope against. Hell, even I was a little worried about what they might bring to the table if they were organizing this dutifully. They did create me after all and must know I'd come to stop them at some point. It wasn't like the magical undead to be caught unprepared. And if I fell, who would step up to save humanity? Who else would have that kind of power and, most of all, care enough to use it?

"You rang?" I floated in to meet with Commander Rudgar in his office.

"Yes. Take a seat. I wanted to talk with you about today's mission at Gestalt."

"What's there to talk about?" I asked. "You were there."

It wasn't that I didn't like the commander or that I trivialized him as a human trying to make a difference in a supernatural world way beyond either of our comprehensions, but I was only here because of Lyle. I didn't want to be a soldier, and I certainly was not his weapon. His orders meant little to me, and I was starting to get the feeling that his self-importance was growing by having me at his disposal to blow up whatever he pointed at, although he had claimed in the past to not want to rely on supernatural assistance. Lyle had warned me when I'd first come here that Commander Rudgar wasn't the kind of person to take no for an answer.

"Hm. I guess I'll skip the chitchat then. I've heard a lot about your entwined fate with the Strigoi, and I'm curious to hear your side of things."

"You want to know if there's any chance I'll turn sides and help those responsible for creating me." I was proud of myself for reading between the lines. A few years ago, I would have been clueless to the subtle mind games. "The answer is no. I'm not on this planet to do anyone's bidding—neither theirs nor yours. But I will stop whoever I feel is in the wrong, even if that means both sides."

"That's good to hear. The world needs more leaders and less soldiers, I say. If people thought for themselves more, it wouldn't be so easy for any one side to gain momentum."

"Okay. I'm glad we're on the same page." I got up to leave, thinking we had resolved whatever had been on his mind.

"I've read your file at length, but I'd still like to know your side of things: your origin and what drives you to make the decisions you do."

Everyone but me had read these files on me. I didn't know if I should be flattered or not that someone had taken the time to write a biography on how I had floundered my way through life.

"The Strigoi created me by mixing up DNA and forbidden magic in their lab. I'm sure the medical technology they used wasn't far off from what we saw at Gestalt. They even had the parasite there that I was fused with to make me immortal." I chatted with the commander for over an hour about what brought me to where I was at that moment. Looking back, I had accomplished more than I had ever given myself credit for.

Yes, I could happily boast that I'd fought a demon and survived a raging dragon, but to me, that wasn't something to put on a résumé—even a supernatural one. It made good conversation at the bar, but it wasn't a life goal I'd fulfilled. The Blackbournes might feel differently, but to me, there was no thrill of battle. The thrill was when it was over, people were safe, and the knot in the pit of my stomach subsided.

"You'll outlive me," he said. "That much is certain. I only hope to stay on this Earth long enough to clean up some of the mess my species has made before the light in the world finishes going out."

"That's a bit ... morbid, and I'm not sure what you mean."

"It's realistic. Dark times are coming. The world was born in darkness, and it will be reborn in it."

"Oh God. Not you too."

"So, you're aware?" he asked.

"I've heard the rumors." No matter where I went or who I talked to, this always came up. Someone or something was always preaching the end of the world. First, it was divine wrath. The gates of Heaven and Hell would spill open in a global war to end all wars. Then it was a single, all-powerful, ancient being who would blot out the sun and extinguish life as we knew it. And finally, religion itself would fade from existence. With no prayers to the beings that created the world, they would starve and die out, leaving the fundamental forces of the Earth vulnerable and unbalanced. The deities once worshiped by humanity were an intrinsic part of all life, as hidden as they might remain.

"It's no rumor." Commander Rudgar typed on his tablet and set it down on his desk. A three-dimensional hologram of the Earth was projected from it in the air between us. "There's a darkness in all of us—every man, woman, and child ... a silent vitriol bubbling over at the work of the same great flame. Humanity is tearing itself apart at the seams."

"You're not blaming it on supernatural or divine intervention?" I was in genuine shock.

"No. It's all our fault and our problem. The world has been in endless turmoil in the past decades with the rise in terrorism. Both sides claim it is a war of passion and cowardice backed by blindness, yet we keep fighting without any clear outcome."

"I'm learning that people are pretty dumb," I said.

"This is all the recent terrorist activity in only the past two years." Rudgar marked points around the globe with a touch of his tablet. Most of them were in the Middle East and Africa, and some were in the United States, the United Kingdom, and Asia. Soon, they were everywhere across the map. "I believe everyone is born with good and evil in them. It's their choice what to do with it. Humans have begun to close their hearts to good and to use evil to keep themselves strong and isolated in a crowd. They outcast themselves, and when the evil boils over as hate, the massacre begins.

"There is no order for humanity any longer. The little you see in the streets is a weak disguise held together by empty smiles. It's spinning out of control. Even the most developed governments struggle to contain their citizens. No one is solving the problem; they only try to drive the issue out of their borders."

Commander Rudgar surprised me. For someone so militaristic, I thought he was looking to solve problems by blowing evil's head off with his high-tech guns.

"I agree about the hate thing," I said. "It's as much of a domestic problem as it is global. People just hate each other for any reason they can find. It's like they're *looking* for a reason to be angry instead of enjoying their own lives. Most of the reasons seem like lame excuses too. I've met supernaturals that were once worshiped as gods, and they didn't really seem to care about all the stuff people think they do."

"I'm glad to hear that from you." The commander actually smiled. "It is no surprise to the governments that we are doing ourselves in. Everyone has their finger on the trigger, waiting for the other to make a move. When families and friends will kill each other, schoolchildren, neighbors, how can we expect there to be global peace to stave off the darkness?"

"The dark isn't always so bad," I said. "It's what you do in the dark that matters."

"Call it what you will, but the more we soak the ground with the blood of our own kind, the quicker we invite our own demise."

"What can we do aside from telling everyone to stop being a dick and get over it?" I asked. Commander Rudgar laughed, and I didn't immediately know why.

"Hearing you speak, I sometimes forget you're really as young as you look because of how powerful you are," he explained. "I will tell you what I think. I believe there are extremist cults that are being offered great power in exchange for spreading more chaos.

"I want to take PROJECT: UNITY to the next level and do more than remedy a situation after it happens and then cover up the problem. I want to go after these hotbeds of chaos and slay the beast at the heart. Whether these humans know and are willingly attempting to aid darker forces, or they are being coerced with all manner of masquerade and trickery, they must be stopped. It is a vicious cycle that keeps feeding into itself and growing stronger by the day."

"So, you want me to stop terrorism across the world." I raised an eyebrow in quizzical disbelief. "Me and a few soldiers. Are you nuts?"

"Not at all. It would be too dangerous, and you can be assured that the closer we get to the heart of chaos, the more the forces of evil will fight to protect it. I want a task force: a mix of mortals and supernaturals working together. We already have the humans and the technology; now we need the supernaturals, and you are our first step."

"Whoa! Wait a minute. I'm not a soldier, and I'm not helping you start an army and cause even more chaos. I want to be left alone," I argued.

"You have a responsibility to this world and all its people—not just human or superhuman. You are too powerful to hide away while everything crumbles. They'll come for you too. You've already helped with Gestalt. They're just one cult with a pretty public image."

"The Strigoi don't work with humans, though," I told Commander Rudgar. "This is an awfully ballsy move for them, but then again, I guess it is cowardly like them to hide behind others too."

"Then you'll need to find out their exact motives when you visit them."

"You're expecting way too much. They don't play well with others; none of the undead do. I'm sure if they could, they'd try to enslave me again."

"You need to persuade them otherwise," the commander demanded. "We don't need to be playing nice if everything melts down into an apocalypse."

"I don't know if I can ..."

"Then find someone to help you. Recruit who you can trust, and I'll make sure you get the support you need."

"I—"

"We'll talk more about it another day. You should be resting." Commander Rudgar was pushing me out of the office to end the conversation before I could debate him anymore. "Have a good night."

"Good night? It's almost morning," I said as the door closed, leaving me alone in the now warm daylight glow of the hall.

Chapter Fifteen

"How'd it go? I thought she might still be here," I asked Lyle when I was back in his room. I had checked on PARAGON ahead of time to see where he and Rebecca were so that I wouldn't walk in on anything inappropriate.

"Nah. You know I'm not like that, man. We had a really good time. I got to learn so much about her. We've been working together for so long and don't really know anything about each other. I could've talked to her all day." I could tell he was still wired. None of us had slept yet, and if I didn't know how to fly, I don't think my legs would have worked to carry me to the room, but Lyle was sitting in bed, bouncing a handball against the wall like he had all the energy in the world.

"Oh, so she gets even better than just an attractive, smart, and accomplished doctor?" I asked and planted my face in my pillow.

"So much better." He let out a sigh of contentment. "It's one thing when someone looks hot or has all the right qualities on paper, but when you get to find out what makes them a person, it's another whole level of sexy.

"I also found out that her father had to retire early due to a stroke, and her family is in jeopardy of losing their house. She feels if she were working in a hospital, she'd be making the money to support them, but we don't really make any personal income, and she hasn't even been able to visit since it happened because she's here all the time. I wish there was something I could do ... like pull a few strings or whatever. Her mom has to get a job just to pay their medical bills."

"That's really sad. I'm sure she'd appreciate anything you could come up with. Maybe sneak her out of lockdown so she can see them."

"Yeah. So, what did you and the commander talk about?" Lyle asked. "I searched for you on PARAGON and saw you in his office."

"The usual: how the fate of the world rests on my shoulders and it's my responsibility to save it. Nothing major. I'll have it done by the weekend."

"Oh. Sorry, man. Sounds like you didn't have a fun night." Lyle jumped up from his bed with way too much enthusiasm. "Hey, you wanna go for pancakes? I'm in the mood for pancakes."

"What the hell? Didn't you just have dinner a couple hours ago? Go to sleep."

"No way. How can I sleep when there's pancakes? Food, women, and justice, man. The ultimate Turner trifecta."

The PARAGON terminal in the room flicked on right as I put another pillow over my head to filter out Lyle. It was Rudgar with a request.

"One more thing, Dorian. Can you find out what Burckhardt wants? You seem to be the only one he isn't hostile toward, and PARAGON has picked him up right outside the base for the past three hours. It's starting to make me anxious seeing as he doesn't normally stay in one place for long. Thanks."

"Not him again," Lyle groaned. "I'm in way too good a mood right now to be brought down by him. Why'd he have to come back? No one wants him here."

"I'll go see what's up," I said and dragged myself back out of bed and into the blizzard outside. I called Noah's name several times without an answer. It was hard to see more than a foot in front of me with the wind whipping snow horizontally past my face. My powers weren't much help at trying to feel anything out in these conditions. The sun was already up but was barely visible through the storm. Still, I couldn't imagine Noah would stay out here like this. As I wandered further from the base, I began to think this was another attempt by Gestalt to impersonate Rudgar to separate us.

I started to hurry back to base when I noticed a large, discolored patch of snow. It was red, and upon closer inspection, it felt mushy compared to the fresh powder that had fallen around it and clumped together in my hand. I dug down a bit until I hit something hard a few inches below the surface.

It was Noah. He was covered in blood, and his body began to sizzle the moment he was exposed to the heavily obscured sunlight. I took off my coat to wrap him in before flying him back to base.

"Oh, no! Don't bring him in here," Lyle complained as I entered his room with Noah's unconscious body bundled in my coat.

"He's hurt," I said and placed him on my bed. His body was covered with patches of frostbite and deep slices that were too uniform to be from battle.

"Take him to Medical then! I don't want him bleeding all over my stuff. It's bad enough he breaks everything—"

"Lyle!" I shouted and turned up the heat to help warm Noah up. "I'll clean him up so it doesn't get anywhere. Relax. If I take him to Medical, he'll be pissed off that other people saw him like this. You don't want him in a bad mood around Rebecca, do you?"

"Fine, but don't use the good towels. I finally smuggled some away from the tech guys during laundry." Lyle left me to tend to Noah. The first thing I had to do was get blood back in him, so I pressed my wrist up into his fangs until I felt the sharp pinch as they slid in. I had seen Noah suffer from ritualistic cuts like these twice before. Both times had been at Aurelia's chateau, and he had been just barely conscious enough to tell me that she'd had him bled out to serve his blood to her guests.

When I thought about it, if he had just come from Aurelia's, then he couldn't have been the one setting off the security system earlier.

A few minutes passed before I pulled my wrist free. I expected Noah to wake up as his wounds sealed and were reduced to red marks, but he stayed out cold. I went into the bathroom and soaked a towel in hot water to start cleaning him with. He still didn't spring to life when I began wiping off the dried blood and burnt skin. Noah hated to be touched, so if there was anything that would make him react, it was that. I knew I ran the risk of him throwing me through a wall, but I felt bad leaving the big idiot like this.

"What the hell are you doing?" Noah opened his eyes halfway. He didn't rip my arm off, so that was good ... surprising, but good.

"Helping your dumb ass," I said with some authority.

"I never asked for your help." He sounded as beat up as he'd looked when I'd found him.

"Yeah? Then why'd you come back?" I asked as I continued cleaning him up. He shoved me away to the floor and got up without answering my question. I hadn't seen his back until now to notice all the welts. Even after taking in a significant amount of blood, they were bad enough to make me cringe. He must have realized what I was staring at when I stayed quiet, because he spun around, giving me an angry look.

"What?" he asked defensively.

"Nothing ... I mean, what happened to you? All the cuts—"

"What cuts?" He looked at himself in the mirror, channeling the blood in his system to heal the remaining marks until they faded away.

"Did she do this to you?" I asked.

"I don't know what you're talking about," he said as he dried the melted snow from his hair with a towel, avoiding looking at me the whole time.

"Why'd you come all the way back here before feeding? You could've died out there in the sun."

"I'm a picky eater. You done with the interview yet?" he snapped.

"Not until I get some real answers." I knew I didn't have the right to keep pressuring him when he was probably hurting more on the inside than anything his body had gone through, but I also wanted him to know that someone cared enough to ask. He didn't take it well, though, and shattered the mirror with his fist before disappearing to who knows where.

I finally settled in for some sleep now that everything had calmed down. Noah wasn't back when I woke up in the afternoon, and neither was Lyle. I wouldn't have been too surprised to find Lyle running laps around the base after all the energy he'd had that morning.

After washing up, I located Lyle on PARAGON. He was in the Medical Ward, of course. Micah wasn't on the base, but Owen was in one of the operating rooms. I flew to Medical just in time to overhear a few of the nurses talking in an exam room.

"It was amazing ... like nothing I've ever experienced," one of the nurses was saying. "Thank God I'm on the pill. It's true what they say about you never know when it could happen."

"I didn't think he could still do it blind. That must've been so weird," said another nurse.

"Oh no. He knew just what he was doing!" The first one began to laugh. "They say when you're blind, it heightens your other senses. He told me it was the best he'd ever had."

Seriously? Owen? He's here less than a day, blind, and in a hospital bed, and he still finds women to hook up with.

I found Lyle asleep in a chair outside the OR where Rebecca was working; he was like a puppy, waiting for its human to return home.

"Wake up, Romeo!" I called out to him. The closer I got, I could see there were drops of blood under his chair. "Are you bleeding?"

"Huh?" Lyle rubbed his eyes and looked down. "It's not mine." He flagged a nurse to come over and take a sample so that PARAGON could identify who it was from.

"There's more of it," I pointed to a seam in the plastic paneling where it was dripping from.

"It's Sanders', Lieutenant," the nurse reported.

"Sanders hasn't been here today that I've seen," Lyle said. "Can you locate him for me and see if he was here earlier, ma'am?"

"PARAGON's log says he was here this morning, but he didn't fill out an incident report," the nurse answered. "He's in his room now."

"Dorian, come with me. I want to check if he's all right."

"I owe you a mirror, by the way," I said as I followed him. I didn't want to lie, but I also didn't want to give him any more reasons to dislike Noah.

Sanders answered the door immediately when we arrived.

"Sanders, what happened in Medical?" Lyle asked. "We found your blood."

I didn't remember what Sanders had looked like without the helmet and suit on, so it was like meeting him all over again. He was of average height and build and was no older than Lyle, but he had a weathered appearance, like he had lived a lot in those same amount of years.

"I must have hurt myself. Everything is fine," he responded.

"That was kinda a lot of blood, man. Where'd you hurt yourself?" Lyle asked.

"My arm." He was wearing a long-sleeved shirt and was making no effort to show us his arms.

"Are you sure you're okay?" Lyle probed further. "Did you hit your head or something? You're acting funny. Come back to Medical with me to get checked out."

"No. I think I'll sleep now," Sanders said and closed the door in our faces.

"I'm concerned about him," Lyle whispered to me on our walk back to the Medical Ward. "I wonder if he got into a fight and doesn't want to get in trouble."

"Maybe it was an embarrassing injury and he doesn't want to say it," I suggested. "Like he sat on his combat knife."

We were halfway to Medical when the warm glowing walls, the terminals, and mounted flat screens started to dim.

"What's going on around here lately?" Lyle griped in frustration. "We're hooked up by solar power *and* a hydroelectric generator that uses the ocean's currents—"

The air began to cool to a chill, and all PARAGON's alarms went off at once around the base, signaling an invasion, but in the dark, there wasn't much anyone could do about it.

"Dorian, look out!" Lyle yelled upon noticing something move in the shadows beside me, but it was too late. I was lifted up into the air as he reached his hand out to grab me away. The heavy dark fog dissipated as quickly as it had come with the sound of a friendly voice.

"Here you are, little chick." Gianni's pleasant smiling face greeted me. His arms wrapped around my waist, raising me two feet off the ground. Gianni was a statuesque man in every sense of the word. I could climb on him and move him no more easily than a bird could a statue.

"Gianni!" I cried out in elation and grabbed on to his shirt collar until our faces almost touched.

"Ah, you missed Gianni?" he asked through a wide grin. He made me laugh, and I couldn't explain why, but it always felt good to be around him. I threw my arms around his neck and kissed him like we had never been apart.

"A little," I said, trying to be coy about it.

"I was gone for long?"

"A little," I said again, now feeling my face turn red from holding back laughter and excitement. I didn't want to tell him I had been counting the days until I'd finally forced myself not to anymore.

"I think you hide from me so I have to catch you."

As he moved in for another kiss, Lyle cleared his throat loudly behind us, jolting me back to reality. I had neglected to notice half of PROJECT: UNITY surrounding Gianni and me in the hall, not knowing what was going on.

"Lyle, sorry. This is Gianluca." I had to squirm my way around to face him with Gianni still holding on to me. "Gianni, this is Lyle—my best friend. And you can put me down now."

"Nice to meet you, man." Lyle put out his hand to shake Gianni's and then waved the all clear to the troops. "I was beginning to think you weren't real."

"These are friends too?" Gianni smiled at the crowd.

"Yeah, you could say that," I told him.

"What place is this? *Palazzo di plastica?*" he asked and wandered off into the crowd, taking notice of a soldier in his full combat suit. "I like this."

Gianni transformed the shadows that made up his clothes into a pure black copy of the PROJECT: UNITY armor. The crowd exploded into gasps of fascination, taking pictures and jabbering to one another. I floated over to him to let him know we needed to show some restraint here, remembering how Lyle had warned me when I had first arrived.

"What is the name?" he asked and put his arm around me before I could get him to stop. "It is to play a game?"

"They're soldiers. This is a military base, Gianni," I explained.

"Oh," he sounded disappointed behind the replicated helmet and then returned to his regular ensemble. "It is *plastica*, no? Like a toy today."

"Yes, you're right." I felt bad, seeing as this was another thing that had also been confusing for me at first, and even more so for someone over two thousand years old. It was times like these that I thought made Gianni feel a bit out of place although he didn't directly express it.

"I want see you alone," he whispered to me over all the chatter. Lyle was trying to get a word in when I turned to tell him I'd be right back, but Gianni didn't wait to whisk us away through the shadows to a very familiar area.

"Do not be mad," Gianni started. "I have no gift for you today. I want come to see you fast, so I hurry."

"You don't need to bring me gifts. All I wanted was to see you too." We sat by ourselves on a stone bench without another soul in sight. Holding hands in the moonlight, we looked out at the steaming pool of water before us. The night sky was framed by a rectangular border from the streets above, with majestic columns reaching up all around in support. We were at the Roman baths in England, where we had first met.

In the short time I had known him, I had learned that Gianluca was filled with romantic sentiment. I noticed how he preferred bringing me to places such as the baths and the Roman Colosseum. These were the last and closest places he felt he could relate to because it was all he had left of his previous life.

"I like to. I think of you many times." He pressed his nose against my cheek and kissed it, making me tingle all over. I missed physical affection more than I'd let myself realize. "Do you think of me? The truth."

"I do," I answered in a hushed voice. Hearing that he thought of me put my mind at ease about the doubts that had started to crop up.

"Stay, a moment," he said and left through the shadows while I sat waiting for him. "For you." He returned to my side with a paper cup of coffee, which he handed over.

"Thank you, but you didn't have to ..." I opened the lid and took a whiff of the contents. "Caramel latté?"

"Your favorite, no?"

"You remembered that?" I fought off the need to start blushing and began to inhale the hot beverage to deflect the urge.

"Of course, is only a sugar and milk." He laughed and put his arm around me. "When I am finish in Yomi, I want to come back to be with you for more time."

"That would be nice," I said, smiling into my drink. "How's it going there?"

"Still danger, but not so much now. The spirit there grow strong again." I could feel the bristles of his facial hair against my skin as he inched closer to my ear to speak softly into it. "I want to see what beautiful thing you practice to make too."

"I, uh, haven't really been practicing." I had forgotten all about working on that skill with everything going on at PROJECT: UNITY.

"Is because you are with the army, yes?" Damn, he was quick. "Why do you go there? You are not a soldier. War is not for you, little one. You tell me this before."

"I'm just visiting my friend," I lied, sort of, and looked away, but he took me by the chin. I didn't want anyone losing sleep over me.

"Dorian, when I go to Yomi, I want you to be safe." He stared me straight in the eyes. There was obvious concern in his expression, and he was being quite firm about it. "When I think of you and your smile, it brings me great joy. I will worry if you are fighting."

"I am safe. It's not a big deal. My friend just wanted to show me where he works." I felt nauseated with guilt for lying, especially because I was so bad at it. How was I supposed to tell him I had been on an operating table being dissected? Or that I had been asked to tackle the universal cause of terrorism in a face-off against an all-consuming evil? He had already pledged to watch over Yomi for me when I'd bargained for the Muramasa that Noah had needed. I couldn't then distract him with worries about me. "Really. I'm fine."

Gianluca tightened his arm around me and kissed my forehead.

"No white?" he asked, tugging the sleeve of my dark blue PROJECT: UNITY hoodie.

"I can't always wear white."

"Hm, I think so." He ran his hand through my hair, rougher each time to be silly, until I swatted him away. "I want you to make a nice art or a building so you can be proud. No fighting in the army."

"I'm not in the army!" I laughed both out of nerves and at how persistent he was being. "I'm just helping them out a little. I don't even have the materials to build anything right now, so there's no point discussing it."

"Ah, now is the truth. You *are* being a soldier ... a little soldier."

"I promise to practice making stuff with my powers again if we can talk about something else."

Gianni made himself comfortable with his head on my lap, the same as he had done back at my apartment the last time he'd visited. We spoke for hours about everything from Lyle and PROJECT: UNITY to how much the world had both changed and stayed the same since his human years.

I could already feel our bond growing beyond the physical attraction or the heroics of battle. It was the little things like the repeat behaviors and building memories that felt natural as we became more open with each other.

"Before I meet you, when I am away from Roma, I dream of it always, my home. Now it is you I think about. I did not know someone like me will have this feeling again. The world always has a new surprise."

"That's really sweet." I smiled down at him and covered his eyes with my hand. I knew he was trying to make me blush again, but I wouldn't allow it.

"How many other worlds do you think are out there?" I asked after some time sitting in peaceful silence and looking up at the stars.

"Very many. But there is still much here I do not see yet."

"Aren't you curious to see what else there may be? There could be others like us. You know... supernatural but not undead."

"Be patient. When you go too fast is when you do not see at all. Go where your passion take you, not curiosity. With curiosity, you can have disappointment, but passion gives you only strength."

"What passion are you following now?" I asked.

"To see this new world with someone in my heart." He held my hand and played with my fingers between his. "My wish is to share the many pleasures together."

"What pleasures?"

"Well ... if you are mine, then many things, but this is not yet. Another time."

"Oh, sex?" I let out a nervous laugh as my mind wandered.

"Tch, no." Gianni appeared to think my choice of words quite distasteful. He didn't come across as someone who would be sexually reserved, but he had also been very respectful of not crossing the boundary between romance and eroticism, so maybe it offended him that I was implying more. "Just a sex is nothing. It is empty ... for being with the *prostituta* or slave. A true pleasure is to share many experience with the one in your heart—to do this with the body and the mind."

"I like the sound of that."

"My favorite is the massage." Gianni's infectious grin had returned. "You, I think, is the coffee." The sun was rising as the city came to life above us with the sound of traffic and pedestrians.

"We should go before the museum staff comes to open," I told him. "Do you have to go back to Yomi?"

"I have more time." He smiled as the
shadows   swallowed   us.

Chapter Sixteen

"He seems like a cool guy," Lyle whispered to me. "I hope he doesn't turn into another Noah around here while we still got the Blackbournes to deal with."

"Trust me, he's *nothing* like Noah," I whispered back. Gianni was deep in an impassioned conversation with Commander Rudgar about war through the ages after already discussing the shadow dimension and demonstrating his powers.

We sat in the boardroom where PARAGON seamlessly translated every word so that Gianni could speak and listen in Latin to make it easier for him to communicate. The technology was just as amazing to me as it was to Gianni, but I still preferred listening to his voice even if I didn't understand the words. It was amusing when he'd slip into Italian or English for a word or phrase that they didn't have in Latin and PARAGON would race to keep up.

"PARAGON's readings are off the charts for him. The computer can't even estimate his limits. Just how strong is he?" Lyle asked me.

"Pretty strong," I answered under my breath.

"That gives a whole new meaning to the term 'power couple,'" he said. "You two could get a lot done together."

Are we considered a couple? Doesn't that take some sort of agreement between us to officiate it?

"He has enough on his plate, and he doesn't like the idea of me going off to war. He's been through it enough to see what happens."

"Yeah, but if you're capable ... two's better than one."

"Would you want Rebecca in battle just because she can shoot a gun?" I asked.

"I'd want her to do whatever she's happy and comfortable with."

Gianni and Commander Rudgar were talking, joking, and laughing over maps that PARAGON had displayed on all the screens. *Who in their right mind has so much fun discussing maps?*

"You are a very wise man, Commander," said Gianni.

"High praise from a military genius such as yourself," Rudgar said to return the compliment.

"Do you guys want some alone time?" I teased. Gianni smiled at me and put his arm over the back of my chair.

"We talk the strategy for war since Roma," Gianni said to fill me in.

"Gianluca is a fountain of knowledge," the commander added. "It's fascinating to get a first-person account of the many tactics of war through history. I feel in humanity's attempt to simplify war with technology, it has actually had the opposite effect.

"I couldn't have dreamt up a better ally to have for the upcoming events. You came at a perfect time to help Dorian in our fight, Gianluca."

"Oh?" Gianni gave me a look with his eyebrow raised and shook his head. "What does this little devil fight? I think he is not the soldier."

"He'll make a great one in our war against terrorism. He's already been a valuable asset at the risk of his own life." Commander Rudgar was trying to pay me a compliment, but he couldn't have chosen a worse way to do it. He went on to explain everything about the "Chaos Cycle" degenerating civilization. "Projected estimates give us within the next few decades before a catastrophic global event."

"No, Commander," Gianni disagreed. "It is more soon ... now. I hear it."

"What are you saying?" Rudgar questioned. The lighthearted mood in the room shifted.

"There is a dark in this places. One I cannot see through ..." Gianni pointed to the same hot spots of terrorism on the globe that Commander

Rudgar had displayed. "I speak with the Great Dragon of the East. Many time, we feel it different here. It is not shadow; it is ... poison. Like ... a... skin that is sick. What is this word?"

"Infection," said Lyle. "You can feel that? That the world is sick?"

"Yes, very, and more all the time," Gianni answered. "The true dark, the shadows, they are part of this world ... all things. They are not bad. But this ... it is very bad. It is not from the world. I hear a voice from it. It is not human, and it does not speak a language, but it always say the same thing. There is no words ... only a feeling, a anger."

"How long do we have?" Rudgar asked.

"Days? Hours? I do not know."

"So what came first?" I asked. "Is it humans' hatred bringing chaos upon the world? Or is it the Strigoi influencing humanity to destroy itself? Who exactly are we supposed to be fighting first? It's an evil version of the chicken and the egg."

"Why chickens?" Gianni gave me a puzzled stare, bringing back some levity.

I smiled at the innocence of his question. "It's just a saying. It means what happened first."

"Do not think about this. I will come to fix the darkness when Yomi is safe."

"I know you love fighting to protect stuff, but not even you can do everything, Gianni," I argued. "What happens if it's all humans at fault? Entire cities ... countries? You can't swallow them all into the darkness. You know that will just cause more fear and chaos."

"I see. Maybe you are right, but I will like to help. You have my strength and my word on my honor as a man of Roman."

"We'll work out the logistics once we collect more intel," Rudgar interrupted. "There's no need to get worked up over who's doing what just yet. As long as we have both of your support, that's all we need right now.

"In the meantime, I'd like to extend my hospitality to you in every way possible, Gianluca. Please, let us know if there's anything we can do to make your stay more comfortable."

Without being asked, I was evicted from Lyle's room, and Gianni and I were given our own to share. I didn't know if this was Lyle still trying to play matchmaker or if he just wanted his room back so he could eventually have Rebecca over.

During Gianni's tour of the base, I had noticed that there was a lack of the usual amicable faces. Some of the smiles and nods were replaced with blank stares as we passed. It seemed almost hypocritical that PROJECT: UNITY had a problem with two guys holding hands but not a floating telekinetic guy with scary eyes. Or maybe it was Gianni they were uncomfortable around. I couldn't see why, though. It was almost impossible not to like him, unless you were Noah.

"Why do they do this?" Gianni was close to hysterics laughing when we got to the gym. He stood watching with such amusement as the men and women lifted weights that I thought he'd fall over.

"They're working out ... to exercise ... be strong ... grow muscles." I tried to find an explanation he'd understand without resorting to PARAGON.

"This makes me laugh. I am sorry." Gianni picked up a two-hundred-pound dumbbell and mimicked the others doing curls with ease. "I do not feel more strong."

"That's because it's for us puny humans, not Spartan bodybuilders," Lyle chimed in.

"He's Roman, not Greek," I corrected with a bit of a laugh at the look on Lyle's face. People stopped their workouts to come watch Gianni have fun making light of the heaviest weights and to challenge him to do more. He was close to a thousand pounds on a barbell when he stopped out of boredom.

"Big deal." A slow, sarcastic clap was heard by the weight rack as Noah appeared out of nowhere. "He's using the shadows to help him. You wanna do something impressive for these monkeys, try lifting like a real man."

Noah proceeded to pick up the entire weight rack over his head with one arm.

"Add that to your file." He sneered. The crowd tried to contain their gasps of awe, seeing as he had just insulted all of them, but a hushed murmur of amazement still managed to sweep through the gym. Always a gentleman, Gianluca showed good sportsmanship by smiling and applauding with enthusiasm.

Once Noah felt satisfied that whatever alpha male need he had was fulfilled, he vanished, letting the weights crash to the floor. Rudgar resumed the tour when order was restored and he was sure that Noah wasn't about to make another spectacle.

"Why not fight? A warrior exercise is much more better. Like this, a gladiator." Gianni pointed to the boxing ring and mats used for sparring.

"They do both," said Rudgar. "Everyone follows a strict exercise and close combat training regimen."

"But I see no sword."

"That's a little ... archaic for our tastes." Rudgar chose his words carefully, but it still elicited a laugh from Gianni, who was having a hard time taking any of this seriously. He changed his formal European-style clothing into the gym shorts and lifting gloves that some of the others were wearing and caused all the ladies present to swoon over his physique.

"You two are pretty serious, huh?" Lyle asked me off to the side while Rudgar continued showing Gianni around. "You guys seem good together. I've never seen you act like this."

"Act like what? You're making more of it than I am. I don't even know if we're considered a couple."

"I know the look ... the way the two of you look at each other. He can't keep his hands off you, and you're always smiling. If I didn't know better, I'd think you were on drugs."

"He does make me really happy ..." I said. "We never came out and specifically discussed being an official couple, though."

"It's not high school, Dorian. Stop overthinking everything and enjoy life." I didn't have much experience with dating to go off of, but Lyle was right.

After the tour was over, Gianni and I decided to retire to our new room with a buffet of food from the mess hall. The bedroom was a duplicate of Lyle's, but it seemed so much more spacious without all the clutter. For a ten-by-ten pod, it appeared to be more than double its size due to the curvature of the walls and the bright white ambiance when the lights were turned up. Gianni had as much fun as I'd had the first time playing with all the lighting settings via the room's PARAGON terminal.

"You like Roma?" he asked as we ate.

"Yeah, it's great," I said, remembering the time we'd spent visiting it together. "I could see myself living there someday."

"I will find you a nice home there to be safe."

"Gianni, stop. I *want* to be here. Having a chance to stop hate around the world isn't just throwing myself in danger for the glory of war. It's personal. I know you want to make up for your past, but I want to fight for my future."

"Okay."

"Okay?" I was surprised by how easily he'd conceded. "You're not upset?"

"No, never. You speak from the heart. This is your passion, then I give you help ... support. I have a promise to ask. Wait for me so you are not to do this alone."

"I'm not sure I can promise that. I never know how long you'll be gone or if you'll come back at all. If something happens, I can't turn down a request for help. I'll try; that's the best I can promise."

We finished dinner and lay in the beds we had pushed together. Gianni still took up most of the space, but I didn't mind getting in close. All those thoughts of demons, hate, and terrorism faded away under the sheets, where there was only room for pleasant thoughts and soothing touches. We stayed quiet for a while until I was nearly lulled to sleep.

"I need to find Vance," I said, fighting my body's call to unconsciousness when I remembered the mission. With sleep also came nightmares, and I didn't want to embarrass myself around Gianni. "The Strigoi in Germany you brought me to once before. He's hiding somewhere else now, and I think he's trying to make more like me to use as soldiers."

"Ohh, more little chicks? Hm, very nice."

I glanced up to meet his suggestive grin with a frown of disapproval. "No, it's not. The Strigoi are making gross mutated versions and using humans to do the dirty work for them."

"I see. We will go soon. This is okay?" I was glad he was taking what we'd said about working together into account.

"Yes, it's perfect." My attempt at evading sleep wasn't going to work, so I decided to put my faith in the positive feelings he brought me and hoped they would also reach me in my dreams. After turning off the lights, I closed my eyes and put my head back down on his chest to let sleep take us both.

Chapter Seventeen

The next day came, and I was alone. My sheets were soaked with sweat, and I felt as if I had been crying not out of sadness but anger. I stayed in bed, worrying that whatever had happened in my sleep had caused Gianni to leave, but I managed to talk myself out of it with the more rational explanation that he'd had to return to Yomi.

On the desk across the bedroom sat a curious ivory lump among a dusting of white roses. I levitated it to my hand and recognized it was a chunk of marble. This must be a subtle hint to keep practicing my craft.

Chipping away at a rock with my powers was a great distraction from all the world's problems. It was not as good as having Gianni himself, but his gift did well in his absence. I was a simple person who was easy to please. Who else would find such enjoyment in getting a rock as a present?

I almost finished rounding out the marble when I realized it had been a few hours, yet I still hadn't been disturbed by someone needing the world to be saved.

I had never used PARAGON's voice control before, because I felt weird talking to a computer, but I was alone in my room, so I decided to give it a shot and see where Lyle was.

"PARAGON, locate Lyle Turner," I ordered. I was met with PARAGON's floating disembodied head on the screen, staring back before finally coming up with zero search results. It wasn't like Lyle to leave the base without telling me. I repeated the process for Commander Rudgar and Noah. No one I knew was coming up, except for Dr. Sullivan in Medical, so I decided to go see if she knew where everyone else had gone.

Along the way, I stopped to ask a guard but was ignored. Ever since people had seen Gianni and me together, they had been acting strangely around me. PROJECT: UNITY cheered and idolized us individually, but once they saw us holding hands or kissing, we were like completely different entities to some of them. It was annoying and hurtful, but I wasn't going to let it get to me.

I got in one of their faces, peering into the black helmet, and repeated, "Where are Lieutenant Turner and the others?"

"I am busy," a man's voice on the other side stated. I didn't need his help anyway. I continued on to Medical, where two female guards were talking to each other in the hall.

"I can't believe you actually did it," said one to the other.

"I know! It's not like me! He said I had the mouth of an angel, and I was the best he'd ever had," the second guard said in a bad attempt at an English accent. "He even invited me to be his guest at his homecoming party."

"He doesn't even know what you look like, Lilia. He's *blind*," the first woman said. "And he's a criminal. What would the commander say if he found out?"

"He hasn't been convicted, and Commander Rudgar doesn't have to know," Lilia said and stopped talking when she saw me approach. Both guards nodded to me as I passed, and then Lilia continued, "Besides, if the commander wasn't okay with him, he wouldn't be keeping him here to get medical treatment."

Owen has been here about forty-eight hours, he's blind, he's in a hospital bed, and he's in surgery most of the time; yet, he's already gotten laid at least twice. How is that even possible?

"Dr. Sullivan," I called after her upon seeing her about to enter Owen's room down the hall.

"Oh, hi, Dorian. What brings you down here today?" She turned and stopped to talk.

"Do you know where everybody is?" I asked. "Lyle and the Commander, I mean."

"Everyone not on guard duty was dispatched to the major Gestalt facilities. It's all over the news that they're under review for a serious breach of ethics and criminal involvement in the creation of bioweapons. Commander Rudgar leaked the information to Interpol, the FBI, and other major government agencies not even a day ago."

"And they just left me behind?" *Maybe I should be thankful I'm sitting one out.*

"I don't think it was anything that interesting." She shrugged and smiled. "No doubt Gestalt emptied all the real important stuff long before. The team is just going to provide backup in case anything pops up."

"All right. I guess it's a day off for me. How's Owen?"

"I was just going to check on him. His eyes are still bandaged, but I think we were successful." I followed her into his room, where she greeted him in the most professional manner she could muster. "Hello, Mr. Blackbourne. How are you feeling today?"

"I suppose about as good as I look, love. Brilliant as a bloody diamond, as always."

"Where'd Micah go, Owen?" I asked.

"Hey, mate. I didn't get to thank you for saving my arse back there. Micah's back home, taking care of family business: Preparing for the incoming shit storm from Gestalt and turning over all the family's finances that Carter was in charge of. I'm going to miss the old man. He made me what I am today."

"An alcoholic, womanizing murderer?"

"God bless his soul. At least he believed in me when no one else did. Now I'm the sixth richest Brit in the world ... and the best-looking too."

"You should feel a bit better knowing that Gestalt is being dismantled as we speak," Dr. Sullivan told him. "The real threat is still out there, but their sights will be on us, not you."

"What would really make me feel better is some extra special attention from your naughtiest nurse."

"Smooth, Owen," I said, disappointed that he was still giving Rebecca a hard time.

"I'm just having a bit of fun. It wouldn't feel right signing over a fortune without tossing some feathers."

"What are you talking about?" Rebecca asked.

"I told Micah if this surgery was a success to invest what we were going to in Gestalt with you instead. A clean three billion euros to the medical staff only, for this lass to use how she chooses. I'm not paying for guns. Never liked them."

"Oh, now you have morals?" I said.

"Mr. Blackbourne, you aren't capable of making any legal decisions like that when you're under the influence of prescription painkillers. Second, I wouldn't take a cent from you."

"How about a British pound?" Owen smirked. "I've signed contracts over breakfast with a stiffer buzz than these painkillers, and your commander didn't seem to have any problem when I offered. Everyone loves money—especially doctors."

"The thought of taking anything from you disgusts me almost as much as the thought of you yourself. I became a doctor to help people, not for the money." Dr. Sullivan turned on her heels and left the room.

"Oh, so you *do* think of me, though?" Owen asked the empty air.

"She's gone, Owen," I told him. "You're really pushing it. Not everyone can be bought."

"She knows I'm joking. The ones that play hard to get just like to have their feathers ruffled a little more than the rest—"

I walked out on him mid-sentence to catch up with the doctor, who was updating her clipboard in the hall.

"I'm really sorry about him. I feel bad for even being remotely associated with them to begin with," I apologized to her. "I guess Lyle seems even better now after that guy, huh?"

"Mr. Blackbourne doesn't get to me, but yes the lieutenant is a real gentleman and a saint by comparison."

"You can call him Lyle around me," I told her. "How'd your date go the other night?"

"Date? Oh, I'm not sure I'd call it a date exactly. Why, is that what he's saying?"

"Uh … no. Not at all. We didn't really get a chance to talk about it, so I figured I'd ask you."

This is bad. Lyle sounded ready to start shopping for engagement rings already. Unless she's just trying to keep it cool so gossip doesn't start.

"He's very passionate about his work," she said. "I can relate to that. He's a very good listener too. I enjoyed us getting to know each other over dinner, but I wouldn't want to presume it was a date. Most of our conversation was work related."

"You sound like me. I think you should just enjoy life and not overthink it. A wise man told me that."

"Maybe you're right. I wouldn't want to send the wrong message and hurt either of our reputations if things didn't work out, though. Everyone living in such close quarters for long periods of time ... it's like we all know when each other takes a breath."

Our conversation was cut short by the lights going out. I wasn't expecting Gianni back so soon, but I wasn't complaining. The only problem was that I hadn't finished carving the marble yet.

After a few seconds in the darkness, I realized that this wasn't Gianni's doing. The emergency lights and PARAGON terminals were lit up just fine.

"Huh, I can't remember the last time we had a power outage," Rebecca said. "I didn't think it was possible with our setup."

She went over to a terminal and typed away.

"Dr. Rebecca Sullivan, please report to the Main Server Room," PARAGON announced.

"What? I'm not on call. Why would I do that?" she questioned. "Put me through to the Server Room, PARAGON."

There was no response from the AI, but a moment later, the power was restored.

"That was strange. There've been an awful lot of glitches lately since upgrading the program. It's a good thing nothing happened during the eye surgery. The automated robotics in the OR have been a blessing. What once took a full team of doctors now only requires one, but I don't want to imagine what would've happened if there'd been a glitch in the middle of the procedure."

"Yikes. Maybe I'll go check it out to make sure nothing's wrong," I offered. "I've never seen the Server Room."

I left the Medical Ward, realizing that I wasn't entirely sure where I should be going as I passed the two female guards from earlier.

"Can either of you tell me where the Server Room is? I think it's on the command floor, right?"

No answer.

"Hello? I know you can hear me. Jeez, you sleep with one English guy and you act like you're guards at Buckingham Palace."

"Move along, please," one of them responded. I couldn't imagine that this was all because two guys were holding hands. Besides, I was sure I could find the place by myself. The base wasn't that big.

I floated down to the bottom floor from the atrium. The atmosphere was so drastically different with most of the team gone. The twinkling twilight walls and moonlight projection above weren't as soothing when you felt like you were in an abandoned spaceship. I was made to feel like I was snooping around any time I passed one of the tight-lipped sentinels.

I wandered the unfinished catacombs of the final floor until I found a corridor I hadn't been to. None of these rooms were labeled anything other than "Restricted," unlike the offices and assembly rooms. I was about to enter the first room when I was thrown to the floor. Something heavy had rammed me from behind, but I was able to float before my face made contact with the metal walkway. I spun an inch above the ground and righted myself to see what had hit me.

"Of course it's you," I said looking at Noah's grinning face. The guards at the end of the hall didn't react; they had seen his stupidity enough times to know not to bother.

"What's up, little shit? Miss me?"

"Not really. What are you doing down here?" I asked.

"I got bored." He shrugged. I could see the blood-drinking Muramasa strapped to his back. Bringing it out from its hiding spot meant he was up to or had been up to something.

"Are you the one messing with the power and causing problems with the security alarms?"

"I don't cause problems; I solve them." The seriousness with which he delivered that line made me laugh.

"That's the biggest lie I've ever heard." I pushed him out of my way and floated over to a locked door marked "Server Room 1" to pry it open. "I thought something serious was going on."

Inside the room sat four members of PROJECT: UNITY who looked as if they hadn't left the basement in years. Firmly cemented in their plush office chairs in front of a slew of computer screens, the techs stared up at the same time.

"This area is restricted. Please leave," said the tech closest to the door.

"Yeah, yeah. I just wanted to make sure everything was fine after the blackout." I took a glance around the room. It looked like we were inside NASA central command. Noah didn't have much to say, and I couldn't make heads or tails of anything in there aside from the power being on, so I left.

"Everyone's acting really weird," I said to Noah as I headed back to Medical. I kept peering over my shoulder, feeling like I would see someone looking back at me.

"Humans are always weird and often smell bad."

"Are you ever going to tell me what that was about out there in the snow?" I asked. "You know … since I saved your life and all."

"That just makes us even for the time I pulled you off the doctor's table because you wouldn't listen to me when I told you not to go."

"I'm pretty sure I've saved your life more than you've saved mine by now. You can drop the macho act; I know it was Aurelia. There's nothing to be embarrassed about. All I want to know is why you didn't take the time to heal before you came back here." He kept appearing down the hall in front of me as we talked... until I said that. I thought he had run off again, but he was standing still a few feet back.

"Because I wanted to get away as fast as possible," he said, trying to make it sound unimportant.

"That badly that you almost let yourself die in the sun?"

"That badly." In his voice, there was the briefest flicker of futility and shame, both of which were uncommon to him. I wasn't going to question him any further. I figured he would dodge answering anything else, but I was wrong again. "She summoned me to Scotland because she needed a lot of blood for some reason."

"I'm sorry. I can't even imagine what you've gone through all these years."

"No, you can't, so don't bother trying." I could tell he was getting agitated, thinking I was patronizing him, but that couldn't have been further from the truth.

"Let me help you—" I started.

"You don't think I can fight my own battles?" he snapped.

"Fighting for your freedom doesn't make it any better if you do it alone. Fight to win, even if that means accepting help."

"It's about waiting for the right opportunity and having patience. I don't want your help, so just worry about yourself." The anger in his voice subsided as he looked down at the Muramasa in his hand. "You've already done enough."

He was gone again as soon as I tried to approach so we weren't shouting at each other down the hall.

Back upstairs, Dr. Sullivan was distraught as she looked around in one of the labs. I had to ask her several times what was wrong before I got an answer.

"There's no blood anywhere. I need blood."

"Uh, excuse me?"

"Sorry. It's just that all our reserves from the blood bank have vanished. We had plenty just before surgery, and now it's all gone. Sometimes R&D will take samples for testing, but they said they don't know anything."

"It was probably Noah." I sighed. "He's back, in case you didn't know."

"There's no way he could have drunk that much blood so quickly. We had several hundred liters."

"Why is it always my fault?" Noah reappeared with his pompous swagger as if our conversation a minute ago had never taken place. I played along for the sake of his ego, realizing that any effort to show kindness would be misconstrued as pity.

"Shut up. I told you something was going on."

"Yeah, your room is covered in flowers. Don't worry about it. I got rid of them for you."

"You better not have touched them." The room shook, but it wasn't my doing, even if I did want to lash out at Noah at that moment. There came a loud bang, and the room shook once more. Noah vanished, and I exited out to the hall. The commotion was coming from the patient rooms.

"A little bloody help would be fantastic!" Owen's yell echoed down the plastic corridor. When I arrived, he had ripped off his bandages and was running from his room in a pair of borrowed sweatpants.

A giant pair of skeletal hands with multiple sets of knuckles reached out, grasping either side of the doorway. Another one of the alien abominations from Gestalt had emerged to pursue Owen. Its featureless cranium swiveled on an elongated neck as it sized up each of us.

My powers rippled through its twitching body the same as they had done to the one in Gestalt's lab, but at least I had the monstrosity's attention on me. When it stood upright in the hall, its wiry frame reached the ceiling like a sickly tree starved of sunlight.

I had no choice but to use the surroundings to my advantage since I wasn't able to get a tight grasp on the creature. I tore up the floor beneath the beast and crushed it together with the ceiling. The creature should have been badly maimed; however, like liquid wax, it oozed from the mess of mangled plastic and metal and re-formed in perfect condition.

Owen was shouting at the guards to do something, but they remained motionless. He grabbed one of their guns, but because he had no implant, it wouldn't fire.

"This isn't what I had in mind when I asked for a bit of entertainment!" he shouted.

Rebecca stepped into the corridor to see what was going on. Something about her presence set the creature off. It slashed at me with its clawed fingers and bounded toward the doctor.

I slowed it down for a moment by ripping an arm off. Even with my powers, grasping at it was like trying to squeeze dough. The severed arm melted into an organic sludge and was absorbed back into the horror's body to regenerate the appendage. Its head turned a hundred and eighty degrees to face me while it kept moving in the opposite direction toward Rebecca. The skin where its mouth should have been ripped open, revealing a wide maw with rows of needle-like fangs and a long, lashing tongue. It screeched in anger then turned its full focus on Rebecca.

"PARAGON, open the door!" Rebecca yelled at the unresponsive terminal outside the lab after the door closed behind her. I used a sharp piece of metal from the floor and hurled it at the monster's legs, cutting them from its body. The legs wriggled across the ground after it as the torso continued crawling toward the lab. My struggle to smash it was no more fruitful than punching water.

The creature stopped when the guards finally took action, but it wasn't the response we were hoping for. They walked right up and were absorbed into it, leaving their empty armor behind like discarded shells. The monster used the fresh carrion from their bodies to generate four crab-like appendages from its spine in addition to rejoining with the legs I had amputated.

Nothing would stop this thing, and Rebecca would soon be cornered. I flew in the way to intercept it, and Owen fearlessly raced between its numerous legs. He was fast—faster than any human—and as he dashed by, I caught a glimpse of his irises, which gave off a faint luminescence.

Having no other ideas, I continued trying to dismember the monster. Its claws cut through me and the plastic walls like paper. Owen leaped toward Rebecca and rolled with her just out of the way as the creature closed in. She grabbed the gun he was still holding and unloaded it into the creature's head, but it didn't come as much of a surprise when the monstrosity shrugged off the bullets and kept advancing.

I was considering my options on how to lure this thing away from everyone and blow it up when it was turned to shreds by Noah, who appeared with his Muramasa unsheathed. He stabbed down into the abomination's detached head, letting the sword soak up the blood as the remainder of the body decomposed around it.

"What took you so long?!" I exclaimed.

"I was putting your flowers back." He withdrew the Muramasa from the dried-out skull and sheathed it on his back.

"Are you kidding me?"

"Yes. You should know by now to lie in wait to assess your enemy."

"People were going to die," I argued.

"Not my problem if they can't take care of themselves." He cleaned the bottom of his boot off on a piece of dislodged plastic paneling.

"I have to go after Vance," I told him. "Do you have any idea where he is?"

"Yeah. Ghent, Belgium. I already paid them a visit, and the Strigoi have nothing to do with this. It wasn't after you. It wanted her." Noah pointed to Dr. Sullivan.

"Bugger has decent taste," said Owen. "I can't say I blame it now that I can see what she looks like."

"Why me?" she asked, ignoring Owen's comment.

"I don't know," Noah said with his arms crossed. "What do you have that an Ancient would want?"

Chapter Eighteen

"That thing was an Ancient?" There were ashes like normal undead remains, but unlike any other, it had parts that hadn't crumbled away to nothing.

"Same aura as one," Noah said. "Probably Carpathian."

The rest of the guards had left the atrium, but there was the sound of gunfire from above. A series of bullets was aimed at us, but Noah grabbed them out of the air, and Owen pulled Rebecca to safety from a stray shot at her feet. The guards had created a kill box out of the atrium, waiting for us to enter.

We retreated into the Medical Ward, except for Noah, who sped off upstairs.

"PARAGON," Rebecca addressed an active terminal. "Emergency override: Shut down all weapon systems on site and lock down the armory."

"Command ... denied," PARAGON responded. The screen blinked, and then pixelated colors appeared. "Primary CPU data breach. Primary CPU compromised. Auxiliary CPU ... off-line. I require emergency maintenance.

"Critical systems failure ..."

There was another screen glitch, followed by a screeching static noise. The voice slowed down and then sped up, fluctuating in pitch and stuttering as it resumed its message.

"P-P-P-P-LEASSSSSE REPORT TO OPERAT-A-TING ROOM 3 FOR DISSECT-DISSSSECTION."

Rebecca stepped back from the terminal in fright. The door to the OR down the hall opened to welcome her in where the shredded corpse of a nurse hung from the robotic surgical arms.

"I told Lyle this would happen," I said. "The first thing I told him when I saw that computer was that it would try to kill us."

"PARAGON isn't sentient," said Rebecca. "It has no mind of its own, so someone had to have reprogrammed it."

"The guards are dead." Noah reappeared with us.

"What happened?" I asked him.

"I killed them." He looked at me with an eyebrow raised like I was stupid for asking. "Trust me, they were already dead if they were under that thing's control."

"This can't be happening! I need to find some way to warn the others not to come back, but PARAGON is our only way to communicate," said Rebecca.

"Have you gone bonkers?" Owen half laughed. "We have to get out of here."

"I'm not leaving," she said with tears in her eyes. "The rest of the team will be slaughtered flying in here blind, and if it can hack PARAGON, then we have a much bigger problem should it get into the armory."

"The Carpathians aren't known for their intelligence," I said. "How the heck is this one able to understand technology as sophisticated as PARAGON to hack it?"

I could tell by Noah's expression that he was trying to figure out a plan of his own. He was also one who had a personal vendetta against the Carpathians for being responsible for killing the woman he loved.

"Dorian and I can destroy it," Noah spoke with confidence as he unsheathed the Muramasa again. "It's going to run out of bodies to absorb after a while if we can keep it here, so it won't be able to heal anymore. Take these since your powers don't work on it directly."

Noah unstrapped his wakizashi from his hips and handed them to me. "Remember to use the sharp end."

I couldn't believe he was entrusting me with them. In the past, he would have stabbed me as near to death as possible just for breathing near his swords.

"PARAGON can be rebooted from the main server room in the basement, but I have no idea how," said Rebecca.

"You'll have to try." I floated myself and the humans down to the bottom floor while Noah sped off to keep the Ancient distracted. Corpses fell from the atrium above, splattering blood as they hit the ground. I thought it was Noah's doing until the blood pooled, and up rose the Ancient from the viscous crimson puddle. It absorbed the many bodies of the dead guards with just a touch before returning to its perfect form.

"Go reboot the computer," I told Rebecca and Owen.

The extra appendages from the Ancient's spine were gone, but two wriggling lumps under its tight skin traveled up its body to the head. Where eye sockets should be, the skin ripped open, and out protruded two bloodshot eyes that honed in on me.

Their gaze gave me a bizarre feeling of vertigo and nausea that steadily increased until I was seeing everything upside down and shaking from side to side. My hands couldn't find their way to the wakizashi at my waist, and I could forget about trying to use my powers.

Noah dropped down right in time and cleaved the Ancient down the middle and then across in four clean pieces.

"Good job," he said sarcastically and punted the Ancient's head. Veins shot out from the base of the skull to ensnare Noah. He spun and sliced them off in midair, letting the Muramasa drink the blood to turn the tendrils to ash.

Noah plunged the cursed sword into one of the remaining chunks of the Ancient to exsanguinate it. The skin turned from a fleshy pallor to a bluish-gray hue. The other pieces melted into organic sludge like they had done earlier, but instead of trying to regroup, it coated Noah's boots and slithered up his body. He tried dashing away and turning to mist, but the gunk stayed wrapped around him, crawling into his mouth and nose and pinning his arms back so he couldn't use the Muramasa.

I attempted to separate them telekinetically, but the Ancient was glued on like a wetsuit.

"Use ... the sword ... the Muramasa," Noah choked out. "Stab us with it."

"It'll kill you too!" I tried cutting off the amorphous Ancient using the wakizashi instead but without success.

"Time is a factor," Noah's words gurgled up from his throat when a bony spike pierced his heart and came inches from my face. He fell to the floor, and the Ancient re-formed with the protrusion through Noah's chest turning into one of its claws. It was injecting some sort of green toxin into his heart that was spreading throughout his veins.

I sent the wakizashi whirling through the air and severed the hideous creature's arms and then used the Muramasa to drain the appendage stuck in Noah so it would crumble to ash. The Ancient turned its attention and caught me in its debilitating gaze. Noah was still lying on the floor unmoving. There was only one thing left that I could think of.

I tackled the Carpathian and flew across the atrium with it as it tried merging with me as it had done to Noah, peeling back my skin and crawling inside. When I was far enough away, I did what I could to tune out the pain and fear. Summoning as much strength within me as possible, I unleashed it in one big psionic explosion. I knew this would render me defenseless for a time by expending all my power in one shot, but I saw no other way to save us.

The Ancient, the walls, and everything within a twenty-foot sphere disintegrated. I was exhausted and barely able to crawl, but there was no sign of the monster anywhere. I dragged myself over to Noah, who was on his hands and knees trembling and vomiting a mixture of blood and gangrenous liquid.

"Are you ... okay?" I asked between labored breaths. I tried helping him to his feet, but neither of us had the energy to move.

"This ... is what I get ... for being a nice guy," he said and collapsed on his back. I followed suit and face-planted next to him.

The room I woke up in was dark, save for an LED lamp on a rolling cart that was just enough to let me see my own breath in the frosty air. I was in a hospital bed, and beside me was another one with Noah. There was no power on anywhere in the room, aside from the lamp, giving off a dead feeling with all the electronics rendered inoperable.

My head was spinning, but I got up to check on Noah. He was in one piece, and his eyes were closed in peace, so that was a good sign. His skin was cut along every exposed inch from the Ancient trying to worm its way inside, and his chest still had a gaping wound where he had been impaled. On top of all that, his mouth was caked with dried blood and that noxious green fluid he had expelled. I couldn't stand to leave him this way, just like when I had found him out in the snow. I wet a towel at the small sink where the doctors washed their hands, and I began to clean him off.

I noticed his swords resting next to the bed. After years of knowing him, he'd finally trusted me enough to hand over one of the few possessions he could call his own. It seemed like we were always saving each other when we weren't pissing each other off. What a weird friendship.

"They're talking about you out there." I jumped at the sound of Noah's voice under the towel.

"I thought you were asleep," I said.

"You just walk up to people and wash them in their sleep?"

I threw the towel down on his face and went to the door to listen to who was talking.

"—never seen anything like it," Dr. Sullivan was saying to someone. "He released a pulse of kinetic energy so powerful it turned some of the area caught in the blast to dust."

"They're talking about you going boom," Noah said, still lying there.

"I figured that."

"Gimme your blood," he demanded. "I can barely move, and I'm starving."

"Before I give you anything, I want to know why you really came here. No bullshit."

"To hang out." The words rolled right off his tongue. Either he was telling the truth or had prepared his lie in advance. I was more inclined to believe the latter.

"You're not getting blood until you tell me the truth. And why did you give blood to the doctor before you left?"

"I'm telling the truth. Don't ask a question if you're just going to doubt the answer. I gave blood so you could use it in case you got your stupid ass kicked again like at Gestalt while I was away. Now give me your blood before I come over there and stab it out of you."

I had trouble deciding if he was genuinely looking after my well-being or using this act of goodwill as a cover for some other scheme. Maybe I wasn't giving him enough credit. In fact, I was as guilty of being as cynical as he was by thinking that there was no camaraderie in the supernatural world after what he had gone through for us tonight.

I sat on the side of his bed, thinking he couldn't actually move, and went to offer my wrist. He surprised me when he grabbed me impatiently by the hair to sink his fangs into my neck.

A bite from an Archios, like Noah, induced a sensation of overwhelming euphoria for both prey and predator. This was meant to keep their meal satisfied, and therefore compliant, but it didn't seem to take effect if he was unconscious like he had been earlier in the night. You'd have to be in a coma not to find Noah physically attractive, regardless of any preferences, but after dealing with his personality for so long, it just made the whole affair rather awkward.

The best I could do was try to redirect my thoughts, but soon a real feeling of my own started coming through. A tiny voice rising up from deep inside of me was filled with panic. Noah was losing himself to his hunger as his wounds began to seal. He was taking too much from me. In this weakened state from burning out all my energy against the Ancient, it was entirely possible for me to die.

"Stop. I'm still weak," I choked out. I tried hitting him in the chest and pulling him away by his hair. My heart rate was fluctuating wildly in reaction to the blood loss.

He removed his fangs from my neck but had to hold me up as I almost fell. He bit his wrist and fed me back some of his blood to stabilize me. "That's why I told you to use the Muramasa. Blowing all your power like that is stupid."

"I was trying not to kill you ..." His blood wasn't making me feel better like it usually did; in fact, it made things significantly worse. My arm was going numb, and the pain in my chest was unbearable.

"Help," I gasped. My whole body was taken with a stinging numbness as my skin turned pale blue.

"What's wrong with you?" Noah looked me up and down. "You look like the ... oh, shit. The Carpathian. My blood must still be poisoned."

He put me on the bed and left the room, returning a second later with Dr. Sullivan over his shoulder.

"Fix him," Noah commanded and set the doctor down. "Hurry. He needs blood."

"We're all out of blood, and we have no electricity. I can't get into the lab where we keep the nitroglycerin pills or any of our medications. I had to shut everything down because we couldn't reboot PARAGON." She came over and examined me just as everything started to go black.

"He's gonna be fine now, right?" Noah's voice sounded so far away as I started coming to.

"*Yes*. Just let him sleep," I heard Dr. Sullivan say, and from her tone, it sounded like she had repeated herself a dozen times.

"I'm awake," I moaned. The lights were back on when I opened my eyes.

"You had a close call, but you're going to be okay, Dorian," Rebecca told me. "Owen was kind enough to donate blood for a transfusion. Luckily, you two have the same blood type, which I remembered from your files, but I think you're already starting to heal again by yourself—"

"I didn't know," Noah barked out of nowhere. "It's not like I did it on purpose. It's his own fault he couldn't heal."

"Yes, I understand." Rebecca was trying to speak calmly and not be confrontational.

"Noah, shut up," I moaned again.

"I don't have to shut up! I'll say whatever I want."

"Please, stress isn't good for his heart right now until we're sure his healing has taken over," Rebecca advised.

"You said he was fine!" Noah shouted.

"Noah! Get lost already!" I yelled at him.

"He was very worried about you," Rebecca said when he finally left us in peace.

"He's an ass. You don't have to sugarcoat it."

"Lyle and the rest are back. He wanted to come see you, but Noah was threatening everybody who came near the room. Right now, they're all surveying the damage and trying to get things back online. We've got basic power, so you should be comfortable in here with the heat on. Just don't overexert yourself."

Dr. Sullivan excused herself to let me rest. My chest still hurt, but mostly, I was feeling frail. With all the nasties I had fought throughout my adventures, the closest I had come to dying had wound up being unintentionally because of Noah.

"I got you food." Speak of the devil, Noah popped back in carrying a tray of breakfast biscuits from the mess hall. "I don't know what slop you like, so I just grabbed whatever."

I wanted to thank him, but I knew by now that he would snap back into arrogant mode as soon as he got validation.

"Why aren't you eating?" he asked. "I'm not feeding you, if that's what you're waiting for."

"I'm not hungry." I changed my tone when I realized how concerned he really was. "I'll eat later."

I moved the tray over to the bed next to me, and Noah took a seat to start cleaning his blades on the unused bedsheets.

"You weren't really going to die," he said, not looking up from his work. I didn't know if he was trying to reassure me or himself.

"Sounds like you would've missed me."

"Don't flatter yourself. I told you I don't want my time I invested in training you to be wasted." A few minutes passed before he spoke again. "You want your pet rock?"

"Pet rock? Oh, the marble I was working on? No, it's fine ... as long as you didn't break it."

"It's from the Italian, isn't it?" he asked, even though I was sure he knew the answer. "And those flowers too. You like that shit?"

"His name is Gianluca, and yes it was a nice gesture."

"How can you still trust that guy? What's so good about him?"

"He makes me happy." I wasn't about to elaborate on my romance to Noah and explain how I felt like a different person when I was with Gianni.

"He seems like a dick."

"And you're not?"

"I do it with style. He's just going to end up using you, and you're gonna need me to save you. He's no different than any other Ancient, even if he isn't undead anymore. They're all the same. Trust me, I know. When he starts talking about changing the world, you'll see."

"I'm not talking about this." I closed my eyes to rest and hoped he'd take the hint and leave.

"At least you keep things interesting to help pass the time," he continued after another minute of silence. "If you died, I'd have to find somebody else to idolize me who's not completely annoying. You could be like that cop you're friends with. He's a real douche."

"Please go away."

"Eat your biscuits, and I'll consider it."

"You're a fucking biscuit." I really wanted to laugh. He was so ridiculous sometimes it was hard to stay angry at the big idiot.

And then the lights went out.

Chapter Nineteen

It was nearly pitch-black, except for some service lights flashing through the window of the door. The PARAGON terminal in the room turned on by itself. The virtual face popped up and glanced around the room, taking note of Noah and me before shutting itself off.

Then came the sound of gunfire.

"Get on my back." Noah knelt down beside the bed so I could climb on.

"What? No. I'm not doing that."

"I can't carry you and fight at the same time." He grabbed my arm and slung me over his back. We stood in front of the door until we realized it was powered by electricity and wouldn't open.

"Well that was a short trip," he said. I hopped down, and my legs almost gave way under me. "Wait here, and don't do anything stupid."

Noah turned into mist and escaped the room. I heard sounds coming from deep in the base. Horrible sounds. Ungodly sounds.

I knew what those sounds meant. The Ancient still roamed the halls, and my sacrifice had been in vain. There weren't many of us left. I couldn't use my powers, and Noah wouldn't be able to defeat that thing on his own, but I still couldn't let him face it by himself. I stumbled around the room, searching for anything that might be useful for defending myself, and I realized that Noah had left the Muramasa behind along with his slim chance at survival. What was he planning on doing with just his wakizashi?

The sound of gunfire stopped, but it only made the howling screams of agony and fright ring out even clearer through the plastic-covered halls. I hid behind the bed, clutching the Muramasa until the floor started to shake. Something was moving outside the door. I saw it approach through the small window. It was the Ancient lumbering by with its lanky body jerking and twitching with each step. It stopped in front of my door and pressed its face against the glass, licking away with its barbed tongue. The protruding bloodshot eyes induced an even more severe madness in my vulnerable state, causing paralyzing spasms along with the vertigo.

The PARAGON terminal flicked on to display the face again and looked right at me.

"TT-T-THISSSS WOULD BE ... WOULD BE ... A M-M-M-MUCH SIMPLER TRANSITION IF YOU COULD C-C-COMPREHEND MY ... MY B-B-BRRRRRRR-BRILLIANCE."

Somehow, the Ancient was still controlling PARAGON and was able to speak through it. The door opened at its command, but it didn't enter. It was mocking me, showing me its dominance over everything and everyone on the base.

My hands shook as I tried to unsheathe the Muramasa just as the Ancient was sliced in two across the torso. It slithered on the ground and kept reconnecting its pieces as I caught a glimpse of Noah slashing furiously at it.

"YOUR-R-R-R S-S-S-SALVATION IS IN YOUR IG-G-G-GNORANCE. TO DEVOU-R-R YOU WOULD ... WOULD BE ... WASTEFUL. YOUR LIMITED-ED KNOWLEDGE IS-S-SSS INCONSEQUENTIAL TO MY PLAN ... MY PLAN. I WILL TERMINATE YOUR EXISS-S-TENCE AT A LATER TIME IF YOU REQU-REQUESSS-REQUEST TO BE SPARED FRR-OM THE SS-S-UFFERING OF LIFE."

The Ancient was still talking through PARAGON, even though it was in pieces. The frantic sounds of all hell breaking loose were still coming from other levels of the base. *How could it be in multiple places at once?* This one we cut apart couldn't be the Ancient; it had to be a decoy, which meant the real one had to be fighting with PROJECT: UNITY right now or still hiding somewhere on base.

"THHH-E COMM-M-M-MANDER WAS CORRECT. THERR-RE ISSS ... THERE IS A CORRUPTION SSSPREADING ON THIS PL-PLA-PLANET."

I went out into the hallway and started stabbing the lumps of flesh with the Muramasa to turn them to ash. I was getting winded, and my head and chest started to hurt. Noah took the sword from my hands and finished the job, but another terminal flickered on in the corridor.

"THAT CORRRRR-UPTION IS MORTAL-KIND ... KIND. THEY ARE IM-IMPERFECT, FLAW-ED-D, SELF-DESTRUCTIVE. THEIR ACTIONS-S-S BRRRRING ABOUT A GRRREATER THREAT THEY CANNOT COMPREHENDDDD, BUT I WILL SS-SSSSOLVE IT."

The terminal let out a digitized screech at the end of the transmission and shut off. My feet stuck to the floor as I tried to run to the atrium. Some of the abomination wasn't destroyed and was regrowing under me. I kicked off my shoes and ran before the fleshy goo could climb up my body.

Noah dashed by, picked me up, and then zipped away in a blur down to the next floor.

"You good?" he asked. I didn't feel okay; I felt on the verge of collapse, but complaining wasn't going to help the situation.

"I'm fine," I said as convincingly as possible.

"Bet you wish you ate those biscuits when you had the chance now, huh?" I know Noah was trying to make light of things, but nothing could bring levity to the situation.

"We have to help the others—"

Noah dropped me hard on the ground. In the glow of the emergency strobe lights, I could see the abomination impaling him with all five of its clawed fingers and lifting him into the air like a doll. It plucked the Muramasa from his hand and went to stab him with it, and in a panic to help him, I jumped in the way.

I was nicked by the cursed blade, and that was all it took to drain away a portion of my fragile life. I was still alive, though, and as long as I had that going for me, I wasn't going to give up. I clung to the creature's spindly arm to try to wrench the sword free from its claws, but my skin started to fuse to its body, making it painful to pull away.

Noah was struggling against the claw that was staking him through the heart. He was trying to reach down to his hip, where his wakizashi were still sheathed. I grabbed one of the swords and sliced off the arm I was on and then the one holding Noah. The abomination's barbed tongue whipped out around my neck to pull me in. I held my hand out, trying to use my powers, but there was nothing left in me.

I flailed behind me with the wakizashi until I managed to cut myself free. Blood trickled down my neck from the puncture wounds left by the barbs. I limped to free Noah, who was still staked by the disembodied arm, but I got smacked away by the creature and went flying over the railing of the atrium into the darkness below. Crashing to the ground caused sharp pangs to shoot through my body, and there was an even worse pain in my face ... then nothing: no sound, no sight, no pain.

"He's got three broken ribs and a hairline skull fracture, and he's lost a lot of blood again. Not to mention ... this."

It was a woman's voice speaking. I thought it was Dr. Sullivan, but I was so disoriented that I couldn't be sure. Was this a dream or déjà vu? I was having a hard time remembering anything.

"What's going on?" I mumbled. It hurt to speak. "Did we win?"

"He's awake." That was Lyle's voice. I was relieved to hear him but was still hoping this wasn't a dream. The lights were out, so that didn't bode well. I tried to get up but was held down.

"You can't get up, man. You've been through a lot," Lyle said. The beam of a flashlight aimed toward the ceiling, and that's when I noticed I was only seeing through one eye. I touched my face and felt bandages everywhere.

"Dorian, it's Dr. Sullivan. You have a skull fracture and some broken ribs. I had to remove glass from your left eye, which is why it's wrapped. The glass was centimeters away from your brain. Any closer, and you could have died." Her voice faded in and out. I was feeling dizzy, and lying down wasn't helping. "It's a good thing I've started the habit of carrying gauze with me everywhere I go."

"Where are we?" I asked. "Where is everyone? Where's Noah?"

"I'm here, kid," Noah's voice answered from somewhere in the room. I strained to look around. Rebecca and Lyle were bandaged too, and even

Noah had his chest wrapped to cover the hole where he had been staked. Without a supply of blood, he had no way to heal himself.

"How'd you get away?" I asked.

"We ran interference." That was Commander Rudgar's German accent. "We managed to take out the roaming intruders with that magic sword of Burckhardt's and some explosives we had onboard the combat vehicles. Right now we're holed up in a storage room on the command floor where there are no terminals or surveillance this Ancient can use against us while it regroups."

"We're all that's left," said Lyle.

"Owen? Shaun?" I almost didn't want an answer.

"Blackbourne is MIA ... presumed dead. Shaun was ... we lost him." Lyle choked up as he tried to get the words out. "That *thing* is still out there somewhere."

"Noah, can you super-speed us out of here?" I asked. "Let it have the base. Drop a bomb on it or something."

"The place is locked down, but I know where it is," Noah said.

"Care to fill us in?" Lyle asked. "Because I've got a brick of C4 left with its name on it even if I have to blow myself up with it."

"It's in the basement."

"We're *in* the basement," said Lyle.

"The real basement. That maximum security jail you have below here. The one you can only get to from the hidden elevator in the commander's office."

"All the C4 in the armory won't get us in," Rudgar said. "The walls are six to eight feet thick of alternating steel, lead, and cement with a fail-safe hardwired to drop it to the bottom of the ocean in case of emergency. Once it's sealed, there's no way in or out, and that's just what that thing wants."

"I'll find a way." Noah vanished.

"I can't believe I'm saying this, but I'm worried about him," said Lyle.

"You should be," I said. "He could probably just mist his way off the base and leave us to die if he wanted, but he's sticking his neck out for us."

"I know ... I'm going after him. At the very least, I can cause a distraction."

"Lyle, don't." Rebecca stood in his way. "I mean Lieutenant ... we need you here to protect what little survivors are left."

"She's right, Turner," the commander agreed. "I can't hold the room on my own in this condition should anything come through that door."

Lyle swelled with a new sense of purpose and sat on the floor next to Rebecca. I'd have smiled if it didn't hurt so much.

My nerves were putting morbid thoughts in my mind. *Noah can't do this on his own. He's got absolutely nothing to gain from this either, and yet I'm always coming down on him for having some selfish motive.*

While lying there, the only method I had of tracking time was the tempo of the throbbing in my head. After an indeterminable number of minutes, another light shone on the ceiling from something in the room. Lyle went to inspect the source and held up one of the tablet devices, which had turned itself on.

"Smash it," I tried to yell.

"It's showing the cameras from the jail. The doors just closed Noah in there with that thing." Lyle sat within view of everyone to watch. Rudgar came over; it was the first time I had seen him since waking up. His arm was in a sling made out of his shirt, and his face and chest were covered in lacerations.

"Do you come to thank me for my blessing of virulence, Archios? I was so hoping to transform that hideous figure of yours into a vision of my own glory." The voice was coming from a humanoid figure facing Noah in the middle of the jail and spoken in tandem by PARAGON. The metal walls of the cell were covered in an organic membrane that pulsed along with enormous veiny structures.

The tall, gangly figure changed from pale gray to a healthier peachy color. Bloodshot eyes and a wide mouth of lethal fangs opened up, letting the tongue out past its lipless grin, where it swayed in the air.

Noah wasn't moving, and that scared me. Giant cysts around the room bubbled until they popped to release duplicates of the Ancient like the ones we had fought.

"Why isn't he moving?" Lyle shouted at the screen as the horrors converged on Noah without any signs of resistance.

"I can't watch this." I struggled to get to my feet, but my body had other plans. "I can't sit here and watch him be murdered. I don't care if I die! I need to try."

"We stand even less of a chance than he does." Lyle held me down, and I started crying out of my one good eye as the sound of God knows what was being crunched on the tablet screen.

"We have to help him!" I pleaded with Lyle.

"Everyone, shut up!" Rudgar shouted. "He's turned the tide. That bastard is doing it! He's winning!"

The commander showed us the screen. Noah wasn't even visible as a blur of hypersonic slashes carved through the nest of monsters, reducing them to a mixture of entrails and ashes. At that moment, I had never been so proud to call him my friend.

The room was cleared, and Noah stood triumphant with the Muramasa resting on his shoulder, reveling in the punishment he had brought down upon the Ancient. He looked in terrible condition, but at least he had won and earned himself all the blood he could drink. I wouldn't even mind listening to him gloat for the next few weeks.

"Oh, no." Lyle took the tablet from Rudgar as he was about to set it down. "Come on! No! It's coming back! All of it!"

Again, the Ancient rose from near nothingness along with its body doubles. They advanced toward Noah, who was too worn-down for a repeat performance. His moves became sluggish and desperate as he was surrounded in the middle of the room. Alarms and metal clanking from the tablet's speakers drowned out whatever was being done to Noah.

"Those sirens mean it triggered the release to drop the jail into the ocean," Rudgar informed us.

"Shut it off," I told them, and when they didn't, I grabbed the tablet and threw it across the room in a rage. "Why are we just sitting here? What are we waiting for? If we're going to die, let's get it over with."

I started screaming for Gianni, hoping he could hear me through the shadows while everyone sat quiet. The little light we had started to go out, and a curtain of darkness fell to bring a sad close to the scene. I became angrier and more frustrated listening to the sound of my own helpless sniffling in the still room.

Too exhausted and unsteady to stand, I dragged myself across the tile floor to the exit and fought hard to dismiss my body's warnings not to. A quick chill sliced the air; I didn't know if it was my body shutting down.

"What is this?! How?" Gianni's voice bellowed in panic above me as the light returned to the tablet and flashlight.

"Don't pick him up," Rebecca warned. "He's injured."

I rolled on to my back and looked up at Gianni, who was kneeling over me. His fingertips glided over my face to inspect the bandages. "Please, Gianni. Help Noah ... he's down ... in a big metal box. Lyle, show him the tablet."

"Gianluca, a word," Commander Rudgar interjected as Lyle showed the screen.

"We don't have time for a word!" I shouted. "Gianni, go! The monster is going to kill him."

"I want it alive." Rudgar's request shocked us all. "I have questions for it that are integral to the safety of millions."

"I ask you a promise. You remember this? You give your word as a man and you lie to me!" Gianni raised his voice and pointed at Rudgar in accusation as his armor took shape from the shadows around him. "I will ask the questions with my sword."

I finally felt I could breathe again, knowing Gianni was here to help. It took only a few seconds for him to return Noah to us before going back to confront the Ancient himself.

"I'm glad you're not dead," I said to Noah. He glanced at me out of the corner of his eye and leaned over to wipe the gunk from his blade on my shirt. I'd let him have that one; he'd earned it.

Everyone except Noah watched on the tablet as Gianni faced off against the Ancient in the sinking prison. There was a brief conversation between them that we couldn't hear as the transmission cut out.

"What did Gianluca mean about a favor?" I asked Rudgar.

"He made a pretty direct request that we not bring you on any missions until he got back and that we evacuate you if there was danger," Lyle answered for him. That explained why they'd left without me to help raid Gestalt with the authorities. Either way, I was screwed, so it didn't really matter in the end.

Noah started to say something derogatory about Gianni, but it was getting harder to concentrate, and the voices in the room dipped in and out until I couldn't understand them.

"Guys, I'm not ... I don't feel well." The feeling of extreme fatigue overtook me and forced me to close my eyes.

"He's going into shock" were the last words I heard from Rebecca before blacking out for the third time   that   day.

Chapter Twenty

I must have been out for some time, because when I opened my eyes, I was back in the Medical Ward with the lights and heat restored.

Everyone was screaming at each other in some intense argument that was making my head pound. It sounded like there was more than one conversation going on at the same time, but I couldn't decipher what any of them were about. Maybe Gianni's voice stood out above the rest because he always had such a pleasant demeanor and it was a drastic change to hear him like this; or maybe it was just that his voice was the loudest and the one that kept flipping between languages.

"You are a child in a warrior body. A weak one with no honor." Gianni was yelling at Noah as they stood face to face, staring each other down. Noah unsheathed the Muramasa as a threat, but Gianni only laughed at him. "You cannot hurt me. I warn you one time. Go away from here."

"What's going on?" I asked. Gianni stopped and came to my bedside.

"I told you this would happen!" Noah shouted to me. "You can't trust this asshole ... any of them. He's doing the same thing he did with Rozalin back in Yomi. When are you gonna open your eyes?"

"Stop!" Rebecca interrupted. "We've seen enough fighting for all our lifetimes today. If you want to fight each other so badly, then take it away from the patients."

"Yeah, this is stupid. The enemy is out there, not in here," Lyle added. There was a moan in the bed next to me. I checked to see Owen sprawled out with a pillow over his head, and when I turned back around, Noah was already gone.

"Someone tell me what happened," I said.

"I am sorry, but that man, he is no man. He is a child." Gianni took my hand in his.

"Gianluca stopped the Ancient and forced it to give back control of the base," Lyle explained. "Noah got pissed off because we kept it for questioning, and he blamed Gianluca, saying that by not killing it, he was conspiring with it. He said this would backfire and then started being his usual self, threatening us and ... yeah, you saw what went down."

"Noah risked his life for us without being asked, and I agree ... I want the Ancient destroyed,"

I said. This was also the second time Gianni had saved Noah and me, and I was sure that it hurt Noah's already wounded ego further.

"I do too," said Lyle. "The commander is interrogating it right now after Gianluca neutralized it and brought the jail back up to shore outside the base."

"It can hurt no one," Gianni assured me.

"Did we find out what it wanted with you, Rebecca?" I asked.

"No, but the Ancient was somehow using the implants from its victims to connect to PARAGON and control it," she said. Rebecca looked miserable, and I couldn't blame her. "That's all the information we've gotten so far. I simply can't believe how we just lost everything ... *everybody*. Seeing all those empty corridors ... I can see the team's faces, even though they aren't there. There aren't even bodies to bury. It's just a ghost town. PROJECT: UNITY is ruined."

"It isn't over for us. There's still you, me, and the commander. We still have the base," Lyle said and put his arm around her. "We know there's an afterlife. Our team isn't physically here, but they're someplace better, watching over us. We have to keep going for them."

"What happened to Owen?" I asked.

"He has a hangover," Lyle said with disgust. "He was hiding in the walk-in freezer and drinking to keep himself warm the whole time."

"Dr. Sullivan," Commander Rudgar's voice came over the PARAGON terminals' blank screens.

"Please, meet me outside the hangar. We need to speak with you."

"We should let these two get some rest," Rebecca said. "Try not to fall asleep with a concussion, but we'll come back to check on you just in case." She gave me the best smile she could manage and left with Lyle.

"I will return, little one," Gianni kissed my hand. "Have a good rest. I go to make sure they are safe."

He disappeared into the shadows, but I wasn't tired and had no intention of lying there with Owen snoring and moaning in the room. I got off the bed, and my body was not happy about it. My head was throbbing, and acute pains shot through my broken ribs. I didn't even want to think about my eye, but fortunately, a new pain in my ankle acted as a nice distraction.

I hobbled out of the room, unsure of what I was going to do. I wanted to find Noah, but he was probably not going to make that easy after what had happened moments ago. The halls were quite haunting with nobody around. The only signs of a brutal conflict that remained were carved into the plastic and steel. I thought of going up to the hangar to see what everyone was doing, but the stairs looked like more than my body could handle, and I wasn't about to trust the elevator, even if the Ancient had surrendered control of the technology on base.

"Stubborn little chick." Gianni caught me and picked me up with both arms as I was about to attempt the stairs.

"I don't want to sit in bed! Put me down!"

Gianni wasn't entertaining my demands as he carried me to my room in the barracks. I gave up trying to fight him, and to be honest, I didn't much mind the extra bit of closeness. It was a good thing he was so much larger than I was, because lying in his arms was like lying on a couch and didn't hurt my ribs.

"Why you do not let me protect you?" he asked. "You do not trust me? Is because of the poison Noah speaks to you? That man has no honor; he is always trouble. A selfish child."

"What? No, Gianni. Noah isn't really like that, and he hasn't changed my mind about how I feel."

"Then let me keep you safe. It is a man's pride to protect what is important to him. Fighting is not your passion. I know you lie to me when you say you want to, but I do not understand why."

"Because nobody likes weakness," I confessed. "I lose people, and they get hurt when I rely on them. I lost my parents because I ran to them like some kid when I should have stood my ground and not gotten them involved in my troubles."

"This is not the truth. Every man has a weakness, or we are not alive."

"Yeah, well now I have a lot of them. I'm mortal now, and I can die. Even if I get it back, I might lose it again. I'm scared of loss. I hate losing things, especially when I don't have much to start with. You don't want to be with someone who can die at any second. You might leave to go to another world and come back and I'll have grown old, but for you, it was only a day."

"No, I will enjoy every second you give to me, no matter how long. I do not count the time. It does not make me want to be with you less. You know my past, but you make me feel like a good man again. I have a hope that I can be in this world. When I meet you, you fill my heart with a purpose. You are my light in the dark, even when a mortal. Strong, weak, it does not make a different feeling for me. I want to be with you for both. We say in Roma *si vales, valeo*: When you are strong, I am strong."

He set me down on the bed once we reached our room, and he put his arm under the pillow to keep my head elevated and hold me close to him.

"When do you have to go back?" I asked. "To Yomi, I mean."

"No." He misunderstood my question of "when," or maybe he was distracted, but either way, I found it endearing. "Yomi will be okay now.

His voice soothed away some of the restlessness until I touched the gauze over my eye. I was almost falling asleep already, even through the discomfort. I wasn't used to pain of this magnitude lasting for so long, but I could handle it.

"It will be better soon," Gianni assured me. This was one time that his words didn't put me at ease. It almost felt as if everyone was expecting my regeneration to come back without question ... everyone but me. I hadn't gotten much in the way of medical treatment other than some bandages. But I knew going to a hospital was out of the question in case my powers returned and sent everyone into a panic.

This made me think of the veterans who would return from war missing limbs ... poor men and women who were decorated as heroes and then discarded: *Here's your medal, now go rot somewhere out of sight.* Like hiding them away so we don't have to look at them makes us feel better about ourselves.

"Wake up, little chick," Gianluca whispered to me and petted my cheek. "You have a bad dream."

"Huh? I was awake." I didn't remember falling asleep. We were in the same position.

"No, I call you three times. Is okay, sleep now." He didn't need to talk me into it. I drifted right off but was woken back up several more times by him checking on me until one final time I woke up on my own.

Gianni was out cold, his breathing slow and relaxed. I was comfortable curled up with him as long as I didn't move, but I'd had enough of lying around. I tried squirming free from the steel girders that were Gianni's arms, but it was no good. He was holding on tight. I called his name, gave him a poke, and attempted to lift his arm up again, but it was no easier than bench-pressing a car. He mumbled something in Italian without waking and snuggled up closer, ending any slim hope I had of breaking free.

I lay there in the dark, trying to fall back asleep, listening to Gianni breathing and the occasional person walking by the room. I didn't know what time it was; the room was cloaked in darkness so black that no light could get through anytime Gianni slept.

Wait a minute. The rooms in the barracks are soundproof. How can I hear people walking in the hallway? In silent anticipation, I listened for the sound again.

There it was: a thumping sound. I had just assumed it was footsteps, but when I paid closer attention, the rhythm was off and didn't always go from one direction to another. Sometimes, it went up above the ceiling or down below the floor. How was that possible? They'd have to be ... in the wall.

"Gianni!" I shouted and had to resort to shoving him. He babbled something in Italian again and hunkered down further under the covers with his face nuzzled in my shoulder. Of course, he had to be the heaviest sleeper the world had ever seen.

I didn't hear the sound anymore, and if it was only the two of us on base, I might have been fine not investigating. I *was* in the safest place in the building—and probably on Earth—but it was the others I was worried about.

"Eh?" Gianni finally stirred. "Oh, sorry ..."

He moved his arm, thinking I was complaining that he was hurting me.

"No, Gianni. I heard something in the walls."

He yawned and rolled over. I thought he was going back to sleep, but the darkness in the room lightened.

"Stay. I go check." He vanished from the room, leaving behind an imposing Roman soldier of solid shadow to stand guard. I climbed out of bed to inspect it close up. The construct was like a mannequin made of black metal. He didn't give this one different textures, except for the horsehair crest on its helm, but it did mimic realistic movements, such as breathing. It even nodded in acknowledgement to me waving my hand in front of its face.

Putting a guard was nice, but Gianni should know by now that I wasn't going to stay in one place. I walked to the door to leave, but the shade moved to block my path. I ducked under it, thinking I was being sneaky, but the shadow picked me up like Gianni would and set me back on the bed.

Well played, Gianni. And here I thought the guard was to keep danger out, not me in. That won't stop me from checking inside the room, though. I just need to remove a panel from the wall, and maybe I can see what was causing the noise. This would be a lot easier if I had a screwdriver or, you know, telekinesis.

There was nothing in the room that I could use, except the guard's sword and spear.

"Can I borrow your weapon?" I didn't get a response. I didn't expect one really, but it was worth a shot. I tried to just take it, but that didn't work either.

"Little one, what are you doing?" Gianni reappeared in the room behind me as I was trying to pry off the plastic wall paneling with my hands. My head hurt from straining against the pain in my ribs. Everything hurt. Being mortal sucked. Why did I ever want to go back to this? "Your nose."

"What's wrong with my nose?" I put my fingers to it and touched blood. "It's nothing. Did you find out what the sound was?"

"Hm, yes. You stay here and be safe. Sleep, okay?"

"Stop, Gianluca! Just tell me what's going on." It was bad enough I was in this position in the first place. I knew he meant well, but I didn't want to be reminded constantly that I couldn't do anything to help.

"Your friends are okay, but the Ancient, it ... hmm ... it escape. Only a piece."

This was bad, and that was an understatement. "You have to find it—"

"No. I know where. It go back to the prison above and wait. I will go to ask, and you stay."

"I want to come with you ... please?" I asked with as much humility as I could muster.

Gianni covered his face and shook his head in irritation as he sank through the shadows. I was left to sit in bed with my jailer watching over me.

In my hand, I played with the lump of white marble that I hadn't gotten to finish carving. Burning out all my power didn't even solve anything. Were my days of saving the world already over?

Chapter Twenty-One

Gianni returned up through the shadows under the bedsheets without a word. He lay there looking up at me until I spoke first.

"Sorry about before. I'm just having a little trouble letting go."

"I know. You lose much in a very young life, but I will not go too. I am happy, and even when you are weak, I am here to be strong for you." He held my hand. "If you feel okay, I take you to your friends. We are going to have a talk."

Gianni brought me to the boardroom, where we sat across from Lyle and Rebecca, with Rudgar and Owen at each end of the table. PARAGON was still off-line, so none of the monitors worked. The room smelled wonderful from a plate of crepes Owen was eating. He was dressed in his hunting armor, which Micah must have left behind for him. I guess the PROJECT: UNITY sweats weren't stylish enough.

"Where'd you get crepes?" I asked him.

"I made them. There's still some in the kitchen if you'd like," he answered between stuffing his face. I hadn't been hungry until he'd mentioned it.

"How're you—" Lyle started to ask me but was cut off by the commander, who was impatient to begin the meeting.

"We've made contact with the Ancient a few times now with Gianluca's help. After some deliberation, and as much as it bothers me to say this, we may be on the same side."

"Throw the bugger into the sunlight and be done with it," said Owen. "I don't need Gestalt coming after me again when the truce is over."

"I can't believe this! I almost get myself killed for nothing?" I shouted so loudly that my head throbbed. "All of you are sitting here with nothing more than a paper cut, and I gave up my immortality, my powers, and lost an eye! People died! Doesn't that mean anything? Where's the justice in this?"

"Our sacrifices weren't in vain—"

I stood up and stopped Rudgar right there. "*Our* sacrifices?! You didn't sacrifice anything! I'm not yours to sacrifice!"

"I understand you're upset, but choices had to be made. Please just take a seat if you want to stay."

"No! You can't just dismiss me now that I've served my purpose. You're giving us a bunch of generic politically correct bullshit to justify your fascination with a new supernatural. If I still had my powers, you wouldn't be so quick to shut me up."

"Dorian, your nose is bleeding," Lyle pointed out.

"Gianluca, maybe it'd be best for you to return Dorian to his room so he can calm down and rest," Rudgar suggested in a firm manner.

"Come. I take you back," Gianni whispered to me. I couldn't believe he was taking the commander's side, but Rudgar had manipulated the situation perfectly, knowing that Gianni wouldn't neglect my well-being.

"Gianni, you don't understand," I said when we were back in the room.

"I do. You trust me, okay? This Ancient is not the enemy. It is enemy with the company that hurt you very bad."

"That thing is lying. It's just saying anything to trick us," I said.

"No. I hear it myself before this. The darkness I tell you I cannot see through, the strange voice with no words. It is a hole to Hell. I speak with the Empress Kamakura before I leave Yomi. We both feel it.

"These hole are opening in the Earth. You cannot see them with the eyes, but they are there.

The Ancient knows this too. If the hole is big, the big demons will come. Just like in Yomi, they will want to eat the souls. The most strongest souls are the best to eat, like the Ancient ones.

"If we let the soul be eaten, then the big demons will get stronger and stay on the Earth. The Gestalt company is control by a demon to catch the strong souls for it. I can feel it. On the map where the company is, that is where many dark places are I cannot see in. The commander show me, and the Ancient. I even check with the Empress Kamakura. It is not a lie."

"Why not just kill the Ancient ourselves before the demons get it then?"

"Because the undead soul go to Hell still. It is the same thing. The Ancient want to stop the demon from coming, so it fight the company you go to. It think your friends are part of it too, but now it stop."

"It only stopped because it doesn't want you to kill it," I argued.

"Maybe. But if it stop, then it doesn't matter. It knows many things about what is happening and the evil coming. You stay close with me, and it will not hurt you." He summoned a towel through the shadows for me to wipe my nose.

"Yeah ..." I just wasn't in the mood for chivalry at that moment.

"Take a rest. I go to explain to your friends now." He left without posting a guard this time. I was still upset, having not grown to appreciate the politics and strategic games being played.

I was hungry and angry and wasn't about to sit around in time-out. I climbed out of bed in agony from my ribs. Any second now, my powers would come back. At least that's what I kept telling myself: *It's all going to be okay. I think.*

"Oh come on," I said out loud, upon limping my way to the circular stairs that wrapped around the whole atrium. Part of the railing was broken on this floor—probably a result of my doing—adding another level of difficulty to my ascent.

"It all starts with the first step." I searched around for the voice and found Noah crouched on the railing of the floor above me. The damage he had taken from his fight had healed, so he must have found blood somewhere.

"Hey, where've you been?" I asked. When he wasn't around, I missed the big idiot, but that usually wore off pretty quickly after he popped back in.

"Around." He balanced on his back with his arms and legs hanging off the sides of the railing to relax. "Guess your powers haven't come back yet. I told you not to do that shit."

"I panicked. I thought you were gonna die."

"Panic is the worst reaction to any situation. Thought even you'd learned that by now. But whatever. You'll get your powers back soon."

"How do you know?"

"I've told you before. It's like a muscle. The more you work it out, the stronger it gets." He flexed one of the mountains he had for biceps. "You just pulled a muscle. Stop being a baby about it."

Maybe he was right. He was always right ... or, at the very least, more often than I liked to admit. It had been only a day, and I was freaking out, but I felt like a huge piece of me was missing, and the pain wasn't helping either.

"You were right about them teaming up. I told Gianluca I agreed with you. They're all down there talking about it."

"I love that sound. It's almost better than total silence. Tell me more about how I'm always right."

"Shut up. I didn't say you were *always* right." I sat on the stairs, feeling winded from the shooting pains running the course of my body.

"You thought it, though. I can read your mind again now that you're a filthy mortal."

"Get out of my head, you jackass! What happened with your blood?" I asked to change the subject.

"Nothing. It's still poisoned, and I can't use it to heal myself either, so I guess I'll always need to feed on fresh blood if I get hurt from now on. Just means you gotta get back to normal soon so I can use you as my blood bag again," he grinned to himself. "I'm just glad my gorgeous face didn't get messed up."

"Yeah, that'd be a real war crime. Speaking of feeding, do you think you could zip me up to kitchen?"

"You got your stupid ass this far. If you want food, go the whole distance. The Italian is making you soft. He's using your weakness to make you dependent on him so that when you're strong again, you'll feel you need him. I'm telling you, he's up to something, and I'm always right, remember?"

"He's not like that. This is one time you're wrong."

"Then why does he never encourage you to do things on your own? I taught you how to survive, but he only holds you back and keeps you in his pocket so that when the time comes, he can pull you out like a card to play. What has he shown you how to do? Explode and burn out all your power so you wind up like *this*? Does that sound like someone who's looking out for you?"

"He showed me how to use my power to create things too."

"Oh that's great. So you can hide in your room and play with rocks. That sounds real useful when the Ancients he's kissing ass with turn on you like they have in the past."

"I don't wanna talk about this anymore." I got up and took a few steps up the seemingly endless staircase.

"Because you know I'm right. He's gathering allies: sweet-talking some, intimidating others. No one is that nice for no reason. Especially not someone with his reputation. He jumped at the chance to guard Yomi, and he doesn't even like me. He knew you couldn't do it, so it wasn't like he was sparing you from that fate. Use your head. It may be broken, but there's still a brain somewhere in there."

"He likes protecting things." I made it up one floor. *Just one more to go.* Noah appeared further up the railing to continue his lecture.

"He likes keeping people under him, like every other Ancient. He's just playing the game well enough to get those other Ancients in his corner too. Has he been showing you how to get by in case your powers don't come back? Or has he been keeping you down and locked away?"

"I'm not really in any condition to be training," I said.

"You thought you weren't in any condition to make it up these stairs, but you just did it on your own. I started to show you how to fight with just your own two fists before any of this even happened. You're relying on him and relying on your powers too much, creating a huge blind spot for yourself. He's even *taught* you how to burn yourself out so it'll happen. How much more evidence do you need?

"If he hadn't shown you that, when you panic you wouldn't rely on something so stupid. You'd get resourceful and pull through like I taught you. If he cared about you like you think he does, he'd be going over every way to cover your weaknesses, not create new ones."

"God, I hate you sometimes." It was getting harder to breathe through the pain pulsing, pounding, and stabbing through every fiber of my body. "Why won't you just drop it and leave me alone?"

"Because I'm not your shadow that keeps holding you back by your ankles. I'm that thorn in your side that keeps you moving forward so that maybe someday you'll be able to play *with* the big boys, like I know you can, instead of being played *by* them." He poked me in the ribs as I passed him, and then he vanished. I almost collapsed, but when I looked ahead, there were no more steps left to the mess   hall.

Chapter Twenty-Two

For someone who was drunk and high on experimental drugs more times than not, Owen could make some great crepes. After having my fill of the leftovers, I went back to rejoin the meeting. The main screen on the far wall was turned on and was showing a video from the detached jail outside.

The metal chamber had been transformed into a throne room of flesh. Discerning the point at which the body of the Ancient was fused with the organic décor was no easy task. Calcified structures resembling bone hung from the ceiling by stretchy ligaments that meshed together to brace the mound where the gaunt figure of the Ancient sat. The tissue covering the walls pulsed with the rhythm of a heartbeat, and a network of gigantic blood vessels traversing the room fed into the living corpse. Where this blood was coming from, I preferred not to know.

The Ancient had altered its appearance once more; there was now a dramatic crest extending from its cranium. It sat crouched, licking the air with its slimy barbed tongue. Elongated arms and legs crossed from its seat, each appendage ending in gruesome claws that clicked together like an impatient pair of scissors.

Its bloodshot eyes changed in the deep recesses of their sockets to impersonate my all black and gray variant when they locked on to me. The emaciated flaps of skin hanging from its sunken chest shriveled into its body as it slowly morphed into a sickly mockery of my image, at least from the torso up.

Gianni barked something in Latin at the screen, and the Ancient let my face melt from its visage and on to the floor, where it was reabsorbed. The rest of the group remained quiet and barely looked at me, but Gianni stood to pull out a chair next to him so I could sit.

"How can it can see us?" I asked. "It can't get out, right?"

"It's secure. We set up a two-way live video feed with audio so we can communicate," said Rudgar.

"Does this thing have a name?" I watched as it continuously metamorphosed itself like a kaleidoscope of meat. The eyes were somewhat human, but what I was looking at certainly was not and had not been in many years at least.

"Who cares what you call it?" Owen put out his cigarette on the table and lit another one. "'Nasty bugger' sums it up quite nicely."

"My kin address me as The Old One of Boundless Flesh," the Ancient spoke with a harsh, almost hissing rasp through the screen and occasionally punctuated its dialogue with inhuman shrieks. "But Vyrlakalos is the name spoken by mortals to express their fear of my malleable anatomy."

"More like disgust. Why does everyone have 'One' in their name?" I asked, directing my question away from the screen. "The Blighted One, The Dark One, and now this thing ..."

"It's an honorific title that older and more powerful supernaturals use to distinguish themselves from others who may have similar but weaker abilities or feats under their belts," Rudgar explained. I was embarrassed that a human knew that and I didn't.

"Dorian Benoit, I have read your file," said the Ancient.

"Everyone's read that file but me," I said.

"Allow me to share an excerpt for you then: *Deemed mentally and emotionally unstable. Frequent hallucinations and stress disorder. A potential threat to himself and others. Must be removed from the general populace. I assign myself sole handler once in our custody. So signed, Lieutenant Lyle Turner.*"

I glared across the table at Lyle, who couldn't look back at me.

"Handler? Unstable?" I raised my voice. "Is that true? That's why you were so invested in looking for me? To remove me from the general populace?"

"Of course not," Rudgar answered. "Let's move on."

"Yes. It is," said Lyle. "I'm not going to cover it up, but it isn't what it sounds like. This was before we found you. You were running around all over the map. The last time we spoke we had an argument. You weren't in a good place ... you had no direction. You're different now. I wanted to find you to keep you out of trouble."

"Whatever. It's because I *am* different that I'm not gonna let that get to me." I was still so angry that I couldn't look at him, so I turned back to the screen.

"Your crimes against my kin pale in comparison to The Dark One at your wing, and yet he guides you all in blindness." The Ancient's words elicited an angered response in Latin from Gianni.

"In English, please," Rudgar requested.

"He threatens my tongue," it explained. "But I fear no darkness, and I cannot be contained. What you see before you is a mere piece of my complete being. I am omnipresent and exist in many locations at all times. Even from a single cell where I lie dormant, I can be reborn upon feeding from the sweet, satiating flesh of my victims.

"The Dark One is where your concerns should be placed for now, however. He was known by another name in our time. He is a murderer of millions ... a true slayer of man. My people's greatest efforts combined only resulted in a fraction of the great Gaius Belisarius' campaign against the innocent souls of Europe, the Middle East, and Africa. His power even felled the Old Gods before turning on his own creators."

"It's lying, right?" Lyle asked. "This is just to get us to turn on each other."

"It isn't true." I lied to cover for Gianni. This was nobody's business and not who he was now.

"No, Dorian. It is okay. I do not hide my past. There is truth, but it was not my control. The men who gave me this power trick me to do the crimes," Gianni explained.

"How do you trick someone into killing millions of innocent people?" Rudgar asked.

"None of this matters, okay? We're not on trial here," I said in Gianni's defense.

"So he gets away with genocide, but I hunt a few werewolves nobody's ever going to miss, and I'm treated like a bloody criminal?" asked Owen.

"He's *changed!* What don't you get about that?" I argued. "It's been a couple thousand years. What do you want to do about it? Slap handcuffs on him and throw him in jail? Or did you forget he just picked it up out of the ocean and threw it to shore like a tin can?"

"Calm down, Dorian. We're not doing anything," Lyle said.

"Thanks, Lieutenant. Don't worry, I don't have my powers back. I'm not a threat to anyone."

"Enough!" Gianni slammed his fist on the table and made the room shake. "We are friends here. Everyone does bad things, but if we change, that is what is important. Even you." He pointed to the screen.

"Why don't you tell us why you had such a grudge against these blokes, whatever your name is?" Owen asked the Ancient.

"I was gathering information. With a taste of an organism's DNA, I can replicate their form to perfection or meld with pieces of the original to keep alive through the power of my blood. To feast upon the brain, however, I am able to integrate all knowledge and memories for myself. After more than three thousand years, my intelligence is limitless and my plans without flaw.

"The other Ancients are blind and arrogant. They ignore their senses and logic, which they instead trade for apathy and indulge in ignorance. They may fall, but I will grow, adapt, and survive. Death is limited and easy to master even for the most basic creatures. Life is the ultimate machine, and I seek to conquer its splendor for my own."

An undead that values life and an articulate Carpathian all in one. I'm not sure which is stranger.

"So you were going after Rebecca because she's got the smartest brain here?" Lyle asked. I forgot she was even in the room. She had been sitting so quietly through the whole discussion.

"No. I was hunting members of Gestalt for information on their Infernal master. I am able to break down my body into microbes to travel undetected on, or in, others. I let you think me defeated in the laboratory so you would bring me back without raised awareness.

"The PARAGON unit was unable to detect such small traces and allowed me to infect and *become* the other members of your army. Once I gained the knowledge to take control of the PARAGON unit, I learned you had a member of Gestalt here for me."

That explained the cold shoulder from everyone when I thought they were acting weird around me.

"Rebecca isn't in Gestalt." Lyle put his arm over the back of her chair in a show of support. "They wanted her to join, but she came to us instead."

"Oh?" It laughed. "Your loyalty to an attractive façade betrays the facts ... as expected from a human."

The Ancient changed once more. Its tongue slithered back down its throat, and the crest of bone retreated into its skull where wavy locks of brunette hair unfurled. Eyelids with lush lashes rolled down from their sockets to veil crystal blue eyes. The skeletal body came to life with plump, perky breasts under milky white skin, and its claws retracted into dainty fingers tipped with red fingernails. A rosy blush filled its cheeks, and its voluptuous lips shifted color before settling on a healthy pink. It flashed a playful smile of pristine ivory teeth and waved at the camera.

"Not bad," Owen nodded. "I'd stay that way if I were you."

"The piddling opinions of mortals are as immaterial to me as an insect's judgment to the sun." The Carpathian continued in a more sultry female voice, "My ever-changing flesh you gaze upon is a resplendence inconceivable by many of even my so-called peers. I evolve ... I endure. Traits meant for creatures of life to adapt to the hardships of generations past I achieve in mere moments. I do not stagnate and wait for death, I do not hide and hope for salvation, I do not pause at others' trite criticisms, and I do not make mistakes, human.

"The one known as Rebecca Sullivan is a registered neurosurgeon for Gestalt Industries. She is the one responsible for developing the neurofeedback loop for their current security system ... the same technology used in your lighting to alter your meager brain functions."

"It's not the same Rebecca Sullivan. There have to be thousands in the world with the same name," Lyle argued.

"It is me," Rebecca said. Lyle turned to her, looking like he had been shot in the heart.

"This is bloody brilliant!" Owen laughed and lit another cigarette. "I'm not looking so bad now compared to all these wankers, am I? Cheers to that. I'm a bloody saint!"

"Shut up, Blackbourne," Lyle yelled. "Rebecca, why? How?"

"Stop overreacting, Turner," said the commander. "It isn't what you think."

"You knew about this?" Lyle asked.

"It's complicated and not relevant right now."

"Like hell it isn't!" Lyle shouted. "You knew about the security system? You *invented* it? My team died because of you, and I was blamed for it! How could you even go to their service when you were the one who caused their deaths on purpose?"

"Sit down, Lieutenant," Rudgar ordered. "She was following orders to supply us with vital information. The mission almost failed because you made mistakes. That didn't change. It was the perfect plan on paper."

"On paper? They're *people*," I said. "Some of those people died. They weren't just names to cross off a roster. They were parents, sons, daughters, lovers. How was the mission 'almost' a failure? Whether we got the information or not, it was still a failure losing them because *you* two wanted to keep secrets and play spy games."

"Dr. Sullivan is, and always was, a double agent. She joined PROJECT: UNITY long before her official record shows because her time was spent with Gestalt in the beginning. We knew Gestalt wouldn't turn her away after she witnessed their experimental drug on the review panel. It was an invaluable opportunity we couldn't pass up and couldn't risk exposing when others had already defected to enemy lines."

"Gestalt Industries binds personnel in contract with their Infernal master," Vyrlakalos said. "An invisible deal with the Devil obfuscated among the mundane paperwork. Once they join, their soul belongs to Hell, and they work only to fulfill a singular purpose: to create an avatar capable of hunting down my fellow Ancient Ones and become a vessel for the demon waiting on the other side of the Gates of Hell. Tell me, how did you break this contact?"

"It never took effect on her for a reason we've yet to discover," Rudgar answered. "All I can guess is that it was the mother of all clerical errors in our favor."

"I'm sorry—" Rebecca said.

"Bullshit!" Lyle kicked his chair into the wall and stormed out. I almost felt bad enough to forget about his little report on me being an unstable basket case.

"Ace meeting," said Owen. "The world feels safer already. At least I'll know a few blokes when I go to Hell."

"I *never* meant for it to come to this," Rebecca said. "The last thing I wanted was for any of our team to die. The PARAGON transmitter they were given to set up on the roof should've also jammed the security signal. It was the same frequency we used for the earpieces later. I checked it myself."

"Let it go, love," Owen told her. "You did what you had to. No one here's innocent. It's a dirty game. That's all there is to it. If you didn't do what you did, someone else would've. So you lied about your previous employment. Women lie all the time about their past. Like that nurse I had a go with when I was blind. I'm pretty sure that wasn't her first time."

"Emotions are unimportant. You are all unnecessary bags of flesh, yet your technology amuses me. I have consumed the minds of those responsible for its design, but I could make use of capable drones to further satiate my undying hunger." Vyrlakalos leaned forward, and the skin on its back bubbled and split open to molt the beautiful outer layer. The heinous alien figure from before crawled back out, shedding the once-attractive remains, which melted into sludge at the base of the throne.

Dr. Sullivan walked out troubled and with her head down. I didn't want to be there anymore than she did. PROJECT: UNITY may have been ruined after all. Shiny gadgets weren't worth a damn without anyone to use them, and a team wasn't a team without trust.

"Hell wants my body now too, eh?" Owen asked, taking a drag from his cigarette and pausing. "They're already getting my soul when I die, but only when I say I'm ready."

"Yeah, welcome to the club," I told him.

"The hunter becomes the hunted," Rudgar said. "Maybe it's time you got a taste of your own medicine to see how it feels, Blackbourne."

"I've rather lost my appetite for the sport as of late anyway."

"Your carcass will serve as suitable bait," Vyrlakalos said. "I will inject a flesh-eating neurotoxin before your possession to render the body infirm. After it begins to decompose with the Infernal host trapped inside, the Dark One will transport the body through the shadows to Hell, where it will be destroyed. A demon can only be vanquished in its own realm, but in its true form will be far too powerful for any force on Earth to defeat."

"I cannot go to Hell," said Gianni. "To go from the shadow I need to be there before or have a path I can see. The dark there is different."

"Then we will go to where one of the Gates of Hell have been opened on Earth. Gestalt Industries has locations not on any map where Hell's influence is strongest. Those nearby have been corrupted to spread chaos and weaken humanity's resolve, making them easier to goad into self-destruction."

"I'm missing the part where I survive as the dashing hero to be showered with wine and women," Owen said.

"You don't."

"Brilliant. Just when I was thinking of turning over a new leaf."

Chapter Twenty-Three

The meeting adjourned on a grim note, and everyone went their separate way, except for Gianni, who stayed with me out in the hall.

"I don't like this plan," I told him as I limped toward the atrium. The painkillers were still working, so the pain wasn't as bad as it could have been. "We just keep sacrificing people, and it isn't solving anything."

"I know. I do not like the plan too," he said. "Do you want a rest? I will take you to the room."

"I want to find Lyle first. I have a pretty good idea where he is."

"Where? I will take you."

"No, I'm okay, Gianni, thanks. You can walk *with* me though. I'm not feeling too bad right now, but knowing you're there to help is enough. I feel like I've lost all control over life at the moment, and I want to take back what I can."

Noah's warning had stuck in my head. I still didn't believe Gianni was doing this for sinister purposes, but suppose I got my immortality back and we were together for a long time? Was it really right for me to be taking advantage of his strength and chivalry and becoming completely dependent on him? At some point, it had to wear thin. The last thing I wanted was for him to resent me and for me to regret it.

Gianni gave me a thoughtful look and then agreed. We walked to the bar, and as expected, Lyle sat drowning his sorrows with rum and cola while watching TV.

"If you're here to give me shit, save it," he said as I took a seat next to him.

"Just tell me why you wrote that stuff about me so we can move on," I told him.

"Because at the time I thought there were no secrets among the team. Rudgar wanted a full background on you. We have one for everybody. It's not like I made any of it up. It was for the sake of honesty, not spite. I just wanted the team to know who they were dealing with and know they were meeting a person … a person who's been to hell and back—not a target or a monster. I figured that was something you'd appreciate."

"Fair enough. I'm over it." Everyone was dead anyway, except Rudgar and Rebecca, whose opinions meant little to me, and deep down, I knew Lyle hadn't meant to be hurtful. "We need to come up with a better plan, so stop drinking. They want to sacrifice Owen as bait to lure out whatever demon was in charge at Gestalt and then kill him with the demon possessing him. You might not like the Blackbournes, but I think you can value the lesson we just learned about needless sacrifices. It's a quick fix that's bound to backfire, and honestly, I don't feel like taking orders from a Carpathian."

"Remember, we cannot let the demon get the Ancient, or it will be more stronger," Gianni added. "For now, the Ancient is not the enemy."

"I should've stayed in the NYPD." Lyle threw his glass behind the bar.

"Camo isn't really your color anyway," I said.

"We don't wear camo. There's nothing I wouldn't give right now to be one of the boys in blue again, though."

"It was an expression, Lyle. Why couldn't you be a fun drunk?"

"I'm not drunk yet, and you're right. I don't like Blackbourne, but I don't want his blood on my hands either. You got any ideas?"

"No, but as long as we have Gianni around, Vyrlakalos won't be a threat. We just have to keep it from getting to Owen so it doesn't go ahead with its plan."

"The Ancient will be no danger," Gianni said. "But I do not think we go to do this so soon. If I cannot see the dark there, the demon will be very powerful. We need the information first and make a good plan. Be patient; this will be a long war, not one battle."

"Turn on the news." Owen came running in with Rebecca. Lyle didn't make an effort to face either of them and handed me the remote instead.

"We're reporting live from Gestalt Industries' biomedical division in Omaha, Nebraska, where authorities have been recovering charred bodies from an underground laboratory. The victims are believed to all be personnel, and so far, there are no known survivors. It's too early to tell if this is the result of criminal activity or a horrible lab accident, but a full investigation is in progress. This comes in the wake of Gestalt Industries' elusive board of directors filing for bankruptcy earlier this morning." The reporter stopped to grab a passing emergency responder for a statement. "Excuse me. Can you give us any insight into what may have caused the fire?"

The worker walked right by the reporter in a daze, and so did several others whom she tried to wave over for an interview. In the background, all the officials were packing up and leaving, but no one was saying anything, and several bodies had been left unattended on the ground.

"It looks like everyone is still in shock here from the tragedy inside one of the world's most beloved companies—"

A fleet of emergency vehicles whizzed passed the camera. I cringed as the reporter barely stepped out of the way, but her luck ended there. With a loud thud, a speeding ambulance hit her head on, sending her body into the air, only for it to land hard, splattering blood. The cameraman dropped the camera, and the report went back to the horrified news anchors in the studio, who couldn't bring themselves to comment.

"What ... the—?" Lyle gasped. Something about seeing that on TV and knowing it was live was even more jarring than dealing with monsters in person. Owen took the remote and changed to another news station, where similar events were happening around the world at other Gestalt labs.

"Look at this!" Owen exclaimed. "It's a bloody mess. I thought Gestalt was done for? It's spreading!"

The TV broadcast cut out and was replaced by the video feed from Vyrlakalos's makeshift throne room. Somehow, it had managed to hack into the systems again.

"Your actions seem to have set things in motion prematurely," it hissed. "Dimensional portals to Hell have begun to open at several locations. Gestalt Industries was a curtain ... a ruse to keep out prying eyes. But it also served to contain their side of things. Revealing them to the human authorities only peeled back the layers and antagonized the real threat that lies buried deep inside."

Owen turned off the TV.

"Chaos ... it is like a prayer for a god. It feed the demons," Gianni said. "I have talks with the Great Dragon of the East. We worry this will come so soon. Now all this chaos will make them strong when it spread."

"Hell isn't being too subtle anymore about their plans," I said. "It won't take long for the public to relate it to the supernatural, and then things are really going to go off the rails."

That was what I was really afraid of. Humanity was historically poor at accepting things that were different, hence the whole reason supernaturals hid in the first place. I had felt bolder about the subject in the past, but now my determination was shaky. We would be fighting a war on two fronts and always having to watch our backs. This all seemed a bit too surreal. I had been told about it happening for a while, yet now that it was here, it didn't feel real.

"This is Rudgar's fault," said Lyle as he headed out of the bar. "He's the leader. Let's see *him* take some responsibility and come up with another secret plan."

"Rudgar deserves all the criticism he has coming to him, but we also need all the help we can get, so let's not start a big fight," I told Lyle and limped after him. Lyle, filled with liquid courage, didn't cave to reason. Gianni snatched me through the shadows and took me to the command floor.

"Oh, not here." Gianni entered the commander's office ahead of me. Inside, the news was on. I peeked into the room past Gianni.

"Rudgar!" Lyle shouted as he came marching down the hall. He stopped when he saw me at Rudgar's desk reading the computer screen. "Where is he?"

"I don't know," I said and started to recite a message he'd left for us. "I realize now that I am not the leader I thought I was. My every effort to improve supernatural–human relations and prevent the spread of chaos has failed. I swore that the day I am unable to act in the best interest of peace I would step down, and today is that day.

"I can't lead a team that doesn't trust where the orders are coming from. I see now that my plan to use double agents and keep secrets from my own men was doomed to fail from the start. This is a war of passion, not cold and calculated risks.

"I've left to follow up on a lead from long ago and hopefully find answers to the many questions I have on how I can better serve our cause. I will be off the grid from PARAGON and place this base, and my trust, in Lt. Turner—a man much more capable of thinking and leading with his heart than I. Before my departure, I activated the distress signal to call all field members back to base, including those from the old base and our satellite bases, for additional manpower. Good luck." The message ended there.

"That son of a bitch left us," I said in shock.

"The weak monarch has fled," Vyrlakalos came over the backdrop screen in the office. "Another must take the crown."

"That sounded too emotional to be the Rudgar I know. Did you have anything to do with this?" Lyle asked.

"No. I would have consumed him to feed my hunger if I knew he was no longer of use. He has taken one of the aircraft and headed in the direction of the Northern British Isles before disconnecting from the PARAGON unit."

"How are you still controlling the technology here?" I asked. "I thought you gave up all the implants."

"I have replicated the modified bacteria's genetic code of the implants and assimilated it into my being."

Lyle shut the backdrop screen as Owen and Rebecca came in.

"Rudgar bailed," I said and turned the computer screen with his message on it so they could read for themselves.

"It does not change what we must do," Gianni said.

"And what exactly is that, mate?" Owen asked. "Just so we're all on the same page: I'm not in favor of being a sacrifice."

"We're not sacrificing anyone," I said. "Can we all agree on that? No one else needs to die. We've lost enough already."

Rebecca nodded and started releasing a flood of apologies that became more and more incomprehensible as she broke down.

"It isn't your fault." Owen, showing a surprising level of compassion, placed his hand on her shoulder. "You were doing your job."

"You know, something's been bothering me about that," I said. "Rebecca said that the PARAGON transmitter they gave Lyle to set up on the roof of the first building should've jammed the security signal. It was the same frequency as the earpieces we used later to protect us, so it wasn't like Gestalt had changed the frequency. I remember seeing Lyle stick it to the wall by the door we entered, so someone had to have removed it after, but there was no one else around, unless they came in behind us without us noticing ..."

Then it hit me. Noah snuck in after us. Did that big idiot have something to do with this?

"What is it?" Lyle asked. "You think we were being watched from the start?"

"Maybe, but I guess there's no point in beating a dead horse." I didn't want the whole group to jump on him just yet ... not until I had the chance to confront him first. "Sorry, let's just worry about moving forward. I think I have a plan. There's someone missing from this team we could use."

"Hi, Vance," I greeted the last remaining member of the Strigoi responsible for my creation. "I have a problem I need some help with."

I'll never forget Vance's fervent ranting when we first met. He went on and on about Heaven and Hell battling it out on Earth. At the time, I'd thought he was a lunatic and that nothing like that would ever happen, but now it seemed a lot closer to becoming reality.

"I've long since paid my dues for granting you the burden of life," he said with one eye on Gianni while speaking to me. "When will you ever leave me alone to my studies? If this is about your immortality, I have no way of repeating the process. You'll just have to wait it out, assuming it comes back at all."

Dressed in arcane vestments adorned with the runic symbols of his coven, Vance's ornate garb didn't blend in well with his new lair. The Strigoi were scavengers of sorts. They took whatever they could find in terms of sanctuary, usually somewhere underground that they could continue to toil away even in the daytime.

This new residence was underground all right—in an abandoned maintenance area of the sewers under Ghent, Belgium. A fine coating of what smelled like excrement lining the stone walls must have dried there after flood waters had evaporated. I wasn't sure how many rooms there could possibly be, but the one we were in was smaller than my room back on base at PROJECT: UNITY and had a single incandescent bulb flickering overhead.

"This isn't about my immortality," I told him. Standing in the corner shadows was his protégé, Heather. She was an equally somber figure, even for one with the body of a young twenty-something-year-old.

"Do you ever blink?" I asked her. "You're kinda freaking me out."

She just stood there, holding a tome and staring at us without moving. She already looked enough like a corpse, as all the Strigoi did; the least she could do was move. I didn't get an answer, though. She turned and left through a door, closing it behind her.

Vance was fidgeting with a four-legged clockwork machine on the floor. There was a human heart encased in glass at its center that looked like it was supposed to be used to power the contraption. Not to pat myself on the back, but this was a far cry from the success he'd had when creating me.

"This is pathetic, Vance. I'm gonna keep this short as usual. Your new place sucks. I have somewhere you can tinker your undead heart out in exchange for your help. It's huge and as remote as you can get with only three humans, Gianni here, and me. There are tons of resources and technology you can fiddle with ... no questions asked. Whatever your twisted mind can come up with."

"What is this about?" he asked. "I'm very busy."

"Since we met, you've just fallen further and further from grace. I'm not going to threaten you, but I know all your little experiments have roots in your survival. Gates of Hell are opening around the world like the legend you told me when we first met. We need a way to seal them. There's got to be some magic you can use like the seal in Yomi against the spirits."

"Dealing with Infernals is strictly forbidden by the council," Vance stated.

"No deal," Gianni said. "We want to stop the demons. Can you do this?"

"Even if I agreed, my magic isn't anywhere near capable of something like what you're asking."

"Then who?" Gianni asked.

"I couldn't imagine. Hell is on a level of its own."

"That answer isn't gonna fly," I said. "You're banking on this piece of crap protecting you?" I pointed to the miserable machine he was working on. "We're all in trouble here. You're being given a free pass and all the help we can provide. You must have felt this coming. You are just as unprepared as we are, but maybe together we can work something out."

"Yes, I have noticed. I suppose it would be in my best interest, but I fear there is little any of us can do. I'll journey with you to this safe haven of yours if only to scout for supplies."

"Good enough for me."

"I'll inform Heather to return to the council in Munich. I'm sure they have begun plans of their own."

"Why didn't you go to them in the first place?" I asked.

"I'm not in the best standing with the coven after the disgrace brought to my family name by Minerva." Disgrace might be downplaying it a bit. Minerva was Vance's aunt and a demon worshiper that nearly triggered an apocalypse. She manipulated her fellow Strigoi into creating vessels for her demonic master—much like Gestalt was trying to accomplish now. Her plan failed and many Strigoi were killed as a result. "Heather is the only one left after our last arcanum was exposed thanks to Noah's meddling with the spirits from the Far East. Coven members believe my presence to be too high risk and disruptive."

"I thought you were an Archmage?"

"Hardly more than a ceremonial title given to any head of an arcanum. It holds little weight when this closet is your arcanum." Vance sighed.

"What is with the undead and their pointless titles?"

Gianni brought us back to base. Traveling through the shadows wasn't a seamless transition like it had been in the past. Unable to go without breathing while I was mortal meant we had to take short "jumps" from shadow to shadow across the continent, leaving me feeling jarred and jetlagged.

I introduced Vance to Rebecca and Owen, who were sitting together on a bench in the atrium. Owen was more preoccupied with "consoling" Rebecca, even though she looked like she was miles away in her own mind. One arm was around her and the other hand was planted firmly on her leg.

"You aren't afraid of me?" Vance asked with a level of cautious disbelief.

"Who the hell over the age of five is gonna be scared of a glorified librarian?" Noah dropped in, quite literally, from the floor above and purposely almost landed on Vance.

"Of course you would be here too," Vance said. "Most humans are skittish creatures is why I asked. That's all."

"You!" I shouted at Noah in anger.

"Yes, me." He looked confused by my outburst.

"Why you are still here?" Gianni asked Noah. He was as tense as I'd seen him since their last encounter.

"To teach you 'the English'," Noah mocked.

"I learn three languages. And you?" I could tell by Gianni's tone and body language that he didn't appreciate Noah's jab. His shoulders stretched back, his eyes narrowed, and his body turned to the side, as if giving Noah only half his attention.

"Nine." Noah smirked. "Fluently. And none of them are obsolete. There's a new word for you: obsolete ... like someone who sleeps for two thousand years because they're too much of a pussy—"

"Noah!" I had to stop him before Gianni sent him into outer space or worse. After I was sure that he was the one who disabled the security transmitter on Gestalt's roof, Gianni could do whatever he wanted to him.

"What? He started it."

"You and I have to talk," I said, leaving the room to be as far out of earshot as possible before the yelling started.

"Something bothering you?" Noah appeared ahead of me on one of the benches out in the hall.

"You took off that transmitter on the roof of the first Gestalt building, didn't you?" I asked, stabbing the air in his direction with my finger.

"Sounds like you already know the answer, so why are you asking?" His voice was low, and he wouldn't look at me.

"Goddamnit! Why? Why would you sabotage us like that? What was the point of putting us through that nightmare? And don't give me any of your *sensei* bullshit."

"I was only trying to mess around with soldier boy and his little posse. I didn't know what that thing was for. I thought it was so they could talk to their computer or something. Come on. I know you don't take them any more seriously than I do."

"People died! I got *dissected!*" I yelled and tried not to show weakness at the painful memory for him to criticize. "I had your back when everyone told me you were a bad influence and only brought trouble, but all you've ever done is make me look like a fool for believing in you. Do you really not care about anybody but yourself?"

"I didn't know any of that was going to happen or I wouldn't have done it, all right?" he yelled back, only looking me in the eye for a brief moment. "It was a mistake, okay? I admit it. I made a mistake. I fixed it though, didn't I? I went back to save your ass. If I didn't care, I wouldn't have bothered, and I wouldn't have left my blood behind with that doctor in case you needed it." Noah vanished without another word, leaving me feeling no better after hearing the truth.

"Okay?" Gianni asked me back in the lab after I had collected myself. Even if he had been listening in on the conversation through the shadows, he wouldn't have understood most of it anyway.

"Yeah, I'm good. Have any of you seen Lyle?"

"He told us to go screw ourselves before you blokes came back, so I was trying to follow through on that until you interrupted."

"He's at the bar," Rebecca said after giving Owen a look of repulsion and removing his hand from her leg. It was starting to feel like I was running a daycare of delinquents—a job I certainly never asked for and was not quite sure how I'd fallen into.

"Rebecca, why don't you set Vance up with somewhere he can conduct his research? Maybe you two and, uh, Vyrlakalos, can think up something."

"Vyrlakalos?" Vance questioned. "You said there would be three humans."

"Carpathian Ancient we gave room and board to outside in the doghouse," I said.

"You're ... you're jesting, right?" Vance, who had just asked the humans if they were afraid of him, was now quaking in his own boots.

"Nope, unfortunately not. It's smarter than most Carpathians. I'd say it wasn't a threat, but this base used to be packed until it ate the former residents. It's in another area and communicates through the screens around the base. We're all in this together, for now, so we just have to make the best of it."

"You're all mad!" Vance ranted. "I want no part of this. Take me back to my sewer, and I'll wait out the last of my days there."

"It'll be fine," I assured him with false confidence. "Gianni is here to protect us, so it won't start anything."

"You can have the R&D lab," Rebecca told Vance. "I understand from your file that you're talented in the occult. I've always considered science and magic to go hand in hand. Science is just our answer, as humans, to what we don't understand about the supernatural."

"What file?" Vance asked. Gianni and I left them to talk so we could find Lyle and fill him in.

"I need to slow down," I told Gianni outside the bar. I was feeling light-headed, and my painkillers had worn off. The energy I had put into confronting Noah wasn't helping me feel any better either.

"You are doing too much. You did not rest for a long time—" Gianni's voice was fading in and out of my head. I missed the edge of a bench I tried to sit on, but Gianni grabbed me.

"No, I just need to talk to Lyle. Then I'll lie down. I'm the only one he'll listen to right now."

"He will listen to me. Sometime it is good to hear the advice from one you do not know." Gianni brought me to our room and put me in bed. "Promise to stay here."

I was torn and frustrated to the point of anger between conceding defeat to my injuries or pushing myself more than my body could handle just so I wouldn't have to depend on anyone. My body, and Gianni, were deciding for me, and that made it worse. I wanted to be in control of my decisions. My power—telekinesis—was based on controlling things, and I didn't even have that anymore.

"Tell Lyle to ... stop drinking." Sleep was starting to take me the moment my head touched the pillow, but I had to get everything out. "And ask Owen to give them the money to fix the base ... Oh, and make sure Vance doesn't run away. He's sneaky like that ... And don't fight with Noah. You just gotta ... ignore ... him. Don't let Vyrlakalos ... eat me."

Chapter Twenty-Four

The room was dark when I woke, nestled under the covers. There was work to be done, but, first, I needed to remember what was going on. I was still a bit groggy, but from what I could tell, my body was feeling much better. The shooting pain in my ribs had dwindled enough that I could lie comfortably at least.

When I reached my arm back, there was a tug. I panicked, thinking something was grabbing me in the dark, and I had visions of Vyrlakalos being under my bed, until I realized it was a tube to an IV.

My body didn't hurt at all. This was amazing. Maybe I should have listened to Gianni in the first place and just rested. I tried to use my powers to retrieve the marble chunk from the desk, but they hadn't returned yet. I thought I saw the marble wobble, but it may have just been my eyes adjusting to the light.

"You look strong." Gianni's voice preceded his entrance into the room through the shadows.

"I'm feeling a lot better," I said as the lights came on.

"You are very brave," he smiled. "I think you can make a good *legatus* or caesar. You are a good leader for your friends. With no powers, you are still very strong. I like this."

"Really? I thought you were trying to keep me weak because you liked being in charge. You always want to do everything for me."

"I protect because I am a man and it is what I like. You know this is not to hurt you. Listen to your heart and not the poison from others. Love is not a competition for who is more strong." I removed the IV and went to wash up in the bathroom while Gianni inspected the IV bag. "*In aqua santias*. In water, there is health."

"It's probably morphine," I explained. "Medicine for the pain."

"Oh? In Roma you go to the baths for healing. I think it feel much better." I was amused at how proud he was of his heritage.

"Did you get to talk to Lyle?" I asked as my memory of the previous night started to come back.

"Yes, little caesar. I go to talk with him now too. He needs many help to lead. Come find us in his room when you are ready."

Gianni left me to finish cleaning up. I removed the bandages around my ribs and unwrapped my eye in the mirror. I was nervous to see what it would look like. I had an image in my mind of it being a gaping hole or split down the middle. My sight was blurred for a short time as I got used to seeing out of it again, but everything was normal. Powers or not, at the moment, I felt invincible.

There was a light tap on the door as I got dressed.

"Oh, you're out of bed!" Rebecca greeted me. She seemed to be in much higher spirits than she had been the previous night. "I came to check up on you. I heard voices but didn't think you'd be up and moving around so soon."

"Yeah, he just left, and I was getting ready to do the same." I let Rebecca in to take back the IV. "I assumed it was you who set this up for me. Thanks. I think my regeneration is back."

"You're welcome. It's really the least I could do to help around here." She forced a smile. "He didn't leave your side for more than a minute, you know."

"Gianluca's really protective like that. I'm sure he spent the whole time worrying."

"Oh," she stopped in the middle of rolling up the IV tube. "No, I meant Noah." I didn't know what to say, and it wasn't like her to crack jokes. "He had all these questions about the morphine like he was scared it would hurt you. I had to reassure him every day that I came back to check on you that it was a low enough dose to not affect your concussion."

"Every day? What are you talking about?"

"You've been out for three days."

"What!? Why would you guys let me sleep that long?"

"You needed time to recuperate, and there wasn't anything you could have done in your condition. We're just getting back on our feet now, so you didn't miss much." Rebecca left, and suddenly, I didn't feel so invincible anymore. I felt useless.

On my way to find Lyle, I noticed a bunch of new faces walking around. The new members passed by in awe of the base and seemed unaware of who I was all over again. This was like the first day of school, with everyone wandering the halls not sure where to find their classrooms.

I spotted Lyle inside a room that wasn't his, and he was packing up belongings into boxes. I knew this wasn't graduation day on the campus. We had to actually deal with the reality of those we had lost, room by room.

"Finally awake, huh?" Lyle welcomed me with a nod. "Good to have you back. It was getting painful watching you gimp around."

"No telekinesis yet for some reason, but I'm healed up. I see we already got help from the other bases. What happened while I was out?"

"Well, don't turn on the news." Lyle sighed. "Several cities where Gestalt had facilities have broken out into bedlam. Riots, school shootings, prison breaks, bombings ... They're calling themselves 'The Congregation,' and witnesses are starting to piece it together. Some people are claiming demonic possession, and you can tell other supernaturals are trying to cover it up, because you never hear from them again or they recant immediately.

"We're screwed if we can't come up with something quick. Panic is spreading like wildfire, and that's only making the demons stronger. There was a video on the Internet that someone took with their cell phone of a man getting shot in the face at pointblank range with a shotgun three times before they put him down. Then he got back up and bit off the shooter's face. The video got three million views in only a few hours before it was taken down. Experts argued it was a hoax or that heavy drug use and bath salts were involved. It's anarchy."

"Bath salts?"

"I don't know, man. The supernaturals are coming up with anything to throw people off. It's just a good thing Gestalt's steroid never made it out to the public, or this would be a hundred times worse."

"But if we're able to close the gates, this all stops right?"

"I hope so. There's no way of knowing for sure. How does a community recover from this, even if we do? I'm having a hard time going through all the stuff to clear out rooms for the new guys. It just feels wrong ... like we're erasing them. This is ... *was* Shaun's room ..."

"I know how hard it is when you don't get a chance to mourn," I said. "Just don't try to block out your feelings no matter how hard they are to deal with. We all need to help each other deal with them together."

"I told him this," Gianni said, upon entering the room in a flash of darkness.

"Yeah, I'm good. Don't worry, no more drinking from me ... for real this time. I've got to act like a commander now."

"You're Commander Turner now?" I asked.

"Co-commander, I guess. Commander Timmons from the other base suggested it since this is my home base and I was next in the chain of command. She only had fourteen people under her in a really low-tech base the size of our hangar. New Zealand was shutting down their operation to join us soon anyway, so it worked out.

"Gianluca's been a real cool guy, talking to me about how to lead while you played Sleeping Beauty."

"Cool guy?" Gianni was puzzled by the expression.

"He means you're a good person," I explained.

"Oh, many thanks. I think you are a cool guy," Gianni returned the compliment to Lyle.

"Are you still not talking with Rebecca?" I asked, not knowing how and when to come clean about Noah's involvement with that first mission.

"We're talking, but I can't trust someone who can keep those kinda secrets like she did without blinking an eye. I understand she was following orders, but it'll never sit right with me. I would've taken a bullet for her too."

"You still would. I know you."

"Yeah, you're right." He sighed. "I'm a sucker; it's who I am. I think she's been warming up to Blackbourne now anyway, so it doesn't matter. He's been playing fetch for her."

"What do you mean?"

"We put his hunting skills to good use like Rudgar had planned. Blackbourne thwarted a bomb threat in Nebraska and brought back The Congregation member responsible for Vance to try and exorcise, but the experiment failed. Doesn't look like they can be saved, but at least it brought down the chaos level in the city, and no one else was hurt. Some cities, like Mesa, haven't been as lucky, and the military has had to interfere to keep the peace. But that's a very temporary solution since most people don't like having tanks in their backyard. I wish we had the manpower to help them all—"

"What is this?" I asked, noticing a medical kit with Gestalt's logo printed all over it in the trash. Inside the kit were empty syringes and small vials of clear liquid. I picked up one of the vials to read the label. "Steroids? Shaun was taking steroids from Gestalt?" Lyle didn't immediately respond and then I put it together. "You were taking them too weren't you?"

"We only did it a few times," Lyle admitted. "It was Shaun's idea when our doctors were researching Gestalt's pharmaceuticals during our investigation before you came. This wasn't the same one that Blackbourne was using and the doctors said it was safe so we gave it a shot."

"Lyle—"

"I know! I know it was stupid. I just wanted an edge so I could be at the top of my game out there. It's hard enough having to be the best on the team so everyone will respect you, but I also had to be good enough to keep up with all the supernaturals too."

The PARAGON terminal in the room came to life with its creepy digital face. I would never get used to that.

"Commander Turner, your presence is requested in Research and Development Lab 4," it announced before deactivating.

"I thought PARAGON was off-line."

"Vyrlakalos restored it to monitor activity related to the demons," Lyle said. PARAGON's screen turned on by itself again.

"Human, I have given you an order. Why do you not do as I command?" It was the same synthesized PARAGON voice, but it was definitely Vyrlakalos on the other end. "Your minor importance is all that keeps you from becoming meat for the slaughter."

"Some people you do not lead," Gianni said to Lyle on our way to R&D. "You show what they want is the same as you, and if you give support, then they will do it with pride. The words they speak are not important. A good leader know what words to not hear. There are many voice in the army, but you only can hear one at a time."

"Good advice, if I don't go crazy first."

"You're in charge now," I told him. "Not that it was run badly before, but Rudgar's military background may have been too closed-minded. He was all about the mission at any cost, even if he had to walk over bodies and work behind backs in secret. You're a cop at heart; you have a lot more compassion for those involved on both ends. Police are meant to defuse situations with the safety of both sides in mind, and the military are brought in to end conflict at pretty much any cost. Rudgar's intentions may have been pure, but I think the more he saw he couldn't proceed how he's used to from the military, the more he had to take risks and make more sacrifices to fill the hole he was sinking into."

"Thinking of it in terms of being back on the force makes me feel so much better," Lyle said, brightening up. "It was so much simpler then, and I was happy. I'm not going to make the same mistakes Rudgar did."

The R&D wing was one very large open area with six smaller individual glass-front labs branching off: three on each side. A floor-to-ceiling flat-screen monitor mounted on the back wall in the middle transmitted video from Vyrlakalos's auxiliary throne room. The main open area was set up with rows of black-topped work stations that contrasted with the white floors, walls, and ceilings, similar to the Medical Ward.

"Please, stop smoking in here," Rebecca was telling Owen as we walked in.

"Can't help it, princess. I'm nervous around this stuff. I have a real sensitive side since Gestalt. I'm a changed man."

"I know. You've told every female transfer you've introduced yourself to."

"I did a little more than just introduce myself to some of the pretty ones," Owen whispered and winked at us as we gathered around.

"Your bedroom wasn't on the orientation, Blackbourne," said Lyle.

"Is that really the extent of your interest in women?" Rebecca asked Owen. "What they look like on the outside? Because I'm starting to regret restoring your vision."

"Of course not, love. I'm an equal opportunist. I'm equally as interested in becoming acquainted with their silky insides." Lyle closed his eyes and took a deep breath. I could tell he wanted to deck Owen but was trying to tune him out like Gianni had advised. "You lads are terrible wingmen," Owen continued. "Micah needs to get his fat arse back over here."

"Where are we at with everything, team?" Lyle asked the room. Vance had isolated himself from the group in one of the labs. It looked like he had his full library of dusty tomes with him. Gianni must have gone back to help him clear it out.

"Vyrlakalos came up with an idea after ... eating the body of the deceased possession victim," Rebecca said.

"A paltry meal to slake my hunger," Vyrlakalos joined the conversation through the screen in its usual manner. "The Strigoi's magic is weak and fallible on its own ... a singularity in need of strength ... a pathogen in need of numbers. The humans have developed technology imprinted in a single cell, and the bacteria is the root of their neural implants.

"Ensorcelling the genetic code to allow self-replication will provide the strength needed. Rewrite the pathogen's code with a spell to banish the host and remove the constraints on growth. The infection will spread and return the Infernal to Hell from the inside out and keep it there."

A Carpathian using disease to combat its enemies ... not the most original scheme on its own, but an ingenious variation on redundancy. This time, I was hoping it would work, though.

"When will it be ready?" Lyle asked.

"The human medical drones must first finish their task. They move slowly, and the limits of their flesh disappoint me. Feed them to me and I shall make better use of their meat."

"We're doing the best we can," Rebecca asserted. Her frustration was almost tangible. "I'm not a genetic engineer, and the staff from New Zealand never worked with this kind of technology." For the sake of using a pun, Vyrlakalos was getting under everyone's skin.

"Come to me and I shall put that brain to better use." The main screen shut, following a ghoulish simper from Vyrlakalos.

"That thing reminds me of a pro at one of my parties," Owen said and lit a cigarette with a

Bunsen burner. "Think she said her name was Priscilla ... or maybe Marissa ... not that it mattered. I was pissed off my arse, of course, and couldn't tell the difference. But the next morning, I swear she turned into some bugger like that. Would've scared me right out of my knickers had I been wearing any. I still think Micah pulled a switch on me for kicks. No other way she could've gotten through our screening process."

"Okay, so ... where are we at with the spell?" Lyle asked. Rebecca motioned to the lab where Vance was hiding.

Vance sat with the lights off, sucking on a pack of blood. He was reading his books by the little light that filtered in through the glass from the main room.

"This Vyrlakalos may be a hyper-intelligent biomass, but it has no comprehension of the occult," Vance spoke softly, and his gaze darted to and from the monitors, hoping not to draw Vyrlakalos's attention. "Before Minerva's betrayal, anything related to Infernals was strictly forbidden. Since then, the council has stated—*encouraged*—that we learn spells to banish them. This is no elementary parlor trick.

"The original undead were created by powerful demons—the Demon Kings of Hell—to use in their war against Heaven thousands of years ago. These original undead are the progenitors of my kind, even preceding the Ancients who founded each of the three covens. But those first undead have long since vanished from this world.

"To give you some perspective, those original undead were hardly more than grunts in Hell's army at the time. The Strigoi have ranked the denizens of Hell based on archaic scriptures as follows: minor, lesser, greater, lord, archdemon, or 'king,' based on the estimated size of their realm and influence on Earth.

"If the original undead were significantly inferior to their masters, I say they would be, at most, as strong as a greater demon. The Ancients today, progeny of those originals, are somewhere near the greater- and lesser-ranked demons on average. Need I remind you that this is all based on conjecture, though, as strength levels fall within a spectrum, not a static tier. There are other factors, such as environment and experience, to account for.

"However, I can be certain that not all of The Congregation are just humans driven mad by the close proximity to Hell's Gate. Some of those running feral in the streets are possessed by minor demons. It is fortunate that the human body cannot be a vessel for any higher-ranked Infernal, for its power is too great."

"So, The Congregation, like that dude who took three shotgun blasts to the face and kept going, was only the weakest level of demon?" Lyle asked.

"At most, yes," Vance said, "as was the one we failed to exorcise. They ramble incoherent messages about a hymn they hear in the darkness driving them to acts of lunacy. Whatever is watching from beyond the Gates of Hell is laying roots here on Earth to help spread its influence.

"We are dealing with a strength beyond our means. Generally, it is said that only an Infernal is powerful enough to defeat another Infernal ... or a Celestial. But now we're getting even further out of the realm of possibility. Nobody has reliably even seen an angel in thousands of years since the last Great War."

"I hear those words in the dark by the gates. The demon inside must be a lord for it to be so powerful I cannot see in its darkness, no?" Gianni questioned. "The Ancient will not work with us if the demon is weak too I think."

"Yes," Vance agreed.

"Do you really think amplifying your spell by having the bacteria repeat it millions of times will work?" Lyle asked.

"There's no way to know for sure, but it's worth a go. You will have to get up close to administer it, but you're going to die sometime anyway."

"Thanks, man. I appreciate the reminder. I'd like a little more confidence going through with the plan, though. I'm not about to sacrifice anybody."

"Gianni, can't you just smash these demons like the ones in Yomi?" I asked. "Or send them all into the dark abyss?"

"Darkness cannot stop darkness. The demons were weak but very many."

"Infernals are masters of inter-dimensional travel," said Vance. "Send them away, and they'll just come back if not properly banished."

"Here are our objectives then," Lyle spoke with authority like a real commander. It took balls to speak with confidence when you were technically at the bottom of the food chain. "Get the banishing spell to Vyrlakalos to enchant the pathogen, figure out a way to weaken the demon just to be sure so it isn't a waste, and find and seal the gate it came from."

"And if we don't, the world is gonna fall into total madness and start the next Great War between Heaven and Hell that reduces the Earth to rubble," I added.

"But how much of that madness is at the hands of our Infernal foes, I wonder," Vance said. "Where is the line drawn between demonic influence and mankind's own inner demons looking for an excuse to lash out? Hatred and chaos, as much as love and order, are part of human nature. I feel this may not be a full invasion but a mere tipping of the scales.

"A match has been struck to ignite the dark side of the soul we all possess. If that is so, then we are all susceptible to the same rage and may be at each other's throats before victory is in sight. It would make more sense for us all to kill each other while the Infernal horde bides their time without any real risk to themselves."

Chapter Twenty-Five

"What's up, little shit?" Noah appeared on the railing of the atrium next to me. Everyone else was busy doing something related to the mission, but without powers, there was nothing I could contribute. Gianni was busy in the Nether Realm, searching for the Gates of Hell; Lyle was rallying and training some of the troops; Vance was scribing the perfect banishment spell; Rebecca was informing the new research and medical staff about the implants; and Owen was busy sexually harassing the rest of the women he hadn't gotten to yet.

"Trying to jump-start my powers. I got my regeneration back but not my telekinesis. I'm going to jump off the railing to try and fly. I figured maybe

I'm subconsciously holding myself back or something."

"Uh, that's not gonna work. You didn't get back anything. I put Vance's blood in your IV while you were asleep."

"Are you kidding me? I thought I was almost back to normal. Why'd you do that?"

"Because *my* blood is poison." He raised an eyebrow.

"Don't think this makes up for anything." I should have been grateful, but I was more disappointed. "I'm surprised Vance was willing to give his blood."

"Depends on what definition of 'willing' we're using." Noah got me to laugh. I didn't know which was scarier: the fact that it was Noah or that my humor was so dark now that I laughed at the thought of him bullying Vance.

"I guess I'm not gonna jump off the railing now that I know I can't regenerate yet."

"Then what was the point of trying to if you knew you had a safety net? A risk isn't a risk if you know you can't fail."

"Because I —" I didn't get to finish. Noah grabbed me by the shirt collar and threw me over the edge, screaming to my death four floors below. In reality, I was less panicked than I should have been. My screams were mostly cursing Noah until I was a few feet from impact and realized my powers weren't going to kick in and save me.

"That brings back memories," Noah said, catching me by the back of my shirt before I hit the ground. People gathered and gawked from the railings. "Nothing makes me nostalgic like throwing you from high places."

I clenched my fists and felt the floor tremble beneath me.

"Hey, it worked." He flashed a cocky smirk and then vanished with a laugh. If reigniting the ember of my power through fury was his plan—and it usually was—it may have been a success.

"This isn't a zoo! Stop staring!" I shouted half-jokingly at the crowd of onlookers, with another tremor that rocked the base.

"What's going on?" Lyle came out from the assembly room with his subordinates craning their necks behind him to see what the commotion was. "Oh, it's you, Dorian. Everything good?"

"Just fine." A moment of anger brought out by Noah led to many of joy. I grabbed a jacket from the barracks and headed outside into the whipping winds. The cold night air smacked me in the face and felt like needles filling my lungs at first breath. My power returned to me with every step. My strides grew bigger. I was running and then vaulting over the ice, further each time, until finally, I was flying again. I could feel it; I was stronger than ever before. A pounding energy surged through my body like an erratic, second heartbeat. I traversed the barren permafrost until I was far enough away from the base to flex my telekinetic muscles without fear of causing any damage or drawing much attention.

With a flick of my wrist, the ice shattered beneath me. I wasn't even trying, and my psionic powers reacted along with my motions. I'd have to be careful until I adjusted to having them again, but for now, it wouldn't hurt to have a little fun.

I flew up high and drew lines in the moonlit ice through telekinetic artistry. I was cracking the ground in larger and larger fault lines several feet deep. If I could hone this to a much smaller scale, there wouldn't be anything I couldn't carve.

Two cracks in the ice met and gave me the idea to see how much I could lift. I spun in the air, creating a near-perfect circle in the ice about a hundred feet across. I lifted it to me; it was nowhere as heavy as I thought it would be.

I sat on my frozen floating island, watching the stars dance around the moon. The power was still building inside me.

"Dorian!" Gianni's voice called from far below.

I peered over the edge, not realizing how high up I was. This was the most I had ever lifted, and yet, it felt so effortless. Over by Vyrlakalos's doghouse were half-eaten whale carcasses covered in some digestive membrane like that which lined the inside of its steel cage.

"Come up here!" I shouted back down to Gianni, who, from that height, was a speck on the shimmering tundra. He rose from my shadow, and I wrote our names together in big letters on the ice.

"Wow, so nice. You are very, very strong. But we go inside, okay?" He was starting to shiver. I set the gigantic ice cube down, and Gianni whisked us away back to our room, where we warmed each other up.

This was probably the last chance we'd have to spend alone like this before our confrontation with Hell.

"Are you tired?" I asked.

"No." His eyes were closed as he pet my hair. It had become a sort of tradition between us anytime we were about to fall asleep. Maybe it soothed him or something.

We stayed quiet. *There must be something worrying him about the mission that he's not saying ... something he found when searching through the shadows.*

"I see the ninja push you to use your powers again. I want it to come from love, not anger," he said.

"Power is power. It's no different than air, electricity, or shadows. It's how you use it."

"I hope this is true and this man—this child—does not change you. I see many men to be poison by hate. I do not want this for you. You are mine, my heart, but he try to take you from me for his games. I am not blind."

"Gianni, are you ... jealous?"

"No. Jealous is for a man with no pride ... too weak to act for himself."

"He just doesn't trust anyone, especially not older, more powerful people. I'm his only friend, but it doesn't mean I'm going anywhere."

"He is a child with no honor, no respect. I do not want blood, but I will fight any who take what is mine. And I will win."

"Nobody's taking anything from anyone," I consoled him. "Why are you so tense? This can't be just about Noah. Is it?"

"I think of the battle ahead."

"You're Gianni. What are you nervous about? You're invincible."

"No man is invincible. I am strong, but I will be a fool if I think I cannot lose. There is more in danger than my life. You are my most big worry, but I know you and the human friends will not stay away."

"I'm more worried about Vyrlakalos turning on us like Rozalin did in Yomi. I already hate the Carpathians to begin with."

Lyle's voice came across the room's PARAGON terminal. "Hey, guys. I need you ... like right now." Gianni transported us to the boardroom, where Lyle was waiting with the others.

"Thanks, guys. Sorry for calling you back again so soon. I hope I didn't wake you or anything," Lyle said to us as Owen sauntered in with a drink in hand and took a seat.

"This is Commander Lisette Timmons," Lyle introduced the dark-skinned woman with a buzz cut and camo gear who was standing next to him at the head of the table. She had that look about her that showed she meant business—something Lyle hadn't yet developed as a leader. "She comes from Nigeria and has been with PROJECT: UNITY at the New Zealand base for six years."

"Ohh, a woman in the army? Very nice." Gianni sounded astonished. I covered his mouth before he could say anything else, and I apologized.

"Sorry, he's ... not from this time period. He missed women's suffrage along with the last two thousand years."

"Very nice, indeed," Owen added and swirled the ice in his glass.

"*He's* just a womanizing misogynist," Rebecca said without looking over to acknowledge Owen leering at her. "He has no excuse."

"Quite the opposite, princess. I love women, and I challenge you to find even one I've been with that wasn't completely satisfied."

"I appreciate the warm welcome," Commander Timmons spoke up. "Where are we with this modified bacterial implant, Dr. Sullivan?"

"We've tweaked the plan from what we discussed with Lyle—"

"It's Commander Turner now," Lyle corrected her. I could feel the suffocating cloud of tension in the room grow thick. We were a mess between all the egos and interpersonal drama. How this group was supposed to pull together to take down a demon was beyond me.

Rebecca was taken aback by Lyle's blunt manner and rushed through her explanation. "Right, yes, Commander Turner. We decided to use a viral instead of a bacterial pathogen. I won't bore you with the details, but the technology was previously unavailable to us until Vyrlakalos acted as a catalyst to allow RNA manipulation in recoding the viral sample. We believe it will be sturdier when infecting a demonic body."

There was total silence in the room until Commander Timmons spoke up again. "Does ... anyone else have anything to add?"

"I had the idea to banish individual cells instead of the body as a whole," Vance said without looking up from a very familiar, grisly tome he was reading. "Previously, we had planned on amplifying a single spell by causing the infection to spread first and then trigger. Instead, the virus will infect a single cell and banish it as it multiplies. We only need a spell strong enough to banish one cell this way."

"Is that the *Grand Grimoire*?" I asked, recognizing where I had seen the unholy tome before. It was given to Vance by Minerva, who received it from her demon master. There was a spell in there that she planned to use so my body could become a vessel for the demon, killing me in the process. It was also the spell book that was used to merge me and the parasite I was infected with to grant me immortality.

"Yes," Vance answered.

"You destroyed it in front of me and Lyle years ago. How did you get it back?" I was furious. The demonic spell book was supposed to have been destroyed because the magic it contained was forbidden with good reason. It was capable of summoning the very demons we were fighting.

"That was a fake so you would leave me alone, but seeing as that never panned out ..."

"What?!" I shouted. My hands shook, and the room quaked along with them.

"I was under the impression I had a 'free pass,' as you put it," said Vance. "How are we to defeat our enemy if we do not know it in the first place? Fight hellfire with hellfire, I say."

"If only a demon can kill a demon, then this just evens the score," Owen said. "I'm using armor made from their skin. What's the big deal?"

"Because that armor can't *summon* them or remove souls or whatever other evil things that book has in it," I argued.

"Look, you know I don't like being lied to either, Dorian," Lyle said. "Let's just ... handle one problem at a time."

"Be calm," Gianni whispered in my ear. "We will take care later."

Commander Timmons was unshaken by all the outbursts, but she glanced around the room as if wondering what she had gotten herself into. "Am I to understand this bioweapon is completed then?" she asked.

"Yes," Rebecca replied. "We've loaded it into a syringe and hollow bullets for Commander Turner's magnetic rifle as backup. There's no need to worry about exposure since the virus is programmed only to trigger the banishment spell once it comes in contact with demonic tissue. The fact that it goes one cell at a time also removes the concern about having to weaken the target's considerable strength first."

"Do we have another plan in case this doesn't work?" Commander Timmons asked.

"Not without sacrifices I'm not willing to make," Lyle said. "We do our best, and if things fall apart, we retreat. No one gets left behind. I'd rather fail and learn from the mistakes than succeed at the cost of teammates. I don't care who you were before this; we're all on the same side now. We're all a team, and that's how I'm treating each of you. I'll die before I leave anybody behind."

"Cheers to that, mate," Owen said and held up his glass.

"Gianluca, did you find where we need to go?" Lyle asked and brought up a map on the table's screens.

"Yes, but … this battle is not for humans. You will all die."

"I'm going. That's not an option," Lyle said. "The more that go, the better the chances are for success."

"Hmm … I see you are a friend of Dorian. Same stubborn head." Gianni sighed. "This is a very dangerous battle. We take only few people so is less to protect."

"My agents won't have the armor or weapons you do without access to the implants yet," Commander Timmons said. "We would only get in the way if Gianluca's information is correct. We can stay outside the perimeter to provide support during extraction, if needed."

"That won't be necessary if we're traveling through the shadows, but it wouldn't hurt to keep a backup method of escape," said Lyle. "So our infiltration team will be myself, Gianluca, Dorian, Vyrlakalos, Owen, and Vance."

"I'll go with the extraction team in case anyone needs immediate medical attention," Rebecca offered.

"I'm a scholar, not a soldier. But that probably means nothing to you," Vance said.

"No, it doesn't," Lyle agreed. "You're Vance, and we need Vance. We need individuals, not soldiers."

"And what of Noah?" Vance questioned. "He is skulking about this facility as we speak."

"Don't worry about him," I said. Similar to Gianni's advice to Lyle earlier, there were some people you couldn't lead but could only share your goals with and let them get there in their own way. Noah was one of those people, but I didn't want him involved in this to cause us more trouble. "Where are we going anyway?" I asked Gianni. He pointed on the map. "Oh good ... Iraq."

"Why don't we just nuke the bloody thing?" Owen asked. "I'm sure there are some for sale on the black market I could get my hands on. It would save us a lot of trouble."

"If you want to talk about spreading chaos and terror across the world, dropping a nuke in Iraq is a sure way to do it," Lyle rebuked. "If the virus *doesn't* work, Dorian can always try to go full meltdown before Gianni evacuates us."

"I'm stronger now," I said. "I might not even need to."

"That'd be awesome," Lyle said. "All right, everyone. Get some rest. We roll out tonight. Meet in the hangar at 10:00 A.M."

Outside the boardroom, some of us lingered to make small talk in the hall. Vance scurried off, but Lyle wanted to more formerly introduce Gianni to Commander Timmons. He figured since Rudgar thought highly of Gianni for his military knowledge, Timmons would too. They did have a great deal to talk about, and after learning about Gianni's background, she was understanding of where he was coming from and that he had not been insulting her when he'd expressed surprise that she was in charge.

I didn't pay much attention to their conversation, though. Owen and Rebecca were having one of their own, which was getting progressively more heated.

"You are such a tough bird to chat up," Owen said, blocking Rebecca's path. "I consider myself a people pleaser, but you're a real challenge. There's got to be something that makes you smile."

"Yes, and it isn't you." She went to move around him, but he blocked her again.

"Why are you so hard on me?" he asked. "You don't even know me."

"I know plenty, and none of it I like. I don't know how much simpler I can make it that I'm not interested in speaking with you," she said. I expected Lyle to come in and say something in her defense, but instead, he wished us good night and left for the barracks.

"Know me how? From some file? People aren't textbooks, love. You can't get to know them from what you've read. Why don't we grab a coffee and chat? I've only been joking around to get a rise out of you because you seem so miserable."

Commander Timmons excused herself from the uncomfortable atmosphere before it got any louder. Gianni put a hand on my arm to take me back to the room, but I wanted to keep listening. He brought us into the shadows, where we watched shrouded from sight.

"Miserable?" Rebecca recoiled. "I've been nothing but polite to you since you've arrived, and all you've done is degrade me and every woman who crosses your path. Life isn't all parties, alcohol, and sex. I'm here to help people, but you wouldn't understand that."

"Oh, I wouldn't? My father beat the piss out of me from the time I was eight years old every time he got plastered. That was every night until I was smart enough to make it out on my own at sixteen. The only man who gave a shit about me and made me who I am died in the same bloody building I was in at Gestalt, and I couldn't do a damn bloody thing about it. Was that in your files?"

Owen was fuming. The wound was still fresh, and as hard as he tried to drown it with booze, it had to come up sometime. I had heard his story before and knew he wasn't as soulless as he may have seemed.

"No … I'm sorry," Rebecca apologized. "I didn't know—"

"Of course you didn't. Because you never gave me a bloody chance. Maybe my humor is a bit off, but I've tried everything I know. I meant what I said back there. I love women, I really do. So, I'm sorry if you fascinate me so much, but I can't help but wonder what goes on inside that pretty little head, because I've never had someone of the fairer sex be so cold before."

"You can't expect to use your money and your looks to open every door for you," Rebecca said. "Say you love women all you want, but you have no idea how to respect them."

"Really now?" Owen's glare was penetrating. "When I was nineteen, I was with my girlfriend, Dawn, for two years before cancer took her from me. Same as my mum … except Mum had lung cancer and Dawn had lymphoma. Prettiest bird on the planet, even in a hospital bed.

"Her parents couldn't afford treatment from the overpriced doctors, so I paid for it all from my winnings in the ring. Up to the very day she died, I carried her in my arms from the limo to the doctor's office for every appointment when she was too weak to walk on her own. I never missed a fight unless it was for her, and my eyes never strayed because I was too busy at her side.

"If you don't believe me, look it up for yourself. The paparazzi had a bloody holiday every chance they got to cash in at our expense. The day she died, I pounded one of their faces in so bad the bloke didn't have one anymore by the time they pulled me off him. Check your records for *that.* I loved her so bloody much that I'm still paying her family's way, even though I can't stand to go see them because they remind me of her."

His hazel eyes burned with a passionate rage I had never seen in anyone before.

"I don't know what to say," Rebecca gasped. "I'm ... so sorry."

"The last thing I want is a judgmental broad's pity," he snapped.

"It isn't pity. I am genuinely sorry for what I've said. But why go around sleeping with everyone like they mean nothing to you but cheap entertainment when you really have a heart?"

"Because it's the only way I know how to make anyone happy when they're around me!" Owen shouted and broke the glass in his hand. Rebecca stood there in as much shock as I was. That was the most emotionally damaged thing I had heard anybody say.

"For just a moment in time, I'm their whole world, and they're smiling because of me," he continued. "There's no sadness, no trouble, and no worries. They feel good, I feel good, and no one is getting hurt. Not once have I *ever* disrespected anyone I've been with. Go ahead and ask them."

Owen walked off, dripping blood from his hand along the way. Rebecca tried to stop him, but he was gone before she could collect herself.

"He is a broken man," Gianni said. "A broken man cannot fight."

"The whole team is broken, not just Owen. Most of us don't trust each other and can't be in the same room without an argument. They came up with a plan fast, but if we can't hold it together to execute it, there's no point. We're kinda declaring war on Hell itself. What happens if we fail?"

Chapter Twenty-Six

Rebecca and Commander Timmons were already waiting with the troops in the dual-propeller helicopter when we arrived at the hangar the next morning. Their uniform was no different from the standard SWAT riot gear. Lyle stood out now as the only one wearing state-of-the-art super-soldier armor. These troops had no idea what we were capable of and gawked at us as I floated next to Gianni. I wouldn't call their stares unfriendly, but it was annoying having to build rapport all over again.

"I hope you guys slept well," Lyle said as we approached.

"Not at all," I answered. Gianni had become mesmerized, watching cooking shows in Italian with me until he'd fallen asleep, but I couldn't close my eyes without feeling anxious about what we were about to face.

"Vance is gone," said Lyle. "Some of PARAGON's surveillance systems are still down for repair, but his lab was cleared out overnight. Blackbourne is missing too. And I'm sure you noticed Vyrlakalos was absent from our meeting and is still unable to be reached."

"How is any of that a problem? That just eliminated the three biggest threats to our success."

"I agree," Gianni said. "We are more strong with few people. Too many emotion is not good in battle."

"I guess," Lyle said, feeling a bit dejected. "I just thought my speech got through to them. I feel like if it was Rudgar giving it, they would've listened."

"Vance played his part, and if we need him again, we'll track him down like always. Owen is better off being left out."

"The Ancient is in the metal box," Gianni informed us. "I can see in the shadows. Wait and I will go there to talk."

"Man ... it's weird not seeing Shaun in the cockpit," Lyle said when Gianni left. "He never liked flying the helicopter as much as the jets, though. He loved those jets."

"Try not to think about it. Keep your head in the game."

"Yeah, yeah I know. I was gonna ask you to hold on to the virus since you don't need to use your hands to fight. We have it onboard in a reinforced briefcase.

"I'm packing serious heat for this. I brought some of everything since we're not sure what surprises they'll throw at us, and I don't wanna get caught with my pants down. Got a grenade launcher attachment for my rifle, EMP grenades to deal with machines, flash grenades, spectral rounds for ghosts, hollow-point silver bullets, cold iron scatter shots, and—"

Someone was groaning between two ATVs in the hangar. Lyle and I headed over to investigate when Owen, dressed in his hunting armor, climbed up, holding on to one of the cars to steady himself.

"Are you okay?" I asked as he pulled out a PROJECT: UNITY canteen, took a swig of something, swished it around his mouth, and then spit it on to the floor.

"Just got to get my buzz back, that's all," he said and held up the canteen. "Martini. Extra dry. Actually, it's just straight gin."

"You're not coming with us drunk, Blackbourne," Lyle said.

"I'm at my best when I'm on the piss. I thought of passing out here so I'd be on time when I woke up, didn't I?"

"Why do you even want to go with us, Owen?" I asked, trying to talk him out of it. "Gestalt is done. You can go back to England and get on with your life."

"I've said it before. I'm already going to Hell sooner or later; I'd rather it be on my terms."

"This isn't a suicide mission," said Lyle.

"Sure it isn't." Owen laughed and boarded the helicopter. "You'll get the money I promised whether I die or not, so what's it matter to you?"

"We don't want your money," Lyle reaffirmed.

"Maybe so, but you *need* it, and it doesn't look like you're in a position to be picking your allies right now, does it? You're on your hands and knees in an alley, and I'm the only john around with a pound to spare.

"I'm willing to settle up on my debt, so if you can put on your big boy trousers and play nice, I'd like to get on with it." He plopped down in a seat next to Rebecca and offered her a sip from the canteen as if their conversation the previous night had never happened.

Gianni rose from my shadow so I was sitting on his shoulders. "We are ready." He nodded to Lyle so they could head out first. "I take Dorian with me."

"Why isn't the rest of the Carpathian coven helping out?" I asked. "If Vyrlakalos is their leader and they were victims of Gestalt's experiments, I'd think they would want in on this."

"She already have an army prepared," Gianni said.

"She?"

We traded cold, hard steel for a sea of warm sand. This wasn't so different from what I'd pictured any other desert—say, in Arizona—to be like. There were dusty rocks, water-starved plants, and a mostly flat, beige landscape with some hills and low mountains in the distance. It was chilly out here at night, but nothing like Greenland. The clear sky wasn't unlike many of the other places I had been. The stars and moon were all there; though they were not in the same position, they were was a reminder that we all looked up at the same universe.

I flew off to take a look around. The metal prison that Gianni transported Vyrlakalos in lay empty nearby. There wasn't a drop of blood or sticky organic residue anywhere, but a series of unusual tracks in the sand all headed in the same direction.

"The dark from here is different." Gianni pointed in the same direction. "My power is not as strong."

We made our way to a campsite wedged in the rocky hillside, where Vyrlakalos's tracks ended, and we waited as the helicopter landed. The only signs of native inhabitants were leftover clothes piled in complete outfits that Vyrlakalos must have shucked the wearers out of like an oyster.

"This has Gestalt written all over it," I said, rummaging through weapon crates and picking up a rocket launcher. "Literally. The hexagon symbol on these is similar to those of their subsidiaries."

"They've been supplying terror cells with weapons for too long," said Lyle as he joined us. "We're only a few miles from the next major city, Mosul, and there are enough weapons here to level most of it overnight. This is exactly what we were afraid of from the start."

Owen was vomiting his liquid breakfast in the sand while the rest of us continued to poke around the camp.

"Blackbourne, go back to the 'copter," Lyle ordered. "You're no good to us like this."

"Sod off. I don't need you telling me what I can do. I've never been better."

"Hmm ... this is a big door," Gianni said, pulling back a camouflage tarp that covered the rocky wall. He was right about that. There was a military-grade blast door in our way ... something used to contain nuclear fallout.

"Think you got the key, Dorian?" Lyle asked. I was about to oblige with the strongest telekinetic force I could muster when Gianni walked up in his full suit of black knight armor and lifted the door with no effort. The mechanism used to move it screeched from the gears being wound the wrong way and breaking apart inside the wall.

"He said *Dorian*," I told Gianni, who just patted me on the head. It was aggravating being dismissed. I knew he didn't want me there, but he could let me do my part. That raging energy from earlier was starting to come back. No matter how many conversations we'd had about this in the past and had come to an agreement, we'd never seemed to make much progress in practice. I was starting to feel that, more than just wanting to be protective, he didn't respect me. I would have to prove to him that I could pull my own weight.

"I thought you couldn't use the darkness in here?" Lyle asked.

"Not for travel," Gianni's voice had a hollow, tinny echo coming from under his helm as he entered the facility. I floated in after him, with Lyle and Owen running beside me as the door slammed down.

Behind us was sand and primitive tents surrounding a campfire, and ahead were hi-tech catacombs straight out of the future. This facility was almost indistinguishable from the others of Gestalt's with its stainless steel walls and unmarked magnetic doors. The structure reeked with a persistent stench of sulfur as if a million matchsticks had all been struck at once. There were no signs of an actual fire anywhere, though. Aside from the smell, a murky gloom snaked through the otherwise well-lit corridors.

"Vyrlakalos is already inside, and the security alarm's been taken care of," Lyle told us after pausing to listen to the radio in his helmet.

Up ahead was a horrid cacophony of hisses and snarls that clashed with gunfire and pained screams. There were no scientists so far—only natives dressed for combat and carrying shotguns, M16s, and AK-47 assault rifles. They were nothing more than thugs doing Hell's bidding. A group of them ran by an intersection, firing madly behind them. One of Vyrlakalos's grotesqueries that had claimed so many of our own scuttled across the ceiling after them.

"I'm so conflicted seeing humans being attacked by monsters and having to be okay with it," I said as the creature pounced on one of the men, undeterred by its body being riddled with bullets. Its tongue sprang out and wrapped around the man's head, pulling it between its jaws to pop like a pimple and then proceeding to suck out the innards.

"Looks like Priscilla is already earning her keep," said Owen.

"You mean Vyrlakalos?" I asked.

"Just keep moving," Lyle said. "We'll let her run interference so we don't get slowed down."

"How is that thing suddenly a 'she' to everybody?"

"She told Gianluca the other day while you were resting," Lyle answered. "At least she used to be a woman when she was human. I'm not sure if it still applies now, but it's easier than trying to pronounce her name each time."

As we walked further down the halls, Gianni's footsteps sounded like mini earthquakes from his heavy armor on the steel floor, and people's death screams mingled with bullets ricocheting off the walls. Vyrlakalos and its army were making short work of the human grunts.

"What exactly are we looking for, Captain?" Owen asked Lyle. "Doubtful that a demon would just be sitting in one of these rooms."

"It's *commander*, and I know. We're looking for an elevator to take us all the way down."

"Why didn't you say so?" I asked. "You should stand back."

I put my fist to the ground and took a deep breath before following through with a punch that rocked the building and shattered the floors beneath us like glass. Gianni didn't seem too impressed … at least he didn't say anything to let on if he was. He jumped down into the hole ahead of us, letting me float the others down with me.

"What is this?" I looked around the enormous cement room filled with wooden crates. It was much darker here, with only hanging incandescent lighting, but it seemed vaguely familiar. There were large machines and conveyor belts everywhere, with catwalks spanning the lengths of the room from above.

"It's a weapon factory," Lyle said. "There have to be thousands of guns and explosives here."

"Why's it look like it's from the forties?" Owen asked as we split up to investigate.

"Because I think it is," I said, remembering why I recognized the place. "The first time I met the Strigoi, they took me to an abandoned military bunker in Germany that looked just like this. There wasn't a weapon factory that I saw, but it was the same exact aesthetic. I know my architecture, and I remember the layout very well. The Strigoi had reworked a lot of the machines there into their own contraptions over the years. They repurposed the whole bunker into one of their arcanums led by a demon worshipper." Now I could see why Minerva had just happened to choose that building to do her work. It already had close ties to Hell.

"It's no coincidence," said Lyle. "That was from the Second World War, and Nazi Germany was suspected of being really into the occult. The Nazis were the terrorists of their day. If it was Hell at the wheel back then like it is now, it makes sense. They've been using Gestalt to manufacture the weapons needed to spread chaos through the Middle East. PROJECT: UNITY has been putting the pieces together for a while. Maybe it was a good thing we caused them to jump-start their plans after all, or they'd have had time to distribute that super steroid too."

"It's all the bloody same," Owen said. "You'll be evil if that's what you want to be. I don't believe someone's organizing it all. Nobody told me to sin. I do what I do because I choose to. People are always looking for an excuse to blame their actions on."

"Well said." Noah's voice came from atop a mountain of wooden crates. "Except the part where most of us can get into your head and make you do whatever we want."

He disappeared from the crates, and then there was a sharp poke to my ribs. "Hey," Noah said, putting away his wakizashi. "I got you something." He held up the *Grand Grimoire* in his other hand.

"No way. Vance is going to be so pissed." I reveled in the thought.

"Good. Now tell me how great I am for getting it, and I'll let you destroy it yourself."

I rolled my eyes and snatched the tome, using my powers. It moaned and hissed like it was alive as I ripped it to shreds and then made it crumble to cinders. "Why are you here?" I asked, remembering I was still angry with him.

"You know me; I couldn't let you have all the fun. Besides, there was a commercial on TV, and I got impatient. You know how I hate to be bored ..."

I stared at him as he kept reaching for excuses. "You're right, I do know you. You're trying to make amends for what you did."

"You shut your stupid face." He pointed at me. "I told you. I'm just here because I'm bored."

"Sure you are."

"Oh, and by the way, the Italian is in a corner out in the hall, mumbling to himself in Latin. I don't know if he's summoning the Devil or trying to order a pizza, but it's probably not productive to the mission. Just thought you should know."

I threw the virus back to Lyle so I wouldn't lose it and flew out the door against his protests about splitting up the team. If something was going on with Gianni that made him want to separate from the group, it was probably too dangerous for the humans.

I sped through the low-ceiling cement halls, searching frantically for Gianni. It was getting humid, and the smell of sulfur and the murky gloom persisted. We were in a desert in a building of metal and cement; what could be causing all this humidity?

My shouts for Gianni were alerting everyone to my location, but I couldn't care less. Guards came out from behind metal doors, shouting at me in Arabic and opening fire on sight. Their cries were quieted as quickly as they came; human bone was no match for my wrath.

As Noah had said, Gianni's voice was coming from a darkened corner. A conspicuous mass of shadows haunted part of a corridor where the gloom was thickest.

"Gianni?" I called into the darkness. The otherwise benign murk that had been present in the air was now starting to feel corporeal as it brushed past me, growing more solid the closer I crept toward him.

"Leave ..." he said from his hiding spot.

"Um, no. I'm not gonna do that. What's wrong?" I was starting to get a little spooked but kept advancing.

"Get out! You must go ..." The shadows parted just enough, moving as a cloak around him, as he brought his fist back and punched the wall with seismic force. His armor had changed in the glimpse I'd caught. Normally, sleek lines matched his musculature in an attractive blend of impregnable strength and beauty, but much of that had been perverted with accents of spikes along his shoulders and knuckles. Claws tipped each finger of his gauntlets, tentacles made of darkness flailed out from his back, and the faces of tortured souls manifested in the shade surrounding him.

When I put my hand out to touch his shoulder, he took me by surprise, grabbing me by the throat in his iron grip. I gasped and choked for breath, but I couldn't get any words out. My powers never had any effect against the shadow matter he commanded, so all I could do was reach out in a desperate plea for mercy.

"You will die!" he roared from behind his helmet. "I will kill you!"

I became even more terrified when my hand brushed against his helm as I tried to touch his face, hoping it would calm him. It warped into the hellish form of an angry, screaming skull. This made me think of all his previous victims in his past life and what they must have seen before their death at his hands. My silent begging was answered, but not by him. Noah appeared and tried bringing down the Muramasa to sever the arm Gianni was grasping me with, but it bounced off his armor with a reverberating shockwave.

"You will never take what is mine!" Gianni bellowed at Noah and then began a fear-inducing tirade in Latin. Noah let loose a devastating torrent of slashes in a vain attempt to find a weak spot in Gianni's armor, but it only took one move of his own to bring Noah to a halt.

Gianni threw me against the wall and summoned his own sword from the dark. Even his weapon was more barbaric now, with jagged edges and chains hanging from the hilt. But the sword was only for intimidation as he simply drew the shadows from inside Noah's heart out into a solid spike to impale him to the floor.

I recovered and immediately flew between them. There was nothing in our arsenal that could do anything to Gianni to even slow him down. "Stop it! Don't hurt him!" I yelled, pleading for Noah's life. I put my face close to Gianni's to get him to focus on me and snap out of his trance. "It's me—Dorian! Remember?"

I tried taking off his helm, hoping it would clear his senses, but we were interrupted by more human minions. Gianni turned his attention toward them and charged down the hall like a rampaging bull. He shoulder-tackled one man against the wall with such force that it turned his body into a mangled paste and sent loose teeth and bone fragments whizzing by my head. The tentacles attached to him tended to the rest of the terrorists, shredding them to pieces as he washed his gauntlets in their blood and basked in the carnage.

Gianni was coming back for us, crushing skulls and rifles under his feet as he dragged his sword behind him, causing a horrible noise against the metal floor. One of Vyrlakalos's abominations that had been in pursuit of the humans crawled along the wall past us. Gianni smashed it like a bug with his fist and tossed the creature into his shadow, where it disappeared. I knew I had to get Noah, and everyone else, out of there before the situation got even worse.

"You're not getting Noah without killing me first." Pulling the shadow spike from his chest was proving ineffectual, as I figured it would have. I had no options left. Gianni pulled me away from Noah when he reached us, but I kept clinging on to his armor, trying to get his attention on me.

"Why are you doing this? Just leave him alone!" I screamed into his helm. He finally stopped before swinging his sword down on Noah and dropped to his knees. I struggled to pry his helm off as he held his head in either pain or confusion before sinking into the shadows below.

"I told you. I fucking told you he was gonna turn on us." When the shadows pinning him down cleared, Noah grimaced in pain from the hole in his chest. "He can pretend all he wants, but I knew it was gonna come out eventually. He's working for the other side. We're getting out of here."

It was hard to argue with what we'd both seen, but I believed in my heart that there was more to it. Noah saw Gianni attack us, but I saw him fighting a voice in his head. "I'm sorry you got hurt," I said with genuine remorse. "Take my blood if you need some and go, but I'm not leaving."

"Don't tell me what to do. You're coming with me if I have to drag you by the hair, and you know I will."

"Why are we always getting the crap kicked out of us?" I sat on the floor, feeling heartbroken and panting from the hot, humid air.

"Because you never listen to me, you little shit." He nudged me with his foot.

"You're the one who unleashed vengeful spirits on us over a dumb sword," I reminded him.

"Stop bringing that up. I told you I had it under control." Noah picked me up by my shirt just as the ground started to rumble. "Your stupid human friends are gonna die if the Italian is going after them. Although I can't imagine why he'd bother. It's not like they're a threat."

"I gave them the virus we needed to banish the demon."

"Of course you did."

Chapter Twenty-Seven

Noah rushed us back to where we had left Owen and Lyle. There were scores of dead littering the floor from the firefight taking place. The body count was piling up, but fortunately our two weren't part of it. Hell may have run out of human minions to throw at us for now, but that wasn't good news. In place of easy-to-dispatch terrorist thugs with conventional firearms, the Infernal forces upped the ante by reuniting us with an old friend from Hell.

It stood fifteen feet tall, with horns and a reddish-black leathery hide covered in spiked protrusions. The demon Noah and I had fought when I had been captured by the Strigoi in Germany was back. The very memory of it made me seethe. It had cornered Lyle, who was taking potshots at it from behind the cover of the large machines in the room. Owen, whether drunk, brave, or some combination of the two, was riding on the demon's head, trying to break off one of its horns with his superhuman strength.

"That's not the lord. We just have to keep it busy until its time runs out!" I shouted to them. "It can't stay summoned on Earth for long." I motioned to push the beast away from Lyle. The result was more than I expected. The demon's chest caved in, so I did it again until all that was left was leathery debris; it was a pleasant new level of destruction.

"Nice." Noah nodded and removed his hand from the hilt of the Muramasa.

"Wow! Never heard you give a compliment to anyone but yourself before," Lyle said, coming out of hiding.

"It *was* for me. I'm the one who trained him."

"Bloody good job either way." Owen came over and messed with Lyle's hair. "The Yankee and I make a good team too. He sprays bullets everywhere to cause a distraction while I get the kill. Sometimes, he even hits something."

"Where's the virus?" I asked Lyle.

"Gianluca came and took it. I thought you guys were going to finish the job without us?"

"Well, you're fucked," Noah mumbled.

"Maybe not. What did his armor look like?" I asked.

"Black?" Lyle looked at me puzzled.

"I mean was it scary and evil?"

"I don't know. There was a lot happening at the time. He just popped in and left with it. I figured you found the target. What's going on?"

"The Italian turned on us just like I said he would," said Noah. "He's evil ... always been evil ... and now he's working with the demons. You don't kill most of Europe and overthrow your creators to become even more powerful and then suddenly decide to be a nice guy after a long nap.

"He says he woke up because he sensed this little shit's power, which just happens to be what that original demon Strigoi bitch was drooling over. He was probably trying to pick up where she left off or use Dorian as his personal guide to sniff out potential threats. He's sleazy and manipulative like all Ancients, and this dumbass fell for it all because of a stupid accent and some flowers."

"I *didn't* fall for anything. He *isn't* evil," I said through blinding anger. This whole place was pissing me off: the demons, these terrorists, Noah ... everything. *Someone is going to get it. The first person, or thing, that crosses me is going to be obliterated. And why is it getting so damn hot?*

"Where's your helmet?" I asked Lyle.

"Got damaged in the firefight. I was getting sick of hearing Vyrlakalos yelling at me over it anyway. So, what are we doing about Gianluca? There's no way we can handle him and these demons at the same time. The guy's a walking tank."

"Bail until we figure out how to kill him," Noah said.

"We're not killing him!" I yelled. The lights flickered, and the ground shook. Glowing pentagrams appeared around the room, opening portals for more demons to climb out of, but they too were laid to waste like the last. Before they could finish slipping the bonds of Hell, my fury once again took form in a wave of unmitigated destruction.

"You're on fire, man!" Lyle cheered. "You didn't even need to self-destruct."

"I feel like I'm literally on fire. It's boiling in here. I'm sweating."

"Really? I feel fine, except for my heart pounding out of my chest from things trying to kill us ... but I'm getting used to that. Maybe you're overheating from your powers," Lyle suggested.

"This is turning out to be a bit of fun," said Owen, lighting a cigarette on a corpse that was still burning with balefire. "I wouldn't mind taking a crack at one of those big buggers again without 'divine intervention' this time."

"I still have the bullets with the virus," Lyle said. "We can still do this. Do you think you can stop ... ah ... distract Gianluca, Dorian?"

"I'll have to try. It was Noah he was more interested in attacking, but that's not too surprising."

Noah cursed under his breath in disapproval and then left without another word. The remaining three of us were about to move out when another portal opened in our path.

"They're going to keep coming, but we can't waste the virus on them." I was going to dispatch this one when a fleshy, pulsating slime dripped from the hole I had created in the ceiling to get down here earlier. In my moment's pause, seven more portals opened behind us. The demons that rose were just as interested in the slime as I was.

The seeping discharge plopped onto the face of one of the demons and then went down its throat. The other demons resumed their assault on us while their friend convulsed. Its skin bubbled into large cysts that popped and oozed with magma-like blood.

The beast started to attack its allies in a frenzy. Its skin was sucked off its frame inside itself while it howled in ungodly agony. The compromised demon's torso burst open to reveal Vyrlakalos. The Carpathian Ancient wore the demon's leathery hide in place of its own, and horns had been added to its crested cranium where a set of crimson eyes with thin slits for pupils glowered at us.

Vyrlakalos's skeletal drones dropped down from the hole to harry the demons but were quickly immolated by their hellfire breath after dealing minimal damage. However, due to its new Infernal skin suit, Vyrlakalos was unaffected by the flames.

"Let's go," I said. "I'm not wasting my energy helping a Carpathian. It can handle itself."

"She's part of the team," Lyle argued and stood in my way. "Like it or not, we're on the same side, and she's held up her end so far."

"But I hate the Carpathians." I looked over my shoulder at the battle. "She" had a massive supply of corpses from all the humans to keep turning into her abominable army. Some were even fused together to create amalgams of two or three drones in one. These fiends were more repulsive with undulating extremities and gaping maws that didn't close quite right from their deformity and were better used to vocalize moans of despair than cause serious harm. They seemed to beg for an end to their unnatural existence as they thrashed at whatever came within range.

"Well, I don't mind a good scrap." Owen charged in, nimbly climbing up the back of a demon. "Get my back, Yankee."

Lyle landed a grenade from the launcher on his rifle into the demon's mouth. The detonation didn't do much, but it gave Owen a few uninterrupted seconds to break off a horn and plunge it into the beast's skull. Vyrlakalos was doing just fine on her own. She was having the time of her undead life, making new hybrid horrors to fight for her out of pieces of the demons and humans lying around, in addition to attaching new parts to her own disgusting body.

Reluctant to help the Carpathian, I chose instead to end the demon that Lyle and Owen were still fighting. Not to be outdone, Noah returned and grabbed one of the other demons by both horns after a quick slit to the throat with the Muramasa. He growled with fangs bared and strained his muscles to snap the demon's neck until there was a crack and it crashed to the ground lifeless.

"That's how you do that," Noah said to Owen and jumped off the body toward another demon. He spun in midair with the Muramasa cleaving through his next victim then slicing its legs out from under it for good measure.

I remembered Noah's wakizashi not doing much to the demon's thick hide back in Germany, but the Muramasa was an exquisite katana containing the soul of one of their own.

The lights in the room went out, and I didn't know if that meant more demons or what, but the sounds of battle halted until they came back on. When they did, Gianni stood in the center of the room, looking as frightening as before. The demons didn't immediately attack until he stuck his sword in one's leg and walked away with a casual stride. The weapon exploded in a sphere of darkness that took out the remaining Infernals who were bearing down on him.

"Leave. This place ... is sick. The dark ... poison," Gianni commanded as he approached. A new sword was forged in his hand as he headed for Noah, who stood his ground.

I floated over to intercept Gianni, but he dropped to his knees, screaming in anguish as he tried removing his helmet again. He pounded the floor with his fists, and his armor grew larger and more ghastly with skulls on his pauldrons and curved-up bladed edges. The floor gave way under him, exposing yet another sublevel into which he disappeared.

I leaped back to Owen and Lyle. Vyrlakalos sprouted bat wings, which were typical of most Carpathians, and flew down to the next floor. I almost went to stop her from provoking Gianni, but he would probably have just done us all a favor by killing her.

"Seems like the big shadow bloke is possessed," said Owen. "It must be the demon lord, right? He's going to come after us if we leave."

"Then we can save him *and* banish it in one go," Lyle said. "I didn't see him carrying the virus, but I still got the bullets."

"He's bulletproof," I said, "even without his armor. The demon lord picked the perfect body as a vessel. He's invincible."

"The dude has to have *some* weakness," Lyle said.

"I'll find one or make a new one while trying." Noah dove through the new hole as a cloud of mist faster than I could tell him to leave Gianni alone.

"When we first met, he told me supernatural light was the only thing that could dispel his darkness," I said on our way down. "But he's still so strong without his armor because he's fused with the Nether Realm like how I am with the energy from the Rift.

"Every pore, hair follicle, and cell in our bodies has some darkness in it, and his can be so super dense that it becomes solid, shields him from damage, and gives him his strength. You've seen him turn shadows into physical objects. That's how his body is all the time, even when he's asleep."

"Maybe you can get him to swallow it," Owen suggested.

"What would happen to Gianni, though?" I asked. "The exorcism didn't work on the guy you brought back to base. I don't want to kill him or trap him in Hell."

"We'll figure something out, man. I'm not jeopardizing anyone," Lyle said. "The virus was changed since that first try."

The cement between levels was several feet deep as if it was supposed to be the foundation of the building. We had to have been a couple hundred feet underground by the time we landed. The floor was in a tight arched tunnel carved right out of the earth, with rough brick or maybe cobblestones embedded in the wall. It was hard to see down there with the only minimal light source coming from the intermittent candles spaced out down the hall in wrought iron sconces. I didn't know who had lit them, but someone who had been expecting us had been kind enough to show us the path.

"What the bloody hell is this now?" I heard Owen say from behind me. You couldn't fit more than one person at a time down the narrow passage. The heat was blistering and humid; I felt as if I was trying to breathe soup. Wasn't it supposed to get cooler underground?

"Catacombs. Real ones," I said as my arm brushed against human bones embedded in the wall. "Sort of."

"What do you mean real ones?" Lyle asked.

"The word comes from subterranean Roman burial grounds. I read a lot about the Roman Empire after meeting Gianni ... Anyway, I didn't think there were any in Iraq. These must've been built for another purpose."

"Kind of a coincidence we've got a Roman bloke and we're chasing down Roman-type tunnels, don't ya think?" Owen asked. "Are we even still on Earth?"

"Why wouldn't we be?" Lyle retorted.

"Well, if we keep going down any further, we're gonna come out the ass end of the globe. I'm starting to sweat in all this leather gear too."

"I'm not hot at all, and I'm in way heavier armor than you," Lyle said. "It's cooler down here than up by the surface."

"I'm close to passing out, I'm so hot," I said. "I don't know how you can't be at least warm. I've been like this almost since we got here."

The tunnel sloped downhill until we reached a more opened-up area that branched off into multiple paths.

"We're not splitting up," Lyle said before any of us could suggest it.

"We don't have to. There's only one path that's lit up, and we're obviously being led down it," I pointed out. As I said that, whispers came from one of the darkened tunnels. "I'm not going crazy, right? You guys hear that?"

"Sure do." Lyle turned on the light attached to his rifle to check out the way ahead. I didn't know why, but I was suddenly very afraid. Up until that point, I had been relatively desensitized to all the gore and nasties that had been thrown at me. The only real thing I had to be afraid of was Gianni, as sad as that was.

The others might not know it, but he had been holding back quite a lot, struggling against the possession. When his mental fortitude was exhausted, our deaths would hopefully be swift. For the others, it meant passing on to the afterlife or whatever the exact process was, but for me, who couldn't die so easily, I feared being thrown into the dark dimension for eternity. I guessed I could always burn out all my power and let myself asphyxiate when turned mortal, if it came to that.

"Dorian," Lyle called and waved his hand in front of my face. "Wake up. There are people down here."

The sound of whispering stopped as we approached an iron door that had been padlocked from the outside. I broke the lock and moved back so that Lyle could shine the light in. People were in there all right: a group of dirty, worn-down men and women huddled together in the farthest corner of the tiny room. Their eyes were big and bright; they were the only things that hadn't lost their luster in the labyrinth.

"They're human," Lyle said with as much disbelief as I was feeling. The whispers resumed in the form of prayers in Arabic. "Do any of you speak English?"

"I ... I do." A man in army fatigues stood. His clothes were torn so badly that there were no recognizable symbols of affiliation. "Take me. Just leave them. Please."

"We're not here to hurt you," said Lyle. "Who are you? Why are you all in here?"

"You're not ... you're not here for the sacrifices?" the man asked. Everyone was staring at me, and then I realized I was still floating.

"Oh, I'm not a demon," I said. The small room was filled with the stench of defecation from lack of anywhere else to relieve themselves for however long they had been locked up. "Why aren't you crazy like the others?"

"We were kidnapped from our homes at night by men of the Devil who were dressed as we were but ten times as strong. They would bring more each night from villages and cities all around. Our cries for freedom filled these tunnels, but as more were brought here, some were removed until only we are left."

"Why were you left, though?" Lyle asked.

"Because we wouldn't become one of them. Some of the ones who came to take us from this room were those captured alongside us. They were our neighbors and family, but they acted as if we had never met when they returned. After a short time in here, many began to lose their minds. It was too soon to be a natural thing ... sometimes in a day or an hour. They only spoke of hate and killing, and they complained that they could feel the heat of the desert under their skin. That's when we knew they were to be taken away again.

"The men still return sometimes and say we will be sacrificed to the pit if we do not join their ways soon. The last of us have not stopped praying to God since we came here. It is the only thing that has kept us sane."

"Which 'God'?" Owen asked.

"If it's keeping them from getting possessed, it doesn't matter who or what they pray to. Good is good," Lyle said.

"That's right," the man agreed. "Only the purest hearts could make it through the belly of the beast without a mark on their soul."

"We have a helicopter waiting outside," Lyle told them. "We're going to get you all out of here."

"You are American?" the man asked him.

"And proud."

Owen sighed and retrieved a smashed cigarette from his back pocket, but he couldn't find his lighter. "Not everyone loves you Americans as much as you think they do, Yankee."

"Not everyone hates them either," the man said. "I've never spoken with one to judge until now, but my only reason for asking is because you wear strange uniforms from any soldiers I have seen."

"Eh, yeah ... It's a long story—" The light from Lyle's gun dimmed to nothing, leaving us in blackness.

"It'll have to wait," I cut Lyle off. I could hear someone moving closer in the shadows down the dark end of the tunnel. I knew who it was; I just wasn't ready to face him and wanted to pretend for a moment that maybe it was someone or something else. "You should probably all start running."

Light returned to Lyle's rifle in time to show us Gianni emerging from the darkness. He barely fit down the hall in height or width because of his armor. How do I defeat him, let alone defend against him?

"Gianni, if you can hear me, don't come any closer."

He didn't respond, nor did he stop advancing. How cruel it was that, without any notice, the person I hadn't been able to get enough of was now the last one I wanted to see.

"Gianni ... please. Just don't hurt anyone. Just go away until we can figure out how to help you."

He wasn't trying to communicate with me like the other times. Instead, he summoned his sword to his hand and started to charge at me. I tried using my powers in desperation to halt his movement, but luck still wasn't on my side. Only a couple of the captives had made it out of the room and back to the junction with Owen. Gianni was already on top of us, and I was forced to throw Lyle and the rest back in the room and close the door to keep them away.

Without the light from Lyle's gun, I was alone in the dark and, once again, terrified of it. I felt Gianni's clawed gauntlet grab my face and lift me up in its crushing grip, digging its nails into my skin. I was helpless without my powers, and even if they could be of use, the level of energy I'd need to take him down would destroy the area around us and bury everyone.

In my panic, I lost the hold I had on the iron door I was keeping sealed so that no one would run out into a quick demise. That was exactly what Lyle did in an attempt to save me. He grabbed Gianni's arm, yelling at him to let me go. Everyone started screaming, and I couldn't understand any of it. All I could think of was being thrown into the void forever and my friends dying. Why had something that had started out so good turned so bad?

I hated the demons, especially the one responsible for this. I mean *really* hated. That surging energy from my anger was coming back, and there was nothing to take it out on without endangering everyone.

Something was going on where Owen had taken his group of rescued captives. I heard a brawl and shouts of panic, but there was nothing I could do.

Gianni threw me into Lyle, sending us falling back into the room, where mayhem continued to build from the sound of screams and prayers, all while illuminated by only a thin beam of light from the rifle that had dropped to the floor. Gianni took a step in with his sword poised and ready to attack both Lyle and me in one swipe. I didn't know if I should still be calling him 'Gianni.' That term of endearment seemed to have expired, given the circumstances, but soon, it wouldn't matter.

There wasn't any room to move in these tight quarters, but I tried to separate myself from the rest to give them a window of escape. We were rats trapped in a cage with a lion. Gianluca brought his sword down. I closed my eyes but didn't feel anything. He dropped to his knees and held his head in agony again, only this time, he was able to remove his helm. Lyle swapped ammo to the virus and held his rifle to Gianluca's temple.

"Wait!" I stopped Lyle before he could take the shot. "It won't work anyway. Just get out with the others and help Owen."

"I'm not leaving—" I threw Lyle from the room so he didn't have a choice, and I closed the door behind him after the captives fled. I was now alone in the dark with Gianluca; I was the last rat left in the cage.

Chapter Twenty-Eight

"Gianni, uh, Gianluca …?" I couldn't see, but I could feel out the room with my psionics and could still hear him from where he was kneeling.

"The dark … is clean here …"

"Is it really you?" I put my hand out into the darkness to touch him and cut myself on the spikes of his armor. He lashed out and grabbed my wrist. I'd thought it was over. I'd thought he had reverted to himself again.

Gianluca jerked me toward him by the arm. I was expecting to be impaled against his spikes or thrown into the Nether. I was no stranger to pain, but it was worse coming from him. There was no such feeling, though—only the touch of his skin. He had managed to dismiss that hellish armor and was leaning against me from on his knees. He was drenched in sweat, and I couldn't tell if he was sobbing or just breathing heavily from exhaustion, but his shoulders heaved with each labored breath.

"If you swallow the virus, it might work to banish the demon, but I don't know what will happen to you ..." I put my hand on top of his head, waiting for a sign that it was safe. He didn't make any more sudden moves, so I hugged his head to comfort us both.

"There, is no ... demon inside me," he said.

I froze.

"What... what's that supposed to mean? You were attacking me on purpose?" I didn't know if I should start running or trying to get away.

"No, I want ... make you leave, but ... the voice. The darkness here. I tell you is poison."

"Gianni, you're not making sense. What about the dark is poison if it isn't the demon? Whoa! Whoa! Gianni?" He keeled over in the middle of me talking. I caught him before his head hit the floor, and I sat with him.

"The Devil ... talk in the shadows ... to put a poison there. The voice ... is very loud. I did not hear anything else." He coughed and groaned, feeling around in the dark for me to come closer. "I cannot even see then. I try very hard for my eyes to find you, but it control me. I do not understand the words it speak, but they make me suffer. I have to fight my body to not make you hurt."

"We have to get you out of here," I said and tried to keep him calm by holding his hand.

"No ... I am stronger here now. Something in this room is pure. The dark is clean. I will never leave you for the Devil to take you away."

"Gianni, you *are* the biggest danger, though ... I can't stop you if you get turned against us again, but we can stop the demon lord with the virus. What did you do with it? The suitcase you took from Lyle."

"I ... do not remember. I do this?"

"It's okay. We still have the bullets. As long as you're safe again, that's all I care about."

"I never want to hurt you ... We talk so much before about who is weak and strong, but I am the weak one. I try, but I cannot stop from being a slave for the evil."

"It's not your fault." I held him as tightly as I could. For the first time since being there, the insidious heat started to wane.

"Yes. Is my anger that let the Devil take me. I am no man if I cannot control this."

"Angry about what?" I asked. "You just wandered away a few minutes after we got here."

"I do not say. Maybe later."

"No, I think it's kinda important if it caused you to almost kill us and take away our key to victory."

"Many thing." He sighed. "I am angry there is much evil today when I think I fix it many years ago. I am angry ... I do not want you to be here where there is danger. You do not need to fight. I feel if my English is better, I can make you understand. I do not feel like a man if I cannot bring us victory with honor. And I am angry the serpent you say is a friend tries to poison your mind. This world is full of darkness I cannot control now ... just like in Roma ..."

The brief respite from the scorching heat came to an end, with the temperature in the room flaring up again. Something cool and metallic moved across Gianni's chest where my hand rested. His shadow armor was re-forming.

"I will kill them. I will kill them all. Everyone who threaten us ... They will pay."

"None of that stuff is true. The thoughts are from the demon. It's turning you against us."

"Then I will kill it before this happen. With only my hands if I need." Gianni disappeared in anticipation of further opposition from me. I didn't know whether any of my words had gotten through to him or if anything could.

I left the room to search for Lyle and the others. The heat was even more blistering now.

The sounds of fighting came from down in the first tunnel through which we had arrived. Most of the group made it back up the hole we had come down. Lyle was helping a much older woman, who couldn't climb on her own, while Owen held off two of the horned demons we had been fighting ad nauseam. The tunnel ceilings were so low that the demons were crammed in almost on all fours.

Owen threw Lyle and the last survivor up the hole as a gout of hellfire was expelled from one of the demons' mouths, incinerating the cramped end of the tunnel in which they were pinned. The fire began to clear by the time I made it close enough to join the fray. Owen stood untouched by the flames, thanks to the demon leather his suit was made of, but it didn't defend against their horns.

I vanquished one of the pair, having to hold back everything inside me not to blow an even bigger hole in the building and kill us all. Owen had no room to move and reached for Lyle's hand to climb out of the tunnel when the second demon impaled him through the chest with one of its horns.

Lyle jumped down and pulled Owen away right as I ended the last demon's time on Earth. Owen lay on the floor, choking on the blood gurgling up in his throat. He was bleeding out so fast that the floor under him ran red within seconds, and there was nothing we could do to stop it.

"No, no, no, no!" Lyle shouted. "You're not dying on me, Blackbourne! You're not going anywhere! Not after you just saved my life. Keep your eyes open."

"You're ... not much to look at ... Yankee."

"I don't care if I die doing it, but we gotta get him to Rebecca on the helicopter." Lyle was frantic past the point of rationale and trying to stop the bleeding with his hands. Someone he couldn't stand was now his cause for impassioned concern. "What about Noah or Vyrlakalos's blood?"

"Their blood is toxic, and if we move him it'll make it worse," I said and ripped my shirt off to use it to stem the bleeding. It wasn't the cleanest, but it was better than letting his insides fall out. Owen wasn't able to keep his eyes open. We took his mask and hood off to help him breathe and propped him up against the wall.

"What happened with Gianluca?" Lyle asked. "Is he okay to bring Owen out of here?"

"Uh, no. He left again. He's not possessed, but he's being 'poisoned,' as he calls it. Something in that room gave him a few minutes of clarity," I explained. "I hate demons. They've officially taken the Carpathians' top spot on my list."

As I said that, a pentagram opened next to us, spitting out yet another demon. I hit it back with so much force that it left an imprint of its remains on the wall down at the end of the tunnel.

"Stop it," Lyle snapped at me. "Since you got here, everything you say is about hating everything. That's exactly what these demons want. You're just feeding them and drawing attention to us."

"Oh, I'm sorry. Am I supposed to 'love thy enemy' or something? It's a little hard to not hate something that's been terrorizing the world, turning us against each other, and killing our friends."

"They're getting to you, man. They're getting in your head like they did to Gianluca and the people they kidnapped. Those people up there who survived did so because they focused on the good and didn't lose hope. They've been here for days and lost everything, but they didn't obsess over what they hate. Hell can't take away your hope if you don't let it."

Maybe that's why the room had had an effect on Gianni. Could their positive vibes have cleansed the area? Once Gianni had started talking about what had made him angry, everything had changed back, and I'd started feeling the heat again like those who'd turned to terror. It had been as if we'd been the ones poisoning the good that had been left over.

"I'm not gonna make it, boys." Owen wheezed and gagged. It was amazing he was still alive for even this long, but it was only because of his supernatural healing. "Tell Micah ... tell him I said to make good ... on that money I was investing in you blokes."

"Tell him yourself," Lyle said back. "You're not dying here. No casualties, no sacrifices, nobody left behind. Just think of it like a bad hangover."

"Not this time, Yankee." Owen couldn't fight to keep his head up or his eyes open anymore. His lips stopped moving when he spoke as blood trickled out of them. "Do me a favor ... get the doc to smile. She deserves to ..."

"I'm going to try and fly us all out of here. He's not healing fast enough." I had never taken passengers with me on a long-distance flight and had never used my powers on so many human-sized objects without destroying them, but I didn't see any other option.

"I've only got one bullet left, and it's the virus," Lyle said. "I had to use the others on the demons while you were with Gianluca."

"You used some of the virus bullets? Did they work?"

"You came and killed the demons I had used them on before they had a chance to take effect."

"We've got to just abort the mission. After I get you all out, I'll stay behind to make sure Noah and Gianni follow. Maybe we'll get lucky and Vyrlakalos will already be dead."

"Dorian!" Lyle yelled. "What did we just talk about?"

As soon as I had said that, another cluster of portals opened to summon more demons. I dealt with them and flew us up to the next floor. "Where are the survivors?" I asked in a hurry to get Owen out.

"I told them to hide here," Lyle said, looking around the ruins of the weapon factory. "Keep going. I can't feel his pulse."

The main power was out when we got up to Gestalt's lab area, but that wasn't a surprise, considering all the structural damage the facility had taken. The survivors had made it all the way to the blast door on their own and were happy to see us arrive behind them. The blast door was closed and had no power supply to open it without supernatural assistance.

"I'm putting you guys down," I told Lyle. "It's like squeezing a muscle. I don't want to accidentally crush you when trying to open this."

It wasn't as easy for me to lift without channeling the anger I'd had before, but it felt good to hear the cheers when I did. The desert sun was up and streamed in, creating a blinding reflection against the shiny metal walls.

"You saved us! Many thanks and blessings!" the soldier exclaimed. "Only the purest heart can stand to face that evil below. Take caution in your wandering down the dark spiral. That which speaks with honeyed tongue holds nothing but hidden malice."

That sounded so familiar, but I couldn't remember where I had heard it before.

"The helicopter isn't far from here," Lyle said as we went to lead the way. "We'll get you cleaned up and checked out—"

The survivors passed us, stepping out onto the sand, and as they did, one by one, they faded from sight. "We are free," the soldier said before disappearing completely.

"What was that?" Lyle looked at me as bewildered as I was. "They weren't real? Ghosts?"

"I don't know. Lost souls, I guess. They must have died down there but were too pure for Hell to take."

"I never liked ghosts, until them, but it still kinda gives me the chills." Lyle stepped out into the desert camp. "I wish I'd gotten their names—"

"Commander!" a woman's voice called from outside. "Stand down, everyone."

It wasn't easy to see with the sunlight blinding us, but I recognized Timmons and her troops guarding the encampment. They had moved the helicopter closer. I went to float out with Owen, but something stopped me. I smashed into an invisible wall and couldn't get through, even with my powers. I had a feeling I knew what it meant.

"Lyle, take Owen." I passed Owen's body through to him. *Maybe I shouldn't say anything.*

Whatever was down there had a hold on me, like it had done to Gianni, and wasn't letting me leave.

"He saved my life," Lyle said to Timmons, who had two of her men take Owen away. "Get him to Dr. Sullivan right now, and do whatever it takes to make sure he survives, even if you have to go back to base. I'm going to reload standard rounds and get another helmet so I can go back in."

"I'll stay here," I told them as a voice hummed to me from inside the hideout. Lyle was back shortly and without good news.

"Rebecca doesn't know if he's gonna make it. She thinks he punctured a lung and he's lost too much blood. But we need to talk." Lyle was understandably solemn. "You can't leave, can you?"

"What are you talking about?" I feigned ignorance. I didn't want to worry him and make this already hopeless situation worse.

"One of the troops saw you. You're getting corrupted by the demons' influence like Gianluca." At least Lyle had a new helmet back on, so I couldn't see his face as he lectured me. "You know what it's like to be discriminated against, but you keep going around saying how much you hate all the Carpathians. The ones responsible for the plague in New York died years ago, and they were manipulated by the demon that tricked their leader."

"Vyrlakalos is a Carpathian, one that killed all your friends and teammates on base. Or did you forget that?" I asked.

"Of course not, and I did hate her, but I had to get over it so I could move on. I still don't like her, but I pity anyone like her that exists only for themselves and can't see any of the good in the world. I don't want my best friend turning into one of them. Being a victim doesn't give you the right to become the villain.

"You're doing the same thing as everyone who ever made you hide because of who you are. Don't judge the group for the actions of a few. Innocent until proven guilty, man. That's one lesson I'll never forget, and the best advice you gave me was to go back to doing things like when I was on the force."

"I wish I had some way to argue that, but you're right," I admitted. I had no basis on which to defend myself.

"Don't make it an argument," Lyle said. "You'll only be trying to justify reasons to hate people, and that's not who you are. You have to let it go."

"All right then. Let's do this."

"Good, so here's where we're at: We have one man down, two MIA, and one big, angry shadow knight that went AWOL. You ready to go old school and do this, just you and me?"

"Sure. I'm not really doing anything else today." I journeyed the hollow chrome halls with Lyle as my new moral compass.

"I still think about her," Lyle said after making our way down to the next laboratory floor.

"Vyrlakalos?" I joked.

"Rebecca, man. I'm trying to tell myself not to, but I can't stop. What happened was as much my fault as hers."

"Can we focus on saving the world?" Maybe it was time I told him that their falling-out wasn't as much their fault as it was Noah's, but I didn't want him focusing his anger on Noah and jeopardizing an already bad situation.

"Come on, man. Don't tell me you're not thinking about Gianluca."

"Of course I am." I was thinking about how to defend myself against him ripping me apart or sending me to the shadows for eternity. "I've been wanting to tell you: Rebecca wasn't the reason the mission failed. You can be mad at her and Rudgar for keeping you in the dark, and I agree with you, but the whole security signal mix-up wasn't because of them or you. Rebecca had the device programmed to block it ... the one you set up outside before we went in. I found out a day or two ago that it was Noah who took it off, not knowing what it did."

I waited for Lyle to start cursing Noah's name. "That's ... that's awesome! That's the best news I've heard in too long," he said.

"So, you don't hate Noah and want to kill him?" I didn't want to poke the bear, but I was surprised.

"Not anymore than I already did. I never liked him, but I dealt with it. I'd expect him to do something like that. Rebecca meant something to me, though, so taking that away really got to me. Does she know?"

"No, I wanted to tell you first, but I was afraid how you'd react knowing Noah keeps popping in."

"Nah, man. I should be thanking him. Better the douchebag you know than the one you don't. I can't wait to tell her, but now I just hope she'll forgive me for acting like a complete dick."

"I'm sure she will, weirdo." Leave it to Lyle to find the bright side in a tragedy caused by Noah's infuriating antics.

We didn't make it far before we ran into the big idiot himself on the second floor of the laboratory. Noah was engaged in battle with a swarm of towering demons. He had some cuts, scrapes, and patches of burnt skin, but he was still moving and slicing just fine to add to the numerous ceiling-high piles of mutilated corpses he had amassed. As the demons' red-hot blood cooled, it fused the bodies into volcanic mounds.

"I'm starting to wonder why Hell has been making this so easy on us," I said. The demon lord was capable of turning Gianni against us within minutes of setting foot into its lair and opening gates around the world to unleash chaos. Why does it keep throwing these weak grunts at us like fodder?

"To piss us off." I let Noah finish his opponents by himself with a spinning somersault through the air, using the Muramasa like a saw blade. I knew how much he hated people stealing his glory, and at that moment, we didn't need any more animosity in the air, but he was starting to look weary. He was mobile enough to keep the

Infernals at bay, although he wasn't moving anywhere near his light-speed standard. "The more we hate them, the stronger they get, and I gotta say it's kinda working."

"You good to go a few more rounds, Muscles? Or you tapping out?" Lyle asked.

"Why's he still alive?" Noah asked me in reference to Lyle. "I need blood, little shit. I'm running on empty, and no blood means no powers or healing."

"There are dead people everywhere," Lyle said. "Can't you just take some from them?"

"No one's talking to you, human. God, you're so annoying. Supernatural blood tastes better and is more potent. I would've ripped your throat out a long time ago if it was all the same."

"Noah, shut up. You can take my blood," I said before things got any more heated. He was always crankiest when hungry and tired, and the atmosphere wasn't making things any better.

"So, you're not mad at me anymore?" he asked.

"No." I sighed in resignation. "I want to be, but I can't in here or I'm screwed."

"Good, because I was gonna bite you anyway." Noah yanked me over by the hair and chomp down on my neck so hard that I yelped. He was either really hungry or really angry, but it didn't take long for the pain to subside and the euphoria to kick in.

"Damn, that tastes good." Noah stopped with his mouth covered in my blood and then bit back down again before the woozy feeling in my head could clear. After another minute, he dropped me like a bag of rocks and stretched.

"You're such a jackass," I told him. He grabbed me again and zipped off to a room in the chrome laboratory.

"We just left Lyle! Go back! He's going to die on his own."

"He's fine. When this is over, you're coming with me," he said. It was dark in the room, with only emergency lighting, which I was getting used to being in by then.

"What do you mean? Where?"

"I'm done with the army bullshit. I was over it a while ago, but now I'm sick of it. You were only going to Greenland to visit, not join the misfit brigade. We're going to go back to Asia ... maybe Thailand. I want to look into perfecting my Muay Thai. Maybe that can be the first martial art you master."

"Uh, no? No to all of that. I'm happy where I am, and I don't think you and Gianni can stay in the same hemisphere without fighting. I'm not going to just visit Thailand with you on a whim."

"Look, I know you thought you had something going with him, but the Italian is either gonna be dead or banished here in Hell after this, kid. He's one of them now. I wasn't telling you he'd turn on us just to be a dick."

"Once we banish the demon lord, Gianni's going to be free from its influence. He heard the demon lord's voice in his head."

"It's not only the demon lord that's making him do this. If it was, don't you think it would've taken us all over?"

"No. It's just because Gianni gave in to his anger."

"Listen to me. I'm plenty pissed that I even came, and I haven't changed. We're already *in* Hell, kid. It's spilled out onto Earth. I thought you knew that. Why do you think the demons' bodies stay around even when killed? Their bodies aren't returning through the portals because we're already here.

"The atmosphere in Hell is as harmful to us as Earth is to the demons. The Italian's soul is already as black as you can get after all the innocent people he's murdered. Whether it was his choice or not, he still did the deed, and pretending he's the good guy now isn't going to change that. If the demon lord has any power over him, it's because he's already turning into one of them from his own evil."

"But that means I am too, then. I'm trapped here. I couldn't get out when Lyle and I went to the surface. Something was blocking me, but it didn't block Lyle. I've been feeling hot when others weren't too, and I heard that's how it starts."

Noah was quietly lost in thought upon hearing that.

"You're not gonna get stuck here," he said. "I'll find a way. You have to do exactly as I say, and I promise I'll get you out. When you fight, do it with purpose and not with anger. Anger leads to hate, and that's what they want. Keep your mind clear even if it means you're not as strong in the moment. Finding strength in hate is pointless, because after you destroy the object of your enmity, you have nothing ... no other focus."

"Okay ..." My voice was shaky from letting my mind run wild with thoughts of Gianni and myself becoming denizens of Hell.

"Just stick close, and I'll pick up the slack. It's better than you slipping further down the wrong path and going on a rampage. It's all about learning self-control like I taught you. The same with not burning out all your energy in one shot. Don't let your emotions drive you. At least if it comes to it, you can be my blood cow when I get hungry."

"Don't call me that. We have to go find Lyle again. Promise me you won't let him die. It'll take a lot off my mind. It can just be between us; he doesn't have to know I asked you."

"You realize it's times like these that are *exactly* why I'm always saying you can't keep human pets."

"*Please!*"

"Fine, blood cow. Just make sure he doesn't get in the way by thinking he's actually of any use, and then you're definitely coming with me to Thailand after." Noah picked me up under his arm and dashed back to Lyle, who was creeping from room to room on his way to the next floor.

"What the hell, man! You guys just left me—" Lyle stopped as the emergency lights and the one on his rifle dimmed following an ominous chill in the air. Gianni rose from the shadows down the hall behind us in his menacing armor.

"Go," I told Noah and Lyle. "I'll handle him."

Chapter Twenty-Nine

The raging titan came barreling down the corridor. I pulled the ceiling, floor, and walls together to section off Lyle and Noah from us so that Gianni had only me in his sights, but it wasn't working. He stampeded right into me and crashed through the barricade I had made.

I had no way of affecting him directly, but I could use the surroundings as a medium like I did when fighting Vyrlakalos. I tried wrapping the metal from the walls around his arms and legs to slow him down. I put all my might—enough to tear apart solid steel—behind it, but he just kept moving forward undeterred.

Noah reappeared with Lyle following behind to help, but it only made matters worse. Gianni started to pull the shadows from Noah's body into his hand to form his sword. I flew in his face to distract him. Shouting into his helm wasn't working this time. He smacked Lyle out of the way and brandished his blade to attack Noah, but I stayed between them. I thought fast and caught Lyle with my powers before he made impact with the wall, which would have emulsified his brains inside his armor.

"You have to remember who I am, Gianni. Block out the evil! That's not who you are!" I kept trying to get through to him until an overwhelming pain in my stomach came over me when I tried blocking him from stabbing Noah. Gianni's sword plunged deep into me, but it didn't stop there. The darkness bled out from the blade and cut like razor wire through my veins. Crystalized shadows pierced my skin from the inside, making it impossible for me to heal.

Noah evaded his own shadow until he was staked by it again. Lyle was unconscious from being backhanded. The taste of blood flooding my mouth was almost nauseating enough to distract me from the horrendous pain coursing throughout my body.

Gianni began to tremble at the sight of what he had done. His armor faded in and out as he struggled to free himself from it, until he was on his knees and then writhing on the ground screaming. He had as much pain showing in his face as I had in my whole body as he held out his hand and returned the shadows to him. Noah was still out cold even when unstaked, and it took a minute for me to get myself on my feet.

Gianni was locked in both physical and mental combat with the darkness, trying to free himself from its hold. I only managed to steal his attention for a moment as he cried out a mournful apology.

"Gianni, you *are* good. I know you are! I believe in you!" I held his head steady against his thrashing.

"No ... My soul will never be clean. I lie to myself to think I am good. Now I lose it all again like I did in Roma." His grimace worsened from the unbearable agony of being torn apart. The same crystalline blackness jutted from his skin, causing him to bleed out from the massive internal trauma.

"Don't give in to it, Gianni!" I was short on new ideas. The ebony crystals protruding from him melted and leaked into his pool of blood on the floor. The blackness expelled from Gianni took form in the image of the hateful armor. I tried to intervene as the two wrestled on the floor, but nothing would slow down the darkness. Gianni was defenseless, weakened, and still bleeding from the puncture wounds.

My interference enraged the animated armor. It swung at me with its sword. Gianni grabbed its arm to stop it, but my throat was already cut and gushing blood. I healed, but something in Gianni's tired eyes looked at me like I was dying. He created his own sword and stabbed the living armor as it impaled him right back.

Gianni was caught on the serrated blade stuck in him, his own sword showing no signs of doing any damage to the rogue shadow.

"We have to get out of here, *now*," Noah said, shaking his head clear as he got up.

"I'm not leaving him."

"Then you're gonna watch him die."

"Take Lyle and go," I said. "But I'm not letting Gianni do this alone."

I tried again to use all my surroundings to at least bind the shadow, but even in full metal restraints, it was overpowering. I wanted to get its attention to take the pressure off Gianni, but even he was telling me to leave again. I got more than I bargained for when the shadow armor punched me in the chest with its spiked gauntlet and grabbed my heart while it held Gianni by the face with its other hand.

Noah pulled me free, tearing my heart out in the process, but he knew it would regrow. My vision kept cutting out as I died and regenerated in Noah's arms as he carried me away. I saw Gianni hold on to the shadow's hand grasping him. The armor began to crystalize, like those that had been stuck in us before, until its whole body was frozen in place. Gianni picked up his sword and shattered the evil darkness with one swing, vanquishing it for good.

I flew back to him as he dropped to the floor, his sword fading away next to him. His consciousness flickered out as he smiled and tried feebly to reach up to me. His body went limp, and his eyes rolled back before closing. I checked for a pulse or breathing, but if there was any, it was too faint to tell—not that he necessarily needed either to still be alive. The excessive blood loss and stab wounds were what concerned me. He didn't heal like I did.

"Don't look." Noah came over to us with the Muramasa unsheathed in his hand. He picked Gianni up by the hair and put the blade to his neck.

"What are you doing?! It's over!" I pushed the katana away.

"It's not over! It's who he is. You heard him. This may be the only chance we get to be rid of him."

I pried Noah's fingers from Gianni, letting his unconscious body slip away into the shadows below. Noah's expression was grim; he'd meant every word of what he'd said and wanted to do. "I would never let him hurt you, and it goes both ways," I said.

"You can't *stop* him." Noah glared. "That's the point. This should've taught you something."

"This confirmed there's good in him, and the good won. I can't stop you either, but I may be the only person who knows the real you anymore, and I know there's good in you too."

Noah checked over his shoulder to make sure Lyle was still out cold. "I'm trying to prevent you from getting hurt in a future that you're too blind to see. He doesn't love you or whatever you think is going on between you two."

"I never said that we were in love. I don't even know what being in love feels like, but I do care about him and only time will tell which one of us is right. Until then, I can only go with my gut feeling and what I saw today." I paused, realizing that Noah's intentions were in my best interest and that he wasn't just trying to make me upset. "I wish you could read my mind so you'd know how much I appreciate you looking out for me, though."

"Whatever." He sheathed the Muramasa on his back and walked a few feet to lounge on some wreckage. "There's no honor in killing someone who's sleeping anyway ... even him."

"You two are a lot alike, you know."

"Now you're just trying to insult me," Noah said and sped off.

"What happened? Are we dead?" asked Lyle, who was still on his back.

"No. Not yet."

Lyle and I headed back into the catacombs to a new area past the candlelit corridor we had meant to take before detouring to save the lost souls. The air down there was thick and musty. I was laboring to breathe, but I was thankful there was any air at all.

I kept stopping along the way to check the red glowing carvings in the cobblestone walls. They looked like the Infernal glyphs that appeared around the portals whenever a demon was summoned. "It's so weird. I can't understand the signs, but the more I stare, the more it kinda starts to make sense," I said. "Like I hear it being read to me in my head."

"Take a look at this." Lyle shined the light from his gun on the wall. We were in a much larger room that reached at least two stories up, with alcoves housing mummified human remains. Some were dressed in simple garb made of scraps of cloth and burlap. Others were posed in such a way to make it appear as if they were watching us or in prayer, but it was the intense quiet that was more unsettling to me after all that action. As we passed, I could hear each flake of dust that fell from the cracks in the ceiling and every drop of wax that hit the floor as the candles wore down. "This looks like Big G."

An enormous mural ceremoniously framed by cobblestone columns lined the wall to our left. The columns glowed crimson from the glyphs carved into them, casting a warm hue upon the picture. "It is him," I said, gazing up at the image of a knight clad in armor born from darkness and evil. Winged humans were flying about him curiously.

I could only hope that he was safe now and resting in the shadows.

We continued onward down a darkening spiral, passing several more murals on the way. These depicted unfamiliar individuals, except that some of them wore recognizable items, such as Nazi regalia and clothing for a Catholic bishop and even a king. Not all the people seemed to be of status, however; plenty were dressed in more plain clothing from various eras: a farmer, a scientist, and a pilgrim woman. None were as particularly threatening as Gianni. "Here's one that looks like you." Lyle stopped short.

"That looks nothing like me." But it did. Only this version of me had fangs, horns, and claws. I was floating over a wasteland that was covered in black wavy lines, and I seemed to be inappropriately happy for the scene. "Hell is just trying to mess with our heads."

I caused a large crack in the picture with my mind, making the wide stone stairwell quake. "Careful!" Lyle warned. "You'll get us trapped down here if this place caves in."

The tunnel walls were closing in the further we traveled down them, until we had to turn sideways to continue. "I hope you're not claustrophobic," I told Lyle.

"Nah, but this might make me." The mysterious boon of lit candles ended, leaving us with only the light from Lyle's gun as I led the way. The stone walls were unusually warm and getting hotter with each step. My head was starting to touch the ceiling, and the tunnel rounded out to form a pipe that reminded me too much of the sewers I had frequented throughout my adventures. I couldn't float anymore, and soon we were forced to crouch and then crawl. The passage was getting narrower and started to angle downward at a steeper slope.

Moving hand over hand was laborious as my elbows scraped against the stone. I had to lie down flat and drag myself forward. I could see a light far down the shaft, but we never seemed to be getting any closer to it. I was starting to have my doubts that this was the way we should be going. If only I could use my powers to open up the path, but I feared a cave-in. The thought of the tunnel collapsing and crushing us wouldn't leave my head.

The walls closed in tighter, and although they were still solid, their texture began to feel like skin. We had to inch our way down, wriggling like insects. I couldn't face up to look toward the light any longer, and I couldn't open my mouth to speak unless I tilted my head down to my chest.

An anguished wail came from the direction of the light. It grew louder and more pained the closer we got. Each time it rang out, the tunnel began to shake violently, and bits of dust and rock crumbled on to our heads. I wanted to go back before we were buried, but we had to be so close based on how loud the sound was getting.

"I think we're at the end," I said to Lyle. The tunnel started to move on its own. It began to ripple like the tide and push us forward where there was no room to fit.

"Hurry! This place is coming down, and I don't want to die like this!"

"There's nowhere for me to go! I'm getting crushed! We have to go back!" My hand brushed against a lump coarser and hotter than the rest of our surroundings. I jerked away, fearing what it might be, but when nothing moved, I used my telekinesis to get a tactile sense of what was ahead. It felt like loops that were linked together; they may have been made of wood or stone. I crawled over them as the tunnel made room for us to squeeze by since I couldn't tilt my head up to take a look. They were metal chains covered in countless years of rust. There were chains anchored above and to the sides of me, making it even more difficult to escape. The wailing turned into howls of unbridled fury, and with every howl, the chains were tugged on.

Lyle and I finally made it to the end, but the mouth of the tunnel was too tight for even a child to escape through.

"I need to crack this open," I said, feeling around the mouth of the hole. "I'll pull you out with me so we aren't crushed."

The rocks around us broke, and as I had feared, the ceiling shifted down.

"Go!" Lyle yelled. I threw both of us out just as the tunnel came crashing down. We were ejected into a cave that was lit up by the walls themselves. It was just like the plastic paneling on PROJECT: UNITY's base, except that the light was an irritating orange and would pulse in and out along with gusts of moist wind flowing in one direction and then back. The dank cave wasn't constructed manually; it appeared to be natural, with stalactites and stalagmites, but I was certain of nothing at this point.

"Whatever's at the end of these chains is ticked off," Lyle said and reloaded his gun. The chains were still being tugged on with the deep growling and screaming that echoed through the cave. There were more of them secured around the rocky columns, some with links as large as those found moored to a ship's anchor or a bridge.

"If we don't put down whatever it is fast, this cave will collapse too."

"How are we supposed to get out?" he asked. I hadn't thought of it and didn't want to start at that point ... not until we were done.

"Hang on." I put up my hand to signal that we needed to stop. There was someone up ahead ... several people ... a lot of people. They were black figures ... larger than humans but roughly the same shape.

"They're not moving," Lyle whispered. I had a bad feeling we were about to be reunited with Gianni's dark side reborn. When the light from the walls pulsed brighter, I was able to get a better look at what was ahead.

"I think they're just statues." I felt out the landscape with my powers. If they were shadow constructs, I wouldn't have been able to touch them like that, but they turned out to be quite solid and immobile. Lyle and I walked over to check them out amid the constant growls still coming from down the way.

"These are Vyrlakalos's creepies," I said. "But what happened to them?"

The creatures were all facing in the same direction and poised for battle, but they were encased in what appeared to be a layer of charcoal.

"And here's Vyrlakalos," said Lyle, inspecting one of the eight-foot figures. Her claws were out and her mouth agape as if she had been about to take a huge bite out of someone. "Now we know where she's been the whole time."

"I guess I'll break her out." I cracked the earthen shell with a light tap of telekinetic energy, but her whole form crumbled into ash. "I didn't hit it that hard!"

"Jeez, she was cooked ..." Lyle pushed over one of the minions, which also broke into chunks. "They all were ... and at the same time, judging by how they're positioned close together in the same stance. I kinda feel bad."

"Don't get too sentimental!" I shouted over the rattling chains and enraged howls, which were getting louder. I may not have liked Vyrlakalos, and I'd been trying not to hate her, but it did also mean that we were down yet another person on our side.

"I'm just saying ... what a way to go. She had that demon skin to make her immune to fire, so whatever did this had to have cooked her from the inside out. I'm not big on killing to start with, but if there's no choice, just do it quick."

My temperature had been climbing again ever since we had gotten down there. I thought I had been doing a decent job of focusing on the mission and not on my emotions. The only stray feelings were caring toward Gianni, so I didn't understand why Hell should be affecting me, unless it was just unavoidable at this depth regardless of my mental state. I decided not to inform Lyle unless he brought it up. Worrying him would only cause a fatal distraction.

The cave seemed to branch into many directions by way of separate pillars and rock formations, but following the chains always led us to intersections where they all converged before branching off again. Occasionally, a chain would snap free and cause what it was fixed around to break. More than once, we had to run for our lives when a load-bearing column would collapse and cause a cave-in, leaving any possibility of backtracking all the more impossible.

"Something's coming up on thermal sight," Lyle said after scanning the area with his helmet's visor. "A lot of somethings ..."

Chapter Thirty

Breaking through the darkness ahead and pouring out from around the corners came a pack of dogs straight out of the Inferno. The sound of mad barking and nails clicking along the cave floor made the dismaying howls from before seem hushed by comparison.

"What is—"

"Hellhounds," I answered preemptively. "Their skin is what Owen's suit is made from. Don't ask me how he got it though."

The hounds were much larger than I imagined. Each was about the size of a rhinoceros, but they moved with incredible agility. Aside from their exaggerated measurements, they would have looked like any other canine if it hadn't been for their four demonic eyes and their breaths of green fire. They barely fit through the passages, but they were smart enough to split up and to each take a different route so that no matter which way we went, we would face a fight.

Lyle was already shooting behind us where one of the sneaky hounds had circled. He bumped into me as he backed away from his target, rapidly closing the distance between us, but the mutt fell to the ground, spewing its molten entrails inches from our feet. According to the Blackbournes, they were supposed to be bulletproof, but it looked like PROJECT: UNITY's weaponry had circumvented that.

The deeper we delved, the more I had to be wary about going overboard with my powers. One telekinetic blast could bring the whole place down on us. In my head, I thanked Noah for training me for close-quarters combat, and then I realized it had been a while since we'd seen him.

A precise telekinetic shot to the forehead was enough to do in one of the hounds; however, I had to pull back even more since the residual energy punched a hole in the cave wall behind it. I never thought being too strong would be such a problem. It wasn't only me, though. The hound's scalding blood was eating through the rock. These things were more of a threat dead than alive.

Lyle and I took out the dogs one by one until we were surrounded by pools of magma on all sides. The ceiling wasn't quite high enough to suspend us in the air safely while fighting, and even if it had been, I couldn't have done both at once. I spun around to check on him at the sound of a shout of pain. The splash back from one of the dog's superheated blood had gotten on Lyle's chest armor, melting it on contact. He was forced to ditch it and leave himself even more vulnerable than he already was.

Next went the helmet. I slayed another of the Infernal canines and flew us both away from the magma licking our heels. We were caught off guard when one of the hellhounds swiped at us from a corridor to the side as we made our retreat. I thought Lyle had been killed when I heard its claws make contact with his helmet. Broken pieces of plastic showered the wall. I lost control and showered the other wall right back with the hound's remains, causing the alcove we were in to shake.

"Careful!" Lyle's voice refocused me as he threw the helmet to the side. I didn't want to tell him that the palpable rage was surfacing. It was becoming a challenge to hear and see straight. I wanted this to be over with. Fast. All I could see when I gazed upon my friend was his own fragile mortality.

"On your right," Lyle said with an ease in his voice that didn't dictate the urgency of being trapped between hellspawn hundreds of feet below ground. "Man, we're good at this. They're retreating."

"How are you so calm?" I asked, and then I saw that the hounds weren't retreating at all but were positioning themselves for a new tactic. "Get down!"

I shoved Lyle to the floor and tore up the bedrock on either side of us to shield against a wave of balefire coming from all angles. The cavern quaked from my attempt to protect us, and the scorching flames persisted long enough to melt away the stone slabs. I couldn't attack the hounds all at once around us without bringing down the cave too.

The green fire broke through. I covered Lyle with my own body and managed to kill two of the Infernal mutts before I began burning alive. The fire was not only unspeakably painful, but it also brought violent and terrifying images into my head … enough to cause a man to lose his mind.

Being immolated was something I feared more than the throes of the Nether Realm or being caught in a cave-in. This was something I had been acquainted with in the past, and the mental trauma had been as bad as the physical.

The fire extinguished in a puff of smoke and the stench of burning flesh and hair. Lyle helped me up as my skin grew back. He had taken out the last two beasts on his own. "Don't do that again," he said. "I never know what you can and can't come back from." He didn't appear as serious as his words sounded; in fact, he was smiling.

A stray hound that must have missed the memo came racing toward us. "I've really, *really* had enough of these things." I propelled myself through the air and grabbed the giant canine by the jaws with my bare hands as it lunged at me. One jerk ripped its skull in two.

"Wow. I didn't know you could do that."

"Yeah. I'm full of surprises," I said. "Come on. Let's go before I get angry."

"Before? Some bad news, though ... ya know because our good luck had to run out some time," he continued and patted a charred scrap of clothing on my shoulder that was still smoking. "I'm out of ammo again except for our 'silver bullet' and some smaller-caliber rounds in my handgun."

"You reloaded when we went up to the surface."

"Uh, and I used it all up. This isn't an action movie, man. I can only carry so much with me. I got a few grenade rounds, but ... yeah, probably not a good idea down here."

"Wonderful." We rushed through the cave faster than we should have, but the snarls and screams were getting louder as we followed the remaining chains, and we wanted to have the heads-up before we were ambushed again.

"That sounds like one big dog," Lyle said. The beast was just around the corner now, and its cries sounded semi-human. "Let me know if you're just gonna rip its face off again so I don't have to bother pretending to help out."

"Oh my God!" I peeked at what we would be facing next. "It's Noah!"

Noah was bound around the neck, arms, wrists, thighs, and ankles by shackles that were attached to the chains we had been trailing. His attempts to break free were what would have crushed us without him knowing.

"I was sort of right," said Lyle. "It's *the* big dog ... not *a* big dog."

"Don't call him that."

There must have been something special about the restraints, because normal iron could never hold him. He was far too strong, even if he couldn't turn to mist due to being blood starved. The chains passed through holes in a stone monolith— the only structure we had seen down there so far that looked to be constructed on purpose. Across from him stood a carved archway at the entrance to a tunnel unlike the rest. Everything from that point on was man- or demon made with brick and mortar. Around the archway was more of the Infernal language I had seen on the upper floors.

"Noah! Noah, it's me. Just … just calm down so I can get you out." I tried to speak as loud as I could over his howls to placate him without yelling. The cave walls were polished to a reflective sheen, driving him madder at the inescapable sight of his imprisonment.

Noah was bleeding profusely from his shackles. The blood dripped down into grooves chiseled along the floor that led to the two pillars of the archway ahead and then just disappeared, absorbed into the stone. His face was wild, feral, and wracked with excruciating agony. Blood leaked from his tear ducts from the immense strain of trying to break himself free.

The fury in his bloodshot eyes was paralyzing, and when they met mine, there was no familiarity between us. He snarled louder and bared his fangs, trying to lash out at me like I was the enemy. Spit dribbled and flew from his mouth as it would a rabid animal. The more he struggled, the more he bled and the more the cave came closer to collapsing. His muscles tensed against the heavy shackles, his biceps close to breaking free by stretching out the metal. I hadn't been this afraid of him since we'd first met.

"Go far back and hide," I told Lyle. "I don't know what's about to happen. I don't know how much of Noah is left in there."

I snapped the collar around his neck and saw what was causing the labored noises that were coming from him. The restraint had a ring of two-inch spikes set inward to puncture his throat where blood pooled before trickling out. These weren't used to bind; they were there to torture. Freeing him wasn't having the calming effect I had hoped. I was scared to release him yet, but I took care of the spiked bonds around his upper arms and legs to start.

"If you're in there, don't attack me when I break these last two cuffs. I'm trying to help you."

He wouldn't speak. My words were returned with frenzied, murderous roars, but I couldn't leave him like this for even a second longer. This was his own personal Hell. Noah wanted freedom. Under all the pompous attitude, he had a heart capable of love and remorse that I had seen, but he hid it away. It was the only thing that couldn't be taken from him if he didn't show anyone he had it. There was one person bent on breaking it, though—his master— and he hated any reminder of his servitude to her. Being chained up like a dog was enough to break his spirit, even without the spikes digging into his body, and it was just enough for Hell to grab hold of him.

I removed the final shackles. He lunged at me and tackled me to the ground, tearing into my shoulder. This was not a bite of desperate hunger and in no way felt good. He ripped the meat from the bone and held my arms down with enough pressure to break them both against the floor. I threw him off me and held him against the wall while I healed, but being restrained again was making him slip further into animalistic lunacy. His glare and deafening war cry had an actual physical effect, causing me to shudder and take a step back. I hadn't been affected by his hypnotic abilities since I'd been mortal, and I had no idea he could use them to induce sheer terror.

In the moment I was stunned, he wrested himself free from my control and disappeared. He pounced on me from behind, digging his fangs into my neck and twisting violently to sever my spine. I had to be thankful that he was too berserk to bother using his weapons, although this was not much better. I knew I had to subdue him before his attention shifted off me and he went for Lyle.

Noah managed to break loose once more because I was concerned that applying the force necessary to keep him in place would do more harm than good. He tackled me from the side, moving at half his normal speed, but it was still enough to slam me into the bedrock. Most of my bones fractured all at once from the collision, causing me to send my own screams of pain echoing throughout the cave. This wasn't helping the anger situation.

He went to pounce on me again, but I had fallen victim to that enough times when he'd been at his best to know how to handle it now. I grabbed his arm and channeled my power into my strength like I had done against the hellhounds, but this time, I used it as leverage to throw Noah to the floor. I pulled back on his arm once his face hit the floor like he'd shown me to make someone submit when I wanted to use restraint. We clashed in hand-to-hand combat like that time out in the snow—only, this time, it was for real. I got on his back and put him in a choke hold so I could wedge my arm into his mouth for him to drink my blood, which would hopefully calm him down if he took in enough to heal his wounds and didn't just use it to beat me into a pulp even faster.

My idea worked until he snapped my other forearm in two and threw me over him and onto the ground. His fist came down and punched a hole in the bedrock, just narrowly missing my head. I'd had enough. I cracked off the top half of the monolith he had been tethered to and smashed it into his skull while I was still on my back. He tumbled across the ground and didn't move after smacking against the wall. I started to worry that I'd gone too far when I saw that his head had been gashed open and the rest of his blood was draining from it. He wasn't turning to ash, so if I fed him blood, maybe the euphoric feeling would bring him to his senses this time now that he was out cold.

I moved him into a more comfortable position and opened his mouth enough to fit my wrist in. I pressed up against his fangs until I felt a sharp pinch, and I let my blood flow down his throat.

The bite did *not* feel pleasing in anyway on my end. I was in enough pain that I had to take deep breaths and keep telling myself not to jerk away as he clamped down. I started to worry about whether what made him who he was might really be gone forever … just like I feared with Gianni. The difference was that Gianni fought tooth and nail to stay sane, knowing that he had someone to stay sane for. Noah wasn't able to hang on. He had no one left. I could only hope that our friendship was enough to bring him back toward the light, but I had my doubts.

I didn't have long to wait for an answer. Noah's brow furrowed and his lips curled as he bit down harder. He sucked the blood from my veins faster than my heart could pump it. I started to shake and felt a sharp pain in my chest as my heartbeat pounded irregularly. Triggering any aggression now by shoving him away would be bad. I had to pry his mouth open just enough to slow his feeding on top of holding his throat with my hand so the blood wouldn't run out of the puncture wounds.

Soon after he started healing, he began to settle down at last. His eyes still hadn't opened, but the pleasant sensation I was accustomed to from his bite was starting to return.

"Noah?" There was no verbal response. He just grunted, and when I tried to reclaim my arm, he growled. I was so glad he was okay. I waited another minute and tried again. "Noah, I know it's you. What happened?"

He grunted again until I pulled him off by the nose.

"I don't remember," he said with his eyes still closed, and then he went back to drinking. "You smell like someone shit in a campfire."

I pushed him away. "If you're feeling well enough to be an asshole again, you don't need any more blood."

"Is it all clear?" Lyle asked from far down the tunnel we had used to get there.

"No. Go away!" Noah shouted back and sat against the wall with his head down. "Why is he still alive?"

"I need to know what happened," I insisted.

"Did you hit me in the head?" he asked and rubbed his temple where the gash had been.

"Stop avoiding my question."

"I don't remember. I got down here and thought I was on fire. When I tried to get back out, everything went black and I was being chained to that rock."

"Who was doing that to you?"

"I don't know. I thought it was the Italian at the time for some reason. Maybe because it was so dark ... I don't know."

Lyle walked up, but I waved him away. I knew Noah would stop talking with him around.

"I heard someone say something about opening that door with my blood." He nodded up to the opened archway. There was a short pause before he said any more. "I'm nobody's fucking attack dog."

I was shocked that that had come out of his mouth so abruptly and worried that he had somehow been able to read my mind the moment I'd thought of it when helping him. "I didn't say you were."

Noah was groaning and holding his head. He punched the ground hard enough to crack it and dug his fingers in until the nails bent back. I pulled his hand away so he'd stop, but he shoved me.

"We're leaving," he said through more growls. "You can't go in there, if that's what you're planning."

"I have to. Lyle and I need to finish this."

He grabbed me, bit into my neck, and then pushed me away again. It seemed to make him recover his sanity for a time, but as with Gianni, the exertion it took to maintain control exhausted him. He slumped over and became unresponsive. I wanted to get him out of there, but the only way to go was forward.

"I'll come back for you when this is over," I told him and shouted to Lyle. "It's up to us, rookie! Let's end this."

"Don't go in there, kid," Noah said quietly enough so Lyle wouldn't hear. "Whatever's doing this is too strong. We'll find a way out of here. We'll even take the human with us too." It wasn't easy leaving Noah there. I had no way of knowing what was ahead and if he would be safe back there alone. Lyle waited by the archway for me. "Let someone else save the world for once. We can train more, and you can always come back if that's what you really want, but I don't want you dying on me just yet... Please." That one word, which I had thought was absent from Noah's vocabulary, cut deep. But I had to keep going.

Chapter Thirty-One

"Cloister of Malice," Lyle read above the archway. I assumed the words spoke to him as they'd done to me in the catacombs. "Doesn't get any more 'demon lord' than that." I stayed quiet and kept looking back at Noah, who was lying there on the ground. I wasn't feeling so powerful anymore. "I feel like you're always the one holding everything together," Lyle said. It was as if he could sense my hesitation without a word spoken.

"What are you talking about?"

"Everyone trusts you. They're not here because of me. Gianluca, Noah, even Owen. The Blackbournes were on our most-wanted list until you came along and turned them into allies."

"You're the reason I'm here and haven't given up," I said. "Just like back in New York when we met." Lyle and I had come a long way since our first inexperienced adventures in the supernatural world, but the strongest people we knew had fallen, and there was no one left for us to fall back on. For all it was worth, I was still the same scared, dirty kid stripped of my self-confidence, and Lyle was just a rookie cop with a handgun. In my mind, we were back where we had started in my Manhattan apartment without a clue about how to survive or what was happening.

"That's why we make a good team, man," Lyle said. "You're my brother from another mother ... uh, well ... you know what I mean."

The crimson hallway into the cloister was another narrow path like the one from the catacombs, only the ceiling was at least fifty feet high. We had to go single file and turn sideways at some points where the stones jutted out of the wall, making travel slow and arduous.

This was not the same stone architecture as above. I couldn't identify any particular style on Earth throughout history that resembled what we were in. The stones had the speckled texture of granite but were an uncharacteristically saturated red for a natural mineral, and they were carved into perfect cubes of varying sizes. They were hot to the touch, and the breeze that had permeated the cave seemed to funnel through in a blistering wind.

Looking back was not a good idea when trying to shield my eyes from the cauterizing gale as it changed directions. The pathway behind us spiraled up into a corkscrew in complete disregard for the laws of time and space. I had come to find that phenomena like this were common in other dimensions, but it was a first for Lyle, who wasn't appreciating that his preferred rules of reality were being screwed with.

"Stay sharp," Lyle said as we neared the end of the hall. "I just need to land a single shot, and that's all we have, so cover me while I line it up."

"*Kill him.*" A cheerful man and woman's voice reverberated through the corridor and my head in unison. "*Dissolve his flesh.*"

Obviously, this had to be the demon lord. I was feeling the heat being stoked inside my gut again.

"It's empty. This place is empty," Lyle said as we exited into a huge cylindrical chamber that was made entirely of the same red cubes.

"*He's jealous of your power. He resents you.*"

We were on a circular platform around the outer edge of the room. Above us were other identical floors I could see up to through the hole in the middle of each. The cloister strongly resembled the layout of PROJECT: UNITY's atrium on base, only the light that mimicked the sun and moon above was down below instead.

"There's no way up or down," Lyle said and peeked over the edge into the dark pit below us. "Good thing you can fly."

"*Your love disgusts him. Your kind repulses him.*"

"Up or down?" he asked.

"I don't care. Just pick one," I said. "We've been going down the whole time. I don't know why you'd even bother to ask."

"Yeah, that's true."

"He pretends to understand you. How can an insect know the suffering of a god?"

The veins in my hand were turning black. I floated us down one floor. The wind blew down into the darkness below and then back out.

"Humans are hateful, arrogant creatures. They choose to shun you for their amusement." The voice was so loud now that I thought Lyle might be able to hear it. My hands were trembling, and the blackness in my veins was spreading up my arms.

"We have to hurry." I could barely hear my own words when I spoke.

"They will never learn to love you. Their lives ... so short. New ones will come, but you will remain. How can you allow such weak, spiteful beings to reign over you? To rot in obscurity is a fate for maggots."

"What? Are you feeling okay?" Lyle asked, looking at my arms.

"He mocks your love. They all mock your love. He covets your power. They all covet your power. He will betray you. They will all betray you."

"Shut up!" I shouted at the voice in my head. "Just get away from me."

"His presence displeases you. Destroy him. Destroy them all."

The entire cloister shook from my anger.

"Sorry, I —" Lyle started to apologize.

"I'm talking to ... the voices in my head." I felt like I was being set on fire from the inside out. The heat was enraging me ... the voices were too. Everything was making me angry. I wanted to shut it all out ... maybe because there was some truth to the words.

"Just ... just, uh, go back. I'll take care of it from here," Lyle said.

"He wishes to control you. First as your leader, then your master. They want to contain you, imprison you, study you. You know it to be true. They have ruled for too long. It is you who should enjoy the sight of them in cages."

"Don't ... I'm fine."

"They seek to conquer. Even each other. Their hatred has no boundaries. When you hide, they will find another. Hate must be released. Everyone hates. Gestalt's crusade has ended. PROJECT: UNITY's crusade has begun. They will expand if you let them. They will suppress your ascendance. They will kill your kind."

I took us down to the last floor, and from midair, we could see it—the demon lord—in the pit. Or I should say, it *was* the pit. A giant breathing orifice was at the bottom of the atrium, surrounded by the final platform. It opened and closed like an enormous camera shutter made of skin. The voices were coming from there. I could feel it. It was still so cheery and confident in its speech.

"That's disgusting," Lyle said. "Is that it? I was expecting more."

"He judges us. He judges you. I judge no one. Malice is impartial, free from prejudice. It is a choice left to the beholder. He stands for what you hate. I sense it in you. A noble cause. One that deserves action. Hate him back. Hate them all back." The same pulsating orange light from the walls of the cave was also coming from down inside the flesh chasm in sync with the breathing and voices in my head.

"Shoot it—fast ... I ... it's in my head—!" My vision cut out.

"The Dark One was whom was meant to be here. He was weak. You are strong. The kings gave him power. He betrayed them. Do not trust the betrayer! They made him undead. They made all the undead. They gave him limits ... restrictions. He wanted more. He sought power he did not deserve. He took it from them. They want it back."

Assuming that any of this was true, it would mean the Nether Lords Gianni claimed to have turned him undead to do their bidding were actually the very Demon Kings who had fought against Heaven. He said he hunted down and defeated them through the ages, but there's no way he could have. This one demon lord demolished us all with seemingly little effort, and the kings were far more powerful by several orders of magnitude, according to Vance's description and the legends that went along with it.

"Dorian!" I heard Lyle shouting, but I still couldn't see. "Put me down! It's me! Don't do this!"

I fought against the influence drowning my mind in irrational feelings of hatred. I could see through the cloudy haze covering my eyes. Heat waves emanated from me. I was dangling Lyle in the air by his neck and couldn't command my own body to stop.

"Please! It's Lyle!" he choked. The only thing I could do was redirect my anger to throw him away from me instead of strangling him to death.

"Get away from me!" I told him in the moment that I could speak. "I'm not in control."

"The Dark One will destroy the humans with our power. We do not want this. It should be you to rule. Put the humans where they belong. The humans belong under you, as insects. Their hate is natural. It feeds us. Kill the Dark One. Kill the humans who hate you. Rule the rest. You decide what is right to hate."

My vision was gone again, but I heard everything happening around me. The trigger pull, the bullet leaving the barrel, piercing the massive quivering lips of the Devil ... and then only silence.

"Yeah! Take that you evil butthole-looking demon! That's for all my friends and everyone else you hurt!" Lyle's cheers of victory may have been premature.

"A false hope in the form of a bullet. Poetic. Pathetic. Where do you seek to banish me? We are already in Hell. We are already here. Your plan has failed. Your hatred still feeds me. You are in my world." The demon lord's dual voices spoke outwardly this time for us both to hear and then continued in my head. *"They all wish to limit your power. They wish to condemn you. They all fear you, laugh at you, despise you, doubt you. You know*

what you are capable of. Great feats. Monumental feats."

The cloister flashed back into view for a brief moment. The platform we were on and all those above us were crowded by hundreds of people. They were the ones from the murals in the catacombs.

I spun in the air until I was dizzy, scanning for Gianni, but he wasn't one of them. They burst into green flames, and from their bodies spawned the same demons and hellhounds we had been fighting on our way there. Lyle was running for his life as the floors above us shifted down to create one giant staircase for the Infernals to reach us. There was nowhere for Lyle to go but around in circles.

"There is no path to walk, to choose. That is the grandest illusion of all... My congregation has been enlightened to this. They accept this. I am an aspect of man. I am man's insidious curiosity. I am innovation. I am creation. My image seared into the minds of the most devout who stand before you. They have been branded. A wondrous gift."

I had to hold on so I could help him. I flew myself to the middle of the room and unleashed my anger on the demons until they disintegrated to nothing. The room was quieted again, except for the praise I earned from the lord of the pit as the little that was left of his congregation was sucked into the darkness below like a deep breath.

"Yes. Feed them to me. A truly marvelous power. A power worthy of true reverence. I can give you more. More power to enact your will. You can choose who the world hates. Hatred will never leave, but it can be directed. Bring equality to the insects.

Show them. Guide them. Hate can be motivating, inspiring. Use it. Usher in a world of balance. I know what you want. You know what I want. This is what we want together."

I knew what Gianni and Noah were feeling now. I was fighting my own mind and body to keep my sanity, but some of the words were starting to make sense to me. There was a numbness encroaching that I was scared would spell the end for me and inevitably for Lyle.

More demons were summoned in. I wasn't even telling my body to fight, but I would see them disintegrate from the telekinetic maelstrom any time my vision snapped back.

"Dorian, listen to me!" Lyle yelled. I caught a glimpse of him holding his arm while he ran under a demon's legs to flee. "Kill the demon lord! Fly down and kill it! It's just summoning stuff to make you mad, and that makes it stronger!"

"He wants you to die. You will die inside me. I would not want that. Give him to me instead. Just a push. He does not have to suffer. Unless you prefer it."

The next time my sight returned, I had Lyle hanging inches over the mouth of the pit while he begged for his life. I was trying to move him away, but it was hurting him when my struggling caused me to clamp down and crush his body. My hearing faded out next and muted his pleas.

"Closer. Offer him and be free. The souls of the pure are invaluable. The incorruptible must be studied. They are a threat to our work. I shall grant

you immense strength to do as you will. Only his soul I require. One insignificant soul."

Multiple tiny, gray, three-fingered hands reached up from the depths of the puckered orifice when it opened to grab at Lyle, who was suspended in the air. I wanted to bring him back in. The sorrowful, nervous look in his blue eyes wrenched at my stomach.

"Do not sympathize with the enemy. His kind made you a victim. Turn the tide. Begin the revolution you desire."

I watched as I dropped him into the pit against my will. The hands reacted quickly to snatch him out of the air and pull him down. I blacked out again as I screamed because of what I had done, and I tried to fly after him.

I battled for control of my body with cries of remorse. I broke free long enough to see that the hands had been cut at the wrists and were flailing in pain, spewing molten blood from the stumps. There was no sign of Lyle, though. My search was frantic. I knew I didn't have much time until I was at the mercy of the demon lord's influence again.

Legions of demons and hellhounds were summoned in all around the room. I looked to where they were headed to see Lyle on a platform across from me, with Noah lying at his feet.

I started to fly to them but then thought it best to keep my distance. Instead, I dealt with the Infernals closing in on their position by crushing them to dust with a scream to hold the others' attention on me. Then I made the critical error of attacking the demon lord directly.

The furnace that had been building up within me exploded in a pale green balefire. My body was vaporized until no part of it remained; yet, even to my surprise, I still managed to revive.

Something wasn't right.

I could see pieces of myself re-forming in midair, but none of them were attached. Strands of blood vessels unraveled, reams of skin unfurled, and my organs and bones floated. I didn't know how I was seeing this, but it brought back the memory of being on Gestalt's operating table, and that brought back the anger along with it.

I had been unmade.

I tried using my powers to put myself back together, but I had no idea where to begin or how the intricacies of the body worked. *Please, I don't want to die,* I thought, hoping someone would hear me. The anger was what kept me from being whole again. Any time I moved two pieces of myself near each other, they repelled and I lost control in my frustration.

"Your anger has blossomed into such beautiful malice. Blind hatred is the most productive. Dull the other senses to see the world for what it truly is. You think yourself immune because you are a victim. A victim searches for strength, and you have found it." It was right. I would have killed those Carpathians that Gestalt was experimenting on when they were just helpless creatures trapped behind glass like I once was. I was letting myself become the prejudiced asshole I hated in other people.

"I just want to live," I pleaded. "I want to love and be with my friends, not get revenge on people I don't even know." This train of thought helped me regain some form of control—enough at least to bring my scattered body close enough for the pieces to begin repairing themselves.

I awoke on the floor beside the edge of the pit, feeling debilitated and anemic. Noah jumped down with the Muramasa in hand, but when he came close, he was also set ablaze. He turned to mist to extinguish the flames and re-formed further back. Again, he attempted to come near the edge from a different angle, but every spot caused the same backlash.

"Ah, Muramasa. I almost did not recognize you hiding in that cage of tempered steel."

As soon as I got up, I was on fire once more. Noah tackled me and rolled out of the way. He managed to avoid being incinerated by popping into mist form at the last possible second, but I burned to death again and had to regenerate all over.

"We can't fight this thing," Noah said. "Anything we do is going to make it stronger. The Muramasa could kill it, but even if you can pull off regrowing from *nothing* like that somehow, we still can't get close enough."

"You cannot fight hate." The cheerful man and woman's voices were very quiet now inside my head, but they grew louder in one sudden burst, making me jump. *"Your soul is forever touched by wrath! You have been tempered for greatness!"*

The platforms above began to crumble down on to us. I used my powers to catch Lyle as the last few blocks beneath his feet were starting to give way. His left arm was broken, and I knew it was my fault whether directly or not.

The demon lord was right; we couldn't fight hate, not with more hate.

"It has to be Lyle," I shouted over the inner voice that was trying to take hold of me again. "He hasn't been affected by any of this. It can't touch the pure. Give him the Muramasa."

"Me?!" Lyle recoiled. Noah was gripping his head and clenching his teeth—signs of the demon lord wresting control of him too. Another legion of its minions spawned in atop the rubble.

"It's always been you, Lyle. You were right about me. I was becoming bitter after being a victim. It's the same thing that happened to The Blighted One, but I'm not going to let it happen anymore."

Noah and I fought back the horde around us, but I could tell by its erratic rants that it only made the lord amused.

"Use this on it." Noah pulled out a syringe of black liquid from his pocket and handed it to Lyle.

"You kept that?" I asked over the calamity, trying to keep my anger in check. It was the Rift parasite specimen we'd found at Gestalt during that first mission. "I thought I told you to destroy it."

"You did, but I guess you forgot I don't take orders from you." He forced a smirk and went back to clutching his head. "And it's a good thing I don't. This thing eats souls, remember? Demons eat souls too; they're full of them. Do the math."

Upon losing control, Noah lashed out at Lyle against his will. I grabbed one of his wakizashi from its sheath and staked him through the heart so he couldn't be used against us.

"It's hero time," I told Lyle over the noise of more demons approaching, platforms falling, and the lord making threats in a friendly tone. I handed over the Muramasa after prying it from Noah's hand. "I'll cover you as long as I can."

"I will pick clean his bones in my bowels for eternity. He will suffer much. You will suffer more."

I scattered the Infernals to make a straight run for Lyle to reach the pit before I started losing my mind. A hellhound caught him by the leg, but my senses were so scrambled that I couldn't even hear him cry out. The next time I regained my vision, the beast had been left dead on the floor by a stab between the eyes, and Lyle was limping onward.

"What worth is one fleeting mortal existence? A meager price to pay for godhood. His death is inevitable. Benefit from his sacrifice. Donate his soul to me and be rewarded the power to change the world to your whim. Be rewarded with an unimaginable power inconceivable by mortal-kind. What friend would rather die in vain? He is no friend."

The demon lord was becoming desperate and frustrated by my refusal to accept its offer. That unfitting benevolent voice was now panged with passive–aggressive undertones as Lyle stabbed the syringe into it. A new batch of probing hands shot out to drag Lyle to his demise. He swung at them with the Muramasa, using his one good arm.

It didn't take long for the parasite to spread through a being with so much nutritious energy to offer. The black veins I had learned to hate the sight of were now much appreciated as they ravaged the body of the Infernal. Its skin became brittle and chalky white and cracked as it opened and closed the aperture of flesh.

"You ANGER me. I grow STRONGER." The voice was no longer pleasant and rang throughout the cloister for all to hear. Two enormous versions of its hands reached out and slammed down as something far larger climbed from the crumbling orifice. More demonic foot soldiers and beastly canines came to their master's aid.

"GAZE UPON THE FORM SEARED INTO THE MINDS OF MY CONGREGATION. BEHOLD—WRATH'S VASSAL! I AM LORD MA'AL, THE INNOVATOR, THE VISIONARY, AND MY HYMN OF INSPIRING MADNESS WILL BE IMMUTABLE!" Attached to the two arms was a gargantuan skull with two faces fused together side by side. Ma'al was weakened, but the parasite wouldn't be enough to end this. I realized that it was too distracted to keep me possessed, and I had to bet the same for Noah, so I unstaked him.

"We have to split up and keep the demons off Lyle, but we can't kill any, or it just makes the lord stronger!" I shouted and flew off. "And don't try attacking the big guy either."

I sped through the horde, dragging as many of the Infernals as I could with me away from the center. Meanwhile, Lyle had cut two of the fingers from the demon lord's hand. Noah dashed back and forth, gathering the attention of small groups at a time by making them hit each other in their attempts to attack him and cutting the hellhounds' legs out from under them to slow them down.

"My unholy congregation already toils on Earth to seed the world with my wrath. The match has been struck. The fuse has been lit. It will all burn. You waste your efforts on me. Humanity will be your damnation. There is nothing so beautiful, so wonderful, as human flesh concealing its own demise."

An exhaust of flame was let loose from the mouths of Ma'al. I couldn't see where Lyle was and just had to hope he was still fighting, until I saw one of the intact demon lord's hands grab him. It was bringing him to one of its faces, but he still had the Muramasa, although his arm wasn't free to use it. I threw one of the dogs at the skull, where it stuck in an eye socket.

"I have corrected their perversions for centuries. Their precious technologies, their advancements, these were but dreams until I showed them how to forge a new reality in my image. Beautiful weaponry and malicious experiments to surpass the boundaries imposed by their maker. I have shown my congregation the secrets hidden from them for years by these untrue gods. Long-forgotten knowledge must be unearthed and lessons lost between generations restored."

This was just enough for Lyle to pull his arm out and stab the demon lord in the hand. The cursed blade didn't discriminate when it came to the type of blood it drank, and it seemed the parasite adapted well to it as long as there was a source of energy for it to sap. With both in play, the hand dried out rapidly and atrophied until it was nothing.

"Whom do you think showed mankind that fire is meant for more than warmth but to smite their enemies in righteousness? Whom do you believe taught them to bottle lightning or harness the atom as a source of spectacular power that divides nations and decimates their foes? Or to even turn their simple medicines into magnificent elixirs of life that remove the frailty of humanity all together? The answer is I."

Lyle fell not too gracefully onto the skull and stabbed the Muramasa into it while holding on for dear life.

"There is no war to win. There is no invasion to thwart. We have never left the Earth. To purge my existence from the world is to undo free will itself. You can never eliminate the quirks of creativity without erasing the mind itself. You can never erase me. I exist in you all. I exist in laboratories, in factories, in the darkest reaches of the mind, which few have the courage to embrace."

Lyle pushed the katana in to the hilt. Lord Ma'al reached for him with its half-amputated appendages. I knew I'd burn again using my powers on it to defend Lyle, but this was it. This had to end here. I pulled the arms away long enough for Lyle to be uninterrupted as my soul burst into balefire and my body was covered in black veins.

"You will make a glorious king in my stead. Absorb my power. Take up my mantle. To slay this

form is no victory. I cannot be defeated. My work will not be stopped. Now I am part of you. Inside you. Go forth and push the wheels of progress. Grind the gears onward until naught but dust remains."

The twin skull of Ma'al cracked and fell into decay, and the voices wavered and faded out as I returned to normal. Noah leaped across the pit and grabbed Lyle before he dropped along with the corpse of Ma'al, which exploded in a mushroom cloud of brimstone at the bottom. With their master gone, the other demons in the cloister retreated into their portals. Noah seized the Muramasa from Lyle's hand.

"Yeah, you better run!" Lyle jeered them while holding his bad arm. "Pretty good for a human, huh?"

The cloister was devastated by tremors that caused the ceiling to hail down as the demons left. I flew up to the hallway we had used to get there, but it was already sealed tight. The temperature plummeted, and the orange light across the crimson walls died out, leaving us in the dark.

"They're leaving because the place is about to crush us," Noah said.

"At least we won ...," said Lyle as we all took refuge together against a wall. "That's what's important, right? Mission accomplished."

"I guess now is a good time to apologize for ... you know ..." I said to Lyle as I shielded us from the falling detritus in the darkness.

"We're good, man. Don't even mention it. I know it wasn't you. What happens in Hell stays in Hell."

Chapter Thirty-Two

Listening to the walls come crashing down around us was bittersweet. We'd done more than banish a demon lord; we'd annihilated it along with its sinister domain and put a stop to its hateful influence over Earth. But there wasn't much we could do in celebration since this would be our grave in the next few minutes.

I was at my limit as the several tons of rock I was holding up turned into hundreds and then thousands. Nobody was saying anything as I started to slip and felt the stone touch the top of my head. Soon, I was lying on my back with less than an inch between my face and the rock.

"To the side," Noah growled as he tried to help. "Move it to the left, where the pit is."

I did as Noah said and redirected the landslide instead of trying to hold it up, but eventually there was going to be more than we could shrug off. Rock was falling faster than I could handle as the catacombs and then the floors above them plunged into the pit. Lyle and Noah were yelling, but no one could hear the other over the noise.

Lights and sirens streaked past us from the Gestalt laboratories that were the last to sink and seal the pit, which was a mangled mess of metal and medical supplies. We had a chance to escape if we could navigate the remainder of the twisted facility ruins that were hanging by a thread above us.

"Go, go, go!" I shouted. Noah raced upward, clamoring over the wreckage as well as he could with us holding on to him. Pieces of the facility below gave way, and we were stuck beneath more that lay ahead.

"Help move this," he told me and started digging a way up through the wreckage. We scrambled up until we could start moving horizontally again. With the whole infrastructure gutted, the mountain that the facility was built into was collapsing too. I barreled through the remains of the corridors, smashing through walls and anything else in our way.

Revisiting the labs let me see the similarities between Gestalt and PROJECT: UNITY more clearly now. Those same mechanical octopus arms used for surgery by Dr. Sullivan were in many of the rooms there, just with a Gestalt Industries sticker slapped on them, and then, of course, there was the security system.

Automated surgical lasers, backlit canisters of alien organs and unnaturally colored bodily fluids, computers plucked straight from the future with keyboards coded in a language foreign to this world ... I was no expert, but the more I thought about it, the more I questioned whether this did all stem from Ma'al or if he had been just calling our bluff.

I was more curious than ever to see the PROJECT: UNITY New Zealand base after knowing their troops used the same armor and weapons that any soldier in a decent-sized country had access to. The technological leap that had happened practically overnight when setting up the base in Greenland had not been their own doing. When I looked at the bigger picture, as Noah had always told me to do, Hell would want PROJECT: UNITY to prosper.

PROJECT: UNITY was the spiritual successor to Gestalt, just like Ma'al had said. The fight between them wasn't one of good versus evil— not to Hell. It was a battle of dominance. PROJECT: UNITY won the prize and, along with it, Infernal interest. How long would it take for the next Infernal to rise and then exert its influence over PROJECT: UNITY? Lyle would never let that happen, but he may not have a choice. The answer was probably better found with another question: How long would it take for PROJECT: UNITY to become an uncontested world power?

"Sunlight! We're almost there!" Lyle pointed to a widening crack in the roof as I levitated him along with me. I burst through, but the helicopter wasn't where we had left it. The encampment and desert around us were being sucked down into the fissure. I spotted the team a few hundred yards away, but Noah stood in the shadows of the facility as more of it fell while he tried to avoid the sun. I boxed Noah in by bending scraps of metal around him and made a mad dash through the air to safety.

"See? I told you I'd get us out," he said, smirking, once we were in the clear. "No thanks to you." I had to laugh, and even he started to, but he caught himself.

"Has anyone seen Gianluca?" I asked over the engines starting.

"He appeared out of nowhere under the shadow of the helicopter naked and unconscious. We had a pilot come and evac him and Mr. Blackbourne back to base," Commander Timmons told me amid the sound of explosions and gunfire in the distance. "The Congregation has formed a militarized insurgent group and started terrorizing a small town a mile west of here. They're all unarmed civilians living there, from what we're hearing from a hacked radio feed. The insurgents are planning to use the town as a foothold to launch a campaign against a major city nearby. We may have trouble taking off."

"We didn't come this far to get shot down by a bunch of terrorists," Lyle said. "Shouldn't they have stopped fighting? We killed the demon in charge and closed the place down pretty good ..."

"Peace is a choice." I looked out over the burning village as we took off. Not far away, the ravenous sinkhole that Ma'al's lair crumbled into finished swallowing the mountain and was filling with sand. "We might've helped push things toward a better balance, but people still have to make their own decisions."

"I know." Lyle sighed. "I just woulda liked a little bit of peace after what we went through."

"People don't know they have the choice until they're shown, and even then, they need to be given a reason to choose something different than what they're used to," Noah said, and threw himself down on a medical cot. "Now shut up so I can sleep."

I sat with my legs hanging out of the helicopter door. It was hot, smelled like smoke and sulfur, and dead bodies littered the ground below. This wasn't much different from Hell. Actually, it was worse. This was heartbreaking to top off the already dismaying ambiance. Mothers cried over the bodies of their children, husbands over wives, and the ones causing it ran around in apathy like they were kids on a playground playing make-believe. From up here, I was starting to see what the Ancients were always going on about—humans being like children. This wasn't a game to me, though.

"I'm going down there," I said.

"They'll see you, and we can't get close to land," said Commander Timmons. "You're going to stick out."

"I'm used to it." I pulled a sheet off an unused cot and threw it around me as I jumped from the helicopter. It was time for someone to step up and make a change. The humans could keep killing each other, and the supernaturals could duke it out behind the scenes, but nothing was being accomplished. Even if we killed every demon in Hell, humans would still be humans unless they were shown something they had never seen before and were given a choice they didn't think they had.

I swooped down to the village, where unarmed civilians were still being dragged out of the ruins of their houses and executed by extremist lunatics. This was making me nervous ... more so than my showdown with Hell. I felt like I was on stage about to perform, but no one was paying any attention to me. The situation was truly abysmal if people were too panicked to notice the floating figure above them.

Bullets whizzed by, Molotov cocktails flew, and trucks lined up in the streets to take hostages while others were on their knees, waiting to be beheaded by the knives at their throats. I called them all to me, turning to claim every weapon as far as my eyes could see. It started with a few bullets and knives being snatched out of the air and pulled to my fingertips. I then dismantled the rifles and crushed the pieces like paper into a growing sphere before me. That got me the attention I was looking for.

There was a pause in the fighting to see where all the weapons were going, and then the familiar gawking I was used to from humans. I thought they would be running for their lives or would have an epiphany about how powerless they really were, like the victims they were making, and that this would cause them to lay down their guns.

"STOP!" I screamed at the top of my lungs, but they didn't cease. Instead, they focused their rage on me. "Are you all really that far gone? If destruction is what you want ... then ...you have my sympathies."

I broke apart the vehicles to free the captives and started sucking everything dangerous into the sphere, including the militants themselves, who were broken down into insignificant dust. All the neutered instruments of war swirled around me as I added them to my collection. Explosions flared out from incendiaries going off when being compressed into the sphere. Not a single hair on any civilian's head was so much as grazed as I quieted the calamity and ended the chaos.

It couldn't end there, though. I couldn't let this be what innocent people had to look to for hope. I had to help them rebuild. Something good *had* to come from this. A feeling came over me that I couldn't shut out. I was inspired by those who stayed true to their peaceful nature, and although I didn't know their fallen, I felt a certain level of empathy toward them because of their pain.

I had no idea how I was doing it, but whatever was happening felt natural. It wasn't a conscious thought controlling my powers; it was raw emotion affecting everything I touched. The damage to the village was being rewound in time. Fires extinguished, and the buildings around me were reconstructed piece by piece using everything I had claimed from the terrorists, including their own ashes, to fill in the cracks. The evil I had silenced would help rebuild this place.

I was as amazed as everyone else. Two months ago, I was having difficulty smoothing out a stone, and now this. It was an awakening inside me that took control and just had to get out.

Everyone was quiet when I returned to the helicopter, but they didn't take long to then break out into an eruption of cheers.

"What was that? Lyle asked.

"I'm not really sure," I said.

"I don't know who any of Rudgar's contacts were in the Pentagon or INTERPOL to help cover this up. Hopefully, they're in PARAGON somewhere ... Blackbourne might be able—"

"I don't want to cover it up, Lyle. That was my whole point. I want the whole world to see ... both of them."

"You're going to have everyone coming after you from both sides though, man. The world is never gonna be the same with things out in the open."

"Let them come. I'm ready. Then I'll know who my enemies are upfront. The world is never going to make progress if we keep doing the same thing. Someone's got to stand up, and who better than us? We can say we've been through Hell and back.

"The supernaturals talk about this 'Apocatastasis' ... how the world is going to reset and everything we know will come to an end. Everyone is waiting for someone else to make a move while the world falls apart around them. History is literally repeating itself, yet no one wants to stop it. I think if we do something different by coming out and unifying both worlds, we can break the cycle."

I couldn't wait to leave the helicopter and see Gianni the moment we landed. Everyone else resumed their celebrating across the base while I headed to Medical. It hadn't been this lively around here for a while.

"Dorian—"

"Where's Gianni? How is he?" I cut Rebecca off as soon as I saw her.

"He's still unconscious," she said, walking me to his room. It wasn't darkened in shadow as it usually would be when he slept. "His vitals are weak but stabilized. Forty-seven bones were fractured, and he received numerous corresponding deep-tissue puncture wounds. His own superhuman durability is working against him in this case. It looks like it isn't entirely from the density of his dark powers as previously suspected since even when not in control of them, his skin is still impenetrable by any conventional means. I wasn't able to give him stitches to stop the bleeding or administer an IV for painkillers and fluids. All I could do was wrap the wounds tightly and change them out as they soaked through."

"That means he's still immortal though, right? That's good news. He would have bled out by now if he wasn't, and he's still super strong." I didn't expect Rebecca to have an answer. I was speaking out loud more to reassure myself. Looking at him in the hospital bed with a respirator on and machines monitoring his vitals was killing me inside.

"I'll leave you to visit and come back later to check the bandages," said Rebecca. "The bleeding has slowed significantly since he arrived, so it should be a while."

"It's okay. I can do it." I thought on it briefly as I held his hand. "Maybe you can show me other stuff to help out with for emergencies." It was about time I conquered my irrational feelings toward the medical profession and clinical atmosphere. I had proved to myself I could contribute more to the world than destruction, and now I had the taste for creation that Gianni was always trying to instill in me. I had been going about using my powers to create all wrong. It took a level of compassion and serenity that I had just never been inspired enough to achieve before that day.

"That would be amazing," Rebecca agreed. "We're short staffed on the medical team, and any extra hands would be appreciated. The fight may be over, but a doctor's job is never done."

"How's Owen?" I asked.

"Sleeping soundly after a few close calls during surgery. We had to set his bones and remove the shards from his vital organs before his healing fused everything together incorrectly. It wasn't pleasant. His regeneration originates from werewolves and is more similar to humans than yours. It won't put everything back into place or regrow lost limbs. All he needs now is some rest, and he should be right as rain. I'm actually about to go check on him again. I'll let him know you were asking for him."

Rebecca went to leave to let me visit with Gianni. "Is it true he saved Commander Turner's life?" she stopped and asked before reaching the door.

"Yes, ma'am." Lyle walked up with his arm in a sling. "And it's just Lyle."

"Lyle's also the one who beat the demon lord by himself." I winked at him as he laughed and smiled, trying to avoid making eye contact with Rebecca in embarrassment.

"I, yeah, I did what needed to be done," he stammered. "I had that magic sword and all ... It wasn't a big deal really."

"Apparently, he's also 'pure hearted,' so the demon couldn't get to him like the rest of us," I added.

"I guess I've just never found a reason to waste my time on hating something that should mean nothing to me when there's so many other things I could be enjoying. I've disliked people before, but I just ignore them. I try to find something about them I like to make it more tolerable if I'm forced to deal with them."

"What about the demons, though?" I asked. "There's nothing good about them."

"I feel the same way about them as I told you about Vyrlakalos. I pity anyone whose entire existence is based on something so depressing. I can't imagine what it'd be like to live my whole life, let alone an eternity, always angry and trying to spread misery. There's got to be some point where they must want happiness. I don't know ... maybe they don't have the choice we have. It just makes me sad for them."

It did put some of this into perspective, especially my own situation. I didn't want to live forever being full of anger over everything that had ever bothered me in my life. "Spoken like a true hero," I said. "Your dad would be proud."

"Are you blushing?" Rebecca asked him with a smile, which of course made him turn even brighter red.

"Ah, no, ma'am, but I do need to talk with you about something if you've got a minute for me." Lyle gave me a thumbs-up and a wink behind her back as they left. Now that my head had cleared, I remembered what Rudgar had said about Rebecca not being affected by the Infernal pact when working undercover at Gestalt. *Could she also be one of the pure like Lyle?*

I sat by Gianni and told him about what happened at the village, hoping he could hear me. He would be proud, I think. I rested my eyes for just a little while, and when they opened again, the room was dark. The first thing I thought of was that Gianni had recovered, but I noticed I wasn't in the room with him anymore. I was on my bed in the barracks, surrounded by the smell of fish.

"Wake up, little shit."

"Stop calling me that," I said in the direction of Noah's voice.

"Why?" he asked. "The Italian always calls you that."

"Little *chick*," I corrected.

"Oh. That's stupid. I like mine better."

"Why does it smell like fish?" I asked. "And how did I get here?"

"You like it?"

"I'm not sure. The way you said that kind of creeped me out." I turned on the light and sat up. Noah was dressed in Owen's leather hunting gear, minus the shirt of course. He was sitting with his feet up on the desk, where there was a plate of food from the mess hall. "Oh God. What are you wearing?"

"I think it's pretty obvious what I'm wearing." He grinned and adjusted the fingerless gloves up his forearms. Everything was tighter on him than on Owen, so it fit like a wetsuit that was one size too small. Good thing Noah wouldn't need to breathe if he ever put on the shirt. "Looks pretty good on me, right?"

"You look like a medieval stripper, and I meant *why* do you have it?"

"Why not? It might come in handy." The top part of the suit was on the desk. The hole where Owen had been impaled was gone, with only a scar left like actual living skin that had healed from a wound. Strange. Could the demon leather repair itself even after being flayed from its host?

"And the tuna?" I looked at the plate.

"Yeah, I don't know ... I thought you might be hungry or something. You're always hungry, fatty." He handed over the plate sheepishly at first, but then his face lit up with a huge toothy grin of self-satisfaction at his wisecrack. "So, Hell was fun, huh?" He jumped next to me on the bed, almost throwing me off.

"That wasn't what I would consider fun," I said and started to dig in.

"Then why'd you go?" he asked. "Life is about what you make it. When you're not having fun, that's a sign you're doing something wrong."

"Thanks, *sensei*, but life isn't always fun. Sometimes you just have to do something because it's the right thing to do."

"If there's a mountain blocking your path, you move the mountain."

"What if I can just fly over it?" I laughed, to which he flicked me on the forehead.

"I'm saying that if you have the strength to do what you really want, *use* it. Don't wait around for someone else to take the lead. Even a pebble can cause an avalanche."

"I thought that's what I was trying to do," I said in between mouthfuls.

"You're just following these idiots around. That isn't what I trained you for. Find your own way so that you'll be happy at the end of the journey, even if it sucks getting there." I knew this was Noah venting his own frustration at not always having a choice in what he did with his life like the rest of us did. "Now hurry up and shovel that slop down your throat faster so we can catch our flight."

"What are you talking about?" I asked.

"Thailand. It's gonna be great. I was thinking we could even check out Brazil after that so I can round out my jujitsu. I wanna start incorporating other variations on styles to keep it interesting since I've already mastered most of them."

"I can't go anywhere right now, Noah."

"Yeah you can. I know you want to punch a few people too. You've got some real potential ... with me teaching you, of course." He shoved me in what would be considered a playful manner for him, but it almost sent me across the room.

"Gianluca needs me."

"Bullshit." Noah sat up, glaring at me. "You promised if I got you out of there and kept your stupid friend alive, this would be over. What's the Italian need you for? He's in a coma and better off that way for all of us."

"I didn't promise that. You came up with the idea to go there on your own and ran with it. I want to be here when Gianluca wakes up."

Noah got up and stood over me, his eyes narrowed and his jaw tightened in anger. "So, you're gonna stay here and play the good soldier boy until the Italian wakes up and turns on you again? Once he starts talking about changing the world and doing things his way, it's too late. What don't you get about that? He *is* that evil that we saw. Hell just dragged it out of him like it did to all of us. When are you going to trust me?" I could tell he was forcing himself to stay angry as his expression changed to one of hurt. It didn't take much for him to feel betrayed, and I understood that.

"Don't say that. You know I trust you."

"The problem is you trust too many other people," he said and collected the rest of the leather armor and the swords he had against the desk. "I knew I'd regret letting my guard down and keeping you around."

"I'll go with you as soon as Gianluca is awake and I'm sure he's okay."

"Don't bother. I'd rather go alone. I was just taking you in case I got hungry."

"I know that's not true," I said, but he was already gone.

Chapter Thirty-Three

Three weeks passed with few signs of progress from Gianni. Every day that went by without him regaining consciousness added to my worry that it might take years or might never happen at all. I felt as if we had been displaced from time while everything else had moved ahead without us.

Commander Timmons was a recruiting machine scouring the map for individuals who'd had brushes with the supernatural to replenish our ranks. Recruits would arrive, and Lyle would parade them through to meet me with all the usual stares of curiosity, fascination, and trepidation. Rebecca came by daily to chat and teach me how to suture a wound or take blood in between giving physicals to the fresh meat and equipping them with neural implants.

Owen had finished recuperating after only two days and had kept his word on the sizable contribution he had pledged to PROJECT: UNITY before returning to England. The money was put to immediate good use on much-needed supplies, repairs, and upgrades for the entire base. After he found out about her situation from Lyle, Owen also paid off Rebecca's parents' mortgage and medical bills so her mother wouldn't have to go back to work. He said it was to settle up his own bill for the medical care he'd received from her and that he hoped it would make it a little easier for her to smile.

Probably the most interesting development was the sudden friendship between him and Lyle. Never would I have imagined seeing the two of them joking like best buddies. Owen was even trying to talk Lyle into coming back to his estate and celebrating in typical Blackbourne fashion with as many combinations of hard liquor and unscrupulous women he could dream up, but Lyle already had his sights on a certain neurosurgeon.

I turned out the lights before taking my spot on the floor beside Gianni's bed, the same as I had every other night. I never slept much, but still, I rested my head on the sheets and closed my eyes. I thought something brushed against my hair as I slipped into a twilight state. I waited to see if it would happen again or if I was dreaming. A few seconds later, there was a weight on my head and the pleasant feeling of fingers through my hair.

"Gianni?" I turned on the lights to see him looking up at me with half-opened eyes and a half smile. I had to hold back from pouncing on him in excitement.

"Is it Heaven?" he moaned with the sound of sleep in his voice.

"No." I laughed and squeezed his hand.

"Do we win? The battle."

"We won. We're back on base. We're safe now."

"You fight the demon? You are so strong, little one. More stronger than me." Gianni tried lifting his other hand, but he winced in pain.

"Actually, it was Lyle who killed it …"

"A human? Wow, very nice. He is the heart of a champion." He was able to move his head to look at his poor, broken body. I could see the pain across his face so clearly that it hurt me too. "This is you, yes? The bandage? I feel you like a dream when I sleep."

"Yup, it was me." I helped him sit up against a pillow, and I removed his breathing tube and pulse monitor. "The doctor has been teaching me more stuff to help out too."

"Soldier, architect, caesar, and *medica*. There is nothing impossible for this little chick. You take good care for me. I am a lucky man." Gianni's eyes were closing again. "My body is very weak, but the dark is clean now. My shadow is more strong. I never feel this so much."

"You have a lot of broken bones and stab wounds from fighting your evil side. The only thing I've ever seen able to slow you down was yourself. You don't have to worry about the corruption in the darkness anymore, so that's what you're probably feeling, I guess ..."

"I ... have no memories. I know when we are in the desert, then I wake up here. There is a voice in my dream ask for my help—a woman—and then I see the sun."

I didn't understand what his dream meant, but there was something else on my mind that had been eating at me since the fight with Lord Ma'al.

"Gianni? The Nether Lords that turned you, were they undead, or were they demons?"

"Undead, I think. They drink my blood." Maybe Ma'al was lying and they weren't the Demon Kings, or maybe they were just incognito to pin their evil deeds on the undead to not draw suspicion from Heaven. They were already hiding behind Gianni. Lyle had asked me how we could be sure it was the good Gianni we'd brought back to base, but I'd had no answer, and that was weighing on me. "Do not worry. They are gone a long time, and the darkness is safe with no more demon in the desert. My mind is very clear ... the most in years."

That still didn't ease my apprehensions. I didn't know if that malevolent side of Gianni we'd seen had been a manifestation of his own suppressed hatred and anger, or if it had been Hell directly taking control of him and his powers. I just hoped it was the last we would ever see of his evil persona ...

"You are unhappy," Gianni said. "I see in your face."

"No, I'm fine. Actually, no, no I'm not. You're right."

"Tell me," Gianni urged.

"This isn't what I thought life would be like," I said. "I don't mean my life; I mean the world."

"Your eyes are open. A boy thinks of a problem in his life, a man thinks of a problem in the world. You are good to learn this very young."

"I'm in my twenties."

"And I am, um, very more old, but I learn this much later. To be a man is not to stop when you are strong and have honor. A man only start his duty to the world when he sees more problem than his own."

"Then I hope the world is ready for me."

Lyle came running into the room, yelling to turn on the TV. "Oh sweet! You're awake!" He stopped short upon seeing Gianni. "You're both gonna want to see this."

"What channel?" I asked.

"All of them! It doesn't matter!" He flipped on the screen mounted opposite Gianni's bed, and the first thing I saw was myself.

"Oh God ... How did anyone have time to take a video?" I stared at the TV, where the news was replaying a clip of me in Iraq. "It's been weeks. Why now?"

"Others have been trying to suppress it," Lyle said. "It's all over the news. There's more clips taken from drone surveillance in the area that was monitoring the terrorists' activity. I think some kid even got a selfie."

"Are you kidding me?"

"You said it was time to stop hiding and to make a change to break the cycle," said Lyle.

"I didn't mean by myself! I had an impulsive moment of bravery."

"Very brave," Gianni said. "I want to do this. The world need us. I like the white toga. You make this for me?"

"It was a bedsheet I threw on because I was half naked again from being set on fire, and I didn't want anyone seeing my face."

"Why this is different from the Colosseum?" Gianni asked. I had forgotten about my display back in Rome only a few months ago. I was doing a terrible job of keeping the secret, but I couldn't stop myself when I felt as if the secret was helping to protect the wrong people.

"He's right," Lyle added. "And with PROJECT: UNITY reborn, things are gonna be different around here. I respected Rudgar as a mentor, but I want us to be a family, not a military. No secrets—only justice. Protect the weak and serve the innocent in need."

"I like this. You have honor like the best Roman," Gianni said to him.

"Thanks, man. I'd like it if you guys would join officially as lieutenants or something. I don't want either of you to feel like you're just add-ons."

"Lyle, you know I'm not really the leader—"

"We will love to do this." Gianni cut me off, answering for us both. "A leader inspire others even without the words. You want to make a change, and that is your power. Destroy, create, is just a step. You are a leader, Dorian. Show your power and the people will follow." There was no point in arguing over a title, so I let it go. Gianni tended to just do whatever he wanted to anyway. I couldn't see myself formally leading anyone, but if it made Lyle feel better and feel supported, I'd play along.

"What's going to happen to all those people who are still possessed and running rampant?" I asked. "There's no way we can track them all down, and the average supernatural can't take them on alone."

"Then we'll have to be the ones to do it," Lyle said. "We'll keep recruiting, expanding, and training anyone who's willing and able."

"How would we even know where to start? They could be anywhere, and we have no idea how many there are or what they're planning next."

"I'm not sure, man, but all I know is that we've got some serious work ahead of us."

Epilogue

"I'm finally home." I knelt before the headstone at my feet, where I placed a bouquet of tulips. So much had changed since I had been back to Boston that I didn't feel like the same person who had left. I wasn't the monster that I thought I was, and I found my greatest strength was what made me feel like an outcast to start with. My telekinetic powers were not so much of a curse now that I had a better understanding of them. The destruction I brought was only a stepping-stone to unlocking the upper limits of my creativity. As I was taught, a road can't be built without clearing a path first. It was the very basics of a forgotten dream that made me feel alive again.

The smell of freshly cut grass across the cemetery lawn brought back childhood memories of summer Sunday afternoons at the park with my parents. For once, I didn't feel like crying or having an anxiety attack from the memory of losing them. It was refreshing to be at peace, but I wished now more than ever that I had shared my gift with them while they had been alive.

Using my thoughts, I etched a picture of us as a family into the headstone, and I put down a baseball that I had sculpted from the white marble chunk in memoriam of our trips to see the Red Sox play at Fenway Park every year.

"Everything is going so fast," I whispered. "I wish you guys were here to tell me what to do." In the months that had passed since our fight in Hell, life had only gotten more confusing.

"Are you ready, little one?" Gianluca called to me from a respectful distance. "It is almost night where we go."

He was eager to continue his search for the voice he'd heard in his coma, but every step forward only brought more darkness. We sought Empress Kamakura's guidance. The Great Guardian Dragon of Yomi had also heard the cry for help and directed us toward the east. Each night, we would scour the lands surrounding the area in which Ma'al had resided, quieting the chaos and looking for clues. But I soon became uneasy with our nighttime ritual. Gianluca took no pause in slaughtering encampments full of terrorists. Even entire cities were suffocated overnight by a sea of living shadow, leaving nothing but empty beds and guard towers.

It was exhilarating at first. Evil was getting its ass handed to it and was losing *badly*. What would have taken a coalition of world powers months and millions of dollars to achieve, Gianluca had been able to do in moments. Prisoners were freed, weapons destroyed, and I got to fly around the barren streets, playing with brick and stone like building blocks to restore a bit of what was lost. More than a few people caught sight of me, and I allowed it to further perpetuate the growing rumor that good things came to good people and that something from above was watching out for them in their greatest time of need.

That lasted a short time. Soon, the killing came too easily, and frustration set in as Gianluca couldn't find the voice calling out to him. He never admitted it, but I was getting to know him well enough to read his face.

Destruction should always be tempered by creation to maintain balance, but as the nights dragged on, Gianluca rushed us from one settlement to the next without stopping to let me rebuild what had been ruined. I wasn't even a participant anymore—just a spectator in my own life again.

Things only got worse when his frustration subsided. He came up with more imaginative ways to keep himself going. Instead of swallowing them all into the abyss, Gianluca would draw his sword and engage in direct combat with the militants. It was hardly a fair fight, and it often left a bloodier, more tortured end for the maimed, but he swelled with pride over his victories and reliving his glory days as a soldier conquering for Rome.

Lyle and the others at PROJECT: UNITY became equally unsettled. They began to argue that humans should deal with human problems if situations were going to be handled with the same brutality as the evil we were trying to stop. I didn't disagree.

The rumors of a divine being watching over the pure of heart changed to those of a devil rising from the dark beneath the sands to quench its thirst for bloodshed.

History was repeating itself, and I was there to witness it firsthand.

"Have you forgotten why we're doing this?" I asked him one night mid-slaughter.

"Of course not!" he declared and raised his sword to the stars above. "We fight for a change to this world and to make this world *ours!*"